A Kiss Before Doomsday

D0974488

ALSO BY LAURENCE MACNAUGHTON

It Happened One Doomsday

LAURENCE MacNAUGHTON

A KISS BEFORE DOOMSDAY

A Dru Jasper Novel

an imprint of Prometheus Books
Amherst, NY

Inquiries should be addressed to
Pyr
59 John Glenn Drive
Amherst, New York 14228
VOICE: 716-691-0133
FAX: 716-691-0137
WWW.PYRSF.COM

21 20 19 18 17   5 4 3 2 1

Library of Congress Cataloging-in-Publication Data

Names: MacNaughton, Laurence, 1975- author.
Title: A kiss before doomsday / by Laurence MacNaughton.
Description: Amherst, NY : Pyr, an imprint of Prometheus Books, 2017. |
    Series: A Dru Jasper novel | Description based on print version record and
    CIP data provided by publisher; resource not viewed.
Identifiers: LCCN 2017008439 (print) | LCCN 2017011876 (ebook) |
    ISBN 9781633882683 (ebook) | ISBN 9781633882676 (paperback)
Subjects: | BISAC: FICTION / Fantasy / Urban Life. | GSAFD: Fantasy fiction.
Classification: LCC PS3613.A276 (ebook) | LCC PS3613.A276 K57 2017 (print) |
    DDC 813/.6—dc23
LC record available at https://lccn.loc.gov/2017008439

For Cyndi.

CONTENTS

Prologue: Driven Apart   9

 1: If You Leave   20

 2: Beneath the Skin   27

 3: The Dead Ride Fast   33

 4: Hot Metal and Gasoline   39

 5: The Damage Done   48

 6: Things That Make You Go Hmm   57

 7: Wake the Dead   68

 8: Kick-Ass Shoes   75

 9: The Way It Never Was   79

10: Hello, Mr. Bones   89

11: Strange Kind of Love   98

12: Love Is a Battlefield   103

13: Found in Translation   112

14: If You Were Here   119

15: Where the Sky Ends   125

16: Never Go Home   132

17: The Way Back   140

18: Darkness Runs Deep   150

19: Who's That Lady?   159

20: Love Me Like a Bomb   167

21: Disco and Doomsday   173

22: The Red Death   180

23: Behind Door Number One   186

24: The Clutter of Our Enemies   195

25: The Man behind the Mask   203

26: Styx and Stones   208

27: Everybody Wants to Rule the World   214

28: As the World Falls Down   221
29: Next to You   229
30: Long, Cool Woman   239
31: The Wild Side   247
32: Back in Black   260
33: Never Let Go   268
34: How the Gods Kill   275
35: Everything Ends   282
36: Kiss Them for Me   288

Acknowledgments   293

About the Author   295

DRIVEN APART

A dark voice inside Greyson whispered that the end of the world was coming. He awoke on a rocky ledge, sprawled beneath a night sky ablaze with alien stars. Burning comets streaked overhead, leaving behind plumes of oily fire. Above, an unearthly sky shimmered with spiderwebs of ghostly light. Below, a jagged cliff dropped away into eternal darkness.

The netherworld.

Bruised and bleeding, Greyson lay on the narrow outcropping, unsure whether he was dead or alive. He stared up at the ethereal lights slashed through with falling stars. Were they the spirits of the departed? Was he among them?

Part of him wanted to give up, just lie there on the rocks and close his eyes forever. Surrender to his injuries. Slip away into the darkness. But Greyson had never been one to give up.

Jaw clenched, he tried to ignore the pain as he rolled over. Every part of his body was cut and battered. His muscles felt as if they were on fire. Gritting his teeth, he struggled to his feet and looked around at the dark cliff face. There was no way off this ledge but up.

Far up.

Steeling himself, he reached overhead, fingers searching for a handhold in the cold rock. With a grunt, he pulled himself up and found a toehold. Taking a breath, he reached up and did it again. And again.

It seemed like hours that he scaled the unforgiving cliff, searching for every crevice and jutting rock he could grip. He panted, too winded to give voice to the pain. As he climbed, memories came back to him in broken fragments.

In the desert, he had tried to save Dru from the Horsemen of the

Apocalypse, but something had gone wrong. He had lost control, become some kind of a monster. Something nightmarish and inhuman. Something fueled by rage.

He remembered seeing Dru's terrified face in the darkness, her long brown hair blowing back in the wind as falling stars plummeted to earth all around them. The anguish in her voice as she called his name. As the monsters closed in around them.

She had fled.

Greyson remembered brief glimpses of a high-speed chase. A bone-jarring crash. The car had tumbled end over end. He had been thrown out through the shattered windshield, over the edge of the cliff, where he had hurtled down into the darkness. How far had he fallen?

Not quite far enough to kill him. But almost.

What had happened to Dru?

He had to find out. No matter what it took. He needed to make sure she was safe.

Just when he couldn't climb anymore, he reached the top of the cliff and collapsed there, panting, every muscle in his body shaking. That was when he found Hellbringer.

The demon-possessed black car, a 1969 Dodge Charger Daytona, lay on its side, smashed. Its pointed nose cone was crumpled inward, revealing one dark headlight. It stared at him like the eye socket of a skull.

Accusatory. Haunted. Lost.

Greyson turned away, unable to face it. He got to his feet and staggered along the top of the cliff, searching for any sign of Dru. Despite the eternal darkness, the hellish skies overhead shed just enough light to see by.

There. Footprints in the dark sand. Dru had circled all around Hellbringer, possibly searching for him, and then headed away. He followed the footprints to the dark mouth of a nearby cave. He recognized it. This cave led out the netherworld through a portal to an abandoned mine in the living world.

If she had searched for him after the crash, there was no way she could have seen him all the way down there. Did she even know he was alive?

He pictured her in happier times, the earnest look in her eyes, behind her dark-rimmed glasses. The integrity in her voice. The slight upturn constantly at the corner of her mouth, as if she wanted to say something funny but was worried it would be highly inappropriate.

A deep need stirred inside him. To get back to Dru. To make things right. To fix things that would otherwise never be fixed.

Beneath a night sky gone mad, he staggered over to the ruined hulk of Hellbringer. The moment he touched the car's hood, a spark jumped between his finger and the steel, connecting them for a split second with a blinding arc of energy.

He jerked his hand away and made a fist, unsure what had just happened.

Like burning coals stirred up from the depths of a dead fire, Hellbringer's headlights began to glow again. Within the cracked, wavy glass, the ruddy glow quickly turned white-hot.

Greyson held up a wounded hand to ward off the blinding glare. This close, he could practically feel the heat from the lights. Brilliant. Searing. But also purifying. Drawing him back to himself, as if a part of him had been missing and he hadn't even known it.

His injured hand, silhouetted in the pure white light, began to heal as he watched. His fingers straightened and strengthened. The swelling shrank away, and the cuts closed, leaving clean, healthy skin.

He lowered his arm and squinted into the headlights, staring back at Hellbringer where it lay sideways among the boulders.

When he summoned up his voice, it came out cracked and gravelly. "Hell of a place to park, buddy."

The demon car flashed its high beams at him.

Gathering himself, Greyson planted both hands on Hellbringer's roof. He had learned from Dru that the speed demon's presence gave him superhuman strength and endurance. But after the exhausting climb up the cliff face, he wasn't sure how much strength he had left.

With a heave that aggravated every complaining muscle in his body, he pushed the car off of its side and back onto its wheels. It landed with a crunch, an eruption of dust, and the rhythmic creaking of steel springs.

Immediately, Hellbringer's dented black sheet metal began to straighten and smooth out. The nose cone uncrumpled. The long spoiler wing above the tail squared up and sharpened to a jet-fighter edge. The smashed windows regrew from the edges of the chrome trim. Hellbringer was healing itself, as it had healed him.

The driver's door screeched open when he pulled on it. He collapsed into the narrow black seat, exhausted, breaths coming hard in his aching chest. But with each painful breath, he could feel his strength returning. As if Hellbringer's very presence made him whole again.

Dru had once explained that his fate was tightly intertwined with the demon car. He never realized just how close that bond really was.

He tilted the rearview mirror and peered at his reflection. Messed up dark hair that could use a trim. Darker stubble. Scratches and bruises that were fading as he watched. That wasn't too strange to accept, considering everything else that had happened to him. But it was his eyes that stopped him.

They were clear and blue. Completely human.

Not the glowing red eyes of a demon.

Hope surged inside him. Dru had done everything she could to break his curse. And here was the proof that she had succeeded. He was no longer one of the Four Horsemen of the Apocalypse. No longer a threat to everyone around him.

Now, he was just a regular guy again. Granted, a guy with a demon-possessed muscle car. But at least he was himself again.

He found his leather jacket on the floorboard, where it had apparently ended up during the crash. He slipped it on, feeling more human by the moment as it warmed against his skin. Beyond the windshield, across the rocky plain, the dark cave waited. It was time to find Dru.

The old brass keys were already in the ignition. As he pumped the gas and reached for the keys, Hellbringer's monstrous Hemi engine rumbled itself to life, growling like a wounded animal that refused to die.

Grimacing, Greyson dropped his hand to the gearshift and shoved it home. The pitch of the hell-powered engine dropped to a guttural growl, and the car crept forward. Its headlights shone across the slate-gray rocks as he drove toward the yawning blackness of the cave mouth.

The rocky ground was almost completely flat, but for a machine that was built strictly for devouring highway pavement, it might as well have been the surface of the moon. Every rise and dip in the uneven stone banged through the car's battered chassis.

Greyson steered carefully into the cave, expecting to have to back out at any moment. But the opening was more than wide enough to accommodate the car.

The thudding of the exhaust echoed off the uneven walls, and the impenetrable blackness ahead swallowed up the headlight beams.

This was no ordinary cave, Greyson knew that much. Somewhere inside lay a portal back to the normal world. The last time he was here, when he had traveled through the netherworld with Dru, she had used her crystal magic to open the portal. Without her magic to aid him, Greyson could only hope that Hellbringer's infernal presence was strong enough to carry them through to the other side.

Otherwise, this would be a pretty short trip.

A gusting wind picked up, buffeting the windshield with bits of grit. But the car's aerodynamic form and tall back wing slipped through the wind like a knife. Hellbringer crept onward, deeper into the cave.

Without warning, the car slowed down, as if something was pulling them back. As if the netherworld itself had grasped them with invisible claws, preventing their escape. Gradually, they ground to a halt in the dark tunnel.

An icy spike of adrenaline pierced Greyson. They were stuck. He had to get them out of here, or they would be trapped in the netherworld forever.

He pulled the parking brake tight to keep them anchored, then floored the long-traveling clutch and fed the gas. The diabolical engine roared, and the white tach needle swung up past 3,000 rpm, but it was no good. The tires let out painful squeaks as the netherworld jerked the car back out of the cave, bit by bit.

He kept the gas pedal down. The tach swept past 4,000 rpm.

The invisible forces of the netherworld continued to pull at them like a hungry creature trying to draw them back in. Trying to devour them.

At 5,000 rpm, the entire car shook. Hellbringer's deep reserves of infernal power strained to be unleashed. Greyson knew the demon car so well that he could feel the right launch moment approaching, the sweet spot in the bell curve of torque that would break them free.

But before they reached it, the invisible force of the netherworld yanked them back. It wouldn't let them go.

At 6,000 rpm, the wailing engine shuddered through the car, drowning out all other sounds. All other thoughts. There was nothing left except the burning desire to go. Greyson kept the clutch planted, waiting for the precise moment to release. The white needle strained forward.

"Steady, buddy." Greyson's feet ached to move. Still, he held on.

Now deep in the red zone, the trembling needle fought its way higher. The engine crackled like an endless peal of thunder. Just when he thought the launch moment would never come, he felt it happen.

Now. Greyson dropped the emergency brake and simultaneously lifted his foot from the clutch.

Hellbringer blasted all of its horsepower into the rear wheels, dragging a howl of tortured rubber from the tires. Clouds of white smoke curled out of the wheel wells. But the car went nowhere.

Fear washed over Greyson. Had he miscalculated? Was all of their torque going up in smoke as the tires burned down to molten rubber? Would the netherworld hold them prisoner forever?

"Go!" he yelled at Hellbringer over the deafening engine noise. "Let's get the hell out of here!"

At his command, the shimmering red glow of hellfire pulsed up around the edges of the long black hood, reflecting off the chrome tie-down pins near the nose. The car's front end glowed like iron in a hot forge, as if the engine itself had become a boiling cauldron of unholy power.

The air in front of the windshield shimmered with heat waves. Hellbringer was a car with the heart of a demon. Greyson felt from the gearshift knob a searing connection directly to its infernal power. It pierced through his body like a needle spiking a nerve, connecting to his very essence and making him one with the machine.

With that, the superheated tires found traction. They bit into the cave floor, breaking the car free of the netherworld's grip. Hellbringer launched down the tunnel at mind-bending speed.

Greyson's head snapped back. The acceleration crushed him into the seat. It took everything he had left to slam through the gears and keep the steering wheel centered as the demon car rocketed toward freedom.

In the darkness ahead, a pinpoint of light exploded into a blinding flare of pure whiteness, painfully intense. Greyson squinted against the glare.

When his vision adjusted, he caught a glimpse of the tunnel walls. They seemed different, somehow. Just as dark, but the texture of the rock had subtly changed. In the blue-hued shadows, the tunnel looked less nightmarish and more real.

Ahead, the tunnel ended in bright sky. The exit was ringed with jagged wooden planks.

Hellbringer smashed through the remains of an old wooden blockade hung with skull-and-crossbones danger signs.

They blasted out of the abandoned mine shaft into broad daylight. Hellbringer's nose went airborne for a moment, then tipped sharply downward. Greyson's stomach dropped as they sailed through the air.

They landed with a tooth-rattling bang on a dry slope broken by craggy brown rocks, wildflowers, and tufted green bushes. Instantly, the car began to skid.

On instinct, Greyson pumped the brakes, trying to bring them to a controlled stop. But they headed down the steep slope too fast. He steered around boulders and pine trees, power-sliding through the dirt. Tree branches scraped and banged off the car's long body.

He got their speed under control just as they burst out of the trees over an old gravel trail that had once been a dirt road. Obviously, no one had driven it for years, and now it was overgrown with hardy grass and cactuses. Greyson brought Hellbringer around in a long, gently slipping curve that landed them safely in the middle of the trail.

With a sigh of exhaustion, he rolled the car to a stop, and only then took his sweaty hands off the steering wheel.

"Let's never do that again," he said.

The car defiantly revved its engine, clearly disagreeing with him.

He took a deep breath. The magical connection to Hellbringer left him drained and shaky. He wanted to get out of the car and walk around, but his legs suddenly felt like lead.

Around them, ranks of snow-capped peaks rose above the rugged green carpet of pine trees, growing bluer in the distance beneath an overcast afternoon sky the color of zinc-plated steel. After the madness of the netherworld's alien stars, Greyson relished the familiar, jagged landscape of the Rocky Mountains.

Ahead, the trail switched back and forth down the steep slope, presumably leading to some cracked blacktop county road, and then eventually civilization.

Greyson realized that he'd been here before with Dru, at this exact spot, after they had walked through the netherworld. Her feet had been red and painfully swollen, and he had made her makeshift bandages with folded-up napkins.

He could picture her sitting barefoot on that boulder, looking up at him with thanks, making some comment about wearing the wrong shoes. But he had been captivated by the beauty of her shy smile, the impish look in her eyes every time she took off her glasses.

The thought of Dru made his breath catch in his throat. Where was she now? Did she even know he had survived? What private hell had she gone through?

He had to find her.

As Hellbringer descended the dirt trail, Greyson reached down to the chrome crank and rolled down the window. A soft June wind whispered through the pine trees and swirled through the car, carrying the tang of a coming storm.

The galvanized sky finally delivered its downpour as Greyson left the winding mountain roads behind and took the highway toward Denver, where Dru had her crystal shop. The endless curtain of rain obscured the city where it sprawled out beyond the rolling foothills at the edge of the grassy plains.

As he drove, the engine let out a constant mournful howl. The windshield wipers slapped back and forth. The highway flattened out and ran straight into the city, and the facts settled on him like an uncomfortable weight. He had just come back from the netherworld. What did that mean, exactly?

Dru would know. She would formulate some kind of potion, do research in some ancient book, or pull a magical crystal out of a drawer. She would be able to verify that he was finally cured. That everything was okay.

Beside him, the passenger seat was conspicuously empty. Without Dru there beside him, nothing felt right.

His heart beat faster as he headed toward her shop. After the long drive, his strength felt as if it was returning, but he couldn't shake a growing uneasiness that something was terribly wrong. The foul taste of danger lurked in the back of his throat, the way it had when the other Horsemen of the Apocalypse pursued them across the desert.

He wrote it off as nerves, telling himself that he was just worried about what Dru would say. After everything they had been through, after all the danger and destruction they'd overcome in trying to break his curse, he wasn't one hundred percent sure she'd even want to see him again.

Something in his jacket pocket prickled his side, like a low-voltage electric shock. He jumped, then quickly fished it out. Much to his surprise, it was a small black rock, a little larger than his thumb. Its polished surface glittered with golden flecks. Dru had given it to him once, telling him that it was protection against evil.

As he held the rock in his hand, it shocked him badly enough to make him drop it in the passenger seat next to him. It had burned an angry red mark on his palm.

He wondered what it meant. Did the rock somehow think *he* was evil? He ran his fingertips over the throbbing skin of his palm as he mulled over that unpleasant possibility.

Over the next several miles, the uneasy sense of impending danger grew stronger. It made him feel itchy and uncomfortable inside his own skin. The closer he got to Dru's shop, the more he felt on edge. What bothered him even more was that he didn't know why.

Greyson stole furtive glances at the rock, not liking the implications.

At last, he turned down the alley and parked behind Dru's shop. Steeling himself for whatever reaction she might give him, Greyson pocketed the black rock, stepped out into the cold rain, and strode toward her door. He wanted nothing more than to sweep her into his arms, feel her brown hair tickle his cheek, see her eyes light up behind her glasses as she smiled up at him.

But was that how it would happen? Doubt gnawed at him as he walked up the narrow gap between the brick wall of Dru's shop and the glass windows of the 24-hour liquor store next door.

With every step he made, his instincts told him to turn back. An angry buzzing swarmed his senses. His eyes burned as if they were on fire.

Something was terribly wrong.

He caught a glimpse of his reflection in the warped glass of the liquor store, and it stopped him dead in the cold pouring rain.

From his reflection, two red-hot eyes glowered back at him.

He peered closer, blinking away the cooling raindrops that pelted his face. There was no mistaking that diabolical glow. "You've got to be kidding me," he whispered.

He was wrong after all. He wasn't cured. He was still a monster. A Horseman of the Apocalypse, and that meant he was a danger to everyone around him.

Everything was wrong. It had all been for nothing.

He reeled back from his own reflection and turned to look at Dru's shop. The windows of the Crystal Connection were boarded up with plywood, wet and lumber-yard musty from the rain. Splinters of wood and shards of broken glass littered the ground, left behind from whatever wreckage had recently been picked up.

The shop was completely shut down. Destroyed. A hand-lettered Closed sign had been stapled to the plywood, and in the pouring rain, the letters ran like blood.

His jaw clenched. So far, he had done a pretty bang-up job of ruining her life. And since none of her cures for him had worked, now he was standing outside her door, getting ready to remind her of yet another colossal failure.

Everything he wanted, everything that was precious to him, was just on the other side of that door. But just standing there in the rain, he could feel the inescapable pressure of the danger he presented to her, and he couldn't ignore it any longer.

So many times, Dru had told him that all she wanted was a normal life.

And he definitely hadn't come back normal. Was it fair for him to ruin everything for her? Was it even safe for her to be around him again? How long would it be before the Horseman inside him turned him evil again?

He didn't know. There was so much he simply didn't understand, and ironically she was the only one he could ask.

Every ounce of him needed to open that door. But he didn't dare. The truth was he didn't trust himself anymore. He didn't trust the demon blood inside him. It had almost destroyed the world once. And if it harmed Dru . . .

That would destroy him.

Even the gold-flecked black rock was fighting him. He pulled the burning hot crystal out of his pocket, ignoring the pain. Dru had given it to him to protect against danger.

Now, *he* was the danger. Which meant that she needed the rock more than he did. To protect her.

From him.

Angrily, he shoved the black rock through the mail slot in her door, trusting that she would find it eventually. Then he marched back to Hellbringer, revved the engine, and took off down the alley. He needed to put space between them. He needed time to think.

He drove off without looking back.

1

IF YOU LEAVE

When the black Lemurian jade crystal came rattling in through her mail slot, it took Dru only seconds to realize what it meant. Greyson was alive.

She ran out into the rain, heart pounding, just as the black muscle car pulled away. Its slitted red taillights seemed to mock her, as if the speed demon bound into its cold steel gloated as it carried Greyson away.

Dru charged down the alley through the pounding rain, heedless of the cold puddles splashing beneath her feet. Desperate to catch the man she loved before he slipped away from her forever.

"Greyson!" she shouted. Had he even noticed her? Maybe in the pouring rain, he couldn't see her through the car's low back window.

She waved her arms overhead, trying to flag him down. Raindrops flew from her sleeves. "Greyson!" she shouted at the top of her lungs. *"Greyson!"*

The icy rain plastered down Dru's long, curly brown hair and spattered her thick-rimmed glasses, making it almost impossible to see. Making the wet alley look nightmarish and surreal.

But she couldn't mistake the car: Hellbringer, a long black muscle car possessed by a demon that gave Greyson supernatural powers. She had fought against that demon car, and then alongside it, finally winning it over from the darkness and enlisting its help to save the world.

And now it was taking Greyson away from her.

She wouldn't lose him again. She couldn't. She chased after him, running for all she was worth.

At the end of the alley, Hellbringer's taillights flashed brighter as the car slowed to a stop.

She couldn't see Greyson through the car's dark, rain-spattered windows, but she could imagine his stubbled jaw brightening with a lopsided smile when he saw her. She could practically hear the creak his leather jacket made whenever he got out of the driver's seat.

She wanted to ask him where he'd been. Find out how he'd made it back. And tell him, finally, that she loved him.

But everything inside her shattered as Hellbringer's tires spun, shrieking on the wet pavement. The black car turned onto the street and rocketed out of sight around the corner, its engine roaring away.

Shocked, Dru ran to the end of the alley, but Hellbringer was already gone, as if it had never existed. Nothing was left but the sound of its engine throttling away into the falling rain.

Dru puffed clouds of fog into the chilly air, trying to catch her breath. Down the length of the empty street, nothing else moved but raindrops hitting the puddles.

Before she'd lost Greyson in the netherworld, he'd been possessed by one of the Four Horsemen of the Apocalypse. The fact that Hellbringer was back now could mean only one thing: the apocalypse was still unfolding. Doomsday was on the way. And the only way to stop it was to break Greyson's curse once and for all.

There was only one thing she could do. Go after him.

She turned and splashed back down the alley, drawing on her last reserves of energy. Panting, she burst through the back door of her sorcery shop, the Crystal Connection. There was no time to waste.

If she was going to find Greyson, she needed help.

"Rane?" she called. "Rane!"

Dru crossed the cluttered back room, looking for her purse full of magical crystals. She left wet footprints as she squelched around ugly plaid armchairs and squeezed through narrow spaces between bookshelves stacked to the ceiling with ancient leather-bound tomes of magic lore.

"Rane?"

Just over six feet tall and rippling with muscle, with a high blonde ponytail and pink workout shorts, Rane would be impossible to miss. But there was no sign of her, even though she'd been in here just minutes before, helping Dru clean up the wreckage of the battle against the Four Horsemen of the Apocalypse. In all likelihood, Rane was upstairs rummaging through Dru's fridge. The woman was constantly hungry.

Dru reached for the door that led upstairs to her cozy apartment over the shop, but an unsettling noise from up front stopped her.

"Rane?" Dru turned and headed toward the front of her shop. What was left of it, anyway.

Since the Four Horsemen had plowed a truck right through the front windows a few days ago, nearly flattening everyone inside, the place was now a boarded-up disaster area. The fluorescent overhead fixtures were destroyed, so now the only light came from a couple of battered table lamps propped up in the far corners. Plus what little rainy-day gloom made it around the edges of the plywood covering the former front windows.

The lamps illuminated piles of broken bookshelves, scattered crystals, and shattered artifacts. The remains of Dru's entire livelihood.

A dark figure rooted through one of the piles, tossing aside handfuls of fragile crystals. As Dru entered, the hunched figure turned, silhouetted by the lamplight.

Dark, gaunt, wrapped in a long black cloak or maybe a coat. Definitely not Rane.

Dru looked around for any crystals she could use as a weapon. In the nearest pile of wreckage lay her dagger-shaped wedge of spectrolite, a naturally protective crystal. She grabbed it and charged it with her own magical energy, amping up its protective powers until the crystal glowed from within, casting a breathtaking rainbow of lights around her.

She held up the crystal and backed away between the waist-high piles of debris. "The shop is closed. For remodeling." She swiped wet hair out of her face. "A *lot* of remodeling."

Still hunched over, the figure staggered toward her. The lamplight fell across his lean face and long, wavy hair. He had a sort of old-fashioned handsomeness to him, but right now he was obviously in pain. Half-crazed gray eyes peered out through his hair, accentuated by black eyeliner.

She recognized him immediately, even without his trademark silk top hat, the kind favored by stage magicians. Or circus ringleaders.

"Salem?" Dru let out a shaky breath and lowered the crystal. "Where's your hat? I didn't recognize you. Almost totally zapped you."

He dismissed that with an arrogant shrug. "Would've been amusing, watching you try. But I have better things to do. Where's your fuller's earth?"

"Seriously? Have you seen this place? I don't even know where my *purse* is right now." She went back to looking for it, frantic to go after Greyson. But how could she? She didn't have a car.

Then again, Salem did. "Salem, where did you park? We need to go after someone. Right now."

From the look on Salem's chiseled face, he clearly didn't believe her. "*Kristalo sorcisto helpos,*" he growled in the sorcerer tongue. "I thought you got your kicks helping sorcerers in need. Surprise, surprise, when I'm in need, you don't care."

"No, I'm just in a hurry, so—"

"Busy redecorating?" He looked around with disdain before returning his attention to her, seeming to finally notice the fact that she was soaking wet. "Are you actually chasing someone?"

Before Dru could reply, Rane clomped down the stairs and strode into the shop, carrying an open carton of milk in one big hand. With the other hand, she powered down the last of a bag of baby carrots. "Dude. You need to start keeping more protein around this place. It's shameful. Why are you all wet?" She saw Salem and stopped short, eyes growing big beneath her pink-striped headband, a fat baby carrot clenched between her teeth.

Salem held Rane's gaze for a lingering moment. A mixture of resentment and hunger flitted across his lean features.

Dru glanced from him to Rane and back, scrambling to think of a way to break the suddenly awkward silence. "So, um, you two don't really talk since . . ." *Since they broke up.*

Rane bit down on the carrot with a crunch that sounded like a gunshot. She chewed noisily.

Dru shook herself back into action. "Salem, look. Shop's closed, so, we'll find your stuff later. This is an emergency." She turned to Rane, who slowly raised the carton of milk to her lips. "The apocalypse is still unfolding. Hellbringer was here. Greyson is alive."

At that, Rane choked and spewed milk and bits of carrots across the floor. Coughing, she set down the milk carton and swiped the back of her hand across her mouth. "*What?*"

"He's alive. We have to go after him!" Dru turned to Salem. "Where's your car? Let's go!"

He folded his arms. "Fuller's earth. I need it."

Rane jabbed a wide finger at him. "You need a swift kick in the ass. For running off with that Gypsy tramp-o-matic, what's-her-name."

"Ember," Dru supplied, instantly wishing she hadn't.

At the sound of Ember's name, Rane's face became a mask of rage. She stalked toward Salem. "And while we're on the subject, you want to know what *I* need?"

"Shut up, shut up, *shut up*." Dru held her hands out like a referee. "None of this matters right now. We're talking about Greyson, here. He's *alive*."

Rane grunted in surprise. Slowly, her face transformed from anger to disbelief. "No way, D. You blew up that whole damn bridge with your crystal. In the *netherworld*, right? *Nobody* comes back from that."

Before Dru could reply, Salem let out a gasp and sagged against a broken bookshelf, holding his side. "Fuller's earth." He lifted one skinny arm and snapped his fingers at her. "Chop-chop."

Rane turned her palms up. "The hell is fuller's earth?"

Quickly, Dru explained. "Once upon a time, fullers were people who cleaned wool. They used absorbent clay to soak up impurities. And mop up spills." She glanced at the orange-speckled milk puddle congealing on the floor between them and forced herself to ignore it. "They lived happily ever after. Now let's go." She took Rane's muscled arm and steered her toward the door.

Salem drew in a shaky breath to speak, but he never got the chance. He slumped over and collapsed to the floor with a clatter of falling shelves and breaking glass.

Rane rolled her eyes. "Oh, here we go with the drama. Seriously? He does this whenever he doesn't get his way." She cupped her hands around her mouth. "Get up, dude. We're not buying it."

He didn't move.

Dru hesitated. Maybe something really was wrong.

She hurried over and knelt next to Salem, hoping this was some kind of joke, some dramatic play for sympathy. But when she shook his shoulder, he didn't respond.

She rolled him over onto his back. Within the depths of his trench coat, his ruffled silk shirt was slashed with four long gashes that stretched diagonally across his chest. The pale skin underneath bore what appeared to be claw marks.

Dru bent closer, easing the slashed fabric open to get a better look. The wounds didn't bleed. They were filled with a black substance, like paint. Or burn marks. And they gave off a foul odor.

"Ugh. What *is* that?" Dru wrinkled her nose. She spotted an old brass magnifying glass lying on the floor nearby. Rane followed her gaze and handed it to her.

The edges of the gashes were ragged and, under closer inspection, appeared to be made up of thousands of tiny, fuzzy black dots that squirmed and grew. "Looks like . . . mildew?" Dru said. "Living mildew?"

"Not living," Salem whispered. His eyes opened up to pained slits. His breath rattled in his lungs. "Undead."

That was the last thing Dru expected to hear. "Undead?"

"The fifth seal," Salem gasped, fighting for air. "The dead . . . rise."

Dru felt her mouth drop open. Beside her, Rane's eyes went wide.

The fifth seal of the apocalypse scroll.

"What?" Dru breathed, desperately hoping she had misunderstood him. But she knew she had heard him right.

Back in the late 1960s, a radical group of evil sorcerers called the Harbingers had sworn to destroy the world and remake it in their own image. To do that, they had started breaking the seven wax seals of the apocalypse scroll, the most powerful magical artifact in existence.

Once they started breaking the seals, it had taken decades for the effects to appear. Most sorcerers, assuming the Harbingers had failed, soon forgot all about them. They didn't know that doomsday was steadily marching closer.

Breaking the first four seals on the scroll had summoned the spirits of the Four Horsemen of the Apocalypse, and one of them had possessed Greyson. Dru had only barely managed to defeat the Horsemen, leaving them trapped in the netherworld. She had lost Greyson in the process. Or so she thought.

If that wasn't bad enough, they hadn't found the apocalypse scroll, either. She had no idea how many of the seven seals had actually been broken.

With a chill, Dru remembered an offhanded comment Salem had once made to her: *"Considering that the streets aren't crawling with hordes of zombies yet, I'm thinking seal number five is still wrapped for freshness."*

But now, Salem's trademark arrogance was gone, and all that was left was his wiry body lying eerily quiet and still on the floor. His bruised-looking eyes were closed.

"Salem?" Rane grabbed him by the shoulders and shook him. He didn't respond. *"Salem!"*

"Give me some room to work," Dru said, quickly unbuttoning his shirt. His chest and shoulders were adorned with elaborate tattoos. He wore a gold amulet on a chain, which Dru batted aside. "Make some space."

With savage swiftness, Rane kicked aside bookshelves and piles of debris to make an open space on the floor. She turned to Dru with the wide eyes of a cornered animal. "Dru, you have to save him. *Do* something!"

"I will," Dru said. There was no way she could go after Greyson right now, but there was no time to dwell on that. Mentally, she cataloged the magical ingredients she would need to try to save Salem. "I'm not going to let him die here. I promise."

She just prayed it was a promise she could keep.

2
BENEATH THE SKIN

As Greyson drove the deserted, rain-swept city streets, he had only a vague plan: go home, get cleaned up, try to figure out what had happened to him . . . and try to put the pieces back together.

How could he still be in the grip of his diabolical curse? Was he a danger to everyone around him? He had to be. Otherwise, why were his eyes glowing an evil red?

He downshifted as Hellbringer rolled up to a stop sign. The wipers swiped back and forth across the glass as the rain pounded down on the windshield, mirroring his emotions.

He couldn't risk hurting anyone, especially Dru. He was determined to put as much distance between them as possible, in case he lost control again. But despite everything, a part of him desperately needed to turn around and head straight back to her.

This wasn't right. None of it was. Especially the foul taste of danger that choked the back of his throat. There was an odd itchiness beneath his skin that he just couldn't shake. He had the sense that something was terribly wrong, and it grew stronger by the moment.

He tilted the rearview mirror down and looked into the sinister red glow of his own eyes, searching for an answer. They just stared back, strange and devilish, revealing nothing.

Hellbringer revved its engine, belting out a growl of exhaust. He could feel its impatience reverberating through the car. The speed demon hated to wait for him.

Ahead, the watery yellow headlamps of several old motorcycles rolled through the intersection without stopping. A half-dozen motorcycles. Then a dozen. They quickly spread out across the intersection, blocking the way, creeping up in a semicircle around Hell-bringer's nose.

Greyson pushed the rearview mirror back into position and frowned. The motorcycle riders, most of them hunched low over their handlebars, were wrapped in some kind of semitransparent gauzy material that trembled and shook in the falling rain.

Thick layers of what resembled spiderwebs wrapped the leather-clad riders to their old, rusted mounts. It was impossible to tell where the motorcycle ended and the rider began. As if they had become one.

The riders filled the street around him, throaty engines barking. From just a few feet away, their pale headlights glared at Greyson.

He dropped one hand to the gearshift and glanced back over his shoulder. For the moment, the street behind him was clear.

One of the riders rolled up to Greyson's window. He lifted one arm from the handlebars as if in greeting, and the gauzy material tore away and fluttered in the wind.

Puzzled, and more than a little apprehensive, Greyson watched him through the window.

Something seemed to awaken beneath the webs that wrapped around the rider. Hundreds, perhaps thousands of wriggling dark streaks swayed back and forth in unison, as if washed by some invisible tide.

Beneath the old-style, visorless motorcycle helmet, there was no face. Only cloudy goggles over a stained skull wrapped in black-speckled webs dotted with rain.

The creature's bony jaw opened wide, revealing sharp teeth. His fingers bent, and sharp black tips pierced through the webs, like claws.

Too late, Greyson realized what his danger sense had been trying to tell him all along. He had misinterpreted the signs.

He wasn't the source of the danger after all. *They* were.

Salem lay bare to the waist on Dru's floor. Alive, but there was no telling how long he'd stay that way.

"Whatever did this to Salem, it's nastier than any undead I've ever seen. Not that I've actually seen a whole lot. But still." Dru felt the sorcerer's clammy wrist for a pulse. She found one, though there was no way for her to time it. Her clock had disappeared somewhere into the wreckage of her shop.

What mattered was that Salem was still alive. For the moment, at least.

Around her, a hundred things clattered and broke as Rane bulldozed a clear area for Dru to work.

Dru knelt down low, studying Salem's corrupted wound, but she couldn't see much. The two battered table lamps in the corners shed little light, and the watery daylight seeping in around the edges of the boarded-up windows didn't help much. Dru pointed to the lamps. "Bring those closer, will you?"

Rane did, ripping their cords out of the wall with a muttered curse. She slammed the lights down near Dru, who scrambled to plug them back in.

Then Rane crossed the room, one fist tight around the titanium ring she'd once gotten from Greyson, and used her power to transform into solid metal. With a faint scraping sound, like a whetstone being drawn across a steel blade, Rane's fist turned into silvery titanium, followed by her arm and her entire body.

Now even stronger than before, Rane reached up and easily ripped the plywood off the windows, letting in the clammy air and what gray daylight there was from the street outside. Cars hissed by in the rain.

When Dru plugged the lamps in, their bare bulbs cast a harsh yellow glow over Salem's narrow face and tattooed torso. Now, she could clearly see that the foul black claw marks cut deep into his skin. They didn't bleed, but the tissue around them gradually swelled as she watched. Whatever was wrong with him, it was growing worse by the moment.

"Salem? Can you hear me? What did this to you?"

He whispered something she couldn't quite make out.

She leaned down closer. His throat worked before he could speak again. "Careless. Didn't realize they were behind me," he said, his voice raspy.

"They? How many are there? What are they?" When he didn't answer, Dru gently shook his shoulder. "Hey. If you don't talk to me, I can't help you."

He swallowed again, his Adam's apple bobbing. "If I tell you, you'll just try to go after them. And get yourself killed. Rather quickly." Beneath the eyeliner, his eyes moved and opened to slits. "Rane would never forgive me for that."

"Well, at least you've got your priorities straight." Dru scrutinized his sweaty face. She could never tell when he was joking. "What's the fuller's earth for? How do I fix this?"

His eyes closed again, and he slumped back.

Rane leaned over them, crowding Dru. "Hey. Hey! What did you *do*, dumbass?" It wasn't clear whether she was accusing Salem or blaming Dru. Or both.

All Dru knew was that she had to figure this out, and fast. But first, she had to stabilize him before he got any worse.

Dru picked up the dagger-shaped wedge of spectrolite she had grabbed earlier. She channeled as much of her own magical energy as she could into the crystal, helping protect Salem until she could figure out what to do next. Gradually, the swelling around his wounds slowed and stopped.

"Talk," Rane said, metal knees clanking on the floor as she knelt opposite Dru. "What's wrong with him?"

"I don't know. I've read about undead black stuff before, somewhere. But I forget where." Helplessly, Dru surveyed the toppled bookshelves. Ancient tomes, some already brittle with centuries of use, lay piled up where they'd fallen. Sorting through them would take hours, possibly days.

Salem didn't have that kind of time.

"What the Faulkner has he been up to?" Dru wondered aloud. "Has he said anything to you about chasing undead? Why does he need fuller's earth?"

"I don't know. It's not like we *talk*." Rane turned human again with a sound like a knife sliding back into a sheath. Her face looked haunted. "I need to *do* something, D. I need to help."

"Call Opal. Put her on speaker."

As Rane dialed, Dru left Salem's side and scrambled over to the messy piles of stuff she had sorted out. Which was only a small percentage of the entire store, granted. But if she could find some copper wire and a few basic protective crystals, she could at least build a magic circle around Salem.

"Hey, talk to Dru," Rane said suddenly, and held out her phone.

Opal's voice crackled through the speaker. "Dru, you know your credit card just got declined? I had to use my own card to buy this stuff for the shop." Traffic sounds and squeaking windshield wipers blasted through the background.

Dru shoveled through the piles of crystals, searching for anything useful. "Opal, I'm sorry, but right now—"

"You're sorry? Honey, I've got bills to pay myself."

"I know. I know. I will pay you back, but—"

"But nothing. Listen, I know things have been hard, okay. But I've got rent past due already."

Rane brought the phone to within inches of her lips and yelled. "*Hey!* Salem's been attacked by undead. Talk to Dru!" She held the phone out at arm's length again.

Opal paused, and the sounds of traffic flowed through the phone. "Salem? Is he okay?"

"Tell me if this rings a bell," Dru said. "Dark claw marks on the skin, human sized. Little black dots that move." As she talked, she sorted through jars and bottles, searching for fuller's earth, but she came up empty-handed. "If I recall, it's kind of like an undead virus. I know I've read about it somewhere. It's a, um, *dirge* or something."

"Oh, my. Look, I'm just around the corner. You try checking in the *Libram of Undeath* yet?"

Dru gazed around at the wreckage of the shop and threw up her hands. "Well, I would, if I had any clue where it was."

"How about the *Folio of the Forlorn?*"

"I have no idea. But I know I've read about this. It's called a dirge, or something. A diverge? Does that sound familiar?"

"The *Folio* was in the bathroom the other day. Under the sink."

"Why is the—never mind." Dru clambered across overturned furniture to get to the back room, which was largely untouched. To her surprise, she found the *Folio of the Forlorn* in the bathroom, under the sink. Its familiar cracked brown leather cover was embossed with slack-jawed skulls.

She brought it up front and flipped through the crackling tan pages, squinting at the thick handwritten passages. "Not a dirge," she muttered. It was something else, something that sounded similar. The word hovered frustratingly out of reach. "Maybe a surge?"

"I'm parking right now," Opal said. Her old car's parking brake zipped in the background. "Sit tight."

"Scourge!" Dru stabbed her finger down on a page with a magic circle diagram, but Opal had already hung up. Quickly, Dru flipped through the pages to either side, scanning the archaic writing. The cure would be intensely dangerous. For all of them.

But if she was going to save Salem's life, she had no choice.

3

THE DEAD RIDE FAST

The undead creature stretched its long black claws toward Greyson's window. He didn't wait to see what would happen next.

Greyson shoved the gearshift into reverse, released the clutch, and fed the heavy gas pedal, sending Hellbringer shooting back out of the creature's grasp.

The skeletal figure, wrapped in layers of black-speckled cobwebs, opened its bony jaw and shrieked in frustration.

Greyson yanked the emergency brake, locking up Hellbringer's front tires. At the same time, he swung the steering wheel hard right, spinning the long black car in the middle of the wet street until it faced the opposite direction.

As Hellbringer's pointed nose came around, Greyson punched it into first gear. He revved the engine and shot directly away from the motorcycles, tires warbling on the wet asphalt.

The gang of undead, now behind him, all streaked after him in pursuit. The motorcycles filled the street behind Hellbringer, trailing sheets of tattered webs like gossamer wings.

Greyson had no idea what these things were. All he knew was that he had to put them as far behind him as possible.

For a few blocks, the street was empty, letting Greyson get almost a hundred yards from the creatures. Then his luck ran out. A slow red pickup hogged the lane.

Greyson swerved around it and into the path of an oncoming old white van. He passed the pickup and swerved right again, dodging vehicles amid blaring horns. Behind him, the motorcycles spread out across the road and the sidewalks on either side, dodging cars, light poles, and a faded couch abandoned on the sidewalk.

Why were they after him? He had no idea. Not yet, anyway. Dru would know, but he wouldn't risk leading them back to her.

He couldn't outrun these things, he realized, not on the city streets. He'd have to shut this situation down before anyone got hurt.

Greyson raced two more blocks and ducked behind a long strip of warehouses, sliding diagonally on the rain-slick pavement before he straightened the wheel and hit the gas again. Back here, among the scattered trailers and Dumpsters, it didn't look like there were any innocent civilians to get caught in the way.

As he charged ahead, the pavement disappeared under the mirrored surface of standing water, lit to a golden glow as the late-afternoon sun briefly emerged from the clouds. The shadows alongside the warehouses grew darker and deeper. Greyson steered into the narrow band of sunlight between them.

Hellbringer shot across the standing water, throwing it back in curtains. The creatures closed in behind like a pack of hunting animals, spreading out into the shadows on either side, boxing him in.

The creature on the driver's side was closest. Greyson decided to take it out first. He watched it in the side mirror for one second, then another, letting the thing get closer until he could see the goggles stretched across its skull.

"Come on," Greyson murmured. Behind the warehouses, he would run out of pavement at any moment. If these creatures ran him into a fence or a dead end, they would have him cornered.

Keeping to the shadows, the goggled creature stretched out one lanky arm toward Hellbringer's flank. Its bony fingers pointed at the car's tall spoiler wing. Greyson didn't know what this thing was planning to do, but he wasn't about to give it a chance.

"Get ready, buddy," he said to Hellbringer. "This isn't gonna be easy."

He deliberately drifted close to the shadows on his left, until the creature was inches away, bony fingers spread wide. Gauzy webbing swirled into existence, filling the space between its clawed fingers.

Now.

Greyson dropped Hellbringer into second gear, ignoring the engine's howl of protest, and flicked the steering wheel a touch to the right, just enough to make the long car lean on its left tires. As Hellbringer's weight shifted, Greyson spun the wheel hard left.

The tires broke their grip on the waterlogged pavement, and Hellbringer slid sideways with a demonic hiss. Its long nose swung around, and the creature that had been reaching for them hit the left fender at breakneck speed.

The creature catapulted across the hood, tumbling high into the air and out into the direct sunlight. The web-wrapped motorcycle and its skeletal rider separated in midair, torn apart by the laws of physics.

Greyson finished the turn wide, swinging out Hellbringer's rear end like a baseball bat, striking a second oncoming creature with bone-crushing impact. Both of the creatures shattered when they hit the ground, hurling up sprays of water that glowed in the sunlight.

Greyson accelerated head-on toward the remaining creatures. They swerved and scattered into the shadows on either side, as if trying to stay out of the sunlight. If the sun bothered them, maybe he could turn that to his advantage.

Hellbringer's fender, crumpled by the impact, slowly smoothed itself back into place. But the demon car's anger rose up, and Greyson could feel it fighting him at the wheel, eager to turn back around and attack the creatures that now regrouped behind them.

"We're not going to stick around," Greyson said. "Not until we know what we're fighting. We need to buy some time first."

That was something that Dru had taught him. Find out more about your enemy. Be prepared. Don't rush into the fight. Don't get cornered.

He wasn't cornered, at least. Not yet.

But he was out of time. As quickly as it had appeared, the sun disappeared behind the heavy clouds once more. The world around him darkened into a gray gloom. The headlights of the motorcycles surged toward him again.

Rane knelt over Salem where he lay on the floor. She looked more worried than Dru had ever seen her. "D, he's not answering me!"

Dru picked her way through the wreckage of the shop as she studied the text of the ancient book, tracing her finger over the diagram of the magical circle inscribed on one of the pages.

"*D!*"

"Still reading."

"Read faster!"

Outside, footsteps splashed. The bell on the wall jingled as Opal barreled through the front door, precariously balanced on purple-sequined platform mules that matched her crushed purple silk top. Her thick black hair was frizzed from the rain, her dark brown skin wet and shining, her arms loaded down with plastic shopping bags.

When she saw Salem lying on the floor, Opal dropped the bags. Her wide eyes went from the black claw marks on Salem's barely rising chest over to Dru, asking her without a word just how bad it was.

Just as wordlessly, Dru gave her a look that said it was bad. *Really* bad.

"Okay, so the *Folio* says the black stuff is called *scourge*." Awkwardly, Dru held up the ancient book, accidentally tearing one of the brittle pages in half. "Son of a—*argh*. Anyway, according to this, the scourge is sort of a super-creepy undead slime from the netherworld. It can ooze around on its own, and it can get inside you. So we have to be careful. It could attack any of us."

"Rubber gloves," Rane suggested.

Opal nodded dubiously. "We just got that biohazard kit from eBay the other day. Still in the box."

Dru set the book down. "No, I wish it was that easy. But we're talking total magical containment. So, super fast, here's the plan." Dru ticked off points on her fingers, one at a time. "Copper wire to weave a containment circle. Spectrolite to protect his soul. Black tourmaline to keep him grounded. Sulfur to negate the evil energy from the scourge when we expel it from his body."

"Expel it?" Rane said.

Opal wrinkled her nose. "That does not sound sanitary."

"Yeah, well, it's not. According to this, after you drive out the scourge, you can briefly dilute it with pure water. But it separates like oil, so you need something to soak it up before it comes slithering after you again. That's why Salem was so keen to get his hands on some fuller's earth, so he had something to absorb it. But we need to start with the circle." Dru held out a hand to Opal. "At the hardware store, did you find any copper wire?"

"Finding it was easy. Paying for it was something else." Opal dug through one of the shopping bags and pulled out a spool of shiny new wire. "Here you go."

Dru took it and hurried around Salem's body, unrolling enough copper wire to create a circle around him. "Now we just need black tourmaline and sulfur."

Opal searched through the various piles of supplies and came back holding up a pair of small crystals, one spiky and glittering black, the other lumpy and bright yellow. "Tourmaline and sulfur. Where do you want these?"

Dru grimaced in dismay. "Those are tiny. Is that all we have?"

Opal put her hands on her hips. "Far as I can tell. You want them or not?"

"Okay, okay." Dru put one on either side of the circle below Salem's right and left hands. "Got to keep the sulfur away from anything flammable, in case it blows."

She bent the copper wire until it broke from the spool, then twisted the ends together. With practiced ease, she bound the copper wire around each crystal, securing it in place. As she did, she felt the magical power of the crystals humming through the wire. It didn't feel like enough.

Salem was growing paler by the minute. There wasn't much time.

Dru matched the torn pages of the book back together and kept reading. "Says here that we can sluice the scourge off of him with pure water. Luckily, we don't have to find a natural spring, because these days it comes in bottles." Dru glanced around at the wreckage of the shop. "Where's all the bottled water?"

Rane's lips pressed together, and she avoided Dru's gaze. "Okay, so, I was thirsty."

Opal folded her arms. "Did you drink *all* the water?"

"Staying hydrated, dude."

Opal shook her head. "I am not going back to Costco right now."

"Maybe there's one bottle left," Dru said. "Look around."

Trying not to show that she was terrified, Dru sat down cross-legged near Salem's head. Exhaling, she touched one fingertip to the warm copper, tapping herself into the circle. She could feel the energy, like an extension of her body, wrapping around Salem. The black tourmaline on one side helped keep his soul anchored, while the bright yellow sulfur on the other side stood ready to negate the side effects of the scourge as soon as she could draw it out.

With her mind clear, Dru reached for the shimmering dagger-shaped wedge of spectrolite and touched it to Salem's forehead.

A sharp breath blew out from between his lips. His eyes rolled back, showing only whites, and his back arched. With frightening speed, Salem's entire body started to convulse.

They had run out of time.

4
HOT METAL AND GASOLINE

Hellbringer shot out from behind the warehouses back onto the street. Greyson steered like mad, dodging the cars that came at him from both sides.

The long black car skidded across the intersection, toward a flat expanse of undeveloped scrub land. He hopped the curb, and they took off overland.

Hellbringer ran arrow straight across the flat expanse of rain-drenched fields, kicking up twin plumes of grass and leaves against the faded blue silhouettes of the mountains behind them.

Moments later, the pale headlights of the motorcycles peered through the weeds behind them. Two creatures, then three, spread out on either side, closing in fast. The rain clung to their web cocoons, making them shimmer.

Ahead, several trailers sat parked at the far edge of the muddy field, bushes growing up around them. To one side, a squat building was surrounded by junk. On the other side, a pile of dirt and construction scraps rose fifteen feet high. All around, a chain-link fence circled the property, lined with old trucks and trailers parked nose to tail, blocking any exit.

Beyond the fence lay the railroad tracks that marked the city limits, and then the deserted county highway that led straight out of town. In the distance, the endless flatness of the highway was broken only by the regular rhythm of utility poles and occasional trees. That was the best escape route. On the open road, Hellbringer would leave those motorcycles behind in seconds.

If only they could get to the highway, he could lead them out of the city and minimize the chance of innocent bystanders getting hurt. Whatever these creatures were, Dru would know how to stop them. But he couldn't reach her as long as he was trapped here, ringed in by the fence and the parked trailers.

Greyson considered trying to make a stand in the abandoned-looking building. But that meant getting out of Hellbringer, and right now the demon car was his only advantage.

He thought about turning around and doubling back again, but he doubted the same bootlegger trick would work twice. Especially with the darkening clouds making it unlikely any more sunlight would help keep the undead creatures at bay.

That left him only one option. Straight ahead.

The pile of dirt was stacked up with enough siding, lumber, and construction scraps to form a crude ramp. If he could hit it just right, it could carry Hellbringer up over the trailers, the fence, and the railroad tracks beyond.

To the highway. To freedom.

Or they could hit the ground in a fiery pile of wreckage. One or the other.

A long shot, but the only one he had.

He aimed Hellbringer's long nose at the scrap pile and pressed the gas pedal to the floorboard. The massive engine wound up, deafening. The acceleration pushed him back into the seat.

Behind him, two creatures closed in, raising their arms to point their bony fingers at him. Fluttering streamers of webbing shot from their fingers, wrapping onto Hellbringer's tail wing, grabbing it like lassos.

If they were trying to drag Hellbringer to a halt, they were too late. The car hurtled toward the scrap pile and hit the makeshift ramp hard, like a punch in the gut.

With a bang of abused metal and a squeal of tires, Hellbringer shot up the ramp and went airborne over the top.

The world dropped away, and for a moment Greyson felt weightless. The creatures behind them, tethered to Hellbringer's tail wing by webs, tipped into lazy cartwheels.

The car sailed clear over the trailers. The razor-topped fence. The rusty brown railroad tracks.

Tires spun through the air as the car crested the arc of the jump and nosed down toward the hard pavement below. Greyson tensed for the impact, bracing himself against the steering wheel.

Below, the rest of the pack of motorcycles swooped in his direction, riding the rocky fringe of the railroad tracks. The pack must've split up and circled around, trying to catch him from both directions.

As Hellbringer hurtled earthward, the motorcycles drew closer, closer, until they roared onto the road right underneath him.

He knew what was about to happen, but there was no way for him to stop it.

Hellbringer hit the road with a crash of steel and sparks, landing right in the midst of the motorcycle gang, crushing creatures and machines underneath. Moldering bones and fragments of metal scattered across the road.

But the car didn't land square. The crushed wreckage beneath the chassis prevented two wheels from touching the ground, tipping the car dangerously to one side. Out of control, Hellbringer skidded sideways to the edge of the road, where the pavement dropped off into the bumpy, wild grass.

Off-balance, the car tipped up on one side. As the tires left the ground, Greyson fought the steering wheel, but it was no use. The big car slid over the edge of the road and down into the grass.

For a moment, tall grass whipped against the window as the car drunkenly rolled over. Weeds and bushes struck the windshield like hail. Hellbringer quickly shed speed as it pounded its way to a stop off the side of the road, wheels up. The entire car slowly rocked, front and back, on its roof.

Dru watched with horror as Salem writhed on the floor. "We have to wash away the scourge! *Now!* We need water!"

Rane tore the room apart. Books, jars, and cans went flying.

Opal wrung her hands. "What about tap water?"

"Not pure enough. Has to be water straight from a natural source." Her torn-up shop offered her nothing but walls stained wet from the rain as it leaked in through her smashed windows. Right then, the solution hit her. "Rain!"

"I'm *looking*!" Rane shouted back.

"Not *Rane*. Rain, rain!" Dru pointed at the dripping wet window frames. "It's natural water. Catch some. Hurry!"

Frantically, Opal rooted through her shopping bags. "I don't have any cups, or bowls, or anything. Hell." She emptied out a bag from the dollar store, dumping shampoo, candy bars, and kitty litter on the floor. Holding the empty plastic bag open wide, she headed out into the cold rain. "Hold on!"

"Hold on," Dru repeated to Salem, whispering it again and again like a mantra over his convulsing body. The copper wire grew hot in Dru's hand, threatening to burn her. "Hold on, Salem!"

Opal rushed over, holding maybe an inch of rain in the bottom of a dripping plastic bag. Rane got there first, her big hands cupped full of water.

Dru wanted to hug them both. But her hands were busy holding together the protective copper circle.

With her mind, Dru reached out through the wire to the yellow sulfur and activated it. Holding her breath, she poured energy into the crystal, making it glow as yellow as a traffic light.

The unseen presence of the scourge reacted with the sulfur, blasting it to pieces.

Dru's ears rang from the blast. Bits of shattered sulfur clattered off the ceiling and walls.

Repelled by the sulfur, the scourge backed out of Salem's body, oozing out through the claw wounds. The black slime wriggled across Salem's pale skin.

"Okay, now the water!" Dru sent her last reserves of energy through the wire into the tourmaline, anchoring Salem's soul against the onslaught of the scourge.

Carefully, Opal and Rane poured steady trickles of rain water over Salem. Purified by the presence of the charged tourmaline, the water sparkled like a stream of diamonds as it fell.

It rinsed away the scourge, exposing clean skin underneath. The flow of water chased black swirls of scourge off Salem until it pooled in a tar-colored puddle next to his body. Hissing, the scourge seemed to come alive, slithering toward the break in the circle where the sulfur had been.

"Dru!" Opal backed up a step. "It's moving!"

"Don't touch it!" Dru said, as Rane moved to stomp on it. "It'll get inside you!"

Dru didn't dare let the scourge escape the circle, or it would turn right back on one of them. As the foul puddle slithered toward freedom, she tore her horrified gaze away. There had to be something she could use to stop it.

Behind Opal lay the pile of stuff she'd bought at the dollar store. Cheap pink shampoo. Brightly colored candy bars. A bag of kitty litter.

Kitty litter.

Dru sprang to her feet, snatched up the bag, and ripped it open. Just before the scourge reached the edge of the circle, she dumped a pile of dusty gray kitty litter on it, burying it.

The scourge let out a muffled squeal and went silent as the litter soaked it up.

Dru stood over it, grinning at the surprised looks on everyone's faces. "Just remembered. Old-fashioned kitty litter, the kind from the dollar store? It's made of fuller's earth."

Opal smiled widely with satisfaction. "See? If I didn't go to the store, this place would fall apart. Mark my words."

Salem's eyes moved under his heavily lined lids. He gasped, then stirred and blinked up at them. "Well," he croaked, "this is embarrassing."

Rane smothered him in a tight hug, rocking back and forth, smoothing his hair down. Seeing them embrace made Dru feel all warm and fuzzy. To a point, anyway, considering it was Salem.

When Rane finally let him go, Salem pointed to the pile of kitty litter. "What are you going to do with that?"

"Get rid of it." Dru stood up slowly, dizzy from the effort of the spell.

Opal headed back to the storeroom and returned with a heavy-duty red plastic bag stamped with a biohazard symbol. "What did I tell you? I said we need a biohazard kit around here. Didn't I say that? And look, it was cheap on eBay." She pulled on long rubber gloves and tugged each one tight with a loud snap.

"Maybe we should double bag this." Dru put on her own gloves and carefully helped Opal sweep the contaminated mess into the bag. There wasn't much more than a couple of fistfuls of clay, but its very presence scared her.

With Rane's help, Salem struggled to his feet and held out his hand. "I'll take that."

"What? *Why?* No." Dru clutched the bag tighter, which she immediately recognized as a horrible idea. She set it down on the floor and backed away. "Why would you want that? It nearly killed you."

Rane nodded. "She's right. Screw that."

Wincing, Salem pulled his torn black shirt back on and buttoned it. "Let's call it scientific curiosity."

"No. Forget it." Dru sagged against the wall, feeling drained. "That undead scourge is going nowhere. Don't worry, I'll keep it someplace safe."

Salem gave her a ghastly smile. "Well, against the undead forces from the netherworld, I'm sure your made-in-China plastic bag is the best defense."

Dru's mouth dropped open in indignation. "By the way, *you're welcome* for saving your life. Now, how did you get into this mess in the first place? Where were you attacked by undead?"

Instead of answering, Salem finished straightening his clothes. "Where's Ember? She should have been here by now."

Dru didn't have to look at Rane to know the hurt look on her face.

The man was impossible. In frustration, Dru shoved her hands into her pockets. She felt the black Lemurian jade crystal that had mysteriously appeared in her mail slot earlier. When she pulled it out, its polished surface glittered with golden flecks of iron pyrite.

Without a doubt, this was the crystal she had given to Greyson. To help protect him.

What had happened to him? Where was he now?

Momentarily stunned from the crash, Greyson crawled out the broken window, looking around for the creatures that pursued him. For now, the road was empty. But the unmistakable droning of motorcycle engines approached from the distance.

Greyson stood up. At his feet, the broken glass reformed, like frost on a freezing winter day. As long as he stayed close by, Hellbringer could heal. But it couldn't flip itself over.

As he surveyed the upside-down car—the dirty frame, the snaking exhaust pipes, the dented metal slowly straightening itself out—Greyson wasn't sure if he could turn the car completely over on his own. Tipping it over when it was balanced on its side, like he had done in the netherworld, was one thing. His connection to the speed demon certainly made him feel stronger than he ever had been in his life. But completely flipping it over? He didn't know if he was *that* strong.

"This would be a lot easier if you could just keep your rubber on the road," he growled. The car didn't respond.

Greyson worked his shoulders, trying to loosen them up, and stepped up to the side of the car. Taking a deep breath, he planted his hands wide against the black metal, tensed, and pushed.

The car didn't budge.

Teeth gritted, muscles straining, Greyson kept pushing until his veins pounded and his vision narrowed to a pale tunnel. His legs began to shake, then his back and arms. Slowly, the car tilted a few inches, but it wasn't enough.

With a painful gasp, Greyson let go. Hellbringer settled back on its roof with an awful crunching sound.

Breath burning in his lungs, Greyson sagged against the side of the car, trying to think up a new plan in a hurry. There were more of those motorcycles out there, and it wouldn't take them long to catch up.

Behind Hellbringer, a long path of flattened grass and bushes marked their departure from the road. Among the scattered bits of motorcycle wreckage that dotted the path, something stirred.

Greyson watched with sinking disbelief as a blackened bony arm rose up from the grass, followed by a cobweb-shrouded helmet. Inexorably, the helmet turned toward him, revealing cracked goggles and a web-wrapped skull. Its jaw stretched wide with a bubbling hiss.

"You've got to be *kidding* me," Greyson muttered.

If he couldn't run, then he had to make sure that these creatures were in no shape to follow him. It was time to finish this.

He searched for something, anything, to use as a weapon. Nearby lay a bent wire motorcycle wheel, sheared off by the force of the crash. Traces of cobwebs still clung to it.

It would have to do. Greyson picked it up in both hands and marched toward the creature.

He was still a dozen paces away when the thing raised its bony fingers and summoned up a gauzy haze of webbing.

Greyson stopped in his tracks. He'd forgotten about that part.

A stream of web shot out of the thing's clawed hand, straight at Greyson. He blocked it with the motorcycle wheel, but the creature pulled its arm back and yanked the tire from Greyson's grip with uncanny ease.

As he watched the motorcycle wheel sail away into the grass, Greyson realized that he had only ever run away from a fight maybe twice in his life.

Right now might make a good third time.

All around him, more hissing limbs clawed their way up out of the grass, reforming into skeletal creatures. Some of them were missing arms, some legs. But all of them crawled directly toward him, closing in with relentless hate that he could practically feel against his skin.

There were just too many of them. And he didn't know how to fight them. Not yet. But he intended to find out.

As he turned to sprint back toward Hellbringer, a streamer of web shot toward him. He dodged to the side, but another web caught his ankle, jerking his foot out from beneath him. He stumbled, hitting the edge of the wet asphalt with his shoulder.

Ignoring the pain, Greyson rolled to the side, trying to get his boot off. More webs hit him, pinning one arm, and then his other leg.

Without any other options, he crawled, pulling himself out onto the wet road with his one free arm.

And then a web caught that arm, too.

He struggled, but the web was too strong. It held him down so tightly that he couldn't turn his head, or even lift it from the wet pavement that dug into his cheek.

Every breath took effort. The web constricted his chest, choked his lungs. With every movement of his ribs, it seemed to grow tighter.

Footsteps approached behind him, clicking on the blacktop. He couldn't turn to look. All he could do was listen.

Boots. Not motorcycle boots, but expensive ones with leather soles. Before Greyson could see who the boots belonged to, the air around him rippled. Magical crackles of energy sizzled all around him, electrifying the webs like a bolt of lightning.

For one terrible moment, Greyson felt nothing but searing pain.

And then he felt nothing at all.

5

THE DAMAGE DONE

D ru gasped. A sharp pain shot through her entire body, fiery and yet cold. She leaned against the wall of the shop to keep her balance.

Opal laid a warm hand on Dru's shoulder. "Honey. You okay? You want to go upstairs, lie down for a few?"

"No." Dru winced as the pain faded to a dull ache, leaving her strangely nauseous. She knew it was magical, but it wasn't from her spell. She didn't know what had brought it on. No matter how much that worried her, she had something more important to worry about.

She met Opal's gaze. "I saw Hellbringer. I think Greyson is alive."

"*Alive?*" Opal's eyes went wide. "How? What happened? Where on earth *is* he?"

"That's what we're going to find out." She turned to Rane, whose muscles flexed as she held onto Salem's arm, steadying him. "Make sure he gets home in one piece, okay? Opal and I are going looking for Greyson."

"We are?" Opal said.

"Right now?" Rane said.

Salem accosted her. "Not one of your better ideas, sweetheart. And in the grand scheme of things, that's saying a lot." He shook his hair out of his face, revealing his usual crazy stare. "Actually, I take that back. Could be a brilliant idea. For someone else. Leave the field investigation to the experts."

Rane snorted. "Yeah, like you're one to talk. Look at you, all messed up."

Dru nodded. "Salem, I don't have time for any verbal ninjutsu. Opal, you remember where Greyson's place is? Let me find my purse." Somewhere in the shop, on one of those piles of wreckage, Dru knew her purse was waiting. She just had to find it.

Rane followed her with a squeak of running shoes. "Dude, hang on. You're going to need me with you, too. In case."

"In case what?"

"In case *anything*."

Dru hesitated. Maybe Rane was right.

Salem came up behind them, putting one hand on Rane's back, the other on Dru's. He leaned close between them, as if sharing an embarrassing secret. "I'm only going to say this once. I know you helped me quite a bit, Dru, which you didn't have to do. And I appreciate that. So let me return the favor." He stared deep into Dru's eyes. "I suggest *not* going looking for your ersatz demon beau."

Dru traded glances with Rane, who was clearly as puzzled as she was. "Why not?" Dru asked slowly. "What do you know?"

He sighed. "The situation is a little out of depth for you and the Brady Bunch." He shrugged. "Just stating a fact. You're big on rules, Dru, so here's a new one for you: no more boyfriends from beyond the grave. Generally unhealthy. Not to mention unwholesome."

"You're unbelievable." Dru studied Salem's angular face. Now that the color was coming back into his defined cheeks, he was starting to look like his old self. For the briefest moment, Dru could see why Rane was so drawn to him. Despite his snarky attitude, there was something enigmatically inviting about Salem's presence. The closer you got to him, the more it seemed as if he had layers and layers of secrets that he could share with you, if you were worthy enough.

Provided you could stand his attitude without strangling him.

Rane nudged him. Hard. "Hey. Are you messing with my best friend? Because, dude, that's not funny."

"Just ignore him." Dru broke out of Salem's reach and went back to looking for her purse. "He'll live, I'm pretty sure. As long as none of us murders him. There are a few crystals I'd like to send him home with, but there's no way I can find anything in this place right now. So just keep an eye on him for a while. Call me if his condition changes."

"You mean if he starts acting funny? Dude, that's *all* he does." With a satisfied smile, Rane draped herself over Salem. She was a full head taller than him.

He ducked out from beneath her. "Hmm, too cozy. I don't do cozy anymore."

Rane bristled. "The hell is that supposed to mean?"

"Just this." Stepping back, Salem pointed back and forth between himself and Rane. "This is not happening again."

After nearly giving up on her purse, Dru finally spotted it atop a pile of wreckage, right between Salem and Rane. Without making eye contact, Dru awkwardly tiptoed between them and picked it up. "Sorry," she whispered, then headed for the front door, motioning to Opal that it was time to go.

Outside, tall boot heels clicked on the wet pavement. They splashed through the rain, coming closer.

Just as Dru reached for the broken door, it flew open and in stepped a dark-skinned woman in a long black leather coat and ripped leggings. Her eyebrow piercings flashed above thick, dark eye makeup as she threw back her hood.

Ember. Salem's new girlfriend.

Ember wasn't her real name, of course, but sorceresses rarely went by their real names.

Unusually fiery, unsettlingly dark, and often mercenary in her allegiances, Ember was one of the few sorceresses Dru actually feared. Not because she was so powerful—most of them were more powerful than Dru—but because Ember was so unpredictable. Add in a frightening dose of relentless ambition, and that made Ember a dangerous aggressor, hungry to take what she wanted from anyone in her way.

"Finally." Salem crossed the shop toward her. "I thought you'd left me stranded here at the kiddie table."

"Had a little trouble on the road," she said quietly to Salem, but despite her thick Arabic accent, her voice cut through the shop. "And you?"

He merely shrugged.

The vulnerability Rane had revealed only moments before instantly vanished, hidden under a steely glare. Rane visibly puffed up, biceps flexing. "He almost got his candy ass handed to him by a zombie. Where the hell were you? Why didn't you have his back?"

Ember's dark complexion flushed. "You cannot possibly speak to me that way."

"Sticks and stones." Salem motioned Ember toward the door. "Just ignore her, and she'll go away."

With both hands, Rane flipped him the bird. "Get over your fancy self, dude. If it wasn't for Dru and the rest of us, you'd be zombie num-nums right now. You need to pay her back."

Salem rolled his eyes. "Fine. I'll just go to the ATM and wait in line behind the unwashed masses who *didn't* devote their lives to conquering the celestial forces of magic."

"Not *money*," Rane said. "I mean start spilling everything you know about the undead."

He squinted, as if pretending to think it over. "Hmm. No."

At the mention of money, Dru had to try hard not to think of the stack of unpaid bills buried somewhere beneath the wreckage of the shop. But at this point, she was pretty sure she was out of business anyway. She just hadn't had time to process that fact yet.

For a moment, the sudden recognition that she was going to lose her shop threatened to overwhelm her. Her eyes stung with unshed tears, and she blinked to clear them.

Now was not the time to lose it. Not here, in front of everyone.

She was so focused on calming herself down that she almost tuned out the rising argument between Rane and Salem.

"Dude, quit acting like you've got some kind of higher calling and the rest of us are beneath you. Dru is the one who makes this all possible." Rane jabbed a finger in Dru's direction. "She's the one who's here every day, twenty-four seven. Reading the books. Brewing the potions. Charging up the crystals. You think that's a cakewalk? She had to sell her *house* to open this shop."

All eyes went to Dru, and she squirmed under the sudden scrutiny. "Well, um, not a house, exactly." She swallowed down the thick lump in her throat. "But I did sell my car. Does that count?"

"See?" Rane said. "This girl has sacrificed. Now she has to ride the bus."

Opal frowned. "I've never seen you take the bus."

Dru held up a finger. "And I am very grateful for the fact that you own a car."

"D!" Rane barked. "Stop helping."

Dru knew she had to shut this down before it spiraled out of control. "That's enough, everybody. Just forget it and go, Salem. Really no big deal."

Rane poked a finger at Salem. "She's right. You're *no* big deal."

Dru held up her hands. "Um, no, that's not what I . . ."

"No big deal?" Salem had turned to go, but he stopped. A cold fury swept over his chiseled features. "No big *deal*?"

"Uh-uh," Opal said under her breath, shaking her head side to side. "Gone too far this time."

Salem's twitching gaze swept across the wreckage of the store. "Let me show you what it means to be a *big deal*."

Like a raven spreading its wings, Salem threw his arms wide. His black trench coat rippled in the silent winds of magic, and sparks of energy flared between his spidery fingers.

An unearthly light suffused the shop, like daylight breaking through a thick fog. The hairs on the back of Dru's neck prickled with the intensity of immense volumes of power flowing in invisible waves around her.

Up and down the length of the shop, toppled bookcases groaned and drunkenly rose up from the wreckage. Like fallen dominoes righting themselves, they shifted back into position and stood straight.

Broken shelves mended themselves. Cracked boards straightened, and splintered wood crinkled as it knitted itself back together.

Dru's breath caught in her throat.

With a hushed clatter, thousands of objects rose into the air around them. Jars of herbs. Bottles of essential oils. Stacks of tan handwritten papers bound together by old twine.

Like a flock of birds taking flight, it all soared and swooped, then landed on the shelves.

The musty smells of herbs and incense swirled and faded as containers reassembled and flew onto shelves. Bottles sucked up their spilled multicolored powders, and corks popped back into place. Open boxes flipped closed.

Wrinkled old maps snapped straight and plastered themselves to the walls. Stacks of books glided through the air and fluttered up into neat rows, lining up one after another. Crystals and fossils tumbled and jostled their way back into divided trays.

Papers uncrumpled. Ribbons slithered. Jars swooped.

Dru stared in awe. She knew her mouth was hanging open, but she couldn't close it. She didn't dare move as the contents of her destroyed shop swirled around her, like snowflakes in a just-shaken snow globe. Through it all, the deep hum of Salem's spell thrummed through her bones.

His thin fingers kneaded the air, sending out unseen waves of magic, warming the shop with an electric tingle. His long coat billowed around him. His face lit with an unearthly glow, making his eyes shimmer white.

The whole time, Ember stood silently behind him, smirking with triumph as she watched everyone's wide-eyed surprise.

Objects flew onto the newly restored bookcases without any rhyme or reason, as if Salem's magic simply plucked the nearest items out of the air and shelved them at random. Apparently, although Salem's restorative powers were incredible, organization was not his thing.

As everything flew back onto random shelves, the sharp contours of the shop emerged from underneath the vanishing mounds of debris.

In moments, the entire mess was put away, more or less. The light fixtures overhead, hanging by their wires, nestled back into place. The shattered light bulbs reassembled and flickered to life. Every surface gleamed, clean and polished.

Sparkling bits of broken glass streaked up from the floor and reassembled into cracked windows. The twisted metal frames straightened and smoothed out. With a squeal like thin ice breaking, the cracks in the glass erased, leaving the windows clean and whole again.

Insulated from the dank outside air, the shop quickly grew warm. The air pressure inside built unnaturally high, making Dru's ears ache, as the unstoppable force of the spell reached critical mass.

All at once, the diffuse light of magic drew back, swirling around Salem like a horde of fireflies until it disappeared back into his long fingers with a sizzling whisper. He lowered his arms to his sides, now so pale and gaunt that Dru feared he would pass out again.

As he swayed, Ember stepped up behind him, steadying him before Rane could. The two women traded glares.

It took Salem a moment to recover. Then he shook himself free, straightened the lapels of his black trench coat and stepped closer to Rane. Everything in his posture radiated aggression. He stopped inches from her, looking up, his pale, crazy eyes locking with hers. One corner of his mouth lifted in a sneer.

"I *am* a *big deal*." He bit off the words. Then he turned to go again, and almost as an afterthought, he added, "Are you?"

He locked gazes with her a moment longer, then shifted his cold look to Dru. "You and I? We're even now. I owe you *nothing*." He turned and marched out of the shop. Ember followed him, sparing only a glance at the rest of them, her dark gaze triumphant.

A shocked silence filled the newly restored shop after the door closed behind them.

"Holy Fantasia!" Dru said finally. "Did you know he could do that?" She turned in a slow circle, staring around at her packed shelves, unable to process all of the emotions she felt. Relief. Elation. Anger. Indignation. Awe.

It was all too much. She had to let it go. Accept it as another day in the incredible life of magic.

"Was he talking about us?" Opal said after a moment. "I think he was talking about all of us. Not a big deal. You believe that?"

"He's just overcompensating." Dru pushed her glasses back up her nose. "Honestly, I don't even try to understand Salem anymore. I just try to save his life every once in a while and ignore his power-hungry, prickly weirdness."

"Well, his prickly-ness needs an attitude adjustment. The man has some kind of Napoleon complex, and that's going to be the death of him someday if he doesn't turn it around." Opal sighed. "Everything's out of order, of course. Take us forever to organize it all. And when I say 'us' of course, what I really mean is *me*."

"Well, you are especially brilliant at organizing," Dru said. She turned to Rane.

Rane stood stock-still, fists clenched at her sides. Though she didn't even blink, a violent tension radiated from her body.

Dru's heart went out to her. She wasn't sure if she should give her a hug, or a moment of breathing room. She knew full well that an inevitable outburst was on the way. Hopefully, it wouldn't involve any collateral damage. Especially not now, the moment things in the shop were finally getting back together.

Inwardly, Dru flinched. Maybe best not to use the phrase "getting back together" around Rane right now.

Dru tiptoed over to Rane. She still stood motionless, her red face wrinkled with anger, her entire body taut.

"Hey," Dru said softly. "That was just his way of being a jerk. Forget about him."

Rane gritted her teeth. "I keep *trying* to forget him."

Dru wasn't sure if it was safe to give Rane a hug or not, so she settled on laying a gentle hand on her arm. "Honey, listen, I love you, and I want you to be okay. Do you need anything?"

A muscle in Rane's face twitched, making her squint. "Yeah. Gotta break something, you know?"

Dru didn't, but she nodded anyway. "Okay."

"Got anything?"

"Breakable? Um, no." Slowly, Dru shook her head from side to side. "But there's a Dumpster out back. Probably has some junk in it."

"Got cinder blocks at home. I need to run anyway."

Dru wasn't sure what that meant exactly, so she just nodded again. Without another word, Rane burst out through the door and launched into an immediate sprint, legs pounding the wet pavement. In moments, she disappeared from view.

Opal cleared her throat. "You still want to go?"

Go find Greyson. That thought crashed down on Dru, shattering the moment. Finding Greyson meant everything. Not just to her, but to the world. If Greyson really was alive, and still driving Hellbringer, then he still had the power of a Horseman of the Apocalypse. And now that the dead were starting to rise from the grave, that surely meant doomsday was on the way.

How much time did the world have left?

Dru nodded. "Let's go."

"Okay, then. Just let me get my keys."

As Opal headed in back, Dru shook herself and looked around. As surreal as it was, she couldn't help but revel in the squeaky-cleanness of her newly restored shop. She wondered if it was possible for this day to get any weirder.

Then she realized the red bag of scourge was missing.

6
THINGS THAT MAKE
YOU GO HMM

Dru scanned the shop's many shelves, looking for the red biohazard bag full of undead scourge. Something like that would be impossible to miss, she figured. But she couldn't find it anywhere. That wasn't good.

"Opal," she called, "did you do anything with that red plastic bag?"

"The kitty litter with the evil undead hoodoo?" Opal called back. "Nuh-uh. I'm not touching that. Why, where did you put it?"

"Maybe it just got moved during Salem's cleanup spell." Dru tried to reassure herself with that thought, but as she walked up and down the aisles a second time, a bad feeling settled in the pit of her stomach. She had to finally admit that the bag of scourge was gone.

Taken. But why?

Salem could have whisked away the red bag while they were all distracted by his spell. That would be typically sneaky of him. But what could he possibly want with that foul scourge anyway, especially since it had nearly killed him?

She tapped her teeth with a fingernail, pondering what it all meant. Could it have something to do with Greyson?

"You still want to go check out Greyson's place?" Opal said, jangling her car keys.

"Yeah. . . ." Dru stared at the shelves a moment longer, then headed back to the cash register and held out her hand for the keys. "Do you want me to drive?"

Opal folded her arms protectively across her ample chest. "No, you can't drive my ride. No telling what might happen. We might end up in the middle of the desert somewhere, crashed at the bottom of a cliff."

"Give me a break." Dru hitched her purse up onto her shoulder. "That was only *one time*."

Opal's purple Lincoln was comfortable like an old sofa, one that's been around so long it's become a constant fixture of life. The car's familiar perfume-laden presence wrapped around Dru like a security blanket, insulating her from the cold, drippy world outside. Though the rain had finally stopped, the heavy gray clouds turned everything outside the color of lead.

Dru couldn't help but dwell on the mystery surrounding Greyson, even as the Lincoln's rearview mirror distracted her with a waterfall of sparkling necklaces, magical charms, and other hanging baubles. Perhaps in an effort to cheer her up, Opal cranked up the head-bobbing hits of C+C Music Factory to mind-expanding volume.

They rolled across town toward Greyson's place like an impromptu dance party in a purple parade float. In the driver's seat, Opal bobbed her head to the music. Her lip-sync skills were flawless.

Dru's phone rang. The screen showed her occasional customer and erstwhile handyman, Ruiz. Like Opal, he didn't have any magical powers of his own, but he came from a long line of sorcerers, and he had helped Dru out more than once.

Maybe *helped* wasn't exactly the right word. On more than one occasion, he had accidentally meddled with magical forces he couldn't control. One time, he managed to burn a permanent pumpkin-shaped scorch mark on her shop floor, triggering a chain of events that trapped Opal and Dru on a runaway magic carpet.

But still, he was a friend.

Dru reached over to turn the music down, earning a scowl from Opal as she answered the phone. "Hi, Ruiz. You're not on fire again, are you?"

"Who, me?" Ruiz said, over a blast of wind noise. He wasn't supposed to smoke in his work van, so he drove around with the window down. "Nah. Not this time."

"Is that Ruiz?" Opal asked, then fluttered her fingers at the phone as if he could see her. "*Hola*, Ruiz!"

"So I just got back into town and somebody told me your shop got all blown up. That's messed up, man. You and Opal okay?"

"Yeah, thanks," Dru said. "Had a big fight with the Four Horsemen of the Apocalypse."

"For real? Wow." He blew out a long breath and talked around his cigarette. "You need some help cleaning up the shop? I got all my tools."

"Oh, thank you. But Salem already cleaned everything up."

"Salem?" Ruiz sounded shocked. "The skinny little guy with the big Abe Lincoln hat?"

Dru wondered where Salem's hat was, anyway. He never went anywhere without it. But something else occurred to her. "Hey, do me a favor. Do you know what a 1969 Dodge Daytona looks like?" She pictured Hellbringer's long, pointed nose and threatening back wing. "It's really old and—"

"Yeah, yeah, I got it. Daytona, sure. Sweet car. Why?"

"I'm looking for a black one with a license plate that says 'HELL-BRINGER.' Or an abbreviation of that, anyway. If you see it, call me immediately. It belongs to a . . . friend of mine."

"Oh. Got stolen?"

Dru hesitated. If she was talking to anyone else, she would try to lie and probably fail miserably. But she could trust Ruiz. "No. It's a speed demon."

"Oh, man. It's dangerous?"

"Only if you get on its bad side. Who I'm really looking for is the driver. His name's Greyson. Tall, dark hair, leather jacket." She hesitated. "His eyes might be glowing red."

"Uh . . . sure, sure. You got it." Nervously, he added, "Hey, tell Opal I said *hola* back, okay?"

After they hung up, Dru contemplated her phone a moment before she put it away. "So this thing keeps bugging me."

"Hmm." Opal sighed and slouched down in the seat. "Something's always bugging you."

"I'm serious."

"And I'm listening."

Dru pulled off her glasses and cleaned them on her shirt. "After the explosion, we couldn't find Greyson anywhere. I thought he was dead. And that just about killed me." Her eyes started to burn, and she blinked to clear away the tears. "Why would he just leave me the crystal and take off? Why didn't he even want to see me? Maybe he thinks we left him behind on purpose, in the netherworld? Do you think he hates me?"

"Oh, honey. You sure it was him you saw? Maybe it was someone else's car."

Dru shook her head no. "I know he's alive. I don't know how, and I can't explain it, but I just know it. Deep inside. Besides, how many cars have you ever seen that look even remotely like Hellbringer?"

"Hmm. Good point."

"So where did he go? Why didn't he talk to me?"

Opal gave Dru a sympathetic look. "The man comes back from the dead, doesn't even call you. Typical."

"Something's wrong."

"Something's *always* wrong." Opal stopped at a light and put on her turn signal. "So where do you think Salem got hit with that undead scourge, anyway? That's some serious trouble, right there."

"I don't know. And it's not like he's going to explain himself to us." Dru played with the gold chains hanging from the mirror. "What is all this stuff, anyway? It's like Mr. T's dressing room."

Opal's eyebrows went up. "That's my collection. What do you think I use my wholesale discount for? Besides, a little good luck charm action never hurt anybody."

"Would if it fell on them," Dru muttered.

If Opal heard, she pretended not to notice. "I don't trust Salem's new girlfriend. What's her name? Ember?"

"Yeah. Me either. Why not?"

"Just don't. Maybe I don't have magic powers, but I do know trouble when I see it." Opal gave her a meaningful look. "Best watch yourself around her."

"Mostly, I'm going to be watching Rane. Trying to make sure those two don't start pulling hair and knocking down walls."

"Only a matter of time." Opal steered the boatlike Lincoln onto a residential side street. "You know, last time I was in Greyson's neighborhood, it was nighttime. Looks even scarier in the daylight."

Dru had to reluctantly agree. Greyson's neighborhood was sketchy at best. Ever since they'd crossed the railroad tracks, the lawns had turned patchy and neglected, mostly bare spots littered with wrinkled newspapers and potato chip bags. Weeds grew up through the cracked sidewalks.

Boarded-up brick houses lurked on every block, most of them tagged with layers of graffiti. They were broken up by one-level apartment buildings that had obviously been converted from old run-down motels.

"It's not so bad," Dru insisted, trying to convince herself.

"So you say. You got your protective crystals with you?"

Dru nodded. "Never leave home without them."

"Mmm-hmm. Unless you do."

"Okay, *hardly* ever."

They pulled up to the curb outside Greyson's place. He lived in a nondescript tan cinder block building that was mostly one big garage, with a small apartment attached. The grass out front was healthy and green, unlike the rest of the block, but it hadn't been mowed in a while. There was no sign he'd been back home since it had all happened.

"It" meaning the battle against the Four Horsemen. And the massive explosion that had left him missing, and his demonic black car, Hellbringer, lying crumpled somewhere in the netherworld.

In her mind's eye, Dru kept seeing Hellbringer's empty driver's seat through a frame of shattered glass. She couldn't shake the image.

The broken glass. The empty seat. The terrible solitude inside her when she knew Greyson was gone.

Gone where, though? Because they hadn't found him then. And if he wasn't here at home, there was no telling where he was now.

Opal turned off the engine and thumbed through the amulets hanging from the rearview mirror. "Let's see. Tiger's eye. Lucky rabbit's foot. Talugh charm."

"Talugh?" With one finger, Dru pulled the charm closer. It was made of a cloudy alum salt crystal wrapped in fine gold wire, tapered like the funnel cloud of a tornado. "Isn't that a charm against bubonic plague?"

Opal dropped her chin, giving Dru a no-nonsense look. "Bubonic plague's a thing. Probably rats in this neighborhood. Rats have fleas. Fleas carry the plague. Get the picture?"

"Yeah, but these days we've got, you know, antibiotics."

"Oh, how did I forget about that? And by the way, can you afford health insurance? Me either." Opal strung the Talugh charm around her neck and nestled it down among the crevices in her crushed purple silk top. "What else do we need?"

"It's not like we're planning on going to war. I'm just going to knock on his door."

"Mmm-hmm," Opal said, clearly not believing her. She pointed past Dru's knees to the breadbox-sized glove compartment. "Got some holy water in there. Any undead limping around, we might need to throw that on them."

Rummaging through the clutter, Dru turned up a small plastic squeeze bottle, the kind used for taking liquids through airport security. "This?" She held it up. "Wish we'd had this when we were working on Salem. But there's probably not enough in here, anyway." She shook the bottle.

"Hey, don't shake that!"

"Sorry."

Opal tucked it in her purse and sighed. "All right. What else do we need?"

Dru patted her own purse, and crystals clinked inside. "We're all good. Let's go."

As they got out of the car into the dank, mud-smelling air, Dru felt a flutter of nervousness in her stomach. It didn't look like Greyson was home. But what if he *was* here? What would she say to him? How would he react?

What had happened to him in the netherworld? Had he come back as the same Greyson she remembered?

Or, and she shuddered to think this, did he come back somehow different?

Halfway up the front walk, Dru froze. A terrible thought occurred to her.

"It's going to be okay." Opal squeezed her arm. "It will."

"Wait. Wait. Greyson comes back, and Salem gets attacked by undead." Anxiously, Dru held out her palms. "Tell me I'm wrong. Please."

Opal seemed puzzled.

Dru cleared her throat and connected the dots for her. "What I'm saying is, what if Greyson *is* the undead? It's too much of a coincidence. Isn't it?"

Opal's eyes went wide. Then she shook her head and dismissed the thought with a wave. "Nuh-uh. Undead can't drive cars."

"Really?"

"Pretty sure. I mean, I never asked a zombie for a driver's license. But I don't think so."

Dru wasn't sure she trusted Opal's logic, but she decided to go with that. "Okay. Let's do this." Steeling herself, she took a deep breath and marched up to Greyson's front door, raising her hand to knock.

But she didn't. Even from here, it was clear that his place was cold, dark, and empty.

The chipped blinds in the window next to the door were tilted partway open, and through them she could see the shadowy kitchen. Coffee cups still sat on the counter, exactly where she had left them however many mornings ago. They hadn't been touched since the day Dru and Greyson had finally joined forces and headed out on an epic road trip that nearly led to doomsday.

Seeing such an ordinary little thing as those coffee cups brought all of her doubts crashing down around her.

What if she was wrong?

What if he really was gone?

Her eyes burned with tears, but she blinked them away. With an effort, she clamped down on her emotions. She still didn't know anything yet. There could be some kind of explanation. He could come driving down the street at any moment.

It was possible, she reassured herself. Anything was possible.

Before she could talk herself out of it, she raised her fist and pounded on his door. There was no response. A dog across the street started barking. She hesitated, then tried the doorknob. Locked.

Standing next to her, Opal scrolled through her phone. "You know, I don't have Greyson in here. You got his number?"

"I don't think he has a phone."

"Come on, everybody's got a phone. Is he on Facebook?"

"No. I checked."

Opal was clearly startled. "For real? You're kidding me. Everybody's on Facebook."

"Rane's not. Salem's not."

"Well, who's going to send them a friend request? It's called social media because you're supposed to be sociable. Not *sociopathic*."

"Rane's fine. She just has issues with boundaries. And impulse control. And, you know, breaking stuff. Hey, that reminds me." Dru headed around the side of the building, where she remembered there was another door. One that Rane had kicked open the night they'd dragged Greyson inside, unconscious, in the form of a demon.

Dru sighed. Nothing was ever easy.

The door stood not quite closed beneath a caged light bulb clogged with dead insects. The wooden frame was splintered, and the dented steel clearly showed the imprint of Rane's size 12 running shoe.

The abused door creaked as she eased it open. "Hello? Anybody home?" Her voice echoed through the darkened garage. It was easily big enough for three cars, but right now it was empty. The smells of gasoline and road dust rolled out through the doorway.

Somehow, she had expected to see Hellbringer parked in the shadows, shiny black and menacing, waiting for her. But there was no sign of the demon car.

Opal stayed planted in the alley, eyes wide. "Dru, I don't like this. Maybe we should call the police."

"And tell them what, exactly? We thought Greyson was dead in the netherworld, but now we've seen his demon car driving around, so maybe they could come break into his house for us?"

"Maybe not in exactly those words."

Without stepping inside, Dru reached in and flipped on the light switch. Carefully, she peered through the doorway. Long chrome bumpers and round air cleaners hung suspended from the walls, jammed between metal shelves packed with parts, spray cans, jugs of oil and antifreeze, and a million little automotive things Dru couldn't identify.

A welding rig sat in the far corner, topped by a dark protective mask adorned with hot rod flames. Red tool chests lined one wall, chipped and grimy from years of hard use. The endless stretch of drawers was broken by colorful stickers advertising unfamiliar brands like Edelbrock and Summit Racing.

Dru was about to step inside when something else caught her eye. Faint sparkling threads stretched across the doorframe. They swooped from the edge of the door up the side of the wall in a great glittering arc, like a giant necklace or net. The strands were so thin that they disappeared if she turned her head.

Strange.

"What?" Opal asked, backing up a step. "You've got that look on your face you always get right before everything goes bananas."

"Not bananas. But I do need to take a closer look at this." Dru fished a frosty cube of ulexite out of her purse and lifted it to her forehead. Her vision swam at first, then steadied as she concentrated, letting her magical energy flow into the crystal.

All around her, colors muted and shadows deepened as the crystal enhanced her vision. Everything around her lit with a soft, inner glow, revealing the ethereal auras hidden from ordinary sight. It felt like looking into a deep underwater cave filled with rippling, refracted light.

She focused on the ghostly strands that stretched across the doorway. In her crystal-enhanced vision, they gave off an eerie glow, as strangely beautiful as they were creepy.

"What do you see?" Opal asked, close behind her.

"Well, it's not a spell." Dru peered closer. There was something everyday and familiar about the way the strands draped, but she couldn't quite place it.

She closed the door slightly, so that the strands went slack. On impulse, she drew in a breath and gently blew. They rippled.

"Cobwebs," Dru said with a sniff, feeling silly. "No big deal."

Still, why were they radiating the cold glow of magic?

She reached out with one finger to swipe the cobwebs away. But much to her surprise, they wouldn't yield. The webs were as tough as steel wires.

"Huh," Dru said. "Opal, do you have anything to cut with?"

"Besides my razor-sharp sense of humor?" Opal rummaged through her purse. "Hmm. How about nail scissors?"

Without lowering the crystal from her forehead, Dru held out her free hand. Opal placed the tiny scissors in her palm.

With some difficulty, Dru got the scissors lined up with the lowest-hanging strand and squeezed. It was like trying to slice through a cable. The scissors refused to cut.

"Holy guacamole. What is this stuff?" Dru tried again, squeezing harder, until the handles of the scissors dug into her fingers. Just when she was about to give up, the strand broke in half with a soft *ping*. The severed ends drifted away like fine hairs, seemingly weightless despite their strength.

"You sure you should be cutting those?" Opal asked, clearly worried.

"Well, I'm not going to just leave them here and run into them later by accident." One by one, Dru cut through the strands of web. "The real question is, how did they get here?"

"Unless it was a spell, must've been some kind of freaky-ass spider, I imagine."

"Maybe. But there are other critters besides spiders that spin webs. There's also bagworms. Tent caterpillars. Bark lice."

"Okay, *now* you're freaking me out. I am not setting foot in that garage. We just need to be clear on that. Just look at my new outfit. You know I'm not about to wreck this." Opal fluttered her hands down to encompass her shimmering purple top, pink velvet pants with pearl buttons, and sparkling purple platform mules. She sighed. "I can't believe I'm saying this, but we've got to get Rane down here. Fighting weird giant bugs is her thing, not mine."

"Rane's a little upset right now. And I know from unfortunate experience that makes her likely to break something important. Besides, we don't know if we need to fight anything at all. Much less giant bugs." Dru cut through the last strand of web. After a moment's hesitation, she pushed against the dented door.

It swung open on abused hinges, letting out a long, ominous creak. Cobwebs all along the edge fluttered free, like ghostly fingers beckoning them inward.

Deep inside the building, something crashed and broke. Goosebumps stood up on Dru's arms. She waited, ears straining to hear another sound, but nothing else came. Everything was ominously quiet.

"Yeah, okay," Dru said softly. "Maybe we should call Rane."

7

WAKE THE DEAD

Apparently, the phone call didn't go well. Opal hung up and stared at her phone as if it held the answer to some existential riddle.

"For real, she told me to cowgirl up." Opal's voice went high with indignation. "I don't even know what goes through that girl's head."

Dru shrugged it off and put away the ulexite crystal. "Good news is, that probably speaks volumes in favor of your mental stability. But I wouldn't worry about it. With Rane, that's just sort of an everyday sign-off."

Opal sighed. "Does that mean she's going to show up and help us, or not?"

"I wouldn't hold my breath. But don't worry, we're not going to get into any kind of trouble. We'll just poke our heads in for a minute and see if we can find any clues about Greyson. Right? We can handle this."

"Why is it that every time I put on a cute new outfit, we end up doing something crazy?" Opal seemed more annoyed than worried. "There's super-powered spiderwebs on the door. You did notice that fact. And it's going to get dark soon."

"It's okay. It's going to be fine." Deep down, Dru knew that Opal was right. They shouldn't go into the garage. Probably shouldn't even stand outside the open door.

But she had to find Greyson and break his curse in order to stop doomsday. She couldn't just walk away. Beyond this door, there could be some kind of clue about what had happened to him. She had to look.

Without the ulexite crystal, Dru couldn't see enchantments, but spotting any other kind of danger would be much easier. Eyes wide, Dru pushed the door all the way open. It creaked.

Slowly, she stepped inside, looking around at the shelves crammed with spray cans of chemicals and jugs of automotive fluids. The chubby red cylinder of what she assumed was an air compressor. A half-rebuilt engine in the corner, red rags sticking out of its eight exposed cylinders. All of Greyson's stuff.

But no Greyson.

At least there were no other cobwebs, supernatural or otherwise, as far as she could see. Dru tiptoed to the center of the garage. "Okay," she whispered. "It's just a garage. Nothing to worry about."

Opal crept up next to her, sequined heels clacking. She leaned closer. "Dru?"

"Yeah?"

"Why are we whispering?"

Dru took in a deep breath, smelling the old oil and steel, and let it out. In a normal voice, she said, "Okay. There's got to be some kind of clue in here that will lead us to Greyson. I don't know what we're looking for, exactly. But something."

"Well, that definitely narrows it down." Opal crossed to the door that led into the rest of Greyson's place. "You know what we should've brought along? Some red zincite. Help your intuition a little."

"Yeah, that would've been a good idea, actually."

"Or at least some staurolite. Know what I mean?" Opal drew a plus sign in the air with her finger, mimicking the cross shape of a reddish-brown staurolite crystal. "A little fairy luck never hurt anyone."

Dru hadn't thought of that, either. She'd just been focused on getting over here as quickly as possible. "Well, I did bring my ulexite for vision."

"Well, you better get on that again, then. Find out if there's any more of those super-webs lurking around. I'm not going to have any bark lice or hoodoo caterpillars dropping anything on me." Opal shot her a warning look, then opened up the door to Greyson's living room.

And screamed.

A withered skeletal figure wreathed in cobwebs lurched through the door. Its empty eye sockets turned toward Opal. Its bony jaw opened wide, letting out a bubbling screech as it raised its long arms.

Still screaming, Opal pulled the bottle of holy water out of her purse and squeezed it at the creature. A thin stream of water shot out, zigzagging across the thing's web-wrapped torso.

The holy water sizzled, releasing a curl of white smoke from the creature. But it didn't slow the thing down. It reached for Opal with long, skeletal fingers that ended in black dripping claws.

Those claws were dripping with undead scourge, Dru realized. That was how Salem had been attacked.

This was possibly the exact creature that had attacked Salem. And the fact that he hadn't warned her would have made her furious, except that she was too busy being terrified out of her mind.

Opal's bottle quickly emptied out, and she ran back toward Dru, her shiny heels clacking. "Dru! I'm all out of holy water!"

"That's because it's only like a sample size!" Shaken into action, Dru fumbled in her purse for Greyson's piece of black Lemurian jade. She wasn't sure how much it would protect them, but it did have some effect against evil.

And this thing was clearly evil.

Just as her fingers touched the crystal, the creature aimed one palm at Dru and shot a stream of webbing directly at her.

Throwing herself to one side, Dru managed to dodge the spray of webbing. But it caught her purse and ripped it from her grasp, flinging it across the garage and trapping it against the far wall under a splatter of webs.

Dru and Opal traded frightened glances.

"*Run!*" Dru yelled, pushing her toward the door.

But Opal only made it two steps before the thing sprayed another stream of webbing directly onto her velvet pants and purple shoes, anchoring her feet to the floor.

Opal struggled, but it was no use. Her legs wouldn't budge. "Dru, don't leave me!"

"Hang on!" Dru ran over to the wall of black metal shelves, looking for anything sharp enough to cut Opal loose. With an inhuman hiss, the creature changed course and came after Dru.

Frantic, Dru rifled through the shelves, but found nothing she could use to free Opal.

"Toolboxes! Toolboxes!" Opal pointed toward the row of tall red toolboxes with their dozens of drawers. "Look for a knife, or a saw, or a blowtorch or something."

But Dru wasn't fast enough. A stream of wiry webs shot from the thing's palms, wrapping tightly around her left leg. Instantly, Dru was stuck, as if her left foot were glued to the floor. She flailed about, but she couldn't lift her foot even an inch.

Dru could only stare, speechless with horror, as the thing lurched toward her with jerky, lopsided steps. Deep within the layers of black-speckled cobwebs wrapped around its desiccated body, hundreds or perhaps thousands of tiny dark streaks wriggled and swam. It looked as if the scourge itself was controlling the creature's motion, pulling its arms and legs like marionette strings.

Despite her terror, Dru watched with clinical interest as the creature approached. She had never seen anything like this before in person. She'd only read about it in her ancient, musty books.

"Dru!" Opal waved her arms. "Stop *studying* it! Do something!"

The thing lurched toward Dru with clawed fingertips dripping black, as if they'd been dipped in paint.

"It's scourge!" Saying it out loud somehow made it even more frightening. She had seen firsthand how quickly the undead scourge had incapacitated Salem, and he was the most powerful sorcerer she knew. If it could overwhelm someone as capable as him, what chance did she stand?

Stuck in place, Dru patted her pockets, hoping she had stashed a random crystal in there. No luck. They were all in her purse, which hung from the far wall, wrapped up like a giant insect lunch.

Opal followed her gaze, then pointed to the shelves behind Dru. "Look behind you!"

Dru pivoted on one foot and pulled everything off the nearby shelves. She dropped it all at her feet, desperate to find anything she could use as a weapon.

Spray cans of WD-40. Sloshing blue jugs of windshield fluid. Plastic quarts of motor oil. A heavy sack full of something called Spill Stop. All of it was useless.

The creature was almost on her. Her heart pounded.

Wait, she thought, and grabbed the bulging plastic sack. The label proudly proclaimed, SPILL STOP: CLAY ABSORBS OIL, FLUIDS & LIQUID SPILLS. SO MANY USES!

Dru was pretty sure this particular use had never been tried before. With trembling hands, she ripped open the bag and plunged her fingers into the dry, dusty clay. It felt just like fuller's earth.

She pulled out a handful and flung it at the creature.

It hit the thing's left elbow. Or where she assumed the elbow was, under the layers of black-speckled webbing.

The creature stopped and turned its empty eye sockets down to stare at the clay. The spatter of ash-colored powder darkened around the edges as it absorbed the speckles of scourge from the webbing. With a crackling sound, the creature's arm stiffened and froze.

This stuff seemed to work, but throwing one handful at a time wouldn't be enough. She needed to find a way to cover the entire thing in powder. Fast.

Her gaze roamed the shelves and fell on the bloated red cylinder of the air compressor sitting on the floor nearby. Just above it, a metal spool bolted to the shelves held a coiled-up yellow rubber air hose. It ended in a vaguely gun-shaped attachment with a chrome nozzle.

Pressurized air. Of course.

Dru grabbed the nozzle and tried to tug it loose, but the yellow hose was hung up on its spool and wouldn't budge.

Opal screamed. "*Dru!*"

Unfazed by its paralyzed arm, the creature lurched at Dru, nearly smothering her with the stench of death. It swiped at her with its good arm, slashing at Dru with black dripping claws.

Grunting, Dru bent out of the way. She yanked on the hose with all of her strength. It stretched taut, creaking slightly, and then something ruptured in the connection between the hose and the nozzle. Air escaped with an angry whistle. The spool popped loose from its mount, clattering to the floor and releasing curls of yellow hose.

As the creature loomed over her, Dru jammed the broken nozzle into the plastic bag and squeezed the trigger. A whoosh of air filled the sack, inflating it to the size of a beach ball. Dru hefted it up, blocking the creature's next swing.

The thing's claws slashed the bag. With an ear-splitting pop, it exploded. A blast of cement-colored dust rocked the garage, choking the air, making it impossible to see.

Dru coughed and sputtered, feeling as if she was drowning in a cloud of atomized concrete. She blinked, trying to clear her eyes, but luckily her glasses had taken the brunt of the blast.

She pulled them off. They looked as if they had been spray-painted in gray primer.

At her feet, the creature lay flat on its back, completely motionless, arms outstretched. Frozen in powdered clay like a toppled statue.

Gradually, the rolling clouds of dust started to settle. The clay coated everything inside the garage in the same thick layer of gray. Including Opal.

She coughed and stared down at herself in horror. "Dru, what in the name of . . . ? What did you just do?" Clouds of elephant-gray clay shook loose from her hair as she spoke.

Dru watched the undead creature closely to make sure that it didn't move again. But it was practically fossilized.

Slowly, Dru grinned. "Check it out! We got it! Yay!" She did a little dance, which was really nothing more than a hip jiggle since her left foot was solidly anchored to the floor. "See? I told you we could handle this."

But Opal paid no attention to Dru or the frozen creature. She just kept looking up and down the length of her body, her gray-painted face horrified. Her voice came out a strained squeak. "But this is my new purple outfit!"

Outside, pounding footsteps approached.

"D!" Rane bellowed. "Where are you?" Puffing, Rane jogged in through the door, wearing clingy pink short-shorts and a T-shirt that said *FLIRTING WITH DISASTER*. "Okay, I'm here. We can get this party start— Uh . . ."

Dru turned toward her and blinked, realizing that thanks to the protection of her glasses, she probably had raccoon eyes. "Hi."

Rane started to say something, but a sudden bray of laughter burst out of her. She laughed so hard her entire body shook. She had to prop her hands on her knees to stay standing.

Opal planted her hands on her hips, releasing twin puffs of dust. "This is definitely not funny."

Which only made Rane laugh harder, until tears streamed down her red cheeks. "Omigod!" she panted, holding her sides. "Omigod, stop it. That's so awesome. You guys . . ." She couldn't finish.

Dru tried not to smile, but Rane's laugh was so infectious she couldn't help it. "Are you just going to stand there, or are you going to help us get out of these webs?"

Rane cleared her throat and wiped at her nose. "Sorry. Sorry." She cleared her throat again. "It's just, you guys are all—" And then her voice dissolved as another belly laugh rippled up through her and spilled out, unstoppable.

Dru sighed. This was going to take a while.

"Wait, wait. Omigod." Rane pulled out her phone. "I've got to get a picture."

8

KICK-ASS SHOES

When Rane finally stopped laughing, she pulled a long car bumper down from the wall and used it to transform her fingertips to chrome. The magic spread up her arms and encompassed her entire body, making her look as if she had just been poured from quicksilver.

Now strong as metal, she tore the webbing off Dru and Opal with a sound not unlike splintering wood. "Damn, it's like this stuff is married to you," Rane said in a booming metallic voice. "Did it all come out of that thing?"

"Yes. Whatever that thing is." Dru brushed ineffectually at her clothes, puzzled by the clay-crusted creature. "I don't get it. Undead scourge tends to accumulate underground, like mold spores. Especially in graveyards. And if too much of it congeals in one place, and you add a dead body, you can end up with a spontaneous undead creature. But this is different."

"Freaky." Rane nudged the clay-caked thing with her metal toe. "So what's the big mystery?"

"Well, I've read that a large enough glob of undead scourge can wrap itself in sort of a web cocoon, and lie in wait indefinitely. Like, thousands of years. You find that a lot in ancient tombs. But I've never heard of webbing around an actual undead creature. That's just weird."

Opal took off her ruined platform mules and sighed at Dru with mournful eyes. "These shoes were only a day old. It's a tragedy."

"At least they went out like heroes," Dru said.

Opal brushed handfuls of clay off her purple silk shirt and glared at Dru. "Told you everything was gonna go bananas. I knew it."

Dru took her by the dusty shoulders. "I'm sorry. I'll get it all dry-cleaned for you. And I'm really sorry that I got you into this."

Opal glanced away for a moment, and when she met Dru's gaze

again, Dru knew that she was forgiven. Mostly. "I know this is what I signed up for. Just freaky, is all."

"I know. Sorry." Dru chewed on her lower lip, not liking what she had to say next. But there wasn't any choice. "Here's the bad news. There's probably a connection between Greyson's disappearance and this creature. I don't know why it was here lurking at his place, and I don't know if this is the same creature that attacked Salem. But there could be more of them. I can't ask you to go any deeper into this."

"But you know I will." Opal hugged her, sending up a cloud of dust. "I'm always there for you."

Dru nodded, glad that they were all alive and unhurt.

Rane rolled her eyes back and jabbed a finger at her own gaping mouth, making a gagging motion. "When you two are done having a Hallmark moment, we've got to figure out what to do with Mr. Bony here." She nodded her silver chin at the undead creature.

It still lay on the garage floor, covered in clay, arms pointed at the ceiling.

"Won't it just turn to dust?" Opal asked hopefully.

They all waited. Eventually, Rane nudged it with her toe again. Nothing happened.

"Nope," Rane said, and turned human again with a sound like metal scraping across concrete.

Dru thought that one day she would get used to Rane's transformation from a shining metal statue back into a six-foot-tall blonde bodybuilder in pink shorts. But somehow, it was always startling.

"Well, we can't just leave this thing lying here," Dru said. "It's too dangerous. Not to mention weird. What do you usually do in a situation like this?"

Rane shrugged. "Just dig a hole and bury it." She poked around the clay-blasted garage. "Greyson's got to have a shovel in here somewhere."

"Just hold on a sec. Considering that the scourge is currently soaked into the clay, you don't want to get that wet. If you bury it, and it rains again, maybe the scourge could escape. I don't know for sure, but we can't afford to take the chance." Dru's mind raced. "I can't think of any spells that would work in this particular situation, though. On a living person, yes, but not this thing."

"Know any chemicals we could use?" Opal asked. "Anything that would react with the clay and turn it into concrete?"

"Or maybe some kind of acid to dissolve it," Dru said.

"Ooh!" Rane's face lit up. "Let's have a bonfire!"

Dru winced. "Under no circumstances. No."

"Let Salem have it," Opal said. "He's the one who took the scourge biohazard bag from us anyway. He wants it so bad, let him deal with it."

"But what worries me is *why* he wants it," Dru said. "What's he up to?"

"Let's totally give it to Salem." Rane pantomimed ringing a doorbell. "Ding-dong. Zombie delivery. Where do you want this? Oh, right here in the kitchen."

Opal made a disgusted face. "That's just not right."

"True," Rane said. "But at the same time, it's *awesome*."

"You would say that. Come on, it's going to get dark soon. Let's just call it a day and go home. We can tell Salem where he can come find this thing."

"No, no, let's drive it over there right now." Rane's features lit with a wicked smile. "I need to see his face when we bring Mr. Bony to his doorstep."

"What, in my car?" Opal's voice went shrill. "Nuh-uh. You are *not* putting that thing in the back of my Lincoln."

"Don't worry. I'll wrap it in plastic first, so it won't mess up your precious disco-tastic shag carpet."

"It's not my carpet I'm worried about, honey. It's the idea of putting a freaky-ass evil, web-shooting zombie in the trunk of my car! Okay? People just don't do things like that."

"Speak for yourself. I do this kind of crap all the time." Rane crossed the garage and pulled a folded blue tarp off a shelf. "Trust me."

Opal turned to Dru, her expression pleading. "Are you going to talk some sense into that girl, or what? No zombies in my trunk. That's a new rule."

"That is a good rule." Dru nodded, thinking.

"What about Ruiz?" Opal asked. "Ruiz has got a van. Let's call him."

Rane gave a noncommittal grunt. "Too many cooks in this kitchen already."

Dru drummed her fingers. Why *did* Salem have such an unhealthy interest in the scourge? Was this the same creature that had attacked him? Were there more of these creatures roaming around the city?

He had said something about the fifth seal. About the dead rising.

"Guys, this is big," Dru said, goose bumps running up her arms. "Salem has been studying all this doomsday stuff for a long time. He probably knows more about the apocalypse scroll than we do. If the dead start to rise all around the world, if hordes of these things start filling the streets, can you imagine? It could mean mass destruction. The end of everything."

"Doomsday," Opal said quietly. The word seemed to fill the garage.

Dru circled around the creature. It lay with its frozen arms raised as if reaching for the ceiling. "We need to find Greyson, break his curse, and stop doomsday."

As she talked, Rane wandered around the garage. "Well, lookie here." She bent down and picked something up from a dark corner, then brought it back to them, holding it high like a trophy. "Guess who's been doing extra credit homework?"

Rane held a black silk top hat, now half covered in clay dust. Just like the one Salem always wore. Until today, when he showed up at the Crystal Connection without it, his shirt slashed open by the scourge-ridden claws of an undead creature. It had to be Salem's hat.

It didn't take a genius to connect the dots. Salem definitely knew something he wasn't telling, and whatever it was couldn't be good.

Opal folded her arms. "Huh. Looks like our man Salem *was* here after all. How about that?"

"Apparently." Ignoring the horrible sinking feeling inside her, Dru pursed her lips and made a decision. "For now, let's leave the creature here—"

"Oh, *man*." Rane kicked a clump of clay.

"—and let's go home and get cleaned up. It's getting late. In the morning, we can go ask Salem some truly uncomfortable questions."

Opal seemed skeptical. "How uncomfortable, exactly?"

Dru chewed it over. "You're going to want to wear your kick-ass shoes."

Opal lifted her clay-crusted eyebrows. "Dru, honey. *All* my shoes are kick-ass."

9
THE WAY IT NEVER WAS

Opal wasn't kidding about the kick-ass shoes, either. She showed up at the Crystal Connection the next morning wearing plush wedge sandals the exact color and sheen of perfectly ripe peaches. She had an amazing velvet skirt to match, which shimmered as she walked by. "Huh. Where's Rane?"

"Not here yet. I assume she stopped to get some food," Dru said absently, rearranging the merchandise on the shelves. Salem's spell had picked up everything, but it was completely disorganized. On the nearest shelf, behind a cluster of candles, statues, and jars of powdered herbs, lay a pair of dead moths. Apparently, Salem's spell had gathered up the dead insects, too.

Anxious about the impeding confrontation with Salem, Dru went into shopkeeping overdrive. She got out her feather duster and worked it toward the back of the shelf, trying to sweep out the dead moths. Preferably without knocking any fragile statues or glass jars to the hard floor.

The bell on the front door jingled as someone came in. Inwardly, Dru groaned with frustration. Now was not a good time for customers. She couldn't see anything over the tall shelves, but she could clearly hear the sharp tapping of Opal's fashionable sandals as she came back up front to greet their visitor.

A man's deep voice said, "Does Drusy work here?"

"*Drusy?*" Opal repeated, sounding amused. The air reverberated with her musical laughter. "All right. I'm here to tell you, that's a brand-new one on me. *Drusy*, really?"

At the sound of her name—her *real* name—Dru felt her cheeks flush. Whoever was up there, he was certainly from somewhere deep in her past, where right now she would prefer he remained. She was already terrified enough about the present and the future. She couldn't handle dealing with any uncomfortable history on top of all that.

She set down the feather duster and considered an escape route, but she wasn't quick enough. With slow footsteps, Opal appeared at the end of the aisle, eyebrows quirked up. "Dru*sy*?" she said pointedly.

"Fine, whatever." Face burning with embarrassment, Dru brushed dust off her clothes as she passed Opal. "Just don't ask, okay?"

Opal's face bunched up with suppressed laughter until she was ready to burst. "No, that's fine. Doesn't matter to me." Then she added, "Just so *cute*. Drusy."

Dru shot her a warning look that was entirely wasted.

Waiting at the front counter was a tall, lean man in an expensive-looking shirt and black designer jeans. His messy ash-blond hair and slender sideburns didn't look at all familiar, but his magnetic gaze zeroed in on her instantly, as if he had always known her.

The angles in his face softened, and his thick eyebrows flashed up for a moment in recognition. "Drusy. Hey, darling." His baritone voice resonated through the shop, making him seem even taller than he already was.

No matter how hard she tried, Dru couldn't place him. When he opened his long arms for a hug, she intercepted him with a quick handshake. "Hey . . . you! I'm sorry. This is a bad time. We're just about to have a . . . meeting."

"Meeting?" He held her hand tight. His grip was strong, but cold, and his cologne hinted at deep pine forests. "Titus," he said, releasing her. "That's all right. It's been a while."

A bolt of recognition hit her. "Holy Hasselhoff, yeah. Titus! Wow. It's been, jeez, ten years?"

"Eight," Titus corrected her. "Almost."

"You look . . ." She didn't know what to say. He had completely changed. The Titus she remembered had been troubled and withdrawn, shy and depressed. He had rarely peeked out from beneath his tattered hoodie.

In contrast, the man standing before her seemed happy, eminently confident, and completely at ease. And he'd obviously been working out.

"You haven't changed a bit," she lied, wondering why she didn't just tell him he looked great.

And then she remembered that it was best not to encourage Titus.

His gaze roamed up and down Dru, and he smiled as if he'd just been handed a tall piece of cake.

Trying to hold off the tidal wave of awkwardness that was doubtless headed their way, Dru pivoted to Opal, who slid onto her stool behind the cash register. "Titus was one of my first customers."

"The very first, I believe," Titus added, not taking his gaze off Dru. "And a good friend, I hope."

Which, for some reason, just made Dru feel guilty. Because to her, he'd just been a good customer. They'd chatted a bit sometimes, maybe had a couple of drinks, but that was it. No matter how openly he had admired her, she had refused to cross that line with a customer.

"You've come quite a long way from selling crystals out of your apartment," Titus said. "This place looks truly amazing."

"Thank you." Dru avoided his gaze at first, then risked a glance up. He was checking out the shop, looking genuinely impressed. But there was something else in his gaze, something intentional. It wasn't just idle curiosity. He seemed to be searching for something in particular.

"So . . ." Opal examined her newly painted cotton candy–pink nails. "Drusy, hmm? Haven't heard that one before." Only then did she give Dru a slyly amused look.

Dru sighed, knowing there was no way to avoid this now. At Titus's puzzled look, she explained. "It's just Dru these days. But yes, my given name is actually Drusy Jasper. Named after a rock, which comes as a surprise to exactly no one. Anyway, jasper, when it's covered with a layer of fine quartz crystals, it's called drusy jasper. It sparkles."

"Aww," Opal said, smiling broadly. "So sweet."

"And quite beautiful," Titus said.

Dru cleared her throat. "And also proof that my mom was always a complete weirdo."

"How is your mom, by the way?" Titus asked, hitting on a subject that Dru truly, desperately didn't want to talk about. "I remember, you were having . . ." Whatever he was about to say, thankfully he changed his mind. "How is she?"

"No idea." Dru shrugged, trying to pretend she didn't care. "Haven't heard from her since she met Blaine the yacht captain and sailed off aboard the USS *Midlife Crisis*."

Titus's thick eyebrows drew together in disapproval. "That is a truly unfortunate name for a boat."

"My first thought, too." Dru chewed on her lip, trying to decide how to handle this. It wasn't as if anything serious had ever happened between them. But still, the way he looked at her now, there was clearly something he wanted to say, and she was absolutely certain it was something better off left unsaid.

The phone rang twice before she realized just how close she was standing to Titus, and how strangely familiar that felt. And how intently Opal kept watching the two of them.

Dru glanced pointedly at the phone. Then, when Opal didn't take the hint, she head-tilted toward it. On the next ring, she finally pointed.

Without taking her eyes off Dru, Opal picked up the phone. "Thanks for calling the Crystal Connection, where we make all *kinds* of connections. How may I help you? Oh, *hola*." She put one hand over the mouthpiece and said in a stage whisper, "I'll just be over there." She slid off her stool and wandered down one of the aisles, smiling into the phone.

Dru quickly came around the cash register to take her place, putting the counter between her and Titus. His very presence seemed to radiate an intensity that rattled her, and even having a few more feet between them made her feel more in control.

She covered her nervousness by pulling her bottle of water out from under the counter. "So. Gosh, it's been so many years. What brings you in today?" She took a sip.

Titus settled one sinewy arm on the counter and leaned a little closer. His dark eyes bored into hers. "The seven Harbingers."

Dru choked on her water. Coughing, she turned away, her mind racing. Something about the way he said their name gave her the heebie-jeebies.

"Just a sec," she croaked, holding up one finger. She bent down under the counter to grab a tissue, and at the same time she palmed her trusty dagger-shaped wedge of spectrolite. The sharp-edged crystal with a rainbowlike shimmer was the best all-purpose defense she had against dark magic.

Not that she believed that Titus had somehow turned evil. But these days, she wasn't taking any chances.

She casually slipped the spectrolite into her back pocket and stood up, blowing her nose. "Sorry about that. Went down the wrong way."

Across the shop, Opal wandered from one aisle to the next, still on the phone. The click of her heels and the murmur of her voice was soothing. Opal giggled.

Titus looked apologetic. "Didn't mean to shock you. But lately there has been so much talk about the Harbingers, especially considering all of these troubling signs around us. The incessant clouds. The strange air. The meteor showers." He seemed to study her, as if looking for any sign of recognition.

The way he stared at her made her unwilling to trust him. She couldn't put her finger exactly on why. Yet at the same time, his sheer presence was impossible to ignore, and a small part of her wanted to give in to that, to tell him everything.

She resisted that urge and did her best to keep her face neutral, but she knew she was a terrible liar. Instead, she hedged. "When you say 'talk' about the Harbingers, who's talking?"

His face showed surprise. "Other sorcerers. People in the know."

She affected a shrug. "So, just rumors. Nobody knows anything for sure. Could be total hooey. Right?" She hated the way her voice rose when she was nervous. "So, okay, let's back up a sec. Back when you first came to me, all those years ago, you were actually trying to get *rid* of your powers."

His smile had a wolfish hint to it. "You were always so good to me. I've never forgotten that."

"Well. Thanks. But here's the thing." She had to be as honest with him as possible, because when it came to magical problems, honesty was crucial. But she could sense an incredible tension within him, and that told her to be careful. "You can correct me if I'm wrong, but if I recall, you used to be kind of miserable with the whole concept of magic. You actually *hated* the idea of having powers. I've never met anyone else like that. Still, to this day."

He watched her intently, without saying a word.

She took that as tacit approval to go on. "Most people, when they're born with powers, they do everything they can to develop them, make them stronger. Personally, I wasn't born with much. Opal doesn't have any. But I always knew that you have some unbelievable magical potential within you. Here, I can tell you right now—" She reached across the counter for her ulexite crystal, intending to look at his aura, but his large hand caught hers.

"Don't," he commanded, and with a pleading look, he let go of her. "I don't need that anymore."

The sudden vulnerability in his face took her by surprise.

"Titus," she said softly, "you never told me what your powers *are*, exactly." She didn't come right out and ask, afraid to push him too far. But she let the unspoken question linger between them.

His mouth worked, as if he was chewing that over. "Things have changed. For me. For you, in fact. For the world. Things are going to start happening rather quickly."

"What do you mean?"

His eyes seemed to light with an inner fire. "Back when we met, I wasn't myself. I felt like . . . well, like a freak. I felt like the universe had punished me for some crime I had never committed. That's why, back then, I asked you to find a way to rid me of my powers. But no matter how many crystals we tried, no matter how many potions, none of that worked."

"I know so much more now," Dru said. "We could try—"

"No. Back then, I didn't know that I was put here for a reason. That I was given these powers for a purpose. Back then, I didn't understand my destiny."

"And . . . now you do?" Dru asked dubiously.

The manic look in his eyes was answer enough. "All of that confusion, all of that angst and regret? That's all in the past." He planted both hands on the counter and loomed over her. "Now, the doubt is gone. I know what I need to do."

"Jeez, wow, that's great. I don't even know what to have for lunch." She attempted a smile. "And here I thought you came in looking for a crystal."

"No. I came to bring one to you." From his pocket, he pulled out a lump of black velvet and carefully unwrapped it on the counter. Inside was a crystal that looked like a delicate rose formed out of coffee-colored rock.

"Hey, wow, that's a nice barite crystal." Dru bent closer to examine it. Truly, it was the finest barite specimen she'd ever seen. Each stone petal of the so-called "rose" was thin and flawless, nestled one against another to form the illusion of a flower cast in stone.

His smile seemed as brittle as the barite crystal. "Do you like it?"

"Well, yeah. Barite is great for detoxification and rebalancing."

"And for cleansing away the past," he added in his deep voice. "Preparing for a new future."

She reached for her ledger. "Are you interested in store credit, or . . . ?"

His shoulders stiffened. "It's a gift," he insisted. "From me. To you."

"Oh, thank you, that's so sweet. But no. Let me buy it from you."

His expression darkened. "Are you playing games with me, Drusy?"

Staring back into the bottomless pits of his eyes was like staring into the eye sockets of a skull. Suddenly, she could hear her own heartbeat thudding in her ears. All of her instincts screamed danger.

"Drusy," Opal said abruptly, hanging up the phone as she came around the corner. Her shoulders shook with silent laughter. "I'm sorry. It's just so *cute*. It really is." She saw the two of them and drew up short, instantly picking up on the tension in the air. "Oh." She gave Dru a worried look.

Titus broke into an easy grin, and it seemed to brighten up his entire face. He backed away from the counter and held up his hands in an aw-shucks shrug. "Of course. This must be so unexpected, after all this time. How rude of me."

Dru swallowed. "Oh, hey, no, it is a really impressive crystal."

"Still. I apologize for the awkwardness."

She waved it off. "Hey, it's not the end of the world."

"No?" He chuckled, and it sounded completely genuine. Whatever darkness she had seen in him, it was suddenly gone, as if it had never existed. Had she imagined it?

Opal watched Titus carefully as she made her way back to the counter and sat next to Dru. "So how come we don't carry any drusy crystals in stock, anyway? If they're sparkly, we should have some. Everybody loves sparkly rocks."

"Over my dead body," Dru said. "Besides, there's just not a lot of demand for it. So why carry it, right?"

"Honey, we've got a whole store full of things there's not a lot of demand for. That's a fact."

Titus abruptly scooped up Dru's fingers in his vast grip. "Drusy. There's something you should know." He leaned closer, eyes burning. "There's going to be a gathering tomorrow night. Everyone who is everyone, all in one place, one night. It's the chance of a lifetime to be among the most powerful sorcerers in the world. You and I, we've known each other so long, perhaps we could—"

"A party?" Dru interrupted him before he could make this even more awkward than it already was. "You know me. I'm just not much of a party girl. I'm sorry."

He smiled, showing too many teeth. "But in fact, you are. I remember."

She felt herself blush. "Well, that's so . . ." She tried to pull her hand away, but she was trapped. "Jeez, you've got really strong hands."

"Didn't I tell you? That's my secret power. Strong hands." He winked and kissed the back of her hand before he released it. "Drusy, darling. Think about it. I'll see you soon."

Then he turned and strode out of the shop, leaving behind the barite rose and a hint of woodsy cologne in the silence after he was gone.

"Mmm-*mmm*." Opal sighed, staring wistfully at the closed door. "For real, we need more of that around here, liven things up a bit. Can you just call him back, have him walk in and out a couple more times in those jeans?"

"You're terrible," Dru said, squirting hand sanitizer onto her fingers. She took a deep breath, trying to shake off the jitters that Titus had left her with.

"The man brought you flowers. That's new."

"One flower. But it's really a rock. Don't read too much into it."

"He's been planning this for a while, you can bet on it." Opal fixed a curious look on her. "So what exactly did he mean about you being a party girl?"

"That's an exaggeration. I'm so not that."

"Mmm-hmm. So, between you two, anything ever get—"

"No, no." Dru shook her hands to air-dry them. "*Noooo.* Definitely not. Not with Titus. But you know, it's so strange. Back then, he used to be so jumpy. Afraid of his own shadow. Now he's all Joe Cool."

"Hmm. Well, I would definitely not kick that man out of bed for eating crackers."

"Trust me, Titus was never anywhere close to my bed."

"Probably closer than you think." Opal's voice dropped an octave. "Drusy, *dahling.*"

"Whatever. Let's put his rock in inventory." Dru spotted her feather duster and remembered the dead moths. She headed down the aisle, duster in hand. "Is it just me, or was that whole thing really, *really* weird?"

"Honey, the only people in the world weirder than the ones we know are the ones we *used* to know." Opal tapped the phone with one long cotton candy–colored fingernail. "Speaking of which, guess who called? Ruiz."

"Ruiz? He's not on fire again, is he?"

Opal chuckled. "Not this time." She sighed. "That man is so sweet, I'm here to tell you."

"That's fabulous. What about Hellbringer?"

Opal gave Dru a meaningful look. "Depending on who you believe, either that car is nowhere to be found, or it tore up half the city yesterday."

Dru traded looks with her. "And who do you believe?"

Opal pursed her lips, obviously thinking hard. "I don't know. I'm not going to believe anything until we see it with our own eyes."

"I like that policy. Let's make it official." Dru pushed the feather duster onto the shelf, and a pair of moths suddenly swarmed out at her, battering their big, ugly wings against her glasses before they swirled away.

"Gah!" Dru jerked her head back and frantically brushed herself off. Then, carefully, she swiped the feather duster back along the shelf, intending to sweep away the dead bugs.

But they were gone. She peeked around behind the jars and short statues, but found nothing.

Dru folded her arms. Something wasn't right.

The dead moths had vanished. Almost as if they had been brought back to life.

10

HELLO, MR. BONES

After Rane showed up, they all set out for Salem's place, which sat within spitting distance of rusty railroad tracks that hadn't seen a train in decades. Dru didn't know who owned the sprawling industrial building, but it was obvious that no one was looking after it. Knee-high weeds grew up through the cracks in the vast asphalt wasteland that was once a parking lot. Graffiti covered every inch of the ground floor, surrounding empty holes where windows had once stood. Dru was afraid to even get out of Opal's car.

"So, I've got to ask. What did you ever see in that man, anyway?" Opal said, echoing Dru's thoughts.

From the back seat, Rane gave her a sour look. "You're kidding, right?"

Opal stopped the car in the middle of the deserted parking lot. "No, I'm serious. I'm not judging."

"You're always judging," Rane said. "Look, for one, he's the most kick-ass sorcerer you'll ever meet, okay? Nobody can stand up to him, besides me. And he's got that whole big-brain thing going on. Besides, he's smoking hot. What did you say about him that one time?" This last was directed at Dru.

"Oh, no." Dru made a pushing-away motion. "You're not dragging me into this."

"No, it was really sweet," Rane said. "You said he was mesmerizing."

Opal raised her eyebrows at Dru.

Dru held up her hands. "What I said was—and this was when you first started dating, I have to point that out—I said, yes, he has the sort of magnetic good looks that make him interesting. If you can get past the guyliner."

"Pretty sure you said *mesmerizing*," Rane said. "Or maybe it was *fascinating*."

Opal's look at Dru became even more pointed.

Dru shook her head. She couldn't win. "But you have to admit, just talking to him kind of hurts. He's like a sarcasm factory churning out extra-strength snark."

"Speaking of factories," Opal said, "why does the man live in one? Or what's left of it?" She leaned over the steering wheel and stared up through the windshield. "You sure this is even the right place?"

"Give me a break," Rane said from the back seat. "I used to *live* here."

Dru and Opal both turned around to look at her.

"*What?*" She glared back at them. "We were in love. It was fine." She got out of the car and slammed the door. Without looking back, she marched across the weed-choked parking lot toward the building.

Dru traded looks with Opal. "Guess it's too soon," Dru said. "How long have they been broken up?"

"Not long enough," Opal muttered, then patted Dru's leg. "Don't worry. I'll keep the engine running for you."

"You're not . . . ?" Dru jerked her thumb at the building.

"Oh, no, no, *no*." Opal dropped her chin and gave Dru a knowing frown. "Honey, I haven't lived this long by breaking into pissed-off sorcerers' bachelor pads. But you go on ahead, really. I'll just be your getaway car."

"Um. Hmm. Okay. You're sure?" Dru took a deep breath, trying to psych herself up. "No, that's totally cool. I'll be with Rane, so I'll be fine. I've been in his place before. What could go wrong?" She hesitated, watching Rane's strong back as she marched away, and then stepped out to follow her.

A series of hollow thumps came from the purple Lincoln as Opal locked the doors. Dru watched through the window as Opal pulled a handful of amulets off her rearview mirror and slipped them around her neck, then quickly fixed her hair and flashed Dru a thumbs-up.

Dru returned the gesture. She chased after Rane, trying to ignore the weeds brushing at her ankles.

With a practiced leap, Rane brought down the rusted metal fire escape ramp. The metallic screech startled Dru. Rubbing her arms, she looked around. There wasn't another soul in sight, but she couldn't shake the feeling they were being watched.

They climbed up to the flat asphalt roof that stretched out under a sky choked with sickly clouds. On the far side, a black metal door led into the top floor of the adjoining building.

"Looks like he's not home. Door's closed, and that means the protective spell is armed," Rane said. "Don't worry. As soon as the door is open, the spell turns off. Watch this."

As she had no doubt done countless times before, Rane crossed the roof, touched the small, grimy window over the door, and transformed herself into solid glass. Only then did she open the door. "Wonder if he's ever figured out this is how I get past his defenses."

Dru stared at Rane, or more precisely *through* Rane, seeing a warped image of the rooftop through her shimmering glass body. It was always a strange sight, seeing Rane made out of glass, so that she was nearly invisible when she stood in shadow. "Wow," Dru said. "Turning into glass must be useful for being stealthy, right?"

"Yeah. Because stealth is *so* my thing." Rane snorted. "Not."

Dru sighed. "Speaking of which, did you ever have a chance to read that Sun Tzu book I gave you? *The Art of War?*"

"Quit trying to educate me, dude. I know what I'm doing." Rane led the way inside.

Salem's place was pretty much the way Dru remembered it, packed with antique furniture, wooden chests, cardboard boxes stacked high with everything from crystal balls to ceremonial masks. It was all one enormous, magical mess.

The far wall was dominated by Salem's doomsday wall, a floor-to-ceiling mess of newspaper clippings, maps, photos, and handwritten notes about the end of the world. Color-coded pushpins and strings connected them all together like some giant vision board for the apocalypse.

Between here and there, the vast maze of musty, old junk and antiques that Salem had accumulated under the broad slanted roof was interrupted by a grisly new addition: a half-dozen large aquariums filled with a whiskey-colored fluid. And in each one floated a handful of stained bones.

Dru wasn't sure they were human until she saw the skull.

Her hands flew to her mouth. Her gaze zoomed from one tank to the next, unable to look away. Skeletal hands floated palm-up in one tank, detached from their connecting arm bones.

A rib cage floated in another tank, stained the color of driftwood.

A grinning human skull sat at the bottom of a third tank, its cranium mottled like disintegrating concrete.

Rane started to step forward, but Dru grabbed her arm. "Don't go in there. Just . . . don't."

Hesitating, Rane stood in the doorway, her glass head turning side to side as she scanned the room. "This is *seriously* messed up. Grave robbing? That's not his style. This can't be what it looks like."

"Maybe. But sometimes, things are *exactly* what they look like." Dru's mind went into overdrive. Salem had shown up at her shop with a wound caused by some kind of undead creature. He had stolen the scourge out from under their noses. And he had always had a fetish for collecting the occult lore of dark sorcerers, including the Harbingers.

Had his fascination with the Harbingers crossed over into something much darker?

What was it Titus had said, unexpectedly reappearing after all these years? He said that other sorcerers were talking about the Harbingers. *People in the know.* Did he mean Salem? Was Titus trying to warn her?

"Hold on. I have an idea. Let me have a look." Dru fished her ulexite crystal out of her purse and pressed it to her forehead, letting her magical energy empower it. After a slightly dizzy moment, her vision took on an added dimension, showing her the ethereal auras within Salem's place.

As she had always suspected, almost everything inside had some kind of magical aura. Salem wasn't any ordinary packrat. Over the years, he had amassed a truly vast collection of artifacts, books, spell components, and who knew what else.

No wonder he came down to the Crystal Connection so often. It was the only place in town that had more magical stuff than him.

She squinted at the aquariums across the room. From this distance, it was tough to make out many details through the distortion caused by the crystal. But she could see something that was hidden to the naked eye: the fluid around the bones was filled with ghostly strands of light.

They twirled and swam in slow motion, as if carried by invisible ocean currents. Thin ribbons of shimmering platinum-white light. Just like the cobwebs at Greyson's place, these threads gave off the cold glow of magic.

Dru lowered the crystal and blinked to clear her vision. "Looks like there are cobwebs floating in the tanks. I bet these bones are parts for one of those undead creatures."

With an icy ringing sound, Rane turned human again. "Are you saying he's, like, *building* one of these things?"

"Looks that way, doesn't it?" Dru stepped into the room and listened, but heard nothing except a train whistle in the distance. The room was filled with the earthy scents of candle smoke and strange herbs, along with a sharply sweet smell like honeysuckle. It was at once unsettling and strangely homey. "Undead scourge is usually associated with necromantic magic. But I never would've pegged Salem for a necromancer. Until now."

Up close, she could see that the rim of each tank was unevenly smeared with dry brick-red paint. A spidery handprint, about the size of Salem's hand, was planted on one face of each tank.

"Finger painting?" Rane sounded puzzled.

After a little hesitation, Dru ran her fingers over the paint. It felt chalky and primitive, not at all smooth and durable like modern paint. "Looks like red ochre. That makes sense. It's a kind of clay that gets its color from oxidized galena."

"Oxy what-what?"

"Here." Dru dug through her purse and pulled out a heavy pair of smooth galena crystals, shiny and round as polished silver spoons. "Iron oxide. It's the same stuff. Only these crystals are magnetized." She pulled them apart with a soft ringing sound. "But essentially, if the galena rusts, it can naturally form red ochre. It's been used to protect graves since pre-historic times."

Rane seemed impressed. "So these are like, what, Neanderthal bones?"

"No, I doubt that. But if Salem is using red ochre, he's done his homework. I never thought of using it to immobilize the undead."

"How about your galena magnets?" Rane nodded her chin at Dru's silvery crystals. "What do you use them for?"

"Mostly, sticking shopping lists to the fridge." Dru dropped them back into her purse. "Let's look around and see what else we can find. We absolutely need to figure out why Salem has these bones, and what he's planning on doing with them. But let's do it fast. If he comes back, I don't want to explain to him why we broke into his place. Again."

"Because he's being a jackwad, that's why." Rane made a face and tapped on the side of the tank holding the skull.

"Don't do that!" Dru whispered.

"Why not? Let's see if it'll do anything. This thing is freaky." She tapped it again. "*Hello*, Mr. Bones."

"Will you stop that?"

"What's it gonna do, bite me?" Rane leaned forward until her nose almost touched the glass, staring back at the skull.

Dru watched, expecting the skull to come alive, jaw snapping. Expecting it to come shooting out of the tank, maybe crashing through the glass, to clamp onto the end of Rane's nose.

But as the seconds crawled by, nothing happened. Finally, Rane shrugged and started wandering around the room, picking up things at random. She frowned up at a black-and-white Sisters of Mercy poster and sniffed. "Look at all this crap. You think his new girlfriend is actually living here? Got enough clothes lying around, anyway." Rane picked up a slender lace-up black velvet blouse and waved it like a flag. "So, do you think she's getting fat?"

Dru paused in the middle of surveying a shelf full of creepy statues and dead insects to shoot Rane a puzzled look. "Who, Ember?"

At the mention of her name, Rane's expression darkened. "Yeah. Little Miss Skunky Junk. You know, the problem with these indoorsy type of sorceresses, they don't get enough cardio. Tend to pack on the pounds."

Dru took off her glasses and polished them on her striped shirt. "This is probably pointless to mention, but I will take a moment to point out that *I'm* the indoorsy type. You do realize I have to spend all my time reading books and brewing potions, right? That's my job."

"Yeah, but you don't have a muffin top like she does." Rane tossed the blouse over her shoulder. "Probably why she's not wearing this. Can't fit into it anymore."

"Oh, don't be mean. I don't think she has a muffin top." Dru settled her glasses back on her nose. There was nothing more she could glean from the floating bones unless she was willing to pull them out of the tanks. And she certainly wasn't. "See if you can find Salem's notebook, or lab equipment that's been used recently. Anything that'll tell us what the heck is up with these vats of bones."

Rane dug through piles of stuff, humming to herself. "*Muffin top city*," she sang softly. "Ooh, look, he kept my old party beads. We got these in New Orleans." She held up strings of shimmering green and purple beads.

But Dru's attention was inexorably drawn to Salem's wall of newspaper clippings, maps, photos, and all the other details he had amassed about the Harbingers and their plans to bring about doomsday back in the 1960s. Decades later, their plan was actually working, judging by the appearance of the Four Horsemen and now the undead.

One drawing in the lower right corner of the wall stood out. It was tacked on top of a stack of other papers, indicating that it had been added recently, possibly since the last time she was here.

It was a ragged square of aged paper, torn out of a centuries-old notebook or journal. It contained an intricately inked drawing of a sinister-looking black urn, its sealed cap crowned with twelve wicked spikes. All around its plump middle, the urn was decorated with elaborate illustrations of destruction.

Horrific creatures clashed with ranks of spear-wielding soldiers, crushing them underfoot. Oceans boiled and swallowed entire mountains, tidal waves seethed beneath a hail of falling stars. The base of the urn was ringed by throngs of the dead and dying, bony arms feebly reaching up from heaps of bodies.

The sight of it all unsettled Dru. She'd seen plenty of horrific drawings in her books, but something about this one bothered her to the core. Mostly because it looked disturbingly familiar.

She took off her glasses again and peered closer. "Now, where have I seen you before?" she asked herself. "Death, destruction, foul creatures of darkness."

"What, Mardi Gras?" Rane appeared suddenly at her side, making her jump, and played with the strings of beads she now wore around her neck. "Oh yeah, that was a hella crazy time. Especially when that giant albino snake got loose, tried to eat some people. Everybody was *freaking* out."

"Not Mardi Gras. This drawing." Dru pointed with the earpiece of her glasses. "This doesn't look like the depraved hallucination of some random madman. It looks intentional. And eerily familiar."

"Huh." Rane glanced at the drawing, then shrugged. "All this freaky old stuff looks the same to me."

As hard as Dru tried, she couldn't remember where she'd seen this style of illustration before. It nagged at her, frustratingly out of reach. "Do you remember seeing any other urns like this one recently?"

"Nuh-uh. Maybe it was in one of your books?"

"Maybe." Dru stared hard at the picture, mentally sifting through the thousands of occult books she'd read, the untold multitude of drawings and illustrations she'd seen, trying to zero in on this particular image. She pressed her fingers into her temples.

Rane looked at her. "So does that head-squeezing thing really help?"

"Well, I don't know. But . . ." Just then, it hit Dru with a flash that sent a chill down her spine. "That's it! It wasn't in a book after all. We saw this in person."

"We?" Rane sounded dubious.

"Remember that ancient tube we found in the desert, at the base of the archway? The one that supposedly held the apocalypse scroll?"

"News flash. It didn't."

"Well, I know the tube was empty. But it was covered with identical illustrations," Dru said, tapping the drawing. "Just like this. About the end of the world."

"Don't get too excited." Rane pointed with a chipped pink fingernail at a line of penciled notations beneath the urn, written in sorcio glyphs. "What about the fine print?"

Dru squinted, puzzling out the enigmatic language of sorcery.

The first symbol was a diamond with one line extended like a tail. Then a pair of concentric boxes, followed by a circle with a segment taken out of it. More symbols followed. She racked her brain, struggling to remember what each symbol meant in connection with the others. "This could take some time. The exact sequence and proximity of the symbols can change the meaning dramatically. It's not as easy as it looks."

"Really? Because it looks like cake." Rane yawned. "Hey, you know who's really good at this stuff? Not me. Let's go get something to eat."

Dru considered snapping a picture with her phone, but magical scripts rarely came out in photos. With some misgivings about stealing, Dru unpinned the scrap of paper and straightened up. If she was right, this scrap of paper held clues that were too important to leave behind. "I'm pretty sure the diamond here means *tenas*, or 'the act of holding.' The boxes mean *sirmi*, or 'protection,' or they could mean that something is literally under guard. This broken circle refers to a piece of something larger or more important."

Dru traced her finger across the line of sorcio symbols, some of them utterly unfamiliar to her, until she reached two words that stopped her cold.

"*Apokalipso voluta*." Dru met Rane's puzzled gaze and felt a wave of excitement. "The apocalypse scroll."

"For real?"

"For real." Dru studied the paper before carefully folding it up. "If we can find the scroll, we can break Greyson's curse and stop the undead. We can stop doomsday."

11

STRANGE KIND OF LOVE

"Come on," Dru said, just as eager to get out of Salem's creepy place as she was to get back to the shop and translate the symbols on the scrap of paper. "Let's go."

But Rane stopped in her tracks, fixated on a charred iron sphere about six inches across that sat atop a crowded shelf. She picked it up and ran her fingers around the rough seam that encircled it. "My cannonball. I can't believe he kept this."

"Your *cannonball*? I don't even want to know." Dru waited impatiently, but Rane obviously wasn't going anywhere. Against her better judgment, Dru finally asked, "Why? Does he have some artillery in here somewhere that we should be worried about?"

"No, dummy." Rane clasped the heavy cannonball to her chest like a teddy bear and sighed. "You remember last October I went on that trip with Salem?"

Dru nodded meaningfully at the cannonball. "That right there is a lovely memento, I'm sure. Can we go now?"

Rane cradled it in her hands. "We found a ghost ship. Under a blood moon." She apparently mistook Dru's irritated stare for interest, because she went on. "Duh, a blood moon makes ghosts go solid. You should know that. And when they've got swords and blunderbusses and everything, that shit gets *real*."

Dru pointed toward the door. "Yes, I've read about that. Now, can we—"

"Yeah, well, you've read about it. I *lived* it, dude." Rane held the cannonball aloft with one hand, muscles flexing. "This old pirate ship damn near killed us. Me and Salem went all *Apocalypse Now* on them. He used his magic to snap the main mast right in half. We ended up fighting the pirates on deck, and it got *brutal*. Pirates coming at us every which way. Then I look up and see behind him these two pirate dudes are rolling out a cannon, and they get it aimed right at his back. Dead center. He's so busy casting spells, he doesn't even see it. I see them stick that red-hot wire down the thing to fire it. . . ." She stared off into space, obviously reliving the moment.

As much as Dru wanted to leave, she didn't interrupt Rane. This was a side of her that Dru so rarely saw, and strangely enough, it felt precious and delicate. For once, the woman stood stock-still, deep in memory, and it would have seemed like a crime to intrude.

When Rane spoke again, her voice was unusually soft. "I was in stone form, but, dude, even I didn't think I could stop a cannonball. Guess I didn't even think about it at all, really. I just jumped. Pushed him out of the way." Her fingers tightened around the iron ball. "When the cannon went off, it was like getting hit by a rocket. Hit me so hard I thought I was dead. Knocked me clear off the deck. By the time I came to, Salem was levitating me out of the water, and the ghost ship was blown to pieces. Burning. Sinking. The fight was all over, and I came this close to drowning." She blew out a long breath.

Dru put a hand on her arm. "Are you okay?"

"Yeah. Good times." She turned the cannonball to show Dru a flat dimple the size of a thumbprint. "See that? That's the impression my ass makes at eight hundred feet per second."

Dru winced. "Did Salem say thank you, at least?"

A flicker of sadness flashed across Rane's face, but it disappeared under a thick layer of bluster. "Nah, he was too busy bawling. Like a *baby*. Thought I was dead. So sweet. I told him, 'Suck it up, dude, I'm fine. Besides, I'm the one that got spanked by twenty pounds of super-sonic iron, and you don't see me crying about it.' Here, check it out." She dumped the heavy cannonball in Dru's hands.

"*Oof.*" She wasn't kidding about the weight. Dru tried unsuccessfully to hand it back. "Okay, can we go now?" she croaked.

Rane's forehead wrinkled. The hurt was plain on her face. "D, why did he break up with me after that? Did he ever say anything to you? Why did he end something that was so good?"

Dru's sympathy warred inside her against her burning desire to get out of this place. "I don't know. Truly." Her heart ached for Rane, but her anxiety was beginning to overwhelm that. "Here. Let's take this with us." She dumped the cannonball back into Rane's hands, silently grateful that she hadn't dropped it on her toe.

"You know what? You're right. Let's just grab all this bad mojo crap and take it back to your place." Rane nodded her chin at the aquariums. "Might have to make a couple trips."

"No, no, that's not what I meant." Dru shook her head violently. "There is no way on this planet that we're driving any of this undead stuff back to my place."

"Why not? Time to get your detective groove on, D. You can CSI the crap out of Mr. Bones here and figure out what the hell our boy's been up to." Rane hefted the cannonball from one hand to the other, as if it were a toy. "Is this because Opal won't let us put any bones in the car?"

Dru nodded, deciding to play along. "Yeah. Let's say that's it. Ready to go?" She turned toward the door.

And just as quickly, she stopped. A lone figure stood in the doorway, silhouetted against the steel-gray sky. Her long black hooded coat hid almost everything except the eyebrow piercings that flashed above her thick black Egyptian eye makeup.

Ember.

"*You.*" Rane's features darkened into a murderous scowl.

Ember slammed the door and approached, holding her flexed hands out to her sides like a gunslinger about to draw. She didn't have any visible weapons, but that didn't matter. Her magic was deadly enough.

"You have no right to be here," Ember said, her Arabic accent thick with barely contained rage. "Leave my home at once. Or I will remove you myself."

"*Your* home?" Rane slowly tilted her head side to side, making the bones in her neck pop. "Go ahead, Lily Munster, try it. The only thing you'll be removing is your *face*. From my *fist*."

"Okay, not helping," Dru said, putting a hand on Rane in a vain attempt to get her to shut up. She smiled at Ember as innocently as she could. "Ember, hi! This is so funny. I didn't know you lived here. We were just looking for Salem, because we found his hat, and—"

"Shut your mouth, shopgirl." Ember slowly circled to the side, keeping about twenty feet between them.

"Shopgirl? Seriously?" Dru said. For an astonished moment, she entertained the notion of letting Rane teach Ember a lesson after all.

Then she watched Rane turn to square off against Ember, stance wide, ready for a fight. This situation was seconds away from turning violent. Dru cleared her throat. "Okay, obviously, this looks bad, us being here uninvited. And I'm happy to explain."

Ember's heavily lined eyes flashed with fury.

"Or we could just leave!" Dru chirped. "Okay, time to go. Rane, come on." When Rane didn't budge, Dru added, "We can work this out later. And we will, I promise. We all want the same thing."

The corner of Ember's mouth curled up in a cruel smile. "Yes, of course," she said to Rane. "You want him back, don't you?"

It took Dru a second to catch up and realize Ember was talking about Salem. "No, no, nobody wants Salem."

Rane shot her a withering look.

"That's not what I meant." Inwardly, Dru cringed. "*Gah*. This is *not* the direction this conversation needs to be going right now. Okay? Everybody just cool it. Let's just walk it off." She motioned toward the door with both hands. "Walk it off, people. Outside. Right now."

In the tense silence that followed, neither Ember nor Rane blinked. The tension built in the still air.

"He does not miss you," Ember said to Rane. Her syrupy voice held a dangerous edge. "It does you no good, chasing after him like this."

"Yeah? How about like this?" With a long metal grinding sound, like a knife edge being honed across a sharpening stone, Rane's muscled body turned the scorched gray color of raw iron. She slapped the cannonball between her hands with a bone-jarring clang.

"Sorry," Ember said with a shrug. "But I am simply unimpressed."

Rane bared her metal teeth. "I'll leave you with an impression, all right."

Dru's knees went rubbery. "Oh, fudge buckets," she breathed. Then, with every ounce of courage she had, she walked into the open space between the two of them, snapping her fingers to get their attention. "Hey! Heads up. Don't do this. No fighting. Nobody's getting hurt. Nobody's getting killed. We're all on the same team, here."

"Really?" Ember said to Dru with mock sweetness. "I always thought your girlfriend here played for the *other* team."

At that, Rane shrugged.

Ember turned back to Rane. "The sad fact is you have always failed with him. And you always will. The sooner you learn that, the better."

Dru's mouth dropped open in shock. "Oh gosh, you did *not* just say that." She turned, seeing the twitch in Rane's eye, and her breath caught in her throat. Even on the best of days, Rane was one eye twitch away from a rampage.

Dru tried to place a calming hand on Rane's arm, but she was too late.

As soon as she took a step to the side, Rane's iron muscles flexed. With blinding speed, she twisted and launched the cannonball right at Ember.

12
LOVE IS A BATTLEFIELD

In the blink of an eye, Ember swirled her voluminous black coat around her body and disappeared, leaving nothing behind but a twist of inky black smoke. The iron cannonball streaked through the air where she had stood, blasting a head-sized depression in the concrete wall.

If the cannonball had actually been fired out of a cannon, it probably would have blown a hole in the wall and kept going. But instead it bounced off the concrete and ricocheted back toward Dru. She instinctively covered her head as the bouncing cannonball whizzed past.

With a flicker of darkness, Ember reappeared on the other side of the room, bending to snatch up an armful of some kind of mesh that shimmered like metal.

But instead of going after Ember, Rane leaped into the air and caught the rebounding cannonball in both hands with a metallic clang. Landing on her feet, she pivoted to face Ember.

With a furious glare, Ember swirled and vanished again.

As if sensing where Ember was teleporting next, Rane spun and hurled the cannonball once more. But the sorceress reappeared for only a moment before vanishing again. The cannonball sailed through the space where she had stood and obliterated an antique wooden desk, sending stacks of yellow papers exploding into the air.

Dru watched in horror. She had to stop this fight before someone got killed. But how?

"*Rane!*" she yelled.

"Busy!" Rane jumped up onto a table, scattering antiques, and caught the cannonball again.

This time, when Ember reappeared, her back was turned to Rane.

Her kohl-outlined eyes flashed wide in fear or maybe confusion, and she disappeared again just as the flying cannonball cracked off the floor where she'd stood, leaving a crater.

The cannonball bounced straight at Dru.

She saw it coming and ducked. It streaked over her head, so close she felt the wind ruffle her hair. The crash of shattering glass behind her was unmistakable, and a sickly sweet stench flooded the place.

The cannonball had gone straight through the line of aquariums, demolishing them. The strange whiskey-colored liquid flooded out across the floor, carrying the rib cage and arm bones of the undead creature like ships on a rogue wave.

Heart pounding, Dru ran for the door. She had no intention of leaving Rane behind, but as long as that killer cannonball was bouncing around, she had to get out of the line of fire. Besides, there was no telling what that foul liquid would do if it touched human skin.

With a swirl of smoke, Ember appeared before her, straddling the top of a workbench. Grinning wickedly, she unfurled the armful of metal mesh at Dru.

Dru tried to duck out of the way, but the metal mesh expanded in midair. A weighted net tangled her arms and legs. Two steps later, Dru crashed to the floor in an undignified heap.

Ember smirked. "Now we will see who—*aiee!*" She broke off in mid-sentence as Rane grabbed the hem of her coat and yanked her off her feet.

"You leave her *alone!*" Rane roared. She swung Ember high overhead, legs kicking in the air, and slammed her down onto her back beside Dru.

As the sorceress gasped for breath, Dru stared wide-eyed at the pool of toxic liquid slowly spreading across the floor toward them. But even more frightening than that, the stained bones of the undead creature started to rebuild itself. Scattered finger bones reassembled into a hand, clattering as it latched onto arm bones that reconnected to the shoulder and then the rib cage. Black oily scourge swirled out of the liquid and streamed across the bones, quickly sprouting web wrappings.

"Problem!" Dru yelled. "Undead!" She struggled against the mesh net, but couldn't get out. Beside her, Ember coughed and gasped for air.

Rane, chest heaving, stood over Ember with her fists clenched. From the single-minded fury written across her face, she was clearly focused on Ember, not the undead creature slowly getting to its feet behind her.

Skull rotating back into place, the creature twitched as the webs built up around its body, layer by layer.

"Rane!" Dru struggled to escape the net. "Creature! Behind you!"

Still breathing hard, Rane finally tore her ferocious gaze away from Ember, who was still coughing. "What?" Then she looked over her shoulder at the creature.

It raised its arms, and its bony fingers stretched into black dripping claws.

Across the room, the door burst open. Salem strode through, long black coat rippling behind him, his gray eyes blazing with a white glow. Without breaking stride, he marched toward the creature, hands steepled together. His lip curled, and he flung his hands apart. Magic sizzled through the air.

An invisible blast of force rippled across the room. With a thunderclap that made Dru's ears ring, the creature exploded into tiny fragments of shattered bone and fluttering webs. Pieces of the creature clattered off the ceiling and walls and tumbled away into the clutter.

Invisible waves of magic, like an unseen wind, pushed the pool of sickly yellow liquid back until it soaked into the scattered papers from the smashed antique desk. Aside from the lingering stench and a nasty stain on the floor, there was nothing left.

The cannonball, finally spent, rolled across the floor and banged into a trash can, denting it.

In the ringing silence that followed, Dru got herself free of the net and tried to pull Ember to her feet. At first, the sorceress resisted. But finally, breathing more normally, she relented and let Dru help her stand up. "Thank you," Ember whispered, avoiding Dru's gaze.

Rane turned to square off against Salem as he strode up to the three of them, seething.

His face twisted with fury. Through clenched teeth, he ground out one word. "*Why?*"

Rane pointed at Ember. "She totally started it."

"She lies," Ember said, her voice rough. She drew in a breath to say more, but Salem cut her off with the wave of a hand.

"Out," he ordered her.

Ember blinked, stunned. She smiled uneasily, as if sure she had misunderstood him.

Dru looked from Salem to the others, feeling confused and more than a little guilty. It took her a moment to summon up the courage to speak, but she had to set the record straight. "It's actually our fault, Salem. We found your hat."

His crazy gray eyes met hers for a moment. "Of course you did. And then you jumped to your usual simpleminded conclusions."

"Well, I don't know about *simpleminded*."

Ember dusted off her coat. "You can't possibly let these two—"

"Out!" Salem pointed toward the door.

Ember looked him up and down, her lip curling in disgust. She leaned toward him. "You will never learn," she said forcefully. Then with a glare at Rane, she swept her black coat around her body and vanished in a knot of sooty smoke.

When Ember was gone, Salem advanced angrily on Dru.

Rane stepped in between them, still in iron form. "You touch her, and I will kick your ass," she spat. "I don't care. I'll kick your ass until it *stays* kicked."

Instead of replying, he just dropped his shoulders and sighed.

Rane waited for a response, but got nothing from him. Completely confused, she glanced over at Dru, who held up her hands helplessly.

Dru cleared her throat. "I think we should just go."

Rane dipped her head so she could be face-to-face with Salem, but he just turned and walked away.

Puzzled, Rane scratched the back of her head with a metallic rasping sound. With a shrug, she headed for the door. "Fine. Whatever. We're out of here."

Dru had so many questions for Salem, but he obviously wasn't going to talk, and she didn't feel brave enough to push him. She turned to follow Rane.

But just as she reached the door, Salem ground out one word: "Wait."

That word was so full of hurt and anguish it sounded like it had been wrenched from the depths of his being. Such raw emotion was so unlike Salem that it startled Dru.

He pointed one long finger at her. "Just you." Then he turned away, avoiding Rane's gaze.

Rane planted her fists on her hips and opened her mouth to retort, but a warning glance from Dru silenced her.

They had reached the edge of something big, Dru sensed. She didn't know what Salem was about to tell her—about doomsday, about the Harbingers, about the undead creature he was keeping in his apartment—but she was willing to go out on a limb to find out. Even though a small part of her warned that being alone with Salem was the dumbest thing she could possibly do right now.

"It's okay," Dru whispered to Rane. "I'll just talk to him for a minute."

Rane's metal forehead wrinkled in disbelief. "Seriously?" She shot a foul look at Salem's back.

Dru nodded.

"Whatever." Rane stomped out the door. Her metal footsteps clomped away across the roof. "I'm going to be right out here," she called over her shoulder.

Salem stood with his back to Dru. The silence settled heavily around them, except for an insistent dripping somewhere in the room. The air smelled sickly sweet.

"Look, Salem." Dru's voice cracked, and she nervously swallowed. "About Ember, I'm really sorry, I feel terrible, we shouldn't have—"

"No. And yet, *once again*, you did." Salem turned around. His gray eyes burned with a murderous intensity that made her flinch. "You have the unfailing habit of stirring up things that should be left alone. It's a talent of yours."

"You know what, maybe you're right, and I'm so sorry—"

"Are you, really?" Salem closed in on her, one slow step at a time. "If you're truly sorry, then you'll make things right again. Sound fair?"

That sounded like a trap. Dru backed up until she bumped into a table covered in clutter. Something rattled over the edge and fell to the floor. "To be fair? We found your hat at Greyson's place. Care to explain that?"

He just watched her, his eyes glittering.

"It's in Opal's car, by the way." She pointed hesitantly. "If you want it back." She cleared her throat. "Look, it's pretty darn incriminating. *And* you have an undead creature in your house, which doesn't bode well. But yeah, still, I am sorry. Sure. Of course."

"Sure? Of course?" He was plainly mocking her. "Too easy. Is your life nothing but an endless chain of commitment issues? Where's your resolve? Your conviction?"

Anger boiled up inside her. She shook a finger at him. "Hey, don't push it, bub. I'm apologizing here, even though I'm not the one who even started this fight."

"Oh, then, my mistake." His black-lined eyes widened theatrically. "Rane came up with this whole plan all on her own, I'm sure. You did your best to stop her from coming here, and yet . . ."

Dru sighed, determined not to get drawn into another one of Salem's head games. "Just tell me one thing, okay?"

"I was *studying* the creature, not creating it. Trying to figure out how to fight it. Because there will be plenty more of them, I guarantee." He scowled at her. "Satisfied?"

"Only if I believe you. Which I'm not sure I do. Look, if you want me to trust you, why don't we work together? Tell me what you need, and I'll get it for you. Crystals? Books? More information for your . . . wall art here?" She waved a hand at his expansive collage of doomsday material.

Salem started to say something and stopped. After a moment, he looked away, and his emotional armor seemed to crumble. He drew in a deep breath and let it out through his nose. In a low voice, he said, "I need you to help her forget about me."

Dru blinked. That was not what she expected. "Huh?"

"You heard me," he snapped. "Do you expect me to repeat myself? Find her a new boyfriend. Someone who isn't fragile. In any sense of the word."

That was so ludicrous Dru couldn't help but laugh. "Yeah, I am *so* not doing that. Hook Rane up with another guy? Are you kidding me? That's like trying to get a kindergartener to adopt a porcupine. Forget it. You can work things out with Ember or not. That's up to you. Just leave me out of it."

Salem rolled his eyes with undisguised frustration. "There is no 'thing' with Ember. There never was. Don't you understand that?"

What Dru was about to say next was immediately drowned out by the giant phonograph needle scratching across her mind. "Wait, what?"

"She's not my *girlfriend*," Salem said, as if explaining it to a child.

"But . . ." Dru pointed vaguely in the direction Ember had vanished. "Then what . . . ? Are you sure? Because I'm pretty sure she is."

"That's what Rane told you," Salem said. "That's what she *thinks*. So keep letting her believe it. For her own good."

Dru folded her arms. "I'm not buying it. Ember is staying here, in your place. You're *living* together."

"She's crashing here while she works things out with her family. We're doing research together." Salem glared. "Honestly, I couldn't care less whether you believe it or not. Just keep Rane away from me."

"You're going to have to give me a better explanation."

"Is that really necessary?" He opened his arms to encompass the wreckage around them. "Rane doesn't know when to back away from a fight. In fact, she has the uncanny knack of creating a fight where none exists."

Dru shrugged. "Nobody's perfect."

"When it comes to the end of the world, when it comes to the forces clashing over doomsday, that's when a full frontal assault is guaranteed to lose. And when the stakes are this high, losing means death. Swift and sure death." Salem's face turned fierce. "I won't watch her die. And I won't let you get her killed."

"That's a little dramatic, don't you think?" Dru said. "Look, you two deserve to be together. You need to be. You were such a good team."

"Once. Not anymore," Salem said. "I grew up. She didn't. It's as simple as that."

"She needs you."

He sniffed. "Definitely an overstatement. And even if it were true, it's still impossible. Because where I'm going now, she can't keep up. I'm sure even you can understand that."

Dru slowly shook her head. "You're an arrogant jerk sometimes, you know that?"

"Sometimes? Hmm. Must be slipping."

"You're underestimating her. And that's sad. Because she has so much to offer, and you're just throwing that all away." Dru headed for the door. "And you know what? I don't need to hear this anymore. I'm leaving. I'm just going to tell Rane—"

"No." Salem's voice stopped her cold. "She's angry."

Dru paused. "Have you been paying attention? She's *furious* with you."

"Good. Rane needs to be angry. Anger is her fuel. It's what powers her through those crucial moments that would crush anyone else. With doomsday on the way, she needs her anger to survive. She can't be distracted by me."

That actually kind of made sense, in a twisted way. But it still didn't seem right. "Don't you think she deserves to know the truth?"

"She doesn't deserve anything. None of us do. If life was about having what we deserved . . ." He broke off and suddenly turned away, but not before Dru could see the hurt and vulnerability on his face.

It was so unlike Salem, so true and raw, that it stunned her to see it. She watched Salem's back as he crossed to a window, narrow shoulders hunched, and suddenly he looked different to her.

He no longer looked the part of the most powerful sorcerer she'd ever met. For the moment, he was just an old friend in pain.

"She still loves you," Dru said softly. "So much. Do you still love her? Because if you do, then this isn't fair."

She couldn't see his face. Over his shoulder, he said, "Fair or not, let her hold onto that rage. Because that's the only way she's going to survive this. Take it away from her now, and she won't make it."

Dru considered that. She didn't agree with it, but she wasn't going to argue with Salem about it anymore. "What about you?"

"Me? Well . . ." He shrugged. "Guess we'll just have to see if you're right."

"About what?"

He turned. A sardonic smile twitched at the corner of his mouth, and his expression hardened into the old, familiar Salem. "About us getting what we deserve."

13

FOUND IN TRANSLATION

Dru cleared out a spot on her battered workbench in the back room of the Crystal Connection. No matter how many times she swore to herself that she would get this place organized, it had a habit of falling into constant disarray. There were always more crystals to catalog, more ancient books to study, more potions to formulate, and a thousand other things that desperately needed to be done.

She studiously ignored the familiar dog-eared yellow legal pad that was scribbled full of to-do lists, begging for attention. Some of those lists went back to the day she opened this shop.

She piled up all of her loose papers on top of the legal pad and set Titus's barite rose on top as a paperweight. There was something about the flower-shaped rock that made her uneasy. As delicate and beautiful as it was, with its paper-thin stone petals, it looked old and dead. It reminded her of a life fossilized in stone, trapped forever, unable to fully bloom.

Titus had taken the opposite view. *"For cleansing away the past,"* he'd said in his deep voice. *"Preparing for a new future."*

What did he mean by that, exactly?

Dru shook her head. None of that mattered now. Not if this scrap of paper from Salem's wall could lead her to the apocalypse scroll, and ultimately to Greyson.

Dru shoved everything else on the workbench aside and made a space to lay out the cryptic drawing.

"What's that?" Opal asked, eating tiny cinnamon rolls out of a wide white paper box.

"A clue I found on Salem's freakishly huge end-of-the-world collage."

"Found?" Opal asked neutrally.

"Well, okay, so maybe I kind of stole it." Dru held up a finger. "But in my defense, you know he's stolen things from me. More than once, and that's a fact."

"Mmm-hmm. I'm sure he sees it that way." Opal delicately dabbed at the corners of her lips with a napkin. "You think he's going to come looking for it?"

"Um." Dru winced. She hadn't thought of that. "Once he sorts through the tidal wave of destruction in his apartment and figures out that somebody took this . . . well, maybe. The list of suspects is pretty short." She scooted her creaky chair in closer to the workbench and switched on her magnifying lamp.

"Better read it fast," Opal suggested.

"Thanks." Taking off her glasses, Dru pulled the lamp down until she could position the fishbowl-like lens over the scrap of paper. The articulated lamp's long springs jangled out a discordant tune as she adjusted it.

Through the magnifying glass, she could clearly see the incredible details in the inked illustration of the urn. Motifs of death and destruction were drawn all around its swollen sides, from its spiky top down to its clawed feet.

Falling stars. Volcanoes. Drowned cities. Heaps of dying victims reaching up in supplication. The urn in the drawing was almost a shrine to doomsday.

Opal leaned in close behind Dru's shoulder, her perfume filling the air between them with the scents of honeysuckle and orange blossoms. "Look at that. The end of the world."

Together, they stared at the drawing in silent horror.

Finally, Opal held up the nearly empty box of miniature cinnamon rolls. "Pecan roll? Last one."

"No thanks." Just looking at this drawing clenched up Dru's stomach. "Give it to Rane. She's had a rough day."

"She already ate half the box. Then she went out for smoothies. Said she'd burned too many calories in the cannonball fight." Opal shook her head. "Can't take that girl anywhere."

As Opal started to turn away, Dru changed her mind and snatched up the last chewy sweet roll. Unfortunately, the delicious blast of cinnamon across her taste buds didn't do anything to banish her worries. The thought of sorcerers working for centuries to bring about the end of the world left a sour taste in the back of her throat.

"What do you make of this?" Dru pointed to the lines of symbols scrawled beneath the urn.

"Better off leaving that alone." Opal folded the empty box in half and crammed it into the trash can. "I don't trust anything written in rat signs."

Dru squinted at the symbols. "I think I can figure it out."

"Even coming from you, those words are terrifying," Opal said. "The thing about rat signs, you get even one thing backwards, we all end up in hot water. And when I say 'we' I'm being generous, because really I mean you. But you know I'll help you anyway." Then she muttered, "Against my better judgment."

She wasn't wrong, but Dru chose to ignore it. "Far as I can tell, this urn was created to hold some kind of fragment of the apocalypse scroll. Not the text itself, but maybe a fragment of paper. Maybe a drip of wax from one of the seals. Something like that. The symbols right here mean 'safekeeping,' or 'finding.'" She tapped a pair of boxes near the end of the line of symbols. "If the Harbingers actually had this urn in their possession, I think they could have used it to find the actual apocalypse scroll. I just don't know how they did it."

With a long, tangerine-colored fingernail, Opal tapped on a pair of symbols buried in the middle of the page: an elongated hexagon beside a triangle. "That's what your friend Salem spray-painted outside our door that one time."

"Do you think he's really a friend?" Dru hadn't said a word to Rane about Salem, but keeping a secret like that didn't sit well with her. Right now, though, she didn't have the emotional bandwidth to deal with that. Doomsday was a bigger priority.

"Sure, he's a friend." Opal gave her a surprised look. "Salem fixed up the shop, didn't he?"

"Well, true. But even if you cut him some slack for being, um, *complicated* . . . he's still kind of a jerk sometimes."

Opal sniffed. "We get rid of all the jerks, we won't have any customers left. So what do these symbols mean, anyway?"

"*Kristalo sorcisto*," Dru said in the sorcerer tongue. "'Crystal sorcerer.'" That struck her as odd. "Huh. Do you think the Harbingers could have had a crystal sorcerer like me on their team?"

Opal put one hand on her hip. "Like you? I doubt it. Lots of sorcerers use crystals, but I have never heard of someone who actually does what you can do, charging them up like that."

But Dru was fascinated by the thought of a crystal sorcerer like her among the Harbingers. "I've never . . . Do you think that's possible? Another crystal sorcerer, back in the 1960s?"

With a long sigh, Opal picked up a heavy-looking stack of books and started reshelving them behind Dru. "Honey, with all the weirdness I've seen walking in this door over the years, nothing would surprise me anymore. If you're going to do anything with those symbols, you just be careful about the way you translate them. Don't burn down the shop." She gave Dru a critical look. "*Again.*"

"That was an isolated incident," Dru muttered. She went back to staring through the lens of her lamp, breathing in the oddly soothing scent of its hot light bulb. As she studied the symbols, a surge of hope rose up inside her. "If the Harbingers weren't just using crystals, but they actually had a real crystal sorcerer on their team, that could really help us."

Opal looked nonplussed. "How, exactly?"

"It means maybe I could potentially undo the things they've done. We just need to figure out how they did them." Dru thought hard, trying to put herself in the shoes of the Harbingers. "Okay, let's think about this. The Harbingers were a product of the late 1960s counterculture movement, right? They were sick of what they considered to be the failings of the modern world. They tried to wipe the slate clean."

"Oh, here we go." With another sigh, Opal settled into one of the ugly plaid armchairs. "We've been over this so many times. What else can we possibly say about the Seven Harbingers?"

"That's it." Dru snapped her fingers, realizing what she'd been over-looking. She put on her glasses, grabbed her notebook, and went flipping back through it. "There were precisely seven of them. Doesn't that strike you as a little odd?"

"Far as I can tell, *everything* about them was odd."

"Yeah, but . . ." Dru kept flipping backward through pages, looking for the first thing she had found about the Harbingers. "Seven. Is it a reference to the seven deadly sins? Or the seven heavenly virtues? Or was it just a coincidence, that there just happened to be seven megalomaniacal evil sorcerers all in one place on the Summer of Love?"

She found what she was looking for and stabbed her finger down on the page. "Listen to this. This is from their actual journal: 'Now, there are seven of us. Seven angels or seven demons? Neither. Seven Harbingers. Seven creators of the new world, because today the world is too sick to survive. The day has come to wipe the slate clean. Do it over, and do it right.'"

Opal shrugged. "Whenever you're getting at, Dru, I'm not seeing it."

"Seven." Dru tapped the page. "Seven angels, seven demons. Where have I heard that before?"

"I don't know." Opal shrugged. "Everywhere?"

"No, no. I read it somewhere. I know it." Dru launched herself out of the chair and searched the bookshelves, skimming over the thousands of ancient bound manuscripts that packed the back room of her shop. "Stanislaus wrote something about seven demons. And there's all that angel stuff in *The Codex of Zipporah*. Gosh, I wish we'd been able to get our hands on *The Compendium of Decimus* that one time. That would've been awesome."

Opal got up and followed her, stopping to pull out a thick, leather-bound book with tarnished silver hinges. "How about *The Libram of Squire Otho*?"

Dru paused. "Didn't they find him dead, drained of blood, in 1609?"

Opal thought. "I think it was 1612."

"Yeah. Not that one." Dru found the padlocked Stanislaus journals and looked around for the key. She dug through the wooden drawers in her workbench, but just as she found the keys, Opal interrupted her.

"Here it is. Lafayette." Opal slid the thick, handwritten book onto the workbench in front of her. On the wrinkled yellow pages, Lafayette had sketched out a seven-point paradigm for tracking down demons.

Dru studied the notes and sketches, flipping back and forth through the pages with a growing feeling of excitement. Although Lafayette hadn't known how to actually implement her idea, Dru did.

She compared Lafayette's paradigm with the sorcio symbols scrawled on the paper she had taken from Salem. The parallels were unmistakable. When she put them side by side, suddenly the pattern became clear.

Those symbols scrawled underneath the urn weren't just cryptic notes, Dru realized. "These are instructions for casting a location-finding spell. Using crystal magic."

Opal's face went through a series of emotions, from mild fascination to shock and finally to worry. "Oh, no you don't."

"Why not? It's perfect." Goose bumps ran up and down Dru's arms. "If I can find this urn and cast the same finding spell, that means I should be able to find the apocalypse scroll itself." And then she hastily added, "With your help, obviously. What do you think?"

The look on Opal's face was the opposite of what Dru had hoped for. "Look, I love you, but I think this is a terrible idea, and no two ways about it. Those Harbingers were into some dark magic, and you don't have any idea what the spell is going to do. Besides, we don't have the urn."

That was true. For a moment, Dru was stumped. She had to have some kind of magical artifact closely connected to the subject in order to use the spell. She didn't have anything related to the apocalypse scroll.

Then a brilliant idea popped into her mind, filling her with excitement.

"I may not have the urn. But I do have this." Dru dug in her pocket and pulled out the smooth oval of black jade. The flecks of pyrite inside it sparkled in the light.

Opal straightened up. "Isn't that the rock you gave to Greyson?"

"Yes it is. If I don't have the urn to find the apocalypse scroll, then I can still use Greyson's rock to find *him*." Dru pointed at the scrap of paper. "Using that finding spell."

The silence in the room stretched out, becoming thick.

"With a crystal magic spell from the Harbingers?" Opal said at last. "You can't be serious."

"I've never been more serious. The Harbingers had a crystal sorceress. *I'm* a crystal sorceress. I can use their spells. Not for evil, but for good," Dru said.

Opal, looking even more worried, bit her lip.

"Greyson is cursed, and I need to find him. This spell is the solution. And I'm going to use it." Dru's throat tightened up at the thought of him, and her eyes blurred with unshed tears. She had almost convinced herself that he was dead and gone. But the moment she had found this rock, she knew he was still alive. The black jade warmed in her hand, and she closed her fingers over it, holding on as tightly as she could.

Opal put one warm hand over Dru's. Gently, she said, "Look, honey. We don't even know that he's still alive. Or where he could be."

"We will find him," Dru swore. "No matter where he is."

14
IF YOU WERE HERE

In the back room of the Crystal Connection, Dru checked her calculations three times before she actually started assembling the crystal circle. Then she checked them again just to be extra sure. Everything seemed to be in order. Theoretically, the spell would tell her exactly how to find Greyson.

Theoretically.

She moved a few stacks of books aside, piling them on one of her plaid comfy chairs, clearing space to lay out a circle on the floor. After measuring out lengths of bare copper wire from the roll Opal had picked up at the hardware store, Dru snipped them off and wove them together. A thick beeswax candle went in the very center of the circle, intersected by copper lines. She checked the angles twice before she laid out the crystals around the circumference.

First, on the left and right sides of the circle, she placed a pair of mossy green teardrops of natural glass. These two tektites, created by the molten rock of a meteorite impact millions of years ago, would project her magical energy far into the distance. As far as it took to reach Greyson.

Going around the circle, she placed a nugget of bright yellow sulfur to absorb any negative backlash from the spell. There was always backlash. She had learned that the hard way.

Next to that, she added a flat pyrite disk, shimmering like a miniature gold record. Not only would it help deflect negative energy into the sulfur, but it also helped synchronize the tektites to make them more accurate.

Then she carefully placed a brownish-red staurolite crystal, which had naturally formed in the shape of a plus sign. According to her research, staurolite would form the core of the spell. But it was also a powerful good luck talisman called a fairy cross. And right now, she needed all the luck she could get.

The final crystal was the polished oval of gold-flecked black jade she had given to Greyson to protect him from the dark side. She took it out and held it in her hands, still warm from her pocket. It took a force of will to place it directly across the circle from her. Even that felt too far away from her.

As Dru worked, Rane returned and leaned against the doorframe, making the wall creak as she stretched her hamstrings. "Why don't we go look at that abandoned mine shaft where we came out of the netherworld?"

"Good idea," Dru said without looking up from where she sat cross-legged on the floor. "Do you remember where the mine shaft is located, exactly? Or which unmarked roads and trails to take to find it?"

Rane shrugged. "Come on, how many abandoned mines can there be in the mountains?"

Dru peered over the top of her glasses at Rane. "About twenty thousand known abandoned mines. And thousands more that aren't on any map."

"Huh." Standing on one foot, Rane hugged her other knee to her chest. "That's a problem."

The golden bangles on Opal's wrists sparkled as she waved her arms to encompass the circle. "Still, I don't know about all this, Dru. I'm sorry, but this spell is too much of a long shot."

Still sitting cross-legged on the floor, Dru twisted the wire methodically around the crystals. "It worked for the Harbingers. They found the apocalypse scroll with this spell, and it wasn't even located in our world. It was hidden in the netherworld."

"My point exactly." Opal planted her hands on her ample hips. "Even if the spell works, you don't know where it's going to lead you. Even if Greyson is still alive—"

Rane rolled her eyes.

"—you don't know what kind of situation he's in," Opal said. "What if he's trapped in the netherworld? Will this spell open up some kind of portal and suck you in? And in that case, what will happen to this shop? More specifically, what about the people standing in it, us being innocent bystanders and all?"

Dru clamped down on her own doubts. "I don't know. I don't. Some of my research is based on guesses, yes, but I don't have any other choice. If there was any other way to find him, I would take it in an instant. But this is it. This is all I have. And I need to do it."

Opal's expression softened. "Honey, I'm just trying to be safe. It's not a good idea to go around experimenting with weirdo magic spells. That's Salem's bag. And look where it's gotten him! The man is clearly insane."

"It's made him really powerful." Dru pushed her glasses back up her nose. "You can't deny that."

Opal didn't say anything to that, but she definitely looked unhappy.

Rane clapped her hands together once, making Dru jump. "Face front, *chicas*. Breakthroughs don't happen inside your comfort zone. Let's do this."

Dru pointed to her. "Yes. That. Exactly."

Opal plopped down into the only plaid armchair that wasn't full of books. "You don't even know for sure this is the spell the Harbingers used. I know you're going to do it anyway, but I'm going on the record right now. This is a bad idea."

"Duly noted," Dru said. The moment the words left her lips, she realized it was something Greyson would have said. Somewhere along the way, she had picked up some of his confidence.

Greyson. At the thought of him, his face flashed in her mind.

She closed her eyes and concentrated, picturing him. Slowly, she breathed out and relaxed, palms resting on her knees.

"Hang on," Rane said, breaking the quiet. "Don't you need to light that candle?"

"I will," Dru said without opening her eyes. "But I have to do it the hard way."

The concept of the spell was simple, in theory: focus on what you were searching for, energize the crystals enough to light the candle, and then follow the smoke as it led the way.

But in magic, as in life, the simplest things were often the most difficult.

Before she had met Greyson, Dru's magic powers were limited. She had always had a little bit of potential, at least sufficient to brew up magic potions and muddle her way through basic crystal circles. But nothing truly spectacular.

Only after his touch had unlocked her true potential did she discover that she was actually a sorceress. His own untapped magical energy perfectly matched hers, and every time they touched, he amplified her powers to levels she had never dreamed of.

Having him by her side, she had come as close as she could ever imagine to feeling unstoppable. But without Greyson there to add his power to her spells, she had to do it entirely on her own.

Just like when she had saved Salem from the scourge, she reminded herself. She could do this. She needed to do this.

She focused on her breathing. *Concentrate*, she told herself. *Concentrate.*

"Dude, it's not working," Rane said loudly.

"Just give her a minute," Opal murmured back.

Dru kept quiet. She steadied her breathing. In, out. Slowly.

She pictured Greyson in her mind. Rugged, handsome, mysterious. Thick hair, stubble, kind eyes. She remembered him leaning over Hellbringer's massive engine, looking up as she pointed out the magic sign painted under the black car's hood.

She remembered him scooping her up in his arms as if she were nothing, and carrying her over the black stone bridge as the netherworld skies exploded overhead like fireworks.

She remembered the moment he had stood chained up in his garage, bare to the waist, fighting to stay human despite the demon inside him. That was the moment when she had first kissed him, and brought him back to his human self. That was when she first started to realize they were meant to be together.

Dru was so lost in thinking about Greyson that she barely noticed when she slipped into the spell. Some deeper part of her mind reached out through the crystals, out into the airy distance beyond her consciousness. Searching for him. Reaching for him.

In the far distance, a spark of life flared bright. *Greyson.*

A jolt of energy flashed through her, at once cold and unbearably hot. She gasped.

Smoke tickled her nose. She opened her eyes to see the circle of crystals glowing like hot coals. In the center, the candle burned with a steady flame.

Curls of smoke swirled up from the flame, changing colors as they rose. Each strand of smoke shimmered a different hue, from emerald green to ruby red, sapphire blue, and a hundred delicate shades in between.

With ferocious intensity, Dru watched the smoke rise, scrutinizing its motions for the merest indication of a direction. Which way was Greyson? Before today, she had never even heard of this spell, and had no idea how subtle the results would be. She couldn't afford to miss anything.

As it turned out, this spell was anything but subtle.

The smoke swirled around the candle flame, gathering thick enough to snuff it out. The moment the flame was gone, the smoke streaked away as if fired from a gun. It stretched out through the length of the shop, leaving a comet-like trail past the cash register, down the main aisle, and toward the front door. Instantly, the smoke slipped around the doorframe and vanished.

Dru shot to her feet and stumbled after it, unsteady from the spell. By the time she reached the door, the smoke was long gone. There was nothing outside but a plumber's van parked next to the empty bus stop. The smoke left no trace.

The other two ran up and crowded in the doorway behind her.

Rane pointed at the parked van. "So, you think he's in there?" she asked dubiously.

"No. West." Dru pointed. "The smoke headed almost due west."

"So, maybe he's in Lakewood?" Opal tilted her chin up and stared into the distance.

Dru shook her head. "I don't know how far away he is. All I know is the direction. So, he's somewhere to the west of us. That's a start."

"So he could be . . ." Opal's brow wrinkled. ". . . in Golden?"

"Hey, let's try the Coors brewery," Rane said. "Do they still do free beer tours?"

Opal covered her face with her hands. "Oh, my God. We are never doing that again. Promise me from now on we're keeping magic and beer tours completely separate."

Rane looked offended. "What? I don't know why you're still mad about that. We caught the monster. We got free beer. Good times."

"Would have been better if you'd caught that thing *before* it chugged down all that beer. And then you beat it up *inside my car*." Opal glared at her. "I still can't turn on my air conditioner."

Rane tapped her temple. "Mind over matter, dude. You just have to decide what matters."

"That's enough. We need to go," Dru said, flipping the sign over to Closed.

"Go?" Opal said. "Where?"

"Hello? West." Dru headed into the back of the shop again and started deconstructing the circle.

Opal followed close behind. "West? *West?* That's not a destination. *West* could be anywhere. We need to try something else. Something a lot more specific."

"I don't *have* anything else. This is it. We don't have any other options left." Dru carefully packed the crystals into her bag, cushioning them so that they didn't scratch each other or the candle.

"Hold on, honey," Opal said, catching her eye. "Are you sure about this?"

Rane towered over her, arms folded, looking equally unhappy.

Dru took off her glasses and fixed them both with a serious look. "Greyson is *alive*. I know it. So we're just going to have to head west and see what we can find. If you have another concrete idea, I'm all ears. Otherwise, this is it."

Rane met Opal's worried look with a shrug. "You know she's not going to give up," Rane said. "How much gas you got?"

Opal sighed in resignation.

"Load up. Gas, weapons, magic amulets, whatever you can think of," Dru said, stuffing her bag. "We have to be ready for anything."

15

WHERE THE SKY ENDS

Dru spent the rest of the warm June day trapped in the car with Opal and Rane, driving west out of Denver, past the suburbs and golf courses, through foothills dotted with horse ranches and small towns, and eventually up into the ear-popping heights of the Rocky Mountains.

Every so often, Opal pulled off the road onto a sandy shoulder, surrounded by jagged cliffs and pine trees. There, Dru laid out the copper wire and crystals, and then focused her thoughts until she could cast the spell again.

Each time, it was harder. She wasn't used to casting powerful spells like this without Greyson's presence boosting her magical power. Doing it alone, she felt as if the well of magical energy inside her was quickly running dry.

But she had no choice. She needed to find him.

Every time the candle went out, the smoke blew steadily west, higher into the mountains, heading directly into the clean pine-scented wind.

Greyson was up here, somewhere. Dru was sure of it. She stared apprehensively up into the endless, unforgiving ranks of mountain peaks. *Greyson, where are you?*

Only after they had gone through the tunnels that led them to the other side of the Continental Divide did Dru start to truly worry. She didn't know how far west the smoke would lead them. It could be taking them as far as Utah. Nevada. Even California.

Heck, Greyson could be on an island somewhere in the Pacific, for all she knew. There was no way to tell until they got there.

Opal and Rane were apparently too busy bickering with each other to reach the same conclusion, and Dru didn't see the need to worry them just yet. She kept staring out the window at the slowly passing mountains, trying not to let her dark thoughts push her over the edge into panic.

How far was she willing to go?

A small voice inside her told her that she barely knew Greyson. She had met him only a week before the Four Horsemen tried to lay waste to the world. In that time, she had barely started to figure out her feelings about him. She still didn't know much about his past or what he was really like.

But every time her doubts reared up, she remembered one crucial thing: he had given up everything to save her. He had offered up his soul to the Four Horsemen to give her the chance to live. And because of him, because of his bravery, she had been able to stop doomsday. At least for the moment.

So how far would she go?

For Greyson, she decided, as far as it took.

She looked across the wide front seat at Opal, who caught her eye and nodded slightly.

Opal had already figured all of this out, Dru realized. She was just waiting for Dru to come to the same conclusion.

Heart swelling, Dru reached across the seat and put a hand on Opal's warm shoulder, which elicited a broad smile.

Behind them, Rane leaned forward between the seats. "What? What did I miss?"

Dru didn't answer. She just let Opal's long purple Lincoln carry them higher and higher into the mountains.

At the very next stop, the smoke changed direction. This time, it pointed up the side of a mountain. Dru looked up, breathless.

This was it.

As Dru packed up her crystals, Rane and Opal surveyed the mountain with different degrees of unhappiness. Stiff from so much sitting, Dru joined them. She shaded her eyes with one hand and leaned back to look up at the imposing slope of the nameless mountain.

Even a dirt hiking trail would have been something, but there was nothing. For the first few hundred yards, the mountain offered only a steep, trackless expanse of dry brown grass and occasional scrub brush.

Above that, the slope split off into a maze of pine-forested ridges broken by jutting brown outcroppings of rock. Far above, the barren peak of the mountaintop soared above the trees, just one mountain among the ranks of peaks that marched off into the distance, some frosted with the last vestiges of winter snow, the farther peaks turning blue in the distance.

"He's up there somewhere," Dru said, scarcely believing it herself. "That's what the spell is telling us."

Opal folded her arms resolutely, shaking her head. "Uh-uh. This is not happening. Sorry, but I didn't sign up for any outdoor adventures."

"You have to," Rane said, as if it was some kind of rule. "We have to follow the smoke."

"Maybe Greyson is up there, maybe not," Opal shot back. "He could be anywhere around here, and that's a big mountain. I didn't come all this way just to fall off of it."

Rane snorted and pulled her backpack out of the car. "You'll be fine. Just watch your step."

"Easy for you to say. You're the one wearing those steel-toed Russian clodhoppers."

"Cool, huh?" Rane clomped one foot up onto the bumper of Opal's car, showing off a pair of olive-green military boots with treads that would put a Sherman tank to shame. "Got 'em on eBay. They came with a free gas mask."

"Okay, let's just think about this," Dru said, pacing between them. Then she caught sight of Opal's apricot-colored suede open-toed sandals and their sparkling copper fringe. "Those are definitely not the right shoes for this."

Opal gracefully turned her ankles to showcase her shoes, making the copper fringe sparkle. "See? Everywhere I go, it's a disco."

Rane rolled her eyes. "Oh, come on. We all knew this was coming. I put on my camos and *everything*."

"Camo doesn't look good on me," Opal said indignantly. The look in her eyes said she didn't think it looked good on Rane, either, but she didn't say it out loud.

"Fine," Rane said. "You stay here. We'll go have all the fun." With that, she turned and marched up the slope.

"Wait! Let me switch shoes." Dru didn't really want to hike, but she had no choice. Quickly, she pulled her hiking shoes out of Opal's trunk and laced them up.

"You go on," Opal said, getting back into the car. "I'll be your getaway driver, in case you come running."

Dru took another look up the side of the mountain slope and snorted. "There's no way anybody could actually come running down that."

"Mmm-hmm," Opal said, with an air of certainty. "We'll just see about that."

"Definitely not running," Dru muttered, and set out after Rane.

As they made their way up the mountain, Dru came to realize that keeping up with Rane was a challenge even under the best of circumstances. Hiking up the wild side of a mountain, lugging a bag full of crystals and rocks, already exhausted from casting spells, was pretty much the opposite of the best of circumstances.

Far above, Rane stood astride a craggy boulder, silhouetted against the coppery clouds as she tilted back a bright pink water bottle and drank.

Dru, meanwhile, struggled to make her way up the steep slope without slipping, scraping her ankle on a rock, or having her legs forcibly exfoliated by thistle.

"I can see why people invented trails," she muttered, panting.

"Don't forget to listen for rattlesnakes," Rane called down, less than helpfully. "It's much better if you don't get bit."

By the time Dru finally reached the rocky outcropping, huffing and dripping with sweat, Rane was sitting in some kind of yoga pose, stretching.

Dru collapsed next to her, convinced she would die before she reached the top of the ridge. "Not enough oxygen up here," she gasped.

"Yeah, everybody says that. I don't know what they're complaining about." Rane held out a thumb-sized foil packet. "Energy gel?"

"I'm okay," Dru wheezed.

Rane waved the packet at her. "You're going to need this more than me, trust me."

"Fine. Whatever." Dru took it just to keep the peace. As she focused on trying to get her breathing back under control, Rane finished stretching and sat up, watching her closely. As the seconds ticked by, Rane gradually leaned closer and closer, still watching.

Dru shrunk away and ate the energy gel, thinking that would end Rane's scrutiny. It actually tasted pretty good.

But that wasn't the problem, apparently. Rane kept leaning closer until Dru could feel the heat radiating off her muscles.

"What?" Dru finally demanded.

"You really think he's still alive," Rane said with uncharacteristic calm. It wasn't a question.

"I know he is," Dru said, after she finally rearranged her thoughts. "I can feel it. Besides, I saw Hellbringer."

Rane shrugged and looked away.

This time, it was Dru's turn to stare. "You don't believe me?"

"Dude, *you* believe it, and that's all that matters," Rane said. "Doesn't matter what I saw back in the netherworld."

With a sinking feeling, Dru asked, "And what did you see?"

Rane brought her fists together and then burst them apart, fingers waggling. "*Boom.* That's what I saw. Big-ass explosion, and Hellbringer went flipping end over end. With us inside it. Lucky for you and me, I had a good grip on you, kept you from flying out. But then I reached for him, and—" Rane abruptly stood up. Her face showing a rare glimpse of pain. "Look, *you* believe he's still alive. Okay?"

A knot of fear hardened inside Dru. "He is alive. I can feel it every time I cast that spell." She hated how small her voice sounded.

"Yeah, that's cool and all but . . ." Rane paced. "I know how it is. When you want something so bad—"

"No." Dru shook her head. "I'm not making this up. Don't even go there."

"I've lost friends, okay?" Rane pointed both fingers at her own chest.

"Good friends. Powerful sorcerers. This thing that we do, fighting monsters, trying to keep the world safe, it's tough. Sometimes we lose."

Her words stung Dru like a slap. Because in a way, they were true. She turned away, blinking her eyes as they filled with hot tears.

"Sometimes," Rane repeated in a low voice, *"we lose.* Okay?"

"Not this time," Dru insisted, her voice thick with emotion. "He's alive. He's up here somewhere. He is."

"Yeah. Or maybe, just maybe, that spell doesn't work. Okay? We've been driving all day, and this smoke keeps changing directions. I'm just saying. We don't know."

"I *do* know," Dru snapped, rising to her feet. "How long have I been doing this? How many books have I read? How many crystals have I researched? You told me one time that the only way I was ever going to get anywhere in this world was if I embraced being a sorceress. Right?"

Rane nodded, somewhat reluctantly.

"And I'm embracing that right now." Dru pointed uphill into the trees. "Greyson is alive. He is in these mountains. And I am going to find him."

As the echoes of her voice died away, she realized she was shouting.

"I'm sorry," Dru added, more quietly.

"No worries." Rane's jaw set in a tough line. "Dude, you know I have your back. I *so* have your back. Right now, I'm standing on top of a freakin' *mountain* for you. Okay?"

"Okay. Right."

"And you know why? Because I've met you. I know you're not going to give up on Greyson. I know how bad you need to find him," Rane said. "So bad, you're liable to dive right over your head into trouble. And someone needs to be there to watch your back and make sure you come out of this thing alive. I've always done that. I always will."

Dru bit her lip. There was an unspoken "but" in there. And it was the last thing she wanted to hear.

"But," Rane said finally, "at some point, somebody needs to tell you when it's time to go home."

Those words hung in the thin mountain air between them, cold and unforgiving.

Dru took off her glasses and wiped her eyes, trying to stop from crying and not exactly succeeding.

"Oh, D." Rane lifted her arms for a hug.

"Don't." Dru stopped her with an upraised finger. She fought to sort through the storm of emotions that ran through her. Anger at Rane for not believing her. Fear that they might never find Greyson. Shame that this was somehow all her fault. She put her glasses back on. "I'm going to cast the spell again."

"Again?" Rane looked surprised. "You look like you're about ready to fall over. You sure you're up for that?"

"What, you have another plan? Because I'm fresh out," Dru said, unpacking crystals from her bag. The candle was burned down to a nub.

Rane looked up at the setting sun, shielding her eyes with one hand. "Going to get dark soon. Trust me, we don't want to be stuck on the side of the mountain overnight. We don't even have a blanket to share."

"I'll hurry." But the setting sun didn't worry Dru as much as the idea that she might have exhausted her magic. If she didn't have enough strength left to cast the spell, one last time, then she would never find Greyson.

16
NEVER GO HOME

It felt like it took an hour to lay out the copper wire on the flat-topped boulder and get the crystals properly aligned. Meanwhile, the sun sank until it barely peeked over the top of the mountain. They were running out of time.

Careful to avoid skewering her legs on the tines of the spiky yucca plants that surrounded the boulder, Dru climbed up and sat cross-legged beside the crystal circle.

She had lost count of how many times she had cast the spell. By now, when she shut her eyes and focused, she could practically see each differently colored crystal through her closed eyelids. But her energy was at an all-time low, and part of her balked at the idea of trying to summon it up again.

She took a deep breath of the painfully thin air and concentrated, clearing her thoughts of everything except trying to find Greyson. She let go of her anger, her doubt, the fiery ache in her tired legs, her worries about the vanishing sun. She acknowledged each of those thoughts and willfully set them aside.

She had only one more chance to find Greyson. She had to make it count.

Summoning up her last reserves of magic, she directed her energy equally through each crystal around the circle. She deliberately went slowly, building the energy inside the crystal as she went along, trusting her feelings for Greyson to guide her.

Her first thought of him was from the very end, after he had been overtaken by evil. In her mind's eye, she caught a glimpse of his fiery demon eyes glaring back at her. Immediately, she pushed that image away. The Four Horsemen were gone now. That wasn't the Greyson she was looking for.

She was searching for the man he really was. The one who had trusted her, embraced her, helped her find her inner sorceress and become who she really was.

She could see him looking at her. She remembered his steel-rimmed sunglasses shining in the sun as they cruised through the New Mexico desert together. She could see the red desert sand and green bushes sliding behind him. See the stubble along his jaw as he turned a warm smile her way.

Was he gone forever? Was he still alive?

Where could he be?

Close. The knowledge burned through her, icy and yet scorching hot, as clearly as if she had heard the sound of his voice. She drew in a sharp breath, fighting for air.

Her magical energy, accumulated inside the crystals, suddenly burst into the center of the copper circle and swirled around the candle. She could feel the crackling heat as the candle flared to life.

She opened her eyes to see the candle engulfed in a multicolored ball of flame. Almost instantly, it burned itself out with a soft pop, leaving behind a bubbling puddle of wax where the candle had once stood. A curl of rainbow smoke streaked away like a living thing, cutting through the mountain wind. Dru knew by now that there was no point in chasing after something that moved so fast. She just focused on the direction.

This time, instead of pointing directly up the mountain, the trail of smoke angled to the right, over rocks and dead grass, up toward a pine-covered ridge.

"Whoa," Rane said as the smoke shot past her and faded away. She took a few steps after it, but something caught her attention and she knelt down on the ground.

Dru swayed, overwhelmed and dizzy. Was that Greyson's voice in her mind? Or, like Rane had hinted, did Dru want to find him so badly that she was somehow imagining it?

"The candle's ruined," Dru said with a horrible sinking feeling. She picked at the quickly cooling wax, trying to peel it off the top of the boulder. "That's it. I can't cast the spell again without it." Reluctantly, she packed away her crystals and folded up the copper circle.

"We've got a problem," Rane said from where she knelt in the grass, studying something on the ground. "We're not alone up here."

Carefully, Dru approached her, not sure what she was looking at.

Rane pointed out a flattened purple wildflower and a curved depression in the dry dirt. "That's a footprint. Leather-soled boot."

"Could it be Greyson?"

"No. A smaller person."

"You mean, like . . . ?" Dru held her hand out at waist height.

"Not a *munchkin*. I mean more like your size. This is too small to be Greyson." Rane stood up and scanned their surroundings, bristling with sudden ferocity, nostrils flared, fists clenched. "Somebody else is up here with us. Maybe a bunch of somebodies."

Dru looked over both shoulders, suddenly wary of the surrounding piles of sharp boulders and the crooked pine trees with their huge, gnarled roots. Until now, she hadn't really felt like they were in danger. Hadn't felt threatened. But the footprint changed that.

"Are you sure? How old is it? Maybe it's from some hiker."

"Shh." Rane stooped and picked up a chunk of granite. With a harsh grinding sound, her entire body transformed into mottled brown rock. When she stayed motionless, she blended perfectly into the mountainside. "Stay here," she grunted. "Stay quiet."

Nearly silently, Rane stalked forward, like a hunting animal, following the direction of the vanished smoke.

Feeling vulnerable, Dru turned in a slow circle, watching every shadow and rock around her with wide eyes. Someone was out there. She could practically feel eyes on her. It made her skin crawl.

She turned back to watch Rane's progress. But Rane was gone.

Dru stood frozen, afraid to stand out in the open, afraid to run and hide.

The pine-scented wind reminded her of Titus's cologne. Where did he fit into all of this? Did he have anything to do with Greyson's disappearance, or was she just desperately reaching for connections that didn't exist?

The wind whispered through the trees as if shushing her. She felt as if the mountain was trying to lull her into lowering her defenses. Somewhere in the shadows, a twig snapped, and Dru had visions of the mountainside coming alive with all manner of creatures swarming out from behind the tree trunks.

But nothing moved.

She fished through her bag until her fingers closed on the familiar length of her dagger-shaped spectrolite crystal. She pulled it out, holding the polished smoky-gray stone like a short knife. Its surface shimmered in the last rays of sunlight with iridescent layers of purple, blue, green, orange, and gold.

Powered by raw fear, Dru dredged up her final reserves of magical energy, with every intention of powering up the protective crystal to defend herself. But she had no idea whether she had enough strength left to do that, or how long the enchantment would protect her.

If she was going to be attacked, she had to wait until the last possible moment. She would only have one shot with this crystal.

For what seemed like eons, Dru stood stock-still, nerves taut. Her legs ached and trembled. Any moment, she was sure, something was going to come charging out of the shadows at her, with steely eyes and snapping jaws.

"We're good." Rane's voice suddenly broke the silence, making Dru jump. Rane came marching downhill from a different direction, changing into human form as she went. With obvious disappointment, she jerked a thumb over her shoulder. "Whoever it was, they headed over the ridge and down the far slope. Long gone by now."

That was when Dru saw the long strand of web strung between two trees easily ten yards apart. It shimmered in the dying sunlight.

"Stop!" Dru held up one palm.

Rane instantly halted, but the sudden stop set loose a handful of small rocks that tumbled and clattered downhill. They sailed past the web, but Dru couldn't tell whether or not they touched it.

Rane's head swiveled left and right. "What?"

"Spiderweb. But probably not from any spider. Let me have a look."

Dru stuffed the shimmering spectrolite blade back into her pocket and dug in her bag until she found her frosty cube of ulexite. With some difficulty, she clambered uphill, closer to Rane's dusty military boots. Then Dru knelt and pressed the ulexite to her forehead.

Powering up the crystal used up the last dregs of Dru's power, leaving her dizzy with exhaustion. Her vision swam as the ulexite altered everything she saw. The colors of the rocks and trees faded, while the shadows around her deepened, tinged midnight blue.

Three ghostly strands of web stretched tightly from tree to tree, running just above the seeds of the dry grass that sprouted from between the rocks. In her crystal-enhanced vision, the web glowed softly, as if illuminated by moonlight.

The strands continued at an angle uphill, past wind-scoured rocks and scrubby underbrush, until they vanished over the top of a nearby ridge. "I don't know if it's a tripwire, or if one of those things just wandered by and snagged some of its web by accident," Dru said. "Either way, the webs lead that direction." Dru pointed, somewhat blindly. While using the ulexite, she wasn't good at sensing motion.

"You think there's undead up there? I was just up there," Rane said flatly, somehow complaining and sounding worried at the same time. "All right, keep that crystal going. Don't turn it off yet."

"Why? What are you doing?"

"You have to spot it for me." Rocks clattered as Rane inched closer. "Where is it?"

Dru clumsily pointed out the length of the web. Rane carefully stepped over it and climbed down beside her. She loomed up in Dru's crystal-distorted vision, looking eerily pale. Her face was half obscured by sharp shadows that didn't really exist. A flicker passed back and forth between them that Dru guessed was Rane waving a hand.

"Dude, can you see me?"

"Yes," Dru said, exasperated. "But not very well. I have to take this crystal down." She could already feel a throbbing headache creeping up the back of her skull. "I'm too tired to keep it going."

"Come on. Follow the trail. Lead the way."

Dru took a few halting steps and immediately stumbled on an unseen rock. Rane caught her arm before she fell.

"What are you doing?" Rane demanded. "Watch your step."

"I can't *see* anything!" Dru said.

"Hello, aren't you using a seeing crystal?"

"It doesn't work that way!" Dru's head pounded. "I have to stop. Right now. I'm totally exhausted."

"No, wait, wait. You have to track down these webs." Rane's head went blurry as she turned to look in all directions. "I need you to spot this."

"I'm not tripping and falling down this mountain." Dru pointed. "The webs go up that way, then they disappear over the ridge."

Rane blew out a frustrated breath. "Fine. Let's piggyback."

"What? No! No piggyback."

"Total piggyback. It's the only way." Rane bent and backed into her, and before Dru could resist, she was suddenly lifted up on Rane's strong back.

With her free hand, Dru hung on for dear life. "Oh, my God. We're piggybacking on a mountaintop. We're going to die." Any moment, she was sure she would slip off and plummet to her death.

"We're not going to *die*," Rane said, striding uphill. "Just follow the web, and if anything moves, yell. We're running out of daylight."

Dru gulped. "The webs go straight ahead." As they swayed side to side with every step, she rested her chin on top of Rane's head. "I hate it when you carry me. You do know that?"

"Yeah. Makes it more fun."

They followed the shimmering trail of web up over the top of the ridge. Beyond, a valley opened up below them, half-hidden in the shadow of the setting sun, now a burning smudge behind the relentless cloud cover.

A gleam of light far below them caught Dru's eye. Something metallic shone in the last rays of sunlight, as the ragged shadows of the mountain peaks climbed up from the depths, swallowing everything.

Dru squinted against her pounding headache. She could just barely make out the brown curve of a dry double-track dirt road. The road, tinted purple in her crystal vision, snaked around the side of the ridge before making a tight switchback into a grove of aspen trees. Their shiny leaves shone like water ripples in the breeze.

And there, in the shadow at the elbow of the road, sat a hunch-backed black car with long chrome-tipped fins. Dru stared at it for several seconds before she figured out what it was.

"A hearse?" she said, making Rane look over her shoulder in surprise.

Rane turned her head to follow Dru's gaze. "Seriously? The hell is he doing here?"

"Who?"

"Salem." Rane shifted Dru's weight. "Damn, I thought those foot-prints looked familiar."

"What's he doing here?" A worried feeling unsettled Dru, tinged with anger. "Did he lie to me? Do you think Greyson is with him?"

The wind carried up a distant burble of engine noise, and the hearse's sharp taillights glowed red. Slowly, the black car eased out from beneath the aspen trees and descended into the deepening shadows.

"The smoke pointed this way, and now Salem is leaving. This can't be a coincidence." Squinting, Dru followed the lines of the double-track road as they snaked back and forth down the side of the mountain, then curved around through the pass and disappeared. "We need to head him off at the pass."

"What are you, the Lone Ranger? We'll never catch up to him."

"I'm serious. Set me down." Still holding the ulexite crystal to her forehead, Dru slid down Rane's back and awkwardly found her footing.

With her free hand, she pointed, tracing the course of the road. "Look. There's nowhere else for him to go. When he gets down to the bottom, he has to go around through the pass. That's the only way off this side of the mountain. If we can get back to Opal in time, we can head back to the fork and catch him as he comes through."

Below them, Salem's hearse steadily rolled toward the bottom of the valley, and the gravel-rattling sound of its tires slowly faded from the mountainside.

"Even if we do catch him, then what?" Rane asked.

To Dru, the answer was obvious. "Then we follow him. Find out what exactly he's up to and why he *really* has undead skeletons in his apartment. And then we make him tell us where to find Greyson."

Even through the crystal distortion, Dru could see the uncertain look on Rane's face. "Are you sure the webs lead down to his hearse?"

"No. The webs end right here." Dru turned around to point out where the shimmering lines of web came to an abrupt end at the top of the ridge, among a jumble of car-sized boulders.

A swarm of web-wrapped undead was already crawling up from between the rocks. Skeletal jaws yawned open, stretching their speckled wrapping wide enough to reveal sharp stained teeth. Their shrouded bony arms ended in blackened claws.

Dru sucked in a breath and lowered the ulexite crystal.

Her vision swam, filling with glittering sparks as she stuffed the ulexite in her bag and pulled out the sharp spectrolite crystal. It was her only defense.

Beside her, she heard more than saw Rane scoop up a dead tree trunk and swing it like a baseball bat. Bones crunched. A creature screeched.

She focused on the knife-like crystal in her hand, willing it to burst into a colorful glow. But the gray spectrolite stayed dark. It wouldn't protect her now.

She had no magical strength left.

"Rane!" Cold fear poured through Dru's veins. She staggered in the direction of Opal's car, stumbling on loose rocks as the undead closed in on her. "*Help!*"

A powerful grip seized her arm, but it wasn't the cold bones of the undead. It was Rane, now turned to stone and looking madder than hell.

Rane bared her teeth. "*Run!*"

17
THE WAY BACK

Streamers of webbing zipped past them, smacking into trees and rocks. Dru tripped and stumbled down the mountainside. Trying to run full speed down a steep slope of dry underbrush and loose rocks was tricky enough, but the lengthening shadows from the setting sun made every step even more treacherous.

Rane held tight to her hand and half steadied, half dragged her down the endless slope. The fear of death cut through Dru's exhaustion and pushed her onward. Together, they charged past thickets of grasping bushes, through stinging clusters of slippery, dry grass, and over rough-edged boulders that threatened to take a bite out of her feet.

Dru wasn't sure which would kill them first: the mountain, or the hissing horde of undead following them.

With every pounding heartbeat, Dru expected to see more of the creatures rise up in front of them, cutting off their escape. Every rock, every tree was a potential hiding place.

Eventually, the sounds of pursuit faded behind them. Dru nearly shouted in relief when she finally spotted the dusty, amethyst-colored expanse of Opal's car waiting at the side of the gravel road. The unmistakable beats of Gloria Estefan and the Miami Sound Machine thudded through the twilight air.

Opal let out a little squeak of surprise when Dru ran full tilt into the side of the car and scrambled inside. Rane got in the back and slammed the door.

A quick look back over Dru's shoulder revealed no sign of the undead. Yet. She was too panicked and winded to explain the danger. Instead, she just pointed down the road. "Go!"

"Told you you'd come running," Opal said. "This is not my first field trip."

Dru gulped air. "Drive!"

"Never listen to me." Opal started the car and sped down the road, spewing gravel behind them. "What happened up there?"

"Undead," Dru said. "Lots of them."

"I could've taken them," Rane said. At Dru's disbelieving look, she added, "What? We only came back here so we could catch Salem."

"Salem?" Opal said his name with the disgust most people reserved for particularly awkward infections. Wide-eyed, she kept watch up the side of the mountain. "If he's here, that's no coincidence, mark my words. That man is up to no good. He knows something he's not telling us."

"You think?" Rane said, turning human again. "That's why I'm going to *make* him tell us."

"Slow down, slow down." Dru waved a hand at Opal, as if that would help. "The pass is just up ahead. And watch out for creatures. That ridge was crawling with them."

They crept up the gravel curve, getting closer to the gap between two ridges where the old double-track joined the road in an angled T-intersection.

In the back seat, Rane leaned forward. "When he comes out, how do you know which way he'll go? He could head right toward us."

"Fifty-fifty chance," Dru said. "And if he does, we've got this direction blocked. He'll have to talk to us. If he turns the other way, we'll see where he goes. Opal, stop right here in the shadow."

As the sun sank, the entire curve of the road was smothered by shadow. Around the bend, the last rays of light were barely visible, shining down through the narrow pass that had probably once been a mule trail, back in the days of Colorado's silver rush.

They waited.

Rane tilted her head to peer up the steep slope. "I know they're up there. But I don't see them."

Neither did Dru. "They might not follow us down here," she said hopefully.

"Yeah, right." Rane kept watch up the mountainside.

The terrifying run down the slope, after the long hike and the endless spell-casting, had left Dru shaky and weak. Suddenly thirsty, she dug around the junk in the car until she found a bottle of water between the seats. She gulped it down.

Just when she thought she had miscalculated Salem's course, movement approached down the pass. The blocky shape of Salem's black hearse, now half tan with trail dust, slowly bounced its way down the rocky double-track. The final bloody rays of sunset sparkled off its chrome trim, shining like rubies, and then the car descended into the darkness with them.

Dru couldn't be sure it was Salem behind the wheel. The car paused at the edge of the road, and she worried they'd been spotted.

Then the hearse's headlights flared to life, and with a clatter of gravel, it turned the other direction and drove away.

"Okay, give him a minute," Dru whispered, "and then we'll follow him at a good distance. But keep your headlights off. With the sun going down, he might not see us."

"Might not," Rane agreed. "Can't see anything out of the back of that thing."

"But he might see our headlights!" Dru insisted.

"Fine, fine." Opal eased the Lincoln forward. "But if it gets much darker, I won't be able to see the road."

"Just go slow. But fast enough to keep up with him," Dru said.

Opal gave her a withering look.

"I don't know. Just drive normally!"

"Just another day at the office." Opal coasted them down a slope and then up the next rise. Salem's sharp red taillights bobbed in and out of sight ahead of them. "Why does that man drive a hearse, anyway?"

"It fits him," Rane said.

Dru nodded. "I can see that. Considering his morose personality, obsession with dark magic, and predilection toward Gothic-style accessories."

"No, dude. It *fits* him. Literally. There's, like, tons of cargo room. Good roof height in back, so he can sit back there with all his magical stuff. And if you need to haul off a dead monster, it's easier to load than a van."

"Oh," Dru said. "That's actually kind of disturbing."

"On so many levels," Opal added.

"Hey, you know, it's part of the job." Rane sounded defensive. "You fight monsters, somebody's got to clean it up. You can't just leave these suckers lying around for the tabloids to find."

"Nobody believes it anyway," Opal said. "Even when they do get photos, everybody thinks it's a hoax."

"Besides," Rane said, "the hearse is big enough, you can sleep in the wayback. If you're on a stakeout. Or, you know, *what . . . ev . . . er.*" The way she stretched out the word made it sound impossibly dirty.

It took a moment for the implications of that to sink into Dru's brain. Where she immediately wished they hadn't. She shook her head, as if that could somehow dislodge the disturbing image of Rane and Salem getting busy in the back of the hearse. "I'm sure you two didn't . . ." She cleared her throat. "You know."

Rane seemed puzzled. "What, hop in the wayback for a little walla-walla bing-bang? Oh yeah."

"Eww. *Eww!* Not another word. In the back of a hearse?"

Rane shrugged. "Like I said, tons of room."

Dru winced. "Ugh. Oh, my God."

"You think *that's* freaky?" Opal said, waggling her eyebrows. "This one time in college, I had these friends who worked at a peanut butter factory, and one night after work we—"

"Look out!" Dru yelled, pointing out the sheer drop-off they were headed toward.

"Whoa!" Opal jerked the wheel, just barely keeping the yacht-sized car on the narrow dirt road. "Honey, don't distract me like that!"

"I'm not the one telling freaky peanut butter stories! Just focus on Salem!"

Opal hunched over the steering wheel, staring out across the night-darkened mountainside rapidly disappearing beneath the evening sky. "I don't see him. I don't see anything. I need to turn on the lights."

"No! Don't turn on the headlights. He'll know we're here."

"Well, he might find out when we drive off the side of the mountain!"

Anxiety gripped Dru. They were clearly the only other car out here in the mountain wilderness. If they turned on their headlights, Salem would surely see them and bolt, meaning all of this effort was wasted. But if they didn't turn on the lights, they could easily run off the road in the dark. Without any guardrails to protect them, the results would be too horrible to contemplate.

A heavy weight settled in Dru's stomach. She had to admit there was no way to win.

"Fine. Turn on the lights."

"Sorry, honey." Opal pulled the light switch, and the gravel road in front of them lit up in their headlight beams.

They weren't alone.

Directly in front of them, in the center of the road, a dark figure stood, feet planted wide. Salem.

Opal screamed and hit the brakes, but Dru knew it was too late. They were surely about to run him over.

Salem's long hair blew back as he raised his arms to point his spidery fingers at them. His eyes glowed white.

Dru's stomach lurched as invisible tethers of magic lifted the car completely up off the ground and suspended it in thin air.

She could do nothing except stare back into Salem's furious face, his skin bleached bone-white by the headlights. With a snarl, he swung his arms to the side, as if flinging them away.

With a nauseating lurch, the car soared off the side of the mountain and hovered in the open air, hundreds of feet above certain death.

Dru realized she was screaming, and so was Opal, so she reached for her. They clung together on the Lincoln's wide bench seat, holding onto each other because there was nothing else to hold onto.

"It's okay," Dru said, over and over, trying to convince herself. "He's not going to drop us." She stared into Salem's enraged features, spotlighted on the road in front of them, searching for any sign that she was right.

"*Hey, goth nugget!*" Rane bellowed, hanging her head out the window. "You're not going to drop us! You're just pissing us off! Why don't you go— *Hey!*" This last was directed at Opal as she buzzed up the back window and clicked on the child locks.

"Don't give him any ideas!" Opal yelled.

Salem motioned again, and the car swung the rest of the way around to the other side of him, so that they were facing back the way they had come.

As they hovered over the gravel road again, this time pointed uphill, Salem closed his hands into fists. Instantly, the car dropped to the ground.

It wasn't a long fall, maybe only a foot or two, but it was enough to flip Dru's stomach completely over. Everything in the car jumped with a bone-jarring bang.

The engine died. They sat in sudden silence broken only by the clattering of the thick cluster of amulets hanging from the rearview mirror as they swung back and forth.

Behind them, Rane broke the silence. "He's such an ass hat. I'm going to teach him a lesson." She opened the back door.

Dru twisted around in the seat and grabbed Rane's arm. "Wait! Wait. He's just trying to scare us."

"It's working!" Opal shrieked.

Dru ignored her and focused on Rane. "If you go out there, it will turn into a huge fight. Like with Ember."

"News flash. When someone picks up your car and dangles you over a cliff, the fight's already started. Now I'm going to go finish it." Rane tightened her fist, the one with the titanium ring, and her body transformed into shimmering metal.

Dru's blood ran cold. This was serious. "Just wait! Just wait, okay? Give me five minutes to talk to him. That's all. I know Salem."

"You think I don't?" Rane barked back. Her metal eyes flashed like the blade of a knife.

As calmly as she could, Dru held up her hands and kept her voice quiet. "One minute, then. Just one minute, and then he's all yours. All right?"

Rane's jaw worked side to side. Then she shut the door and turned to Opal. "Time her." She bit off the words.

Opal made a face. "I'm not timing her. Are you crazy? I'm about to back us all the way down this mountain. I've had enough of this." She turned the ignition key. The starter whinnied, but the car didn't start.

Dru put a calming hand on her wrist, stopping her. "Just one minute. I promise. Just pop the trunk for me."

"The trunk?"

"Just trust me." Dru slid out of the seat before either of them could argue with her. She circled around to the back of the car and lifted the trunk lid. In among the clutter of shoe boxes and garment bags, she found Salem's black silk top hat.

She smacked the clay dust off it as she crossed the dozen yards of dirt road that separated them. Silently, she hoped this little peace offering would work. He'd had this hat forever. It had to mean something.

Salem stood with his half-unbuttoned black silk shirt tucked into black leather pants over boots with wicked-looking metal toes. His long hair fluttered freely in the wind. Without his hat, he looked less like a stage magician and more like a rock star. Dru could almost understand why Rane had such a thing for him.

Except for the fact that he looked ready to murder them all.

Dru took a deep breath and held out the top hat. "Here. Brought you something."

After a tense standoff, Salem finally took the hat. He scowled at her for a moment before he looked down and gently brushed off the last traces of clay dust. It made little clouds in the beams of the headlights.

Dru adjusted her glasses and clasped her hands in front of her. "So, um . . . Mind telling me why you were at Greyson's place?"

"I do mind." He carefully placed the hat on his head and swiped his finger around the brim. From beneath the hat, his eyes glittered. "Let's call it professional duty and leave it at that."

"Uh-huh." Dru tried to ignore the butterflies in her stomach. "So, funny coincidence. You're out here in the mountains, and they're kind of full of undead. Why is that?"

"They're not close enough to worry about," he snapped. If the presence of the undead came as any surprise to him, he didn't show it. "What do you want?"

"Okay. Listen, we don't have to be on opposite sides here. Can we just be friends again?"

The corner of Salem's mouth twitched. "I've always preferred being enemies," he said with an air of impatience. "It makes *so* much more sense."

Dru couldn't keep the shock from showing on her face. "Salem, we've always been friends, I thought. We've never been enemies."

"Really? That's a new one. Allow me to count the ways." He paced back and forth across the road, ruffled black shirt shining in the headlights, his shadow dancing far behind him. "First, you lied to me about your demonic boyfriend, Greyson."

"Well, in my defense, all I did was omit certain details—"

"You *stole* from me. On more than one occasion."

That stung. "Truth be told, you actually stole certain things from me first. Including the journal of the Seven Harbingers, which you took apart and pinned up on your wall. So, I was just trying to—"

"You followed me here," he said.

"We're looking for Greyson."

"You've been gossiping about me behind my back."

"Hey, you're the one who broke up with Rane. Remember?" Dru jabbed a finger at him. "And she's my best friend. That makes you fair game for trash talk. That's a girl code exemption."

"You broke into my home. My private sanctuary."

Dru cleared her throat. "Are you still hung up on that? Because really, it's not like we went through your bedroom drawers. We just had to get a few things that—"

"Things that belonged to *me*."

Dru felt her own patience rapidly disappearing. "Let's get one thing straight, buddy. When it comes to doomsday, we're in an emergency situation here. Okay? Social mores go out the window just a little bit when the fate of the world is at stake."

Salem stared at her for an uncomfortably long time. Long enough for her anger and defensiveness to fade away into a little bit of shame. Maybe she had treated Salem badly, after all. It was true that saving the world was a matter of epic importance. But that didn't make it right to forget who your friends were.

"Doomsday," he said at last. "Well played."

For once, Salem didn't sound the least bit sarcastic. That made her feel even worse.

"Look, for what it's worth, I really am sorry," she said. "I am. I normally don't treat people like that. I never meant for you to come to any harm, or to violate your personal space or . . ." Her confidence withered under the intensity of his stare. Quietly, she added, "Is there any way we can go back to being friends? We could help each other. We can work together."

He folded his arms and glared at her in silence.

Behind Dru, a car door slammed. Heavy footsteps marched up beside her and stopped. Rane, arms folded like Salem, looked him up and down. Her jaw was set in a tough line, but at least she was in human form. Dru hoped that meant she wasn't about to start a fight.

Salem's gaze cut over to Rane, and something in his face softened. For the briefest moment, Dru saw real vulnerability pass across his sharp features. Beneath the all-black outfit, the long, wavy hair, and the guyliner accenting his crazy sorcerer eyes, there was a regular guy next door gazing with real longing at the girl he regretted leaving.

The night air seemed to go still around them, as if the world was waiting for Salem to make his move. Dru held her breath, not daring to crack the fragility of this moment.

"Dude." Rane's flat voice broke the silence like a rampaging bull crashing through a rodeo fence. "Are you wearing leather pants? That is *so* hot."

Salem sighed and rolled his eyes. Just like that, the magical moment was gone. The wind picked up again, carrying particles of dirt through the headlight beams as he turned on his heel and strutted away uphill. "Fine. Come on. Might as well show you," he said without looking back.

"Yeah! Let's see it," Rane called after him, hands on her hips. Her lips quirked up into a smirk as she watched him walk away.

"What do you think he's going to show us?" Dru whispered, worried.

Not taking her eyes off Salem, Rane leaned closer. "I don't know. But if things get hot and heavy, just be cool, okay?"

"*Seriously?*" Dru couldn't keep her voice down. "In the *hearse?*"

"Not in the hearse," Salem called from the darkness ahead. "Under the mountain. That's where everything is about to happen."

18

DARKNESS RUNS DEEP

Salem stood at the edge of the mountain ridge and pointed out into the night-darkened abyss. "There."

Dru walked up beside him, ignoring for the moment where he pointed. Instead, she studied the sharp angles of his face in the faint reflected glow of Opal's headlights.

She had known Salem for years, and despite his insufferable attitude, she still felt that deep down he was a good person. But he had too many secrets, too much anger, too much ego. She had never entirely trusted him. Could she trust him now?

The wind whispered through the sparse pine trees, making branches creak and bushes rattle. The air rapidly cooled as the night closed in around them, stripping away the warmth of the day.

Rane marched up, crunching gravel beneath her military boots, and planted herself between Dru and Salem. Muscles bulged as she folded her arms. "I don't see anything."

Dru looked, too. "Me either."

Salem sighed and pointed harder. "Over there. In the moonlight."

Dru took off her glasses, polished them on her shirt, and put them back on. Following Salem's outstretched finger, she squinted into the far distance, where the silvery light from the cloud-shrouded moon spilled down a rough slope.

"Do you see the entrance?" Salem asked.

Dru squinted harder, seeing nothing at first. Where he pointed, there was just a rough cliff face and possibly the ghost of a road.

Then she spotted it. A wide archway was cut deep into the rock, as tall as the pine trees that surrounded it, and twice as wide. The curve of its ceiling was much too even to be natural, but all she could see was a solid black shadow within.

"What is that?" Dru asked.

"That," Salem said, dropping his arm and turning to face her, "is exactly where you need to *not* go. Let me handle this."

"Excuse me?"

"That's the source of the undead. The mountains around here are crawling with them, and you two princesses are lucky you haven't run into any yet, or you'd both be dead."

Rane snorted. "Whatever, dude, we already—"

Dru kicked her in the ankle before she could reveal to Salem that they had already stirred up some kind of undead nest.

Salem looked up at her suspiciously. "Already what?"

Dru stepped in. "Obviously, we already knew there were undead creatures around here. What we need to know is, what is that?" She pointed toward the mysterious tunnel entrance. "Some kind of a mine or something?"

"Judging by the Fort Knox–style blast doors sealing off the entrance, my money is on a nuclear bunker from the Cold War," Salem said. "Somebody has been busy with obfuscation spells, keeping it hidden from casual observation. What's inside is anyone's guess. But everything points to it as the epicenter for doomsday."

And it was exactly where the smoke had headed, Dru realized. Greyson was inside there somewhere. But why? And what was keeping him there?

Rane pointed at it with her chin. "So how did you find it?"

"Good point," Dru said. "How did you know where to look, exactly?"

"The undead they sent after us were practically an open invitation. In fact, I believe they *were* an invitation." The look on Salem's face suggested he was surprised she hadn't come to the same conclusion. "I got here by tracking the sorcio glyphs on the creature's hands. Didn't you?"

Dru had a momentary flashback to Greyson's garage, especially the hissing creature's outstretched claws, dripping black with scourge, as it reached for her. With her feet webbed tightly to the cold concrete floor, she hadn't been able to escape. She'd barely been able to fight back. She pushed away that suffocating thought and focused on what Salem was saying.

Sorcio glyphs. On the creature's hands.

She hadn't thought to look there. But apparently, he had studied the creatures much more thoroughly. Which explained why he was keeping them preserved in his apartment.

"Huh," Dru said nonchalantly. "Well, *yeah*. Of course. The old glyph-on-the-zombie-hand trick. Everybody's heard of that one."

Rane pursed her lips. "Yeah," she said in a flat monotone. "We totally did that, too."

Salem's gaze ticked over to Rane and then back to Dru, looking slyly amused.

"Wait. Did you say that the undead were *sent* after us?" Dru asked, alarmed. "Who would do that? And why?"

"You're supposed to be the big brain around here. Go home and figure it out." He turned to leave.

"Whoa, whoa, wait a minute." Dru chased after him and stepped in his path. "How do we get inside that atomic bunker?"

Salem's eyes glinted in the moonlit gloom. "*You* don't. *I* do."

"Come on," Rane said behind him. "That's not fair."

Salem moved to go around Dru, but she refused to step aside. She knew that the smoke had pointed this direction. They were so close, but there had to be something Salem wasn't telling them.

"What's inside the bunker, Salem? I'm not budging until you tell me. I will get up inside your grill in all kinds of ways. You know I will. I'm crazy like that."

Salem's spidery fingers wiggled at his sides, as if they had a life of their own. "You should learn to leave these things alone. You don't want to be part of what comes next."

Dru leaned closer. "What . . . is in there . . . Salem?"

His mouth twitched, and finally he uttered one word: "*Volvajo.*"

"Ooh. Sounds dirty," Rane gushed. "What's it mean?"

It took Dru a moment to place the word. It wasn't Spanish, Italian, or any other common language. It was sorcio, the language of magic. "Volvajo is a masquerade," Dru said. "Isn't it?"

"Oh, very good." Salem looked unimpressed.

"But it's competitive," Dru said, trying to remember what she had read about it ages ago in *The Primer on Dread Things*. "In a volvajo, all the sorcerers are trying to outdo one another. It's like a tournament. Sorcerers keep competing until the end, and the best of the best team up and form a new group."

"My prediction?" Salem said. "It's not going to end well. It never does."

Rane made a face. "How come I've never gone to one of these Volvo parties?"

Over his shoulder, Salem said, "Because everyone's terrified to invite you, buttercup."

Rane snorted. "'Cause I'd win."

"As far as I know, there hasn't been a masquerade since 1969," Dru said with a growing feeling of alarm. "Not since the one that formed the Seven Harbingers. Isn't that right?"

Salem looked briefly uncomfortable. "There have been a couple since then, actually, but these days, they're more of a second-rate talent show. At best, the world wrestling of sorcery."

"You weren't invited to those, were you?" Dru asked, getting a perverse sense of satisfaction from the flash of anger that passed over Salem's face. But it quickly faded as she thought of the possible motives for gathering so many sorcerers in a masquerade right now. "Is someone trying to put together a new team of sorcerers? A new Seven Harbingers?"

"Frankly, I'm shocked," Salem said, deadpan. "Here it is, doomsday unfolding around us, and someone's grabbing up the end-of-the-world power all for themselves? Scandalous."

Dru was about to retort when she was interrupted by the scritching sound of an unseen bat flying overhead. She took a deep breath of the clean, invigorating mountain air, rich with the scents of pine and crystal clear mountain streams. It seemed so impossible that evil could be so close by.

Titus had known about the masquerade, she realized. He wanted to bring her. *"There's going to be a gathering tomorrow night. Everyone who is everyone, all in one place, one night. It's the chance of a lifetime to be among the most powerful sorcerers in the world."*

"Tomorrow night," Dru said, earning a surprised look from Salem. "That's when this masquerade, this volvajo, is happening, isn't it? We have to get in there."

Salem shook his head in seeming disbelief. "You really don't know what needs to be done, do you?"

"Not *exactly*. But so what? We can handle it as a team. And face it, you could use the help. Your 'invitation' practically killed you, and it might have succeeded if it weren't for us."

He nodded, almost imperceptibly. "Managed to catch me by surprise. That won't happen twice."

"Speaking of which, what happens to the people who do fall victim to these so-called invitations? If they aren't strong enough to fight off the undead . . ." Dru thought through the implications of that. "If these masqueraders only want to invite the most powerful sorcerers, then this would be their first test, fighting off the undead. If the sorcerers don't survive, then they don't qualify."

Rane's face showed her horror. "Dude, that's messed up."

"Thins out the competition." Salem sniffed. "Notice a drop in customers lately?"

"Wait," Dru said. "That creature we found at Greyson's place. That was an invitation to him? These things just, what, wander around looking for sorcerers to accost? Why didn't any show up on my doorstep?"

Rane ripped the top off another packet of energy gel. "You've got all those protective crystals around the shop, right?" She slurped up the packet.

"That's true," Dru said. "With that protective grid of crystals in place, the shop is locked up pretty tight, energy-wise."

"Oh, I'm sure that's it." Salem's sarcasm was painfully obvious. "Otherwise, you would've been a shoo-in for the top ten." He shook his head. "Try to understand. You wouldn't fit in. One look at you, and they'd know you're not in the in crowd. They'd eat you alive."

Dru let out a nervous laugh. "Of course, you don't mean that literally . . . right?"

He pointed at Rane. "And you, you would start a fight the moment you walked in the door."

"You say that like it's a bad thing." Rane tossed her hair back and gave Salem a sultry look. "So why don't you take me to the party and keep me out of trouble?"

Salem looked a little startled, but he tried to cover it by turning back to Dru. "You should take her home. We're done here."

"You're not taking your new girlfriend, are you," Rane said to his back. It was a statement, not a question. "How come?"

Though he had his back to Rane, Dru could easily see the look of irritation and awkwardness that passed over Salem's features, and it was priceless.

"It doesn't matter," he said.

"Aww," Rane said with mock sympathy. "Had a little spat, did ya?"

"She has her own agenda," Salem snapped. "I don't control her. I'm not responsible for her."

He wasn't dating her either, Dru thought. She desperately wished he would just tell Rane the truth.

"Ooh." Rane swaggered back and forth along the far edge of the dirt road. "Somebody's not getting treated right. That's too bad."

Salem sighed and squeezed his eyes shut. When he opened them, Dru could see the weariness there. Although he put on a tough face, she could tell he was nearly as exhausted as she was.

Levitating Opal's car must have taken a lot out of him. And who knew how much other magic he'd been casting lately? Why would he expend precious reserves of energy on a stunt like that? To frighten them away.

"Do you really have that low of an opinion of us?" Dru asked softly, too quietly for Rane to hear. "Why are you trying so hard to scare us off?" She glanced past him at Rane, who watched them with puzzled curiosity. "You're really trying to protect her, aren't you?"

A moment of fear flashed across Salem's features. If she didn't know him so well, she would have missed it. But that look was unmistakable.

His eyes narrowed to dangerous slits. "I used to like you so much more when I thought you were harmless and easily distracted."

Despite his harsh tone, it was obvious he still deeply cared about Rane. Dru couldn't tell if it was actually love or not, but he certainly seemed to fear for her safety. That was jarring, since Rane was physically the toughest person Dru had ever met.

But if she was right, and Salem was truly trying to protect Rane, that meant that things were extremely dangerous. Whatever was inside that mountain rattled him enough to try to warn them away, in his own special way.

"If this is going to be bad, we need to stick together," Dru said softly. "How many years have I known you? I can tell when you're worn out. Come back to the shop with us, and I'll fix you a potion. We can talk."

"Don't presume you know a thing about me," Salem growled back. "I'm not some kind of cripple."

"Okay, first off, we don't use that word anymore. It's not nice," Dru said. "And second, are you kidding me? Don't shut us out like this. We could be stronger together."

He leaned so close to Dru that she could feel the heat of his breath. "For her safety, and yours, just forget all about Greyson. Get her out of here and don't come back." For once, he sounded completely sincere. "If you do anything for me, do that."

Then his sincerity vanished like a puff of smoke, and he turned to Rane with an elaborate bow. "Good night, cupcake. It's time to go home."

"You and me," Rane said. "Right here. Tomorrow night."

His eyebrows went up. "Thanks for the offer, truly, but no." He turned and strutted away into the darkness.

Dru watched, pained, as Rane's expression went from hopeful to disbelieving to indignant.

"Bastard." Rane kicked a rock the size of a cantaloupe. Dirt exploded into the air around her foot, glowing in the headlight beams, and the rock shot away into the darkness. "Why does he have to be like that?"

"Because he's Salem," Dru said, coming over to her and standing close. Together, they listened to the whinnying sound of Opal trying to start her car. "Listen. I'm not supposed to tell you this." Dru hesitated, thinking maybe she shouldn't.

Judging by the eager look on Rane's face, Dru knew she couldn't back out now.

"Okay." Dru kept her voice low. Just because Salem was out of sight didn't mean he couldn't hear her. "Listen, Ember isn't really his girl-friend. She's just staying with him while she figures things out with her family. They're not sleeping together."

The car whinnied again, and then the motor started, steady and reassuring.

"Uh-huh." Rane's skepticism was obvious. "They're not sleeping together. Is that what he told you?"

"Well, yeah. But I believe him."

"Really? Why?"

Dru opened her mouth to reply and realized she didn't really have a good reason. It was just a feeling. And it was more than likely she was wrong. She hung her head and sighed.

Rane lightly backhanded her across the shoulder. "No sweat, D. That's what he does. Gets inside your head. Come on, before Opal leaves without us."

As Rane marched back down the slope toward the glowing head-lights, Dru hurried to catch up. "Wait, wait. I've got a plan to find Greyson. Although I have to warn you, it could be really dangerous."

Rane's eyes turned fierce. "Does your plan involve kicking asses, spe-cifically Salem's and his new girlfriend's?"

"Something like that. Only better."

"What could be better than that?"

"The smoke from the spell headed straight toward that bunker, right? That means Greyson is in there." Dru pointed into the distance. "We know where the entrance is. We know when the door will be open. Tomorrow night, we'll get inside, crash the party, and find Greyson. Then I can break his curse for good, and we'll stop doomsday. And save the world."

Rane gave her a look that was equal parts adrenaline and uncertainty. "Yeah, I don't know."

They reached the car, and Dru stopped before she opened the door. "We can do this, right? It's a plan?" Tentatively, she held up one palm. "High five?"

Rane gave her hand an unenthusiastic slap, but the impact was still hard enough to sting. "You heard what he said. We'd never fit in."

"Oh, yes we will. When it comes to dressing up, we have a secret weapon."

"Yeah? What?"

Dru just smiled and opened the front door of Opal's car.

19
WHO'S THAT LADY?

The next morning, Dru didn't open up the Crystal Connection. She handwrote a sign that said "Closed for Makeover," and then thought that might be a little too on the nose for her plans. So she made up another sign that said "Closed for Renovations," which wasn't exactly true either. She crumpled that one up too, and just left up the regular Closed sign. Then she went straight into the back room to prepare a miniature version of her Greyson-finding spell. She gathered penny-sized crystals and wove a tiny copper circle she could roll up to fit in her pocket.

After that, she headed over to Opal's place.

Opal's fashion collection—as she called it—took up almost the whole upstairs of her house. Over the years, every bedroom had been transformed into a giant walk-in closet, filled with racks upon racks of brightly colored clothing. The walls were stacked up to the ceiling with shoes.

Dru stared wide-eyed at the endless racks of clothing packed into every available space. Colorful swaths of fabric and beaded curtains draped the walls and doorways, creating a cozy sitting space around plush chairs shaped like giant high-heeled shoes. The music was already thumping when she arrived.

Opal made her sit down next to her in a shoe chair and leaned close. "I must've misunderstood something. When you said you needed help dressing up for a masquerade party, that's one thing. I'm all about that. But are you actually planning on going undercover with Rane?"

Dru shrugged awkwardly. "I don't know about 'undercover,' but—"

"To a sorcerers' masquerade party. To try and find Greyson, so you can save the world. All stealthy and secret-like. And you're planning to bring *Rane?*"

"Well, when you put it that way . . ."

Opal looked at her as if she'd lost her mind. "This is a bad idea. I know this for a fact. And there's going to be alcohol involved?"

Dru winced. "Rane's not always that bad."

Opal sat back in the high-heeled shoe chair, her eyes wide. "You *are* kidding me. Every time I let you talk me into doing something with that girl, it always ends with—" Opal's voice dropped an octave, "—'Ma'am, you're going to have to come with us quietly.'"

"This time it's going to be different, I promise." Dru spied a plastic bag of giant foil-wrapped breakfast burritos sitting on the mirrored coffee table. "Is she here?"

A muffled crash sounded behind one of the beaded curtains. "There's no room in this stupid place!" Rane yelled. "And nothing fits!"

"It's okay, honey," Opal called back, wringing her hands. "You just keep looking!" To Dru, she said in a stage whisper, "This woman is a walking disaster zone. Lucky for you, I've got a lot to work with. I've been collecting fashion for a long time."

Dru decided there was a fine line between collecting and hoarding, but she decided not to say anything. Instead, she unwrapped a breakfast burrito and bit into it, savoring the buttery taste of hot eggs and potatoes. She could've done with far less greenery—asparagus, spinach, and other vegetables—but sometimes, Rane had an obnoxious fixation with being healthy. Even with her burritos.

"Hey, Rane," Dru called after a few bites. "Thanks for breakfast! It's yummy."

"Hey! D!" Another crash resounded through the room, and Rane ducked out under the beaded curtain, wearing a fringed silver halter top and a skin-tight gold lamé skirt.

"Oh, sure," Opal said, folding her arms. "You've been in there forever. But the moment Dru shows up, you come out of the closet."

"What are you trying to say?" Rane twirled in front of one of the many mirrors, ducking her head to try to see herself. "This top sucks. But, dude, I am rocking this miniskirt."

"You do realize that's not actually a miniskirt?" Opal said.

From her six-foot-plus height, Rane looked down the length of her body to the shimmering gold skirt. "It is now."

"Take that off before you bust a seam," Opal ordered. "If you stretch that out of shape, it'll never be the same."

"Chill out." Rane strutted across the room and slurped down half a smoothie through a straw.

Chewing, Dru set down the burrito and wiped her hands with a napkin. "Okay. We have to think strategically. There are going to be a bunch of sorcerers at this party, all of them wearing masks. Nobody's going to know anybody. We need to look good, but not so good that we draw too much attention."

Rane made a face. "Screw that. I'm going to draw some attention."

"Same here," Opal said, drawing a circle with her finger to encompass all of them. "We are all going to look smokin' hot, don't you worry about that."

"You're not coming with us," Rane said. She picked up Dru's burrito and ate half of it in two bites. With her mouth full, she said, "This party is for sorcerers only."

"Don't be mean," Dru said.

"What?" Rane said around the burrito.

Opal shrugged. "Doesn't matter. This is a masquerade party. Nobody's going to recognize me. I am going to be completely incognito. Besides, if there's one thing I know, it's how to handle a bunch of out-of-control sorcerers." She gave Dru a pointed look and motioned with her eyes toward Rane.

Dru waved off the stub of the burrito when Rane tried to hand it back to her. "Opal's right. We need to stick together. And we need to be in disguise. Because if I go in looking like normal, everybody's going to recognize me."

Rane chewed. "So what's the plan?"

"The volvajo is more than just a masquerade. It's a competition. So, you get up there and compete, keep the judges and the audience occupied. I'll sneak off to look for Greyson."

"Her in a cage match?" Opal said. "Uh-uh. That's a bad idea."

Rane's eyes gleamed. "No, it's a kick-ass idea. I like it."

"You would." Opal pushed herself to her feet. "Come on, then. Let's start looking absolutely fabulous." She took them on a meandering tour of her fashion racks. "Now remember, this is my collection. Loaning you my clothes is like loaning you my puppy. You have to take care of them. Promise me."

"I promise," Dru said solemnly.

"Yeah, it'll be fine." Rane made a heart-crossing motion, then grinned wickedly the moment Opal turned her back.

Opal didn't notice. "Kids that come into the Crystal Connection these days, you see what they're wearing. They don't know how to dress up. But a true sorceress is ready for any occasion. Like your friend Salem. He has his own sense of style, even if his choices are too predictable."

"He wears black," Rane said unnecessarily. "And that's all he wears. But the leather pants, that's new."

Opal pulled out a rich nutmeg-brown wool men's coat and expertly folded a boysenberry-purple silk square into the front pocket. "Somebody should tell that man he needs a little pop of color. See? Like that."

Rane wasn't looking. She turned around, straining the seams of the silver halter top. "Seriously, how old are these clothes?"

"Some are new. Some are vintage. All of them are precious," Opal said with a sniff of pride. "True fashion never goes out of style."

"Pretty sure it does. That's why they call it *going out of style*."

Dru meant to intercede, but she found herself entranced by a pair of calf-high metallic boots that shimmered a rainbow of colors, reminding her of an exotic crystal. Carefully, she pulled them down from the shelf, surprised at how heavy they were. Only then did she realize that they had thick glittering platforms and towering high heels.

"Ohh . . ." Opal sighed, placing a warm hand on her arm. "Honey, those are just perfect for you. Make you look like the crystal princess of the dance club. Go ahead, try them on."

"Yeah, no." Dru shook her head in refusal. "There's absolutely no way I could walk in these things. I'd break my leg."

"Trust me. Those boots are so you." Opal guided her to a seat and helped her zip into the boots.

Dru stood up, shocked at how steady and powerful she felt. "Wow. I feel so tall." She found a mirror and turned around in it, admiring the boots.

Opal grinned. "Love them, don't you?"

"Where did you get these?"

"On clearance. Come on, let's find the rest of your outfit."

"Funky Town." Rane read from the end of the boot box. "Exotic Supply. Hey, wasn't that that old stripper store on Broadway?"

"Exotic Supply," Opal insisted, pointing. "Just what it says."

"I'm wearing *stripper* boots?" Dru couldn't keep the alarm out of her voice.

"Go-go boots," Opal corrected her. "Relax, honey. This is a serious party. Nobody here's got time to waste on second-rate shoes."

With that, Opal led her on a whirlwind tour of the fashion collection, trying and discarding dozens of outfits. Rane gave each one a thumbs-up or thumbs-down, which Opal largely ignored. But there was one outfit that made them both smile knowingly.

Before Dru knew what was happening, she found herself draped in a short A-line dress that practically exploded with silver hexagonal sequins. They made soft chiming sounds as she moved, reflecting a million points of light at everything around her.

Opal stepped back and looked her up and down with a critical eye. "How are you feeling about that one?"

"A little naked." Dru tugged down at the hemline. "Do you have anything maybe a little longer?"

"You've got the legs for it. Might as well work them." Opal snapped matching sequined armbands just above Dru's elbows. Short, gauzy sleeves draped down around her forearms, leaving her upper arms and shoulders bare.

"Wow." Dru flapped her arms. "That's a little weird."

Rane, hands on her hips, nodded and gave Dru an exaggerated wink. "Smoking hot, D."

"Hang on." Opal searched the shelves. "I've got a choker collar around here somewhere, too."

"Absolutely not. No choker collar."

"Thought you wanted more clothes on? That's what I'm doing." Opal snapped the sparkling choker around her neck. "That okay?"

Contrary to Dru's expectations, she could breathe just fine. She nodded.

"Can't wear T-shirts and jeans every day," Opal said with a smile.

"Why not? That's why I have my own business."

But Opal was already headed over to Rane. "Your turn, honey."

Despite Rane's initial look of panic, Opal knew what she was doing. She expertly replaced Rane's too-tight skirt and top with a draping gold minidress that clung to Rane's athletic silhouette as she moved, flattering her at every turn.

Rane uncomfortably shrugged left and right in the mirror. "This thing's from the eighties, isn't it? Look at these crazy shoulder pads."

"Already took the shoulder pads out, sweetie," Opal said. "Those are your shoulders."

"Huh," Rane grunted. "Guess those delt raises really pay off."

While they were getting used to their outfits, Opal put on a satiny tangerine dress with swirls of peacock blue and apple green. She teased her black hair up to a truly magnificent volume and planted a supernova-colored fake flower just over her temple.

"Question is, which shoes? I'm thinking animal print," Opal announced. With a sweep of her hand, she indicated a wall shelved with outrageous shoes. There was an entire section of animal print: tiger, cow, giraffe, cheetah, zebra, and ones Dru couldn't hope to identify.

Rane picked up a pair of fire-engine-red pumps with mottled black dots. "No animal on earth looks like this."

"Ladybug," Dru said, proud she'd figured it out. "Right?"

"Think I'm going to go with the honeybee platforms," Opal decided after much consideration. She picked up a pair of high-heeled sandals adorned with narrow black and yellow stripes.

With more than a little fuss, Opal straightened Rane's long blonde hair and let it be, then worked Dru's curly brown hair into an asymmetrical updo, letting it fall casually to the side.

"Now that's your look," Opal said when she was done. "That's what the real Dru is like."

"Like I just spent the night riding around Las Vegas on the back of a motorcycle?" Dru put her glasses back on. "No, I like it. Really."

Opal tapped one long pink fingernail on her hair dryer. "You ever think about contacts?"

"Sure. I think the last thing on my agenda is poking my own fingers into my eyes."

"Hmm." Opal frowned. "Everybody's going to recognize you with those glasses. You got a prescription for contacts once, I remember. Still got those lenses in the back of your medicine cabinet?"

Rane came over to stand behind Opal. "No, no, keep the glasses. You've got that whole smoking-hot librarian thing going on."

"Is that really a thing?" Dru asked.

Rane slowly looked her up and down. "It is for you."

"Now we need masks." Opal crossed the room. "It is a masquerade, after all. And I've got a whole crate full of masks. Been waiting years to use them. Let me get them out."

"Hold on. How about these?" Rane slipped on a gold metal visor with a horizontal slit across the middle. She swiveled her head from Dru to Opal and back again.

Dru nodded her approval. "Kind of Trek-y."

"That's actually a headband," Opal said, "not a mask."

"Yeah, but on my ginormous face, it works. And bonus? It's made out of metal." Rane touched her fingertips to the brass. With a metallic ringing sound, her entire body transformed into shiny brass. "See? Useful."

"She's got a point," Dru said.

"I suppose," Opal said grudgingly. "But that's still not a mask."

"Check it out. Vogue." Dru framed her face with her hands. "Strike a pose."

Moving like liquid gold, Rane mimicked her. Then she started to dance, putting her hands up to raise the roof.

"Don't you raise my roof for real!" Opal called. "I just got new shingles." She rummaged around in the semi-darkness beyond the beaded curtain, the swirls of her dress rippling like the spots of a hunting cat. A moment later, she returned wearing an apricot-orange masquerade mask ringed with fluffy feathers.

For Dru, she held up a sparkling mask covered in small mirrored squares. Dru took off her glasses and put on the mask, turning her face to squint in the mirror.

Suddenly, without her glasses on, showing so much skin, she felt dangerously vulnerable. All of her insecurities bubbled to the surface at once, and she was absolutely certain that the entire party was going to be a colossal failure.

Opal came closer, putting a hand on her shoulder. "Oh, honey, what's wrong?"

Dru pointed at the mirror, and her voice came out as a squeak. "I look like a human disco ball."

With a metallic chime, Rane turned human again. "Trust me, you look totally hot."

"Red hot. Atomic hot," Opal added. "Let me tell you, it's a good thing they've got a bunker under that mountain, because you are going to hit that party like a bomb."

"You really think so?"

Rane grinned, showing sharp teeth. "What she said. Like a bomb."

20

LOVE ME LIKE A BOMB

The adrenaline rush of playing dress-up quickly wore off. During the long drive into the mountains, Dru started to have second thoughts.

As twilight faded into night, the endless peaks around them disappeared into the black sky. Blinking against her uncomfortable contact lenses, Dru stared out the car window at the towering mountains. With every mile, the peaks seemed to close in tighter around them, imprisoning them. The rocky cliffs grew taller and steeper until it seemed as if the washed-out cones of Opal's headlight beams were drawing them onward, pulling them ever deeper into a pitch-black tomb.

Was she making a terrible mistake tonight? Crashing a sorcerer masquerade party—if that was what it really was—sounded a lot less like a good idea the closer she got to it. So many things could go wrong. So many deadly things. Was she willing to risk getting her friends killed?

But if she couldn't find Greyson and undo his curse before the scroll's seventh seal broke, the world would come to a fiery end. What other choice did she have?

Beside her, Opal bobbed her head along to the timeless musical stylings of Salt-N-Pepa, tapping her long nectarine-orange fingernails on the steering wheel. If she had any misgivings, she didn't show them. But she did wrinkle her nose.

"What's that smell?" Opal asked. She leaned forward and peered over the top of the dashboard as if afraid that something would crawl out of the vents.

Dru sniffed. Through the cloud of Opal's citrusy summertime perfume, she picked up a sickly and pungent odor. She reached over and turned down the stereo. The unmistakable crinkle of aluminum foil came from the back seat.

They both looked over their shoulders at Rane, who clutched a paper bowl containing a hearty mix of speckled rice and glistening brown chunks. She waved a plastic spoon. "Carb loading," she said cryptically.

"Oh, no," Opal snapped. "You are not eating that in my car."

"Too late," Rane retorted, chewing.

"What *is* that?" Dru tried not to make a face. "Smells like bananas and blue cheese."

"Smells like feet," Opal said, rolling down her window. "Goat feet. Maybe camel."

Rane leaned close between the seats, speaking rapidly. "This is going to be a high-energy night. Right? Right. So I need to make sure I'm loaded up with carbs. That way, if anything hits the fan, I'm not hitting the wall. That means muscle glycogen, and plenty of it. You know?"

"Well, sure. Obviously." Dru had only the vaguest idea what Rane was talking about, but she decided not to ask. Unconsciously, she reached for her glasses, and realized they weren't there. She folded her hands in her lap instead, feeling slightly awkward.

Rane pointed into the bowl with her white plastic spoon. "Oatmeal, plantains, sweet potatoes, wild rice, cherries, beets. Agave syrup too, 'cause of the low glycemic index. Do I have any potato skin stuck in my teeth?" She bared shining, carnivorous-looking jaws.

"No, you're fine." Dru sighed. "It's just, I was thinking—"

With her spoon, Rane shoved a chunk of something earthy and banana-like into Dru's mouth. "*Stop* thinking. You do that *all* the time. Seriously. Enough."

Gagging, Dru looked around for a napkin, but she'd left her big purse at home.

"Don't you dare spit that out," Opal said, raising a warning finger. "My upholstery has been through enough already."

Reluctantly, Dru chewed. It was kind of buttery and bitter, like Brussels sprouts, but honey-sweet. She swallowed. "Ugh. Oh, my God. Water."

Opal held up a bottle, and Dru chugged half of it down. "Look, tonight could be dangerous. I think that—"

"*No.*" Rane waved her spoon like a threat. "No more thinking. You want different results? Do something different. You want to find the majordomo behind all these undead? Less thinking, more ass kicking." She shoveled up a huge spoonful and chewed. "Trust me. You'll thank me later."

"Yeah, okay. Great pep talk," Dru said, without enthusiasm. She drank more water and swished, trying to wash the syrupy taste out of her mouth.

Opal looked over at the two of them. "I'm just finally glad to get to go to a decent party. One with magic. It's been too long."

Dru swallowed and stared out the window again. "If it even *is* a party. Salem could've been wrong. Or lying."

"Well, that would be embarrassing," Opal said. "Just don't let me drink, okay? I'm driving."

Foil crinkled in the back seat. With her mouth full, Rane added, "Don't let her dance, either."

"Hey." Opal swatted at the air. "You better hope it's all about the dancing, and not zombie fighting, or nobody's going to have a good night, I promise you that."

"They're undead, but they're not zombies," Dru corrected her. She watched through the window, but saw no sign of the creatures. Still, she knew they were out there, somewhere.

Eventually, Opal pulled off the desolate mountain road into a dirt washout that had been created by spring runoff from the ice-covered mountaintop. At the moment, the washout was dry, and Dru hoped it stayed that way. She had no intention of trying to push Opal's massive purple car out of the mud.

"I don't see a parking lot," Opal said.

"That's okay," Dru said. "We'll be sneakier this way."

"I don't have sneaky shoes on," Opal complained as they got out of the car.

With a certain amount of difficulty, they hiked up a flat stretch of patchy meadow until they found a bare track that in decades past had been a gravel road, now abandoned. Pulse pounding, Dru watched the darkness, sweeping the light of her cell phone back and forth across the dead grass and dry brush.

Ahead, the dark mountainside rose like a fortress. At its base, a wide tunnel beckoned them inward. Easily big enough to swallow a semitruck, the tunnel led a couple dozen yards into the mountain before it ended in floor-to-ceiling steel doors.

An unearthly full-moon-yellow light seeped from between the thick, saw-toothed edges of the open doors. They looked like the jaws of some great beast lying on its side, ready to snap shut and devour them.

Dru paused just short of entering the tunnel, and Opal and Rane stopped on either side of her. Directly above them was a faded stencil: CLEARANCE 18 FT 5 IN. On either side of the sign was a black-and-yellow radiation symbol. Dank, cold air wafted out of the tunnel. Standing just outside, in the pure mountain air, Dru wasn't sure she could summon the strength to step forward.

In her platform boots, she felt about a foot taller, but that just made her feel somehow detached, as if she had become someone else. Someone crazy enough to crash a masquerade of sorcerers in a secret nuclear bunker beneath a mountain full of undead.

"Maybe this is a bad idea." Dru's words echoed back to her in a cathedral-like whisper, as if a chorus of ghosts mocked her.

"I didn't get all dressed up for nothing," Opal said, but she sounded a little unsure.

"Shh," Rane commanded, holding up a hand. "You guys hear that?"

Dru listened, straining her ears. She could hear nothing but the mountain wind, their breathing, and the whine of her own nerves.

She shook her head. So did Opal.

"Right. Exactly." Rane held out her open palms. "Pretty freakin' quiet for a party. Right? I don't like this."

"Hmm." Opal cocked her head. "Maybe Salem got the date wrong?"

"None of this was lit up last night, or we would've seen the lights from across the way. No, this must be the place. And tonight is the night." Dru took a deep breath, and before she could stop herself, she stepped into the clammy tunnel. She felt an unsettling change in the air, as if she'd stepped into another world.

After a moment, the other two followed.

"This is a trap," Rane announced, her voice echoing.

Opal shushed her.

"Maybe," Dru admitted quietly, without breaking stride.

"*Maybe?*" Rane insisted. "How come the entrance isn't guarded? Where is everybody else? Where did they park?"

"I don't know," Dru said. "Maybe we're early."

Only as they crept toward the doorway did Dru understand how truly huge the doors were. Massive enough to swallow a freight train. Probably a good three feet thick, she estimated. Past their black-and-yellow-striped teeth, the tunnel continued, illuminated from within by the ghostly glow of evenly spaced caged light bulbs that led into the distance down a gently sloping tunnel. Eventually, it disappeared around a wide curve.

Dru paused outside the doors and dug her ulexite crystal out of her bag. With a quick press to her forehead and a burst of magical energy, she surveyed the entire entrance. Much to her surprise, it was clean. "No magical wards, no sorcio inscriptions, nothing. That's so weird. There's nothing protecting the entrance."

"Freakishly big-ass door, but no guards," Rane said. "Fishy."

"Now, if we go in there," Opal said, "and there's nothing but a bunch of bored NORAD boys in jumpsuits and security badges, how are we gonna explain all this?" Her wrists jangled as she waved to encompass their outfits.

Dru thought about it. "We'll just have to run."

"Or act drunk," Rane said. "I could do that."

"Hell no, I'm not doing either. I'm ready to party. Here. Masks on." Opal handed over Dru's sparkling disco-ball mask and Rane's brass visor. With that, she put on her own feathery Mardi Gras mask, stepped between the doors, and set off down the tunnel, honeybee-striped heels clicking on the polished stone floor. "If the air force is in here waiting, they better watch out, because Opal's in the house. It's *going* to be a party."

Dru traded looks with Rane through their masks.

"Don't look at me, dude. You're the one who wanted to bring her." Rane looked a little bit like a gold robot as she turned and followed Opal into the darkness.

Dru hurried to catch up, and the three of them walked side by side down a tunnel easily as wide as a two-lane road.

In her little party bag, Dru didn't have much room for crystals, so she had carefully selected a handful of her best. One of them was her trusty dagger-shaped spectrolite crystal. She rested her fingers on its smooth surface, ready to light it up at the first sign of trouble.

Up ahead, the tunnel branched. The left branch continued deep into the mountain.

On the right, a faded warning sign just above eye level stated, TUNNEL 13—RESTRICTED AREA.

Another open saw-toothed blast door waited. Beyond, the darkness was punctuated by flickers of light, the distant beat of thumping electronic music, and an ocean-like wash of voices.

Cautiously, Dru stepped between the yawning doors. As soon as they were inside, she realized they had dressed for exactly the wrong party.

21
DISCO AND DOOMSDAY

Tunnel 13 widened out into a cavernous darkness at least the size of an aircraft hangar, but much stranger.

Sorcerers in black leather costumes and horned masks clustered in groups beneath roaming spotlights. They talked, sometimes danced, or just glared at one another.

Against one wall, a movie projector splashed grainy black-and-white film clips across the bare rock: snowy ancient graveyards, dead forests, nuclear explosions. A relentless assault of death and destruction.

Overhead, two small stages stood atop metal scaffolding, fifty feet apart. On the left stage strutted a woman in a gauzy black dress and glittering mask. In anger or defiance, she pointed a finger over the crowd at the other stage.

There, a black man with bare, muscled arms and a wolf mask motioned to her in what was unmistakably a challenge.

In the crowd below, the roaming lights shone down on shiny black skin-tight outfits, glittering spikes, washed-out faces hidden behind masks. Each costume had a theme, of sorts: a knight, an angel, a bird, a truly terrifying clown.

Dru had hoped to blend in. But this crowd was far darker and scarier than she had ever imagined. She traded glances with Rane and Opal. "Abort! Abort!" she whispered. "Let's sneak back out before anyone sees—"

At that moment, a spotlight zoomed over onto Dru, temporarily blinding her. Her sparkling outfit scattered points of light in all directions, simultaneously making her the center of attention and filling her with mindless panic. For a moment, the pounding of her pulse in her own ears drowned out all other sounds. A sea of black masks turned to stare at her.

She had no doubt that she, Opal, and Rane were all painfully visible to everyone in the vast underground chamber. All of those unfriendly faces. She decided there was only one thing she could do.

Turn and run.

But Rane's large hand pressed against the small of her back and shoved her forward, forcing her to walk directly into the masquerade.

In three strides, they were out of the spotlight and back in the gloom. Dru was too blinded by the light to see much except masks looming out of the darkness.

"Strut it," Rane growled into her hair. "Act like you own this stupid place."

Dru tried, but the sudden spotlight had rattled her. She made an abrupt turn and circled the edge of the vast room, trying to stay away from the overwhelming crowd.

They found a clear spot by a bank of old-fashioned monitor screens, the rounded glass kind, all of them dark and dead. Beneath the monitors ran a bank of control panels with lights that flickered on and off as if they'd been short-circuited. If this place had been some kind of a nuclear bunker in the past, it hadn't been maintained in decades.

"I like this place," Opal said cheerfully, looking around. "Good music. I see some people have drinks. All the leather's not really my thing, but one time I had a boyfriend who was into it, so . . ."

"I think I'm going to be sick," Dru gasped. She leaned against a control panel, careful not to touch any buttons. Just in case.

Opal's concern was obvious even through the orange feathered mask. "Oh, honey, you okay?"

"No! This is not what I expected." Dru had to raise her voice to be heard over the thumping music, but she tried not to shout. "I don't know. When sorcerers come into my shop one at a time, that's one thing. But so many of them in one place, wearing masks, it kind of freaks me out."

"Don't worry, nobody can recognize us." Opal pointed at her own gigantic feathered mask with both index fingers. "Totally inconspicuous."

"We've got company." Rane's normally flat voice carried an unmistakable warning. She stepped in front of Dru and Opal, intercepting a stout figure as he approached out of the gloom.

"Hey, Rane." He gave her a little wave.

The brass visor made her expression difficult to see, but it certainly wasn't friendly.

"So much for inconspicuous," Dru muttered.

The man's face was hidden by a silvery cloth whole-head mask with teardrop-shaped eyeholes and openings for his lips and the tip of his nose. Still, Dru would have recognized his dumpy work coveralls anywhere.

"Ruiz?" Dru stepped around Rane. "What are you doing here?"

"Dru? Is that you?" He peered closer at her. "What happened to your glasses?"

"Don't worry about that. Worry about all these freaky sorcerers." She pulled him back into her little corner by the control panels. "I'm not saying this to be mean, Ruiz, but you don't have any magic powers. And this is strictly a sorcerer-only party."

"Except for me," Opal said with a pointed look at Dru.

Dru held up her hands. "Well . . ."

Ruiz shrugged, unconcerned. "Opal told me, and I thought it could be fun, you know?"

Dru gave Opal a withering look, but Opal somehow avoided her gaze.

Ruiz went on. "I didn't know this was supposed to be some sort of top secret party. Freaky place, right? Sorcerers keep getting up on those stages, having some kind of contest."

Dru looked up. The man in the wolf mask was gone, replaced by a stick-thin girl who brought her arms overhead in a ballet-like movement. A swarm of tiny gold lights, not unlike fireflies, swirled into existence around her.

"No way I can do that," Ruiz said. "I'm just going to hang out down here with you guys. That okay?"

Inwardly, Dru groaned. Ruiz's grandmother had been a sorceress, and it was obvious that Ruiz wished he had inherited her powers, which explained why he was always coming down to her shop. That, and it gave him a chance to chat with Opal.

But right now, she was worried about his safety. She leaned close, trying not to get weirded out by his silver head-wrapping mask. "Look, Ruiz, this masquerade is all about sorcerers competing to be the best of the best. There's serious magic going on. If you get dragged up there, it could get dangerous super fast."

Opal nodded. "That's why you're supposed to have an invitation. Carried by a zombie."

"Not technically a zombie," Dru pointed out.

"Zombies?" Inside the teardrop-shaped eyeholes, Ruiz's eyes went round. "Oh, man, nobody said nothing about zombies. When do we get to see them?"

"Yeah," Rane said. "I'm here to kick some zombie ass. Let's do it."

"No, no, no." Dru made a patting-down motion with her hands, as if that would somehow keep this whole situation under control. "We don't want to see them. Hopefully there aren't any down here. And they are not technically zombies." Dru shook her head. Better to let that one go. "Ruiz, tell me you didn't bring anyone else down here with you. Did you?"

"Bring anyone? No, man, I don't know nobody else. Who would I bring? But let me tell you something. There are some foxy ladies here tonight." He gave Opal a sidelong glance. "I was thinking about, you know, this music's pretty good for dancing—"

"I could use a drink," Opal said.

"I could get you a drink," Ruiz said quickly.

"No drinks," Dru insisted. "Oh, my God. We're on a mission, people."

"They got to have drinks around here somewhere." Ruiz turned around in a circle, standing up on his tiptoes to peer over the crowd. His silver whole-head mask reflected light off the back of his skull.

"Ruiz," Opal said, "what are you supposed to be, anyway?"

"El Santo," Ruiz said, sounding as if it was obvious. "*El Enmascarado de Plata*." At her confused look, he added, "What, you don't like wrestling?"

"Oh, *yeah*!" Rane brightened up. "I had a Santo comic book when I was a kid."

"Yeah?" Ruiz nodded. "Santo was the best, man. Number one *luchador* in the world."

"Wrestled an alligator," Rane said proudly, as if she'd done it herself. "Least in the comic book he did, anyway."

"No, that was for real, I think. He really did that. You know my cousin did that, too?"

Despite her brass robot-like visor, Rane's face radiated disbelief. "Your cousin wrestled Santo?"

"No, no, an alligator. There's a place down by the sand dunes you can go, across from the UFO watchtower. You pay a few bucks, and you can jump in the pit and wrestle a real live alligator." From inside the silver mask, Ruiz's tongue nervously licked his lips. "But you know, he's already missing a couple fingers, so I don't know that he should do that. Tempting fate, you know?"

"Let's do that." Rane bumped a fist into his shoulder. "You and me, we should go."

Ruiz backed up a step and pointed at his own head. "Is just a mask, you know. I don't know about real wrestling, okay? Especially giant reptiles."

Rane shrugged. "Basically like wrestling anything else. Just got to watch out for the teeth."

Dru couldn't stand by and listen anymore. She balled her hands into fists. "Can we just focus, just for a second, on stopping doomsday? We aren't here to party. We're here to find Greyson. Now, whoever's in charge of this masquerade, we need to find them, follow them, and see if they'll lead us to Greyson."

Opal and Rane nodded.

Ruiz held up a finger. "I'll be right back. Oh, Opal, what do you like?"

She gave him a slow smile. "Surprise me, honey."

"Okay, okay, good." He rushed off into the crowd.

Rane cupped her hands around her mouth. "Find me a bottle of water, dude." But Ruiz was already gone.

In his place, Salem appeared from the crowd, wearing his exact usual outfit—black ruffled shirt, black trench coat, black top hat. The only addition was a black domino mask. And his leather pants.

Dru's heart sank. This was not going to be a fun conversation.

He looked the three of them up and down, frowning at Opal's animal print, Rane's gold lamé, and Dru's shimmering calf-high go-go boots.

"What are you supposed to be," he said finally, "some kind of Swedish disco super group?"

Rane sniffed. "Look who's talking, Houdini. Hey, I didn't see any cars outside. Where did everybody park?"

"Funny. If you'd had an actual invitation, you would know. You didn't drive up the dirt road and then have to walk, did you?" Salem turned his crazy eyes to Dru. His gaze roamed up and down her body, but not in a lustful way, more as if he was examining some strange new species of insect. "Did you really have nothing better to do tonight than the *exact* opposite of what I said? I told you to stay away."

Dru stood up straighter. "Well, you're not the boss around here."

From the curl of his lip, he seemed to find that amusing.

"So you can either help me find out who the boss *is*," she said, "or maybe you can just get lost."

"Or both," Opal said.

Salem turned to Rane, who stared back fiercely.

"Did you come here alone?" Rane asked.

"You didn't," he said.

"Don't mess with me, dude. Not tonight."

An unsettling prickle at the back of Dru's neck gave her the feeling she was being watched. She looked all around, seeing nobody watching her. Then she looked up.

There, on a shadowy balcony just above the edge of the light, a looming figure in an elaborate red costume watched her from the darkness.

He was dressed in a blood-red double-breasted jacket with long tails and shimmering gold trim. The shadowy eye sockets of his skull mask stared down at her with eerie intensity.

Dru nudged Salem's elbow, drawing a hostile look that she promptly ignored.

"Who's he?" She nodded her chin up toward the man in red. "Do you know him?"

"He's the one in charge here. If you need a formal introduction, then that's your cue to go home," Salem said acidly. "Leave this up to the real sorcerers. Now where have I heard that before? Oh, I remember: every conversation we've ever had."

"So he's the one running this thing," Dru said, not expecting an answer.

Above, the man in red turned and strode away into the darkness, followed by the ripple of a cape that flowed behind him like blood.

22
THE RED DEATH

As Rane traded insults with Salem, Dru leaned close to Opal. "If I'm not back in five minutes, get Rane and come after me with guns blazing."

The feathers on Opal's orange mask quivered. "When Rane talks about her guns, you know she actually means her biceps, right?" She tapped her upper arm for emphasis.

"Just . . . I'm going after the guy in red, okay? If he's in charge, and Greyson is in here somewhere, this guy has to know about it. Come after me in five." She left the relative safety of the control panel nook.

"'Lot can happen in five minutes," Opal called after her.

Dru threaded her way through the black-leather-clad crowd, looking for some sort of staircase or ramp up to the balcony. She moved fast, since she needed to find a way up there before the man in red got away.

Unexpectedly, she found herself facing the man in the wolf mask. He swayed in front of her, inviting her to dance. Tribal-looking tattoos swirled up the well-defined muscles of his bare arms. His dark brown skin shone as he danced, maybe with sweat, maybe with some sort of magical energy.

She didn't have time for this. Waving an apology, she ducked around him and headed closer to the rough stone wall, hoping she could thread her way around the periphery of the crowd.

But her path was blocked by the bulk of the terrifying clown in black leather. He wiggled his white-painted eyebrows and started jumping up and down in front of her, his belly flopping, the jingle bells on his three-tasseled hat bouncing ever higher.

Dru stopped dead, looking for some break in the crowd, some escape route. But there was no way around him.

The clown opened his mouth and let out a wet pink slab of tongue that wiggled as if it had a life of its own.

Heading out on her own was a mistake, Dru realized. She had to get back to the control panel, back to safety. She never should have separated from the others.

The crowd parted behind the leather-clad clown. He stopped jumping and froze as a red glove clamped onto his shoulder. Visibly flinching, he moved aside.

The glove belonged to the skull-masked man. He stepped up to Dru and gave her a slight bow. Despite the height of her sparkling platform boots, he towered over her.

His mask covered most of his face, so that only his lips and strong jaw showed beneath. He held out one red-gloved hand. "May I have the honor of this dance?" His voice was surprisingly deep.

The stiff formality of his gesture, contrasted against the thumping electronic music, made her laugh. "Not what I expected you to say." She held up a hand to wave him off. "Thanks, but I'm a terrible dancer."

"I find that impossible to believe." He took her hand in his, and at the touch of his red leather glove, the music abruptly changed. A classical string arrangement sprung up, a resonant cello quickly joined by lively violins.

The next thing she knew, his cool gloved hand had curled across her ribs, and he lifted her right hand into the air, making her gauzy arm cuff flutter. She had just enough time to realize that they were about to start dancing, and then they were off.

He led her onto the dance floor and into an elegant waltz. It was all Dru could do to not stumble and fall. Her brain scrambled to remember directions from long-ago dance lessons. Something about stepping in the shape of a box. Her mind conjured up a confusing diagram of black-and-white footprints connected by dotted lines. None of it helped.

Luckily, her feet hadn't entirely forgotten. After a few unsteady steps, she eventually found her rhythm. She was able to keep up with him, as long as she didn't overthink it.

Meanwhile, everyone watched them.

In fact, so many pairs of eyes followed their waltz through the spot-lights that Dru had to stare up into the skull mask to blot everyone else out of her consciousness. She couldn't give in to the crushing panic that came with being the center of attention.

After what seemed like an eternity, they left the spotlights behind, and other couples danced around them. Oddly enough, no one else seemed to be moving to the same beat.

"Everyone is hearing different music," Dru concluded. "That's why it was so quiet when we first got here. It's some kind of enchantment, isn't it?"

He tilted his head in acknowledgment. "Of course. But then again, I was enchanted the moment I saw you." From the shadows inside his skull mask, his eyes met hers.

She turned away, her mind racing. This was all happening too fast. She'd just gotten here.

Who was this man in the mask? What did he know about this moun-tain? Or the undead? Was he responsible for Greyson's disappearance? Or was he innocent?

She couldn't just ask him outright. Possibly he was the pinnacle of evil. Or equally possible, he could be a crucial ally. There was no way to know. She had to get more information out of him first.

"We haven't been properly introduced," she said quietly. "Do you have a name?"

"I'm afraid I'm not allowed to tell. It is a masquerade, of course." His face was turned slightly away from her as he led her across the dance floor, slipping effortlessly through the crowd. "Your costume is breathtaking. I can't resist a guess. Could it be Titania, the fairy queen?"

"Could be Dolce and Gabbana for all I know."

His lips curled up in a smile. "But there is a theme. You must tell me, or I will be heartbroken."

"I'm the crystal princess. Either that or *Sex and the City* with sparkly stripper boots." She winced. "Just so you know, in my head, that did not sound even remotely that dirty."

His only response was a slight smile. From the depths of his skull mask, his dark eyes met hers again, and then glanced away.

She cleared her throat. "And how about you? What's your theme?"

"You must try at least one guess," he said, sounding disappointed.

She looked him over. He was tall by any standards, looming over her even in her heels. And despite the elaborate costume, she could tell he was much more athletically built than most sorcerers she'd ever met, Rane and the wolf-mask guy notwithstanding. Under her left hand, the velvety fabric of his sleeve hid a rock-solid arm. His grip was gentle, but firm and unyielding as he led her through the waltz.

"Um, Skeletor?" she said. "Was that the guy who fought Captain America?" She winced again, wishing she could force herself to stop talking. "Okay, I have to warn you, we could be here all night."

"Indeed? Then I will do my utmost to keep you guessing." He led her in a new direction. The pace of the music became somber, and he slowed down their dance to match it.

Despite her misgivings, Dru felt herself getting caught up in the beautiful music and the magic of the dance. A poignant piano joined the soaring strings and made her feel somehow more alive. In this rare moment of beauty, the rest of the insanity around her faded away, until there was nothing but the dance, and she started to lose herself in it.

"*Je suis la Mort Rouge qui passe*," he said softly in French. From within the skull mask, his dark gaze caught hers. "I am the Red Death that passes you by."

Under the intensity of his gaze, her voice failed her for a moment. She swallowed. "Edgar Allan Poe. Creepy, but nicely done. Wait, in that story, didn't everybody die?"

"Poe never shrank away from the inevitability of death." His eyes glittered. "You are a fan of the classics?"

"Had to read them all in high school. Nevermore. Ha." She saw a hint of confusion in his eyes. "Just a little . . . never mind. You're really good at this whole masquerade thing. Is this your place? Did you put this all together?" She deliberately avoided his gaze, knowing subterfuge was not her strong suit.

Only then did she realize they had circled halfway around the room. On the nearest stage, a woman in a shimmering onyx-black dress and a black horned mask threw her head back and exhaled a furious plume of emerald-green fire. The flames curled and roiled like living hands grasping out toward the crowd. Someone cheered, and a few sorcerers clapped.

"Who are the judges?" she asked the Red Death. "I don't see any."

"There are none." He sounded amused, as if the very idea was ridiculous.

"Well, that doesn't make sense. Someone has to be in charge. Isn't that the point of this whole masquerade? A great big sorcery competition, to find the best of the best?"

"I suspect you yourself have nothing to prove. Your powers are beyond compare."

She felt herself blush beneath her mask. "Yeah, I don't know about that, exactly."

"Your modesty is quite becoming."

Knowing she was being flattered and trying to ignore it were two different things. She cleared her throat. "So if the contest doesn't actually have judges, if no one is in charge, then why put on the show? What's the point of it all?"

"A distraction to occupy the troublemakers," he said. "Those stages are an obvious avenue for the frustrated and arrogant to put their angst on display. It allows them an opportunity to vie for the admiration of their rivals and enemies."

Dru could hear more than a little frustration and arrogance in his voice, but she decided not to call attention to that. Maybe this was an opening to learn more about what was really going on underneath this mountain.

"Well, when it comes to winning admiration from your rivals, that's not a bad way to go," Dru said carefully. "Every sorcerer I've ever met is drowning in angst. Maybe if they knew the real reason they were here . . ."

"Angst is simply ambition that's been denied too long, until it has soured from zeal into pain." He waltzed her away from the stage. "We all need to suffer through a certain amount of pain in order to reach our ambitions."

"And what's your ambition?" she asked.

He gave her a sharp look. "To save the world. Isn't yours?"

Booming lightning flashed overhead, making Dru jump. A branching blast of energy zigzagged over the crowd, leaving tree-like afterimages on her vision. In the wake of the deafening boom, the crowd roared with approval, and the woman on the other stage—wearing a black-and-gold harlequin costume—took an elaborate bow. Then she held out her hands and slowly pointed toward the unseen ceiling hidden in the darkness overhead.

Glittering sparkles began to drift down from the sky, fluttering into the light like metallic snow. A few scattered flakes quickly multiplied into a twinkling snowfall, sprinkling everyone with shimmering specks.

The Red Death tilted his head back to admire the falling sparkles. They fell into his slicked-back hair and gathered on the red velvet of his coat. "I believe the Harlequin has won the popular vote." His words were drowned out by another roar from the crowd.

The waltz music finished with a flourish, and he released her, bowing deeply over her hand. She expected to find herself relieved at the end of the dance, but instead she was oddly sad that it was over.

"Wait, you never answered me," Dru said. "Is this your place? Why the masquerade?"

He smiled enigmatically. "In many ways, you're just like me, Ms. Jasper. Your happiness peaks when everything becomes complicated. I would not take that happiness away from you." With that, he backed away, his dark eyes boring into hers, as if he wanted to say more.

A touch on her arm startled her. Opal sidled up next to her, her face clearly showing alarm. "If you're done playing Jane Austen, we've got a big problem."

"Hold that thought." Dru held up a finger for her to wait a moment. She turned to ask the Red Death for another dance, but he had already vanished into the crowd.

Only then did she realize that he had called her by name. He knew who she was.

The question was, who was he?

23

BEHIND DOOR NUMBER ONE

Dru plunged through the crowd, going after the Red Death. She needed to find answers. She ducked between half-sloshed dancers and those who still stood around staring upward, entranced by the falling sparkles. The air smelled bitter, like the smoke after a fireworks display.

Opal followed close behind her. "You looking for Rane?"

"No, the guy I was just dancing with. Did you see which way—"

"Forget him. You better hurry and find Rane before Ember does, or else there's going to be hell to pay. And I mean it. With all this magic around, if those two start a fight, mark my words, somebody in here is bound to get killed tonight."

Dru pulled up short and surveyed the crowd. No sign of anyone she knew. "Ember is here, tonight?"

"I don't know. But Rane took off, saying she was going to cage-match that girl soon as she found her." Opal stayed close as they made their way through the crowd and came out on the shadowy edge of the room.

Dru searched, but there was no sign of the Red Death. She had lost him. She sighed and turned to Opal. "All right. Which way did Rane go?"

"I don't know. All I did was get one drink—just one drink, mind you, and *damn* this is good. Here. Try this." Opal thrust out a vast martini glass festooned with a shimmering metallic pink umbrella, a curlicue of shaved lemon peel, and some kind of fluffy cranberry-colored tropical flower.

Dru eyed it suspiciously. "What is it?"

"A zombie."

"A *zombie*? Seriously?"

Opal cocked her head to the side. "What's wrong with that?"

"Never mind." Dru waved it off. "Where did you even get this?"

"Ruiz. That man's so sweet, isn't he?"

"He is," Dru agreed. "Does he know you already have a boyfriend?"

"No I don't. Not since recently."

"What happened recently?"

"End of the world started?" Opal propped her free hand on her hip. "You remember when those meteors started going crazy, and I found out doomsday was on the way, and I tried to call that man, and he wouldn't pick up the phone?" She took a long drink through the straw and smacked her lips. "Turns out he's not as commitment-minded as he says. Got a little somebody else on the side. And I don't play that game. So that's it. We're done."

A wave of sympathy washed over Dru, tinged with guilt for not knowing this already. "I'm so sorry."

Opal took another drink, holding the shiny pink umbrella away from her orange feathered mask. "Got some girl named Karri who likes to text absolutely everything in those little smiley faces."

"Emojis?"

"Like trying to read texts from King Tut's tomb. But all those hearts and winky eyes don't leave much to the imagination. I know what she's saying to him."

Dru gave her a hug. "I'm so sorry, sweetie. Jeez, I can't believe Diego would do that."

"Diego?" Opal shook her head, making her feathers shake. "No, Diego was way back. This is Leon."

"Leon?" Dru scratched her head. "Um, I don't . . . Did I meet Leon?"

"Well apparently, now you don't have to. And he's not getting his phone back, neither." Opal swirled her drink in her glass, making the curlicue of lemon peel bounce. "You see Rane anywhere? Should be easy to spot her, even in this crowd. I don't know what on earth that girl said to Salem, but he's about ready to go nuclear."

Dru's stomach clenched. She'd be lucky if she didn't spend the entire night trying to keep her friends from murdering each other. "Okay. Where's Ember?"

"I don't know. Do I look like I'm on team Ember?"

"What I mean is, are you sure Rane and Ember aren't already beating each other up somewhere, right this second?"

Judging by the way Opal's eyes went wide, she obviously hadn't thought about that. Her face cycled from horror to worry to indifference. Finally, she shrugged. "I give up. I can't be that girl's keeper. She'll get herself into trouble no matter what we do." She touched Dru's sparkly dress with her index finger. "You just need to make sure we don't get kicked out of this party."

"Wait a sec. Are you just asking me to handle this so that you can go off and party?"

"Don't be ridiculous. I'm going to party no matter what you do." Opal sucked down another straw full of her drink and started swinging her hips to the music.

Ruiz shuffled out of the crowd, grinning inside his silver *luchador* mask. He clasped a pair of gigantic drinks in his hands, and held one out to Dru.

"Keep it," Dru said with a sigh.

So many worries swirled around her. Where was Rane? Was she okay? Dru had no idea. Opal and Ruiz were too busy chatting to be any help. If she was going to find Rane or the Red Death, she would have to do it herself.

Taking care to avoid any more dance floor entanglements, Dru crept around the periphery of the room. No one was wearing red. The mysterious stranger seemed to have left. But where could he have gone? There were no other exits from the cavernous chamber.

She walked by an alcove hung with gold-framed paintings, some of which she vaguely recognized from history books. A few stuffed animals stood in eerie silence, including a polar bear and a mountain goat with epic three-foot curved horns.

She passed a row of bronze statues holding lit candelabras aloft, and then the old film projector. It blasted out grainy black-and-white footage of trees and houses being swept away in a hellish explosion. Something about the projector was broken, so that it spewed shiny streams of spent film onto the floor, piling up in a dark mass. Two drunk sorcerers, arms around each other, fell into the seaweed-like mass of film, laughing and spilling their drinks.

Past that, the shadowy rock walls were free of any decoration, and since this was obviously where the interesting stuff ended, Dru almost turned back. But something caught her eye.

At the edge of the light, a rectangular area of the rough rock wall turned smooth. It was a slightly darker shade of gray than the rest. Dru looked it over as she stepped closer. It was just barely big enough to be a door. Surreptitiously, she turned her back to the now-distant crowd and slipped her ulexite crystal out of her bag.

Pressing it to her forehead, she tried to blot out the noise and confusion behind her and focus. The crystal tingled slightly against her skin as her energy flowed into it. Her vision warped and shifted, giving her a truer look at the wall.

It was a door, all right. A sliding metal door, not quite like an elevator door. It was painted gray to blend into the rock wall, and in the gloom, it was nearly invisible. An empty gap the size of a drink coaster showed where there had once been some sort of a keypad or lock built in at waist height, now filled with a tangle of cut wires. The sliding door was open about an inch along the left edge.

Carefully, Dru wedged the fingers of her free hand into the gap and pushed. The door didn't budge.

She pushed harder, until she groaned with the effort. Gradually, the door started to give. It slid open another fraction of an inch, and something in the broken machinery inside the wall hissed out air. She paused to take a breath, thinking she needed a better way. There had to be a trick to it that she was missing.

From behind her, long fingers seized Dru's shoulder and yanked her away from the door.

Dru's breath caught in her throat as she lowered the crystal from her forehead. It took only a moment for her vision to clear, but in that moment her entire body went cold with fear for her life.

But it was only Salem. Behind his black mask, his wide eyes looked even crazier than normal. "What exactly do you think you're doing?"

"I found a way in," Dru said, hoping that was enough explanation.

"Hurrah for you." He looked past her, quickly taking in the details of the door. Then he gave her a calculating look and carefully said a single word: "Why?"

As she slipped the ulexite back into her bag, she briefly considered making up some kind of excuse, but then decided that honesty was probably the best policy. Especially since she knew she was a lousy liar.

"I'm looking for Greyson, and everything points into this mountain. Obviously, he's not here at the party. But if the Red Death is running the show, then he knows where Greyson is. And this is the only way he could've gone."

Salem sighed and gazed off into the empty space slightly over her head. "Don't you need to go tumble some rocks or something?"

"Really? You're going to be like that?" A surge of anger rose up inside Dru. "You know what? That's it. I've had enough. You can insult me all you want—"

"Oh, good. I've been waiting for your permission."

She gritted her teeth. "You know, if you're not going to help me, maybe you could at least stay out of my way. Is that too much to ask?"

He made an inarticulate sound and rolled his eyes. "Fine. Go explore where you don't belong and get yourself killed. If you insist on taking this to its logical conclusion, I can't stop you."

Dru hesitated. Maybe he was right. Heading through the secret door alone was a risky move. "Where's Rane?"

He shrugged. Dru didn't know whether that meant he didn't know, or just wouldn't tell her.

But every minute she stood here arguing with Salem, the Red Death was slipping farther away. And with him, she was losing her best chance of finding Greyson. She had to go in. Summoning up all of her courage, she stepped around Salem, heading for the doorway.

He grabbed her arm, his movement almost nonchalant, but his grip was tight. "Oh wait, I just remembered. Of *course* I can stop you."

"Salem, for Pete's sake, let me go. I have to get in there."

Salem looked skyward, making an exaggerated thinking face. "How about . . . hmm . . . *no?*" He pushed her away from the doorway again and stood in front of it, arms folded. "If you want to stop doomsday, leave it to the big kids. You have a habit of getting yourself into trouble and making other people come bail you out."

"You're not going to have to bail me out, Salem."

"Oh, don't worry, I wouldn't bother. Just don't drag Rane into this, that's all I ask."

"I'll have you know that when it comes to getting into trouble, Rane does not need my help."

He leaned closer, invading her space until his crazy eyes stared deep into hers. "Exactly." There was no mercy there.

She couldn't stare back for long before she had to drop her gaze. She didn't know how far she could push Salem before he snapped, and the direct approach wasn't working at all.

More than anything, she wished she could say something scathing and acerbic, but she was too worried about Rane and Greyson to spar with him anymore. She had to find another way in.

Dru turned and slowly walked away, glancing back to see if he would follow her. But he just stayed put, arms folded, as if he was waiting for her to go away.

She gradually retraced her steps, passing the projector and its growing heap of discarded film. She waited there, hoping Salem would lose interest and leave, but he still blocked the door, glaring at her from a distance.

She kept walking. By the candelabra-holding bronze statues, the creepy stuffed animals in the next alcove caught her attention. In particular, there was something oddly familiar about the goat with the yard-long horns that curved magnificently from its forehead almost back to its shoulder blades.

It was an Alpine ibex, she finally remembered, dredging that fact up from somewhere deep in her reading. There was some sinister significance to a dead Alpine ibex, but she couldn't remember what. Something to do with sorcerers. It was important.

As she struggled to remember it, one of the bronze statues leaned down close to her. "Dude," it whispered.

Dru jumped. She clapped her hands over her mouth, stifling a scream.

The bronze statue grinned. It was Rane. With her hair, skin, and dress all transformed into bronze, she blended in perfectly with the real sculptures. "Check it out. I've been watching this whole scene, and nobody even knows. Pretty trick, huh?"

Knowing it was only Rane didn't help calm down Dru's pounding heartbeat. She desperately wanted to slap Rane, but resisted the impulse. The woman was solid metal, after all.

Dru darted around behind the statues and hid in the shadows. "Did you see a guy in red go through that door?" She pointed into the distance, at the wall behind Salem.

"Couple minutes ago, yeah. Why, do we need to kick Mr. Red's ass?"

"Maybe. Maybe not. I don't know yet."

Salem glanced over both shoulders. Apparently satisfied that Dru was gone, he surreptitiously waggled his fingers at the door. It began to slide open.

A fluttery feeling ran through Dru's stomach. "Okay. The door's open. Now I have to get in there."

Rane shook her head no. "How are you going to track Greyson without your candle and all your crystals?"

Dru held up her heavy little bag. "I made a travel size. Little tiny copper circle, little crystals. I even found an old birthday candle to use."

"Aww." Rane's bronze expression melted. "Was that from the time I made you a birthday cake?"

"That was a cake?" Dru said, unfondly remembering the heavy bacon-flavored brick Rane had given her for her birthday. "What did you call it then? A protein loaf?"

"Chicken cake." Rane shrugged. "Same diff."

Wrinkling her nose, Dru pushed away the memory. She motioned toward the doorway, where Salem was peeking inside. "I need to get in there, but Salem's being a total son of a Bieber."

With clanging footsteps, Rane stepped down from the platform of statues. She rolled her head side to side, making her neck pop. It pinged like hot metal. "Don't worry. I'll take care of him."

Dru suddenly envisioned the resulting mayhem and waved her hands urgently. "No! No. Don't. Let's just go get Opal and put our heads together."

Rane rolled her shoulders, loosening them. "Relax. I'll get him out of your way in sixty seconds flat."

Dru put her hands on Rane's metal biceps, which were strangely as warm as skin. "Please, please, please, I'm begging you, do not start breaking things in here. This is a highly charged situation. Don't blow things up."

Rane snorted. "What's wrong with blowing things up?"

"Let's try something different, okay? You remember that book I gave you, Sun Tzu, *The Art of War*? Did you ever have a chance to read that?"

"Yeah. I settled down by the fire in my slippers, smoked my pipe, and read about some dead Chinese guy. What do you think?"

"There's a part in there about baiting the enemy. Causing a distraction. That way you can win without actually fighting."

"Pshh, whatever, dude." Rane gave her an annoyed look, but then she apparently spotted something out on the dance floor that brightened her up. "Wait, good idea. I like it. I'm going to go all Sun Tzu on Salem's ass."

"That's the spirit." Dru pumped a fist overhead. "Okay, let's think up a plan."

"There you go with all the thinking again. Just watch and learn, cowgirl. Watch. And. Learn." With that, Rane turned human again and sashayed out along the edge of the dance floor, her short gold lamé dress rippling in the light. She strutted straight past Salem, who pulled his head out of the open doorway and turned his whole body to watch her go by.

Then Rane walked right up to the tattooed guy in the wolf mask and greeted him with wide eyes and a glowing smile.

Even from this distance, Dru could clearly see her say, "Hi there!" The wolf's response was instant interest. She took his arm and led him farther onto the dance floor, swaying to the beat as she went.

Salem watched them go, his attention riveted on Rane, his shoulders hunched and tense. At his side, his fingers clenched into fists.

Dru watched, morbidly fascinated, as Salem stepped away from the hidden door and followed Rane into the depths of the dance floor.

Bait the enemy, Dru thought. Rane was using strategy instead of full frontal assault, and it had worked spectacularly.

The moment Salem was out of sight, Dru darted out from behind the bronze statues. She ducked inside the open door and descended the shadowy metal staircase behind it, alert for any glimpse of the Red Death.

24
THE CLUTTER OF OUR ENEMIES

Dru expected the steep, rusty staircase to somehow lead to the balcony overlooking the dance floor. But instead, it went down, flight after shadowy flight of flaking metal steps with punched-out diamond treads.

Dru finally paused on the fifth or sixth landing, trying to get her bearings. The stale air was decidedly chilly and close. The stairwell was lit only by occasional caged bulbs that seeped a sickly yellowish light, leaving deep shadows where the metal stairs crisscrossed one another.

She thought about heading back to get Rane, maybe even Opal. But she couldn't risk Salem stopping her again. If she was going to have any chance of finding Greyson, she couldn't go back. She was on her own.

She got out her phone and switched on the light, shining it around her. Decades of dust and tiny fragments of broken concrete had accumulated in the corners of the metal landing. On the wall, stenciled number and letter codes, military-looking, told her nothing. She kept descending.

Finally, one of the landings yielded a rust-spotted steel door the color of charcoal. A string of six letters and numbers was stenciled in yellow paint in the exact center of the door.

Though it certainly seemed abandoned, the steel doorknob and strike plate in the frame were shiny from recent use. Someone had been coming and going through here on a regular basis.

She listened at the door, one ear pressed up against the chalky paint that covered the cold metal. No sound except her own breathing. Every muscle taut with fear, she eased the door open.

Beyond, nothing moved in the still, cool air. Everything smelled of stone and water and decay.

The ceiling was easily twenty feet overhead. The rough rock was spotted with round splotches that resembled mold but were more likely minerals accumulated from seeping groundwater.

Rough floor-to-ceiling stone columns loomed out of the darkness, like the ruins of an ancient civilization. They stood ranked one after another, in evenly spaced rows that stretched far beyond the range of her phone's flashlight.

Whatever this place was, it was impossible to gauge its size. But it was huge, and largely empty, except for random-seeming debris: stacked wooden pallets, racks of black steel drums, giant spools of wire. They were all covered in deep layers of grime, as if they had been dredged up from the bottom of the ocean, and draped in cobwebs.

She passed by a rusty metal grate that ran from floor to ceiling. Behind it stood the massive blades of a motionless fan, each one zebra-striped with streaks of corrosion.

A red symbol loomed out of the darkness. Someone had used bright red spray paint to put three interlocking circles on the nearest stone column, just above head height. The symbol was something she didn't recognize.

She turned in a slow circle, shining the light from her phone. She spotted another symbol in the distance, then another, marking one particular line of columns leading away into the darkness.

More unfamiliar symbols: spiky triangles, wavy lines, hash marks. She vaguely recognized them as ancient sorcio signs. But she didn't know the meaning of any of them, except for one: a circle with a pair of arrows pointing away from her. She knew that one.

Escape.

She stood frozen, ears cocked to listen for any hint of danger.

Nothing broke the silence but the sound of her own breathing and the metallic whisper of her sequined dress as she turned one way and then the other.

Was it a warning? A back door? There was no way to know.

As far she could tell, she was completely alone in here. If she was going to cast another spell to find Greyson, she had to do it soon, or else risk getting lost in this maze.

Here was as good a place as any, she figured.

She took off her disco mask and knelt down on the stone floor. Taking a deep breath, she emptied out the contents of her heavy little evening bag. She set aside her translucent rectangle of vision-enhancing ulexite and her sharp dagger-shaped wedge of iridescent spectrolite.

Carefully, she unrolled the six-inch copper circle she had earlier woven out of thin wire. It was a delicate task, because copper wire hardened over time and became brittle once manipulated into shape. But she was able to smooth it out onto the floor without breaking any of the strands.

Then she set out a selection of tiny crystals she had carefully chosen to fit into the miniature circle: tiny teardrops of tektite, a yellow polyhedron of sulfur, a penny-sized disk of gold pyrite, a chocolate-colored cross of staurolite.

Greyson's polished oval of black jade went onto the circle opposite her, dwarfing the other crystals, but the size difference couldn't be helped. She needed his particular crystal in order to find him. She just hoped that the exceptional clarity of the other smaller crystals would balance everything out.

In the very center of the crystal, she placed the tiny pink birthday candle from Rane's protein loaf cake, wedging it into a crack in the stone floor.

Placing her hands palms-up on her knees, she closed her eyes and tried to clear her mind to cast the spell. But she was so nervous to be in this strange, cold place, so worried about getting caught alone and undefended, it felt impossible to focus on the spell. Besides, she was still rattled by everything that had happened in the ballroom.

She didn't even know for sure whether she was on the right track. What if she had been casting this spell wrong all along, and it was just leading her on a wild goose chase? What if it was leading her *away* from Greyson?

What if Rane was right and he really was dead and gone?

No, she thought. He was alive. She knew it, even if she couldn't explain why. They shared a connection that even she didn't understand.

She didn't have a shred of evidence that he was still alive, except for this smooth black jade crystal. But she could *feel* him, somehow. She could sense his existence as surely as if he stood right there before her, in the flesh.

He was alive. And it was up to her to find him.

"Come on, guys," she whispered to the tiny little crystals. "Don't let me down now."

Pushing aside all her doubts, her worries, her fears, she concentrated on visualizing Greyson.

His kind eyes. His friendly smile. His broad jaw covered in dark stubble.

She imagined his creaking leather jacket, his scuffed boots, the musky scent of his shirt tinged with a hint of motor oil. The reassuring strength of his arms wrapped around her.

But most of all, she focused on the way he made her feel safe in a world that was anything but.

How many times had he put himself in harm's way to save her? How much had he sacrificed to save the world from the Four Horsemen? He had lost everything.

She had to find him.

She had to find him *now*.

All at once, magical energy surged through her, as if a match had been thrown into a pool of gasoline. It flowed out of her and into the copper circle. Heat washed over her, as if she were sitting too close to an open flame.

She heard him whisper her name. *Dru.* For a moment, it felt as if he were right there next to her, his breath hot on her ear. Through her closed eyelids, she could see a tiny pop of flame.

She opened her eyes just as the little candle went out. A curl of prismatic smoke rose from its blackened tip and streaked past her left shoulder.

Surprised, she watched the smoke head down a dark tunnel, nearly opposite the way she had been going. Grabbing her phone, she scrambled to her feet and chased after the smoke, but it disappeared into the darkness, eluding her faint light.

Dru stared into the darkness of the tunnel. For as far as she could see, its apex was caked with a thick accumulation of minerals, making it look like the throat of some slumbering Leviathan waiting to swallow her.

"That's just great," she whispered, suppressing a shiver.

She quickly went back and gathered up her crystals, stuffing them into her little bag. In her haste, the coin-like disk of pyrite slipped out between her fingers and rolled away across the floor. She chased after it, trying to catch it, but the gold-metallic crystal dropped into a crack in the floor and vanished.

She shone the light of her phone down after it, down inside the deep stone crack, but the crystal was gone without a trace. No way to get it back now.

"Fudge buckets," she whispered fiercely. Scratch one spell kit. Missing even one of the crystals meant she couldn't cast the spell again.

Frustrated, she rolled up the copper wire and stuffed it back into her bag. She would just have to find Greyson without it. At least now she knew which direction to go.

The tunnel sloped down at a gentle angle, curving slightly to the right. Smaller tunnels intersected it, each one at a different angle.

Ahead, a warm firelight-orange glow seeped out of one of the side tunnels. Dru's heartbeat picked up. She edged toward it, staying close to one wall until she could peek around the corner.

Inside, she was shocked to see an elaborate study. A crackling fireplace dominated the long wood-paneled room, crowned by an elaborately carved mantelpiece cluttered with knickknacks. Gilt-framed oil paintings peered down. Leather-upholstered chairs were scattered around the room, beside side tables with reading lamps and crystal glasses. A glass-fronted collection of iridescent insects hung on one wall.

But most of all, what caught her attention were the books.

Shelves and shelves stacked high with old books, all sizes and ages. Some were relatively recent, barely used, spines unbroken. Others were well-worn. Then there were the older tomes, impressively thick and heavily bound in time-darkened leather. A few were ancient, nothing more than stacks of calfskin held together by primitive leather stitching.

Irresistibly, Dru felt herself drawn into the firelight by the comforting presence of the books. They enticed her, mesmerized her, made her mind hungry. She knew a sorcerer's collection when she saw one, and this one was huge. She couldn't even imagine the volumes of mysteries contained within their pages.

She gave the rest of the room a cursory glance on the way to the nearest bookshelf. The center of the library was dominated by a vast table covered in charts, maps, and blueprints. She looked them over carefully, trying to understand the layout of this labyrinthine fortress. But without any frame of reference, she had no idea how to orient herself.

The corners of the blueprints were held down by old books. On impulse, she flipped open the cover of the nearest one. Its title stared back at her in an elaborately illuminated medieval text.

The Scripture of Ephraim.

Her jaw dropped open. Heart pounding, she slammed the cover shut.

It was one of the Wicked Scriptures. Just reading its text reputedly messed with a sorcerer's head in all kinds of unpleasant ways. If a non-sorcerer was unlucky enough—or foolish enough—to read the entire thing, the result would be insanity. Or death.

According to the rumors, anyway.

Back in the Middle Ages, when demon summoning was much more common, the Wicked Scriptures pretty much topped the list of most banned books you could feature in your library. Just having the book in your possession, it was rumored, was enough to curse you. It would draw evil forces into your life that would eventually warp your mind and your soul in fiendish ways.

In other words, the thing was a magical weapon. Using it as an office paperweight was kind of like propping up a leg of your coffee table using a land mine.

The Wicked Scriptures had supposedly all been burned and scattered to the wind centuries ago, in a concerted effort to stamp out demon summoning and related atrocities. As much as Dru detested the idea of burning books, she kind of agreed with the medieval scholars on that call.

But she had recently learned that this one-of-a-kind book had somehow survived the ages. It had been uncovered in the 1960s by the

Harbingers, the radical group of seven fallen sorcerers who had devoted their lives to bringing about doomsday.

And now it was here. What did that mean?

She quickly scanned the shelves, looking for other forbidden texts. Perhaps the *Formulaes Apocrypha*, which was a disturbing study in the nature of primordial destruction. Or the *Treatise Maleficarum*, practically a Who's Who for the pits of hell. All of those books collected by the Harbingers had been auctioned off from their mansion in New Mexico.

Then a memory became crystal clear. The Alpine ibex. She remembered seeing it on the auction list.

That auction was how Greyson had ended up in possession of Hellbringer. That was how this whole doomsday thing had started. Everything was starting to click into place. Someone had bought the Harbingers estate at auction and brought it all here, underground. Who would do such a thing?

As she passed by the carved wooden mantelpiece, one of the knick-knacks stopped her cold.

It was a black urn, no bigger than a human skull, its round cap crowned with twelve sharp-looking spikes, like shark teeth. Glossy like wet ink, it shimmered with illustrations inlaid in silver. Spear-wielding armies. Horrific beasts with snapping jaws. Oceans boiling. Stars falling. Heaps of human skeletons.

Dru swallowed. Her palms tingled.

This was it. The urn in Salem's drawing. The one that contained a fragment of the apocalypse scroll. The thing the Harbingers had used to find the scroll in the first place.

She didn't dare touch the urn, but she studied it closely, blinking against the uncomfortable contact lenses in her eyes. Every detail matched the drawing she had swiped from Salem's wall. If this was a forgery, it was extremely convincing.

Before she could talk herself out of it, she swiped a linen napkin off one of the side tables and used it to carefully grasp the spiked top of the urn. To her surprise, it popped off easily. The seal had already been broken. Mustering up her courage, she peered down inside the urn.

It was completely empty. Not even a speck of dust. Someone had already taken the fragment.

In frustration, she banged the lid down and tossed the napkin. That was when she saw the barite rose sitting beside it.

A beautiful specimen, each round nut-brown petal perfectly formed, like a rose turned to stone. Just like the one Titus had brought to her shop.

Could all this—the books, the artifacts, the entire nuclear bunker—belong to Titus?

It struck her again how much he had changed over the years. She couldn't wrap her head around the transformation she had seen in him, from the scrawny, painfully shy guy in the hoodie to the confident powerhouse with the sophisticated vocabulary. What had he found here, deep down inside the mountain, that had transformed him so completely?

Titus was the Red Death, Dru realized. He had to be.

But why did he possess all of these dark artifacts that had once belonged to the Harbingers? Why was he collecting them? What was his ultimate plan? And what was his connection to Greyson?

What did it all mean?

Without warning, a voice boomed out behind her, raising goose bumps on her arms. "Hello again, Drusy."

25

THE MAN BEHIND THE MASK

Knowing there was no escape, Dru faced the booming voice. In the tunnel doorway stood the Red Death. With one graceful move, he stripped off his skull mask.

His slicked-back ash-blond hair sparkled with glitter from the ball-room. Without his mask, she could now clearly see his slender sideburns and the angles of his face. The way he carried himself, the confidence of his stride, practically radiated power.

His dark gaze fixed on her, unblinking, as he crossed the room. "I see you've discovered my inner sanctum. Please, make yourself at home." His baritone voice resonated through the open room, coming back in soft echoes.

"It is impressive." Dru turned in a slow circle, her frightened brain madly trying to come up with an excuse for being in here. "I had no idea this was all yours."

"Of course you did. That's what brought you in here." He stripped off his flowing red cape and draped it over the brass fittings of a leathery antique globe, easily the size of a beach ball. The fabric clung to the globe as it settled, making the earth look as though it were bleeding.

When he stood close to her, her heart beat faster, mostly because all of this added up to something she was afraid to face. She couldn't look him in the eye and pretend he didn't scare her.

It took all of her strength to lift her gaze to his and ask him the one question that was burning inside her.

"Where is Greyson?"

Titus seemed puzzled. "I'm sorry, were you expecting . . . ?" He glanced back over his shoulder before facing her again. "It was me in the mask." He jabbed a red-gloved thumb into his broad chest. "We were dancing?"

"Yeah, no. I know. I got that. That's not what—"

"That was me," he insisted. Then, with an awkward hint of jealousy, he asked, "Who's Greyson?"

Dru blew out a long breath, mentally grinding gears as she tried to reverse her entire line of thinking. "Okay, enough with all of the theatrics." Dru waved her hands to encompass the soaring shelves of ancient books and cryptic artifacts that surrounded them. "Really impressive theatrics, by the way," she added grudgingly. "But that's not the point. I cast a finding spell. And it led me down here. I know that Greyson is somewhere in this mountain. And you're going to tell me where he is."

Titus stared at her for a moment, one eyebrow quirked up. Then he burst into an earnest laugh. "I would if I could. I have only the vaguest idea of who's here tonight, or where all they might've gotten to. You're the exception to that, of course."

"That's because you led me down here." She didn't phrase it as a question.

"When you put it like that, you make it appear unseemly." He sounded a little wounded. "I'm just making sure you don't get lost in here. This fortress is completely overwhelming, miles of tunnels. Utterly enormous. It's bigger than any sorcerer's sanctum I've ever heard of." Titus swept his gloved hand in a wide arc to encompass the rest of the mountain. "And it's all mine. Would you like to see it?"

"Um, no, not so much." The words came out of her mouth before she realized that, in fact, this would be the perfect way to look for Greyson. But not with Titus. She had to figure out a way to ditch him and explore on her own.

"Come on. We can go look for your friend. In fact, we should. Before he gets into any trouble." Titus crossed the room and reached into a bookshelf. Silently, the entire shelf swung open like a door, and Titus disappeared through the gap.

"Seriously?" Dru said, regarding the secret door. It seemed a little too obvious. Still, she badly wanted one in the Crystal Connection.

She wasn't sure what to do next. One of her personal rules was to never go with a sorcerer to a second location.

That applied double, she was pretty certain, in any situation that involved, A) a secret underground lair, B) stacks of apocalypse paraphernalia, C) an old friend stalking you in a skull mask, or D) all of the above.

Nobody else knew where she was. Even if Rane, Opal, or even Salem did come looking for her, they wouldn't know how to find the library. Or how to open the secret door in the bookshelf.

Titus reappeared a moment later, looking concerned. "Not to frighten you, but I have to warn you, there are some uncomfortable and decidedly dangerous areas down here. If your friend has wandered into the wrong place, he could need a hand. We should go find him. Are you coming?"

She looked Titus up and down, trying to reconcile the guy she once knew—the haunted, furtive, scrawny young guy in the tattered hoodie—with the imposing, red-dressed sorcerer standing before her now.

Nothing about him added up.

Even though she didn't say anything, her hesitation was enough to tip him off. Her distrust of him sat awkwardly out in the open between them.

"I see," he said quietly, studying his boots.

"Titus, it's not that I don't trust you." Except, of course, that was exactly the problem. She didn't trust him one bit.

"You don't have to explain. I understand."

Suddenly, she felt guilty, and she wasn't even sure why. "Do you, really? You've changed so much. I mean, you disappear for years, and then you just show up with a fortress full of apocalypse stuff and throw this massive party that's actually really *weird*, and I'm just . . . I'm just worried about you. What's going on with you? Honestly."

He seemed to consider her words carefully. His dark gaze lifted and moved about the room, from one bookshelf to the next. "You're right, of course," he said heavily. "I don't even know where to begin to explain myself."

"You don't have to explain. Just tell me you're okay, and help me find Greyson."

A pained look flashed over his features, but he quickly buried it under a self-confident smile. "It's true, I have spent an inordinate amount of time collecting and studying the work of the Harbingers. Figuring out exactly what they did, how they set in motion the events leading up to doomsday. On the surface, of course, it must seem insane."

"Well, I don't know about *insane*, exactly. Because there aren't any 'normal' sorcerers," Dru said. "But it all kind of depends on why. Why all the dark magic stuff?"

"Better to know than not." He shrugged one of his wide shoulders, making the tassels on his gold epaulets shake.

"Save the world," Dru said. "Did you mean that?" At his questioning look, she explained. "When we were dancing, you told me that your ambition was to save the world. Did you mean that, honestly?"

"Absolutely." He drew in a deep breath through his nostrils, standing straighter and taller. "I believe that's the entire reason I was put here, on this earth. To save it." He stated that as a fact, without any trace of arrogance or boasting, which Dru found strangely charming. "And I think the same about you."

"Me?"

"Is it any coincidence that you're here, now, at this critical juncture? You're the best at what you do. And that's what the world needs most at the moment. Perhaps we can even work together." His dark gaze lit up. "Come on. Let's go for a drive."

"Drive?"

"You'll see." Gently, he took her hand and led her into a downward-sloping tunnel that was littered with bits of broken concrete. With every step, the air turned colder and clammier, but his presence was bright and confident.

"I should go get my friends," Dru said over the sound of their footsteps echoing in the tunnel.

"We can pick them up along the way, if they don't mind riding in the back." He indicated a doorless little open-top Jeep painted a flat dark blue with yellow numbers stenciled on the side. The knobby tires had turned brown with age, and the gasoline can strapped to the back looked nearly rusted through.

Titus turned apologetic. "In my defense, this wasn't my first choice, but it was already down here, and it is ridiculously useful." He held out his hand. "Your chariot awaits, darling."

Dru shook her head. "Uh-uh. This thing doesn't even have doors."

He quirked up one eyebrow. "And you dressed up to come dance in a sorcerer masquerade in the middle of the night—inside a nuclear bunker—because you prefer to play it safe?" His sarcasm had an almost physical presence.

She looked deep into his eyes. She could see pride there, and hope, and a hint of amusement. And perhaps the fear of being turned down. But she didn't sense any dishonesty.

"I'm going to regret this," she sighed. Carefully, she gathered her short sequined dress and, with his help, climbed into the rattletrap Jeep. It smelled of old mud and dry-rotted fabric. Tiny white stenciled letters below the grimy windshield proclaimed, MAX SPEED ON BASE 25 MPH.

Titus came around to the driver's side and wedged his long body into the tiny flat-cushioned seat. "Trust me. You'll be fine."

"Oh, yeah," she said, gritting her teeth. "I do this sort of thing every night."

The engine coughed to life, and they trundled away down the dark tunnel.

26
STYX AND STONES

With Titus at the wheel, they puttered through one tunnel inter-section after another. In between pools of light from the caged bulbs, the Jeep's faint yellow headlights swept along curved stone walls strung with power lines and pipes.

At this point, Dru had no idea which direction the smoke had pointed. So she did her best to memorize the route. She strained her eyes in the darkness, searching for any sign of Greyson, whatever that might be. She didn't see another soul down any of the tunnels.

Titus pointed left and right as the Jeep grumbled its way through the maze. "Down that tunnel is the old main control room. Auxiliary control rooms in every wing. The power plant is that direction, the better part of a mile away. There's even an electric subway system that connects the individual wings. Too cumbersome for my purposes, but I could get it working again if I had to."

"Have you explored this entire place?" she asked over the sound of the motor.

He hesitated. "Not all of it. Not yet. But we can still look for your friend. What's his name again?"

"Greyson." Dru clung tight to a steel handle bolted into the blue-painted dashboard, certain she would be flung out at every turn. "Who built this place? How did you find it?"

"Once upon a time, our fair government believed the world was about to come to an end, courtesy of the Soviet Union," he said, with a touch of amusement. "They were right, in a way. Just not about the Soviets."

"Was everything like this when you found it, with the lights and everything?"

He nodded. "Some of it still worked. Most of it didn't. I had to . . . enlist some help." The hesitation in his voice told her there was much more to that story, but he didn't explain.

He went on about the structure of the bunker and its many levels. As he talked, he waved a red-gloved hand, proudly pointing out details around them. In the passing lights, she studied his angled face. An uncharacteristic enthusiasm lit his features, a boyish joy that was impossible to ignore.

It was so refreshing to talk to a sorcerer who actually valued her presence. So unlike the torture of constantly dealing with people like Salem or Ember. She could get used to this.

As the tunnel opened up into a larger chamber, he pulled the Jeep over near the left wall and stopped. "This is truly astonishing." Without further explanation, he turned off the engine and climbed out, making the Jeep's springs creak. Cautiously, Dru did the same.

The floor in the center of the chamber was split by a rectangular pit easily large enough to swallow a city bus. Wet sloshing sounds echoed up from below. Titus walked toward the pit, but Dru hung back.

"This place gives me the creeps." Dru turned to peer down the shadowy intersection of tunnels, each one marked by stenciled numbers and letters that were incomprehensible to her.

Something tickled her hair. She brushed at it, only to realize too late that it was a hairy, thick-bodied spider. With a brief scream, she jumped back. The spider dropped to the ground and scuttled around her feet, only to accidentally meet an untimely end beneath the platform of her sparkling go-go boot as she tried to get away from it.

Dru froze for a moment, hands clenched, then quickly backed up to the Jeep. Her footsteps echoed in the tunnel. At Titus's sharp look, she felt embarrassed. After clearing her throat, she said, "Nice place. Really."

"It doesn't need to be nice. It just needs to be *functional*. Getting this bunker operational again, and getting all of these sorcerers safely inside, it's been an all-consuming project. The most important accomplishment of my life."

Dru leaned against the Jeep. "This party? Tonight?"

"It's much more than just a party." His voice trembled, just a little. "This is a new beginning, for all of us. When I learned about the impending doomsday—the apocalypse scroll, the Four Horsemen, all of it—I knew that I had to get this place working again. So I could gather together the most powerful sorcerers I could find, and give them all someplace safe to stay."

"Safe from . . . ?"

"Doomsday," he said, as if the answer was obvious.

"Safe from doomsday?" Dru couldn't keep the skepticism off her face. "Don't get me wrong. This place does look pretty secure, so kudos for that. But isn't doomsday sort of an all-encompassing thing? It's not like you can just hide underground and wait it out."

"Can't you?" The look in his eyes suggested that he knew something she didn't. "How do you suppose the Harbingers intended to survive the apocalypse?"

"Hmm." Dru shrugged. "I figured they were suicidal. If doomsday rolls around, the world just comes to a fiery end, everybody dies, and that's it. That's the end. Right?"

"Except that death isn't always the end." Titus gave her a meaningful look, then circled around to the far side of the pit. From a peg on the wall, he took down a caged light bulb attached to a coiled-up length of grimy cord.

Dru swallowed, not liking where this conversation was headed. "What does that mean, exactly?"

"Allow me to demonstrate." Titus switched on the bulb, the click oddly loud in the silence of the cold tunnel. It cast harsh shadows up at his face, reflecting off his sharp cheeks and prominent eyebrows, and throwing his eyes into darkness. For a moment he seemed to have the grinning face of a skull.

Then he lowered the light into the pit, unspooling the power cord hand over hand, and as the light faded, his skull-like grin once more became a reassuring smile.

But it didn't reassure her at all. A wave of fear rippled through her as she added everything up.

Undead. Mountain fortress. Collection of Harbingers lore.

No matter what Titus implied, the two of them were not on the same page.

Slowly, she edged away from him. "What's down there in the pit?" she asked, although she already suspected the truth.

He shrugged in a self-deprecating way. "I have a confession to make. All those years ago, you kept asking me what my power was, and I always said I had a good reason for not telling you."

"I tried to treat you, find a crystal to cure you. That's why you came to me, Titus. To help you get rid of your power. That's what you wanted. You *hated* your power." She quietly added, "Almost like you were afraid of it."

"I was," he admitted softly, still unwinding the cord. "But that was because I didn't understand. But now, my power has been accelerating far beyond what I ever hoped for. Every day, it grows. Look."

As he lowered the bulb, Dru finally crept forward to see. The descending pool of light revealed an arched tunnel below theirs, running perpendicular.

In the darkness, something glittered. Dru glanced back at the Jeep, verifying that the keys were still in the ignition. Then she cautiously stepped closer to the edge of the pit.

She feared it would be full of undead. But she was completely wrong.

It was water, she thought at first. An underground river flowed through the tunnel beneath them. But as she watched the waves reflecting in the light, she realized that the liquid was much too viscous to be ordinary water. And it had an unpleasant sickly sweet smell.

Titus unspooled the cable until the light hung mere inches over the surface. The thick liquid seemed to react to the presence of the light, rippling away from it at first, and then dimpling to form a depression. The liquid actually appeared to be moving as far away as it could from the light.

It was only when he lowered the bulb another inch and the liquid let out a goose bump–raising squeal that Dru finally figured out what it really was.

"Scourge." She backed away from the pit in horror.

As she backtracked past the dead spider, it stirred. Its flattened body swelled back into shape. Its crooked legs straightened, and it lifted itself up and scuttled away into the shadows.

Just like the dead moths in her shop. Something about Titus's presence brought them back to life.

That, or the river of inky blackness running beneath them.

"Undead scourge," she breathed. "A river of it. Oh, my God."

Titus looked pleasantly surprised. "Oh, good, you're already familiar with the scourge. That's a relief. All my life, I've been able to summon up this stuff, but it took me years to figure out what it actually is. I didn't know there was even a name for it until I discovered the Harbingers' books." He pulled the light up, winding the extension cord around his forearm. When he was done, he hung the light on the wall. "In retrospect, I should have just come and asked you. I would've saved both of us an inordinate amount of trouble."

Dru kept backing away until she bumped against the old Jeep. "Why did you invite all those people here tonight, really? It's not a sorcery contest after all. Is it?"

Titus just folded his arms and frowned, keeping the open pit between them.

"I don't know what you think you're doing," Dru said, "but that stuff could kill everyone in here, including me and you. It's deadly."

"Only to someone who can't control it."

His words seemed to hang in the air.

It took a moment for the implications of what he was saying to sink in. Even then, Dru didn't want to believe it. "Are you turning people into undead? Turning *sorcerers* into undead?"

"Not the living. Not yet." Titus unfolded his arms and circled around the pit, an eager look on his face. With every step closer, the heels of his polished boots echoed off the stone. "For years, I've been waiting for the right moment to tell you about this. About my power. To raise the dead. To give motion and purpose to otherwise lifeless bones. To make them servants of the human race. First, to rebuild this bunker. Then to rebuild the world."

She backed up a little more, along the length of the Jeep. "You know, you're right. You should've told me all this a *lot* sooner."

As if sensing the panic rising inside her, he stopped and held out his empty hands in a placating gesture. "It's all right, Drusy. I promise, it's all right. Believe me. I would never allow you to come to harm." He smiled. "Will you trust me?"

Absolutely not, she thought.

But she slowly nodded her head yes. "Sure."

He smiled again, looking not the least bit convinced. "You'll see. Just remember, they won't hurt you."

Her breath hitched in her throat. "Who?"

He looked over her shoulder at something behind her. The hairs on the back of her neck stood up.

Whispers of movement echoed through the tunnel. Though she couldn't tell what it was, she knew there were a lot of them.

Heart pounding, she turned to look.

The dark tunnel behind them was full of slow, shuffling silhouettes. Gradually, as they approached the light, she could make out the outlines of heads, arms, legs. A silent crowd flowed out of the tunnel, surrounding her.

And every single one of them was a skeleton shrouded in scourge-speckled webs.

27

EVERYBODY WANTS TO RULE THE WORLD

*D*ammit, Dru thought. *Never leave a party with a sorcerer.*

Despite how angry she was at herself for getting caught in this situation, most of her was actually terrified out of her mind. But if she gave in to that fear, she was as good as dead.

She decided to go with being mad instead.

She had her spectrolite dagger and a handful of other crystals in her evening bag, but she was outnumbered at least twenty to one, not counting Titus.

No matter what, this was a fight she couldn't win. Instead, she'd have to talk her way out.

She pointed an accusatory finger at Titus. "You told me you wanted to save the world."

He looked incredulous. "I do, Drusy. Absolutely. Why do you think I gathered everyone together here tonight, secure inside this bunker? I'm doing everything I can to save the very best parts of the world. Including you."

"Yeah, that doesn't sound like we're talking about the same thing."

"No, you don't understand. I used to hate my power. *Hate* it. I used to think I was some kind of . . . *freak*, for lack of a better word." The anguish was plain in his voice. "Summoning up this tarry black oil from the depths of the earth to animate the dead? What good could possibly come of that? When I first met you, I was desperate to get rid of my power. I didn't embrace it. I thought it was pure evil."

Dru nodded. "You're not wrong about that."

"But I *was* wrong. Don't you see? I wasted so many years of my life trying to fight against it, not realizing the entire time that it is a precious gift. The most precious of all." He paced back and forth between the rectangular pit and the crowd of lifeless, web-shrouded creatures. "I spent all of my life up until now feeling like a pariah. Feeling like the universe had punished me for some crime I never committed. I tried so many ways to become 'normal' again. I fought so hard it nearly killed me. Do you have any idea what that's like, how heartbreaking that is?"

"I do, a little bit," she admitted, trying to ignore the twinge of sympathy she had for him. At his pleading look, she felt compelled to explain. "I had this boyfriend. He was a dentist. Drove a Prius. I was thinking about buying a house in Highlands Ranch. It was all so *normal*."

Titus gave her a puzzled look. "You? Living in Highlands Ranch?"

She threw up her hands. "It was a sensible plan B, if the crystal shop kept losing money. And then, I don't know, we could've found a safe, quiet neighborhood and—"

"No. There's no place safe." He cocked his head slightly, his dark gaze piercing her. "You had to know that after you found out about the Harbingers, and doomsday. And then everything changed for you."

And I met Greyson, she thought, *and then I changed.*

She shook her head. "How long have you been studying the Harbingers? How much do you really know about them and their plans?"

"At first, I imagined they were tilting at windmills. Ask any of the older sorcerers, and they will tell you the Harbingers' experiment was a mad lark. An unqualified failure." He pointed at the rectangular pit over the river of scourge. "But when I saw how much of *that* I could summon, just with my thoughts, how I can make it flow into the bones of the dead to give them function again, that's when I knew this was bigger than just me. That's when I knew the Harbingers must have truly broken the fifth seal on the apocalypse scroll."

Slowly, Dru shook her head, trying to keep her voice level. "I don't think you understand. The fifth seal allows the dead to rise from the grave."

"Precisely." A manic grin split his face, revealing white teeth.

"This is different, Titus. These are monsters. Not people rising from the grave. These are undead *creatures*."

"But they have *risen*." He threw his arms wide. "Look around you! What do you see? The dead, risen from the grave, each one shrouded in white, just as it's written. And it's all because of me."

Pulse pounding, Dru slowly looked around at the horde of undead that surrounded them. The creatures all stood hunched somewhat asymmetrically, skulls and ribs wrapped in black-speckled webs that seemed to tremble and writhe with a life of their own.

Strictly speaking, he did have a point. These dead had risen. In a way.

"The moths," Dru realized out loud. "There were dead moths in my shop. After you left, they came back to life. Just up and flew away. That was you, wasn't it? You made that happen just by walking past them."

"An accident, of course. But just imagine what I can do intentionally." His bright smile was seductive, almost infectious. His presence felt like a physical force, a hot, invisible light bathing her. She shrank back.

Titus followed, stepping closer. "The first four seals of the apocalypse scroll released the Four Horsemen," he said. "And the fifth seal raises the dead from the grave. And thus it has multiplied my powers a thousand-fold. Like a force of fate, spread out through the atmosphere of our entire world. It will change everything." His smile widened until she could see the outlines of the skull beneath his skin. "Don't you see? My power, it's not just some random chance. I'm here for a *reason*. My entire *life* makes sense now."

Dru quirked an eyebrow at him. "So you're actually trying to tell me that this whole thing about the dead rising from the grave—you think this is all about you personally?"

His chest seemed to puff up, straining the brass buttons of his red double-breasted coat. "Why else would I be cursed with such a dark power? This horrifying reversal of life and death, upending the natural order of things? If it's a curse, I never did anything to deserve it. Never." He made a violent sweeping-away motion with his hand. "But it's not a curse. That's what it took me years to realize. This power isn't a burden.

It's a key. The key to life *itself*. The key to the continuance of the human race. The key that unlocks a new world after doomsday. One that will rise from the grave of the old."

She watched him as he turned in a semicircle, gazing out at his horde of gurgling undead with something like fatherly pride.

Clearly, Titus was insane.

"But now, everything has changed. I'm not afraid. I'm not ashamed. I'm a *savior*." He strode toward her, his gloved hands balling into fists at his sides. "At this very moment, I am the most important sorcerer in the *world*."

"I know a few people who might disagree with you about that." She stood her ground, but his looming height meant she had to tilt her head back to look up at him.

His baritone voice dropped to a menacing growl. "The world is dying, Drusy. No one can stop that. But after doomsday, I can bring it back."

"Or, and this is just an idea, maybe we could stop doomsday from happening in the first place. Ever think about that?"

He didn't seem to hear her. "You and I, together, we can remake the world, even more so than the Harbingers intended. We can raise it up from the ashes into something newer. Something brighter. Something better."

She couldn't hide her disgust. "You mean to create a world full of monsters?"

"No, no. Not monsters. Servants. An army of labor to rebuild the world into something beautiful and lasting. The Harbingers intended to make a new world for themselves. But I will make it for *all* the sorcerers. For everyone. For you." He lifted one cold, gloved hand and cupped her cheek. "Especially you."

It took all her willpower not to flinch away. "Titus—"

"Shh." He leaned closer. "I know. It's hard to let go. I've loved so many things in this world. There's been so much beauty, and truth, and wonderful things to celebrate. But none of that matters anymore. They're all going to go away." His dark gaze bored into hers. "The world *will* come to an end, Drusy. All things must. This is just its time. So we must say our good-byes and let it all go. A new world awaits us. Together, we will create a new Garden of Eden." He was so close she could feel his breath on her lips. "And you will be my Eve."

She knew the kiss was coming, and every fiber of her being rejected it. Rejected him. Rejected everything he was trying to accomplish.

Even as she tried to think of some stinging retort, some brilliant escape plan, a little voice inside her warned her that talking wasn't enough anymore.

She had to *do* something.

Her hand darted into her evening bag and pulled out her short spectrolite dagger. The crystal blade flared to life, fueled by her adrenaline and fear, bathing them in a swirling rainbow of light. The creatures nearest them backed away with a gurgling hiss.

Titus pulled back to arm's length and looked down. Much to her own surprise, she had the crystal pointed at his solar plexus. It seemed so cruel, so crude, to threaten stabbing him. It was so unlike her. But she was panicked. She didn't know what else to do.

"I'm sorry," she whispered. "But you're completely freaking me out. You need to back off. Right now."

"You despise me." He looked crushed. "All along, I thought you were better than that."

"No. No, I don't *despise* you, Titus." That much was true. If anything, she felt sorry for him. "Look, see it through my eyes, all right? It's all kind of terrifying."

His gaze burned with an inner fire. "No, it all makes sense. Don't you see?"

"I see that you've somehow worked out this entire doomsday scenario to revolve around you. And it doesn't. I'm sorry." She regretted the words the moment she spoke them, but she couldn't stop. "Your power is freaking creepy, and you need to count me out."

He looked wounded. "Drusy . . ."

"And stop calling me that, for Pete's sake! It's just *Dru* now." She backed along the length of the old rusty Jeep, shaking with adrenaline. "We can talk later." *Or not*, she thought.

He looked genuinely sorry. "Don't go just yet. Not until you hear me out."

"Already did. Not buying it." Still holding out the glowing spec-trolite like a knife, she circled around the back of the Jeep, putting it between them.

"Drusy . . . *Dru*. I had to show you, in person. Would you have come here, had I told you everything before? Would you have trusted me, had you known the reality about my power?"

She couldn't bring herself to answer that question out loud. They both knew the truth.

His expression turned hard then. "I can't let you leave. I can't let you go back out into the world, knowing you won't be safe there."

"Something tells me we don't share the same definition of the word *safe*." She reached the driver's side of the Jeep, and silently hoped she could remember how to drive a stick shift. Slowly, she lowered the knife. "I'm sorry, Titus."

"No, you aren't." With a fierce scowl, he motioned toward her with both hands. Behind him, the undead creatures raised their black-clawed hands. Strands of webbing whirled into existence in their skeletal palms.

"Oh, fudge buckets," Dru muttered. She dropped to all fours beside the Jeep, instantly ruining her dress on the dirty stone floor.

Strands of webbing streaked through the air all around her, striking the Jeep and the stone wall with wet smacking sounds.

Titus had parked just a couple of feet from the wall, giving Dru barely enough cover to keep from being surrounded by the undead. She reached into the Jeep and fumbled with the controls, pumping the spindly gas pedal with her palm and twisting the key until she got the Jeep started.

But without windows or even doors, the Jeep provided little cover from the barrage of webbing. She was forced to crouch down next to the tire to avoid getting caught.

She yanked at the grinding controls until the Jeep started to roll backward. Hunched over, she scrambled to stay alongside the Jeep, using its bulk as cover.

A rope of webbing shot beneath the Jeep and caught her knee. A knobby black tire rolled over the long strand of web, yanking her to the floor.

She slashed at the web with the glowing spectrolite crystal. To her surprise, it cut through the webbing like a hot knife, freeing her. She scurried to keep up with the rolling Jeep, her head ducked low.

Another sticky white lasso of webbing wrapped around her boot, making her stumble, and more webs quickly caught her shoulder and wrist, immobilizing her arm.

Before she could accept what was happening, she found herself toppling to the floor, quickly being encased and immobilized by webs. At the last moment, she closed her fingers around the spectrolite crystal, willing it to go dark.

There was a chance she could use it to cut herself free. But not here, not now.

The Jeep lazily rolled away, engine chugging and filling the air with the foul stench of burning oil, until Titus strolled over and shut it off. He picked up her bag of crystals from the ground and tossed it in the back of the Jeep.

Then he loomed over her, arms folded. His hissing horde of undead crowded in behind him.

"Okay," she said, struggling against the webbing. "If you really want, I guess you can call me Drusy."

28

AS THE WORLD FALLS DOWN

At Titus's command, the horde of hissing undead hoisted Dru up and carried her away down the tunnel. She fought against the moldy-smelling webs that wrapped tightly around her entire body, leaving only her head exposed. But it was no use. No matter how much she writhed or strained, the webs wouldn't give.

The only good news was that the web cocoon protected her from direct contact with the black dripping claws of the undead. But that was cold comfort.

Everywhere the sticky webs touched her skin, they had a disturbing numbing effect, making her arms and thighs feel uncomfortably hot and rubbery. Like going to the dentist, only a hundred times worse. The cocoon felt as if it was draining the energy from her body, short-circuiting her magical power, leaving her exhausted and disoriented.

Her fingers closed around the knife-shaped shard of spectrolite crystal she had hidden in her palm. It wasn't much, unless she could charge up the crystal, and right now she didn't have the strength. If she could find a way, then there was a chance she could cut herself out of the cocoon. But first, she would have to get away from this staggering horde.

Which wouldn't be easy, considering she was currently crowd surfing above the undead.

Dru expected them to carry her all the way back to the library, but instead they made a detour. They crossed a set of rusty, narrow-gauge railroad tracks set into the ground and headed down a smaller tunnel lined with surprisingly ordinary-looking apartment doors.

Here, the mountain rock that formed the tunnel was clean and polished. The doors were painted a happy modern orange. Evenly spaced overhead lights eliminated the shadows, making the place look more like a boring tech startup or a self-storage facility than an abandoned nuclear complex.

Everything here seemed almost normal, she thought. If you didn't count the crowd of hissing, limping undead led by Titus in his candy apple–red Sergeant Pepper uniform.

The undead carried her through a door into a round chamber that had been halfway transformed into a studio apartment of some kind. A small kitchenette with expensive but unused appliances sat half assembled beside a stack of furniture still wrapped in plastic.

Titus motioned toward a padded bench jammed up against one wall, and the creatures deposited her there. With a dizzying jolt, she found herself sitting upright, spine pressed against the rough stone wall. She tried to shift her position, but she was unable to do much more than wriggle inside the swaddling webs.

One by one, the undead creatures filed out the orange door, leaving her alone with Titus. Her gaze darted around the room, frantically searching for anything that could help her. Any sharp edges. Any heavy blunt objects. Anything that could be turned into a weapon.

Nothing. The place was as dull as an empty U-Haul truck.

Except for the artwork. Opposite her, hung directly from the raw granite wall, was an amateurish painting of a sprawling space capsule–white mansion shaped entirely of curves and domes. Its dark round windows stared skull-like out across a landscape of scattered creosote bushes that dotted the reddish hills of the New Mexico desert.

Dru recognized the place immediately. The Harbingers mansion.

The place where she, Rane, and Greyson had first encountered the evil magic of the Harbingers. Where they had nearly died. And where she had first discovered that she was in way over her head, facing a foe she could only barely comprehend.

Some things never changed.

Alone with her now, Titus clasped his hands behind his back and followed her gaze to the painting. "It's not my style, personally. But it was painted by one of the Harbingers, I believe. That makes it rather priceless, don't you think?"

She gave him a disbelieving look. "Priceless? You're kidding."

He shrugged. "Matter of opinion, I suppose. But it was in the estate auction with everything else. So I thought, well, why not?"

Angrily, Dru struggled against the webbing. All she accomplished was racking her leg with a painful muscle knot. She groaned in frustration.

Titus looked apologetic. "It's quite tight. I wish you wouldn't."

"Yeah, I don't give a Jar Jar Binks what you wish," Dru snapped. She was fed up with all the double-talk and veiled hints. It was time to lay all of her cards on the table. "What did you do with Greyson? I know he's down here somewhere."

Titus shook his head. "I'm sorry, who?"

She glared at him. "Don't lie to me anymore," she said through gritted teeth.

He crossed the room, picked up a plush orange cushion, and gently wedged it behind her back, easing the discomfort of the rough granite wall. His dark eyes were kind. "I have never lied to you, Drusy, not once," he said softly.

He seemed sincere, but she wasn't willing to give an inch. "Greyson. Red eyes. Leather jacket. Amazing hair. Has a really badly behaved car."

"Oh, the Horseman," Titus said, as if that explained everything. "Trust me, he's no friend. You're better off staying as far away from him as possible."

"So you *do* know him!"

"We've never been properly introduced." Titus pulled up an expensive-looking stool and sat down in front of her. "He's the only Horseman I could find. The other three seem to have vanished. He wasn't easy to capture, but one is all I need."

Her heart leaped. Greyson was alive.

Burning hot tears leaked out of the corners of her eyes. She didn't bother blinking them away. They ran in tiny rivers down her neck and into the webs.

She wasn't crazy. She wasn't wrong. She wasn't alone.

Greyson *was* down here, somewhere.

She would find him, she silently swore to herself. No matter what.

Titus apparently mistook her joy for worry, because he laid a comforting hand on the part of the cocoon that wrapped over her hands. "Oh, don't worry. You're completely safe, I promise. He's not going to get you. I have the Horseman locked up tight, in preparation."

It didn't seem as if it was possible for any more alarm bells to go off in her head, but they were clanging like an air raid. Quietly, Dru asked, "In preparation for what?"

He gazed at her as if she were the most delicate thing he had ever seen. "We're going to build a beautiful world together. I've never been more certain."

He really was obsessed with her, she realized.

"Titus, focus on my words. Tell me the truth. Why do you need the Horseman?"

"To finish what they started." He glanced over his shoulder at the painting, and his voice swelled with admiration. "What no one seems to fully appreciate about the Harbingers is just how many magical breakthroughs they engineered. They weren't afraid to break the rules, in fact even completely rewrite the rules. They opened doors that no one knew even existed."

His admiration of the Harbingers made her skin crawl. "They set out to *destroy* the *world*. Kind of wipes out any other accolades, doesn't it?"

"Point taken. But think for a moment about the reasons why they were so driven." He ticked them off on his gloved fingers. "Environmental destruction. Nuclear proliferation. Moral decay. Corrupt governments forcing millions to starve. Can you blame them, truly, for trying to start over?" He stood and paced the room. "Imagine a world where magic is no longer hidden in the shadows. We will no longer be a sideshow or a curiosity, none of us. We won't have to hide in the dark anymore."

"You make it sound like sorcerers are repressed," Dru said. "Like we're some kind of second-class citizen. But it isn't like that."

He gave her a pitying look. "You have your powers, Drusy. But you haven't lived the life of a sorcerer. You don't know what it's like, having this unstoppable power inside you that alienates you from everyone. Forces you to lose everything you value. Everyone you trust. You don't know what it's like to have to live in the shadows of the world that doesn't accept you."

"Kind of do," she insisted. "Because all my life, I've been surrounded by full-fledged sorcerers like *you* who didn't accept *me*."

He dismissed that with a wave of his hand. "We can create an entirely new world where the possibilities will be completely unfettered by the laws of physics. Consider the speed demon, Hellbringer. It fixes itself. It never needs maintenance. Never needs fuel." He paused, as if savoring some delicious taste. "Isn't it brilliant? What if every vehicle in the world were like that?"

She tracked him as he crossed the room. "We're on the eve of doomsday, and you're worried about *gas mileage*?"

"You're missing the point. The new world will be ruled by magic. Powered by it. Magic *itself* will be the driving force for good." Titus threw his arms wide, and the gold tassels on his red uniform shimmered. "You and I, we can accomplish so much more than anyone ever has before. We can realize the dreams that the Harbingers only imagined. But better. We can make this world a good place again."

She stared up at him. "You talk a lot about doing good. But you have no idea how far you've gone over the line, do you? It's like your good and evil meter is completely broken."

He looked amused. "The concept of evil is a modern construct. It won't apply in the new world. When we are finally free to live in a state of pure magic, there will be no good or evil. There is only what you do, and what you don't do."

Dru chewed on her lip. "Okay that, right there, sounds suspiciously evil."

He looked directly into her eyes. "Last week, there were four Horsemen of the Apocalypse. Now there's only one. And I have him." The gold flecks in his dark brown eyes practically shimmered with excitement. "With his doomsday energy at hand, I can increase the power of the scourge one hundredfold."

"For . . . what, exactly?"

"Drusy, doomsday is going to happen," Titus said, with utter certainty. "One way or another, the world will end. I'm just here to make sure it ends properly. A controlled landing, if you will."

Dru imagined grabbing him by his gold-braided lapels and shaking some sanity into him. But that wouldn't do any good. And in her cocooned state, it wasn't going to happen anyway.

Fortunately, years of customer service experience had taught her that when she most wanted to scream, that was when she needed to put on a smile instead.

"You know what, Titus? We could do that," she said in a soothing tone, watching as his shoulders relaxed and his sharp features softened. "We could work together. I can see it. You and me."

"Yes." His voice seemed to fill the room.

"You're powerful, Titus. You're resourceful. Obviously, you know what you're doing. Just the existence of this place proves that. And you have like a whole army of dead guys to do your bidding. Which is, you know, *really* impressive."

The look in his eyes told her that he was going to try to kiss her again.

She shrank back against the granite wall, speaking quickly. "So here's my idea. Instead, you and I can team up to *save* the world. We can find the apocalypse scroll. Reseal it. And stop doomsday. We can do it. I know how. Or at least I have a pretty good idea."

"Drusy, you don't understand—"

"I'm not kidding," she insisted. "I know how the Harbingers found the scroll in the first place. I figured it out. You think you've been studying the Harbingers stuff? Well, so have I." She hedged. "Maybe not exactly as in-depth as you. But still. I know how."

He shook his head. "No. It's impossible. The apocalypse scroll is . . ." Suddenly distracted, he looked over his shoulder at the orange door, then crossed over to it and poked his head out into the tunnel. He frowned.

Dru leaned forward, constrained by the webbing, dying to know what he was about to say. "The apocalypse scroll is . . . *what*? Talk to me, Titus."

"You can live in a state of denial if that's what you choose. But that's not going to help anyone." With stiff movements, he returned and put the stool away, avoiding her gaze. "Unfortunately, our guests are becoming restless. Right about now, those who are still conscious are starting to wonder why they can't go home. It's time I welcomed them to their *new* home." He looked her up and down. "You seem uncomfortable. Let me get you a drink. It will make all of this so much easier to understand. And the effects aren't permanent, I promise."

A leaden worry landed inside Dru's stomach. "Effects? What effects?"

His expression hardened. "I'm sorry, Drusy, but I can't trust you with everything just yet."

As she looked into his cold eyes, she thought about Opal and Ruiz sipping on those huge tropical-looking drinks. A spike of fear shot through her.

Had Rane had anything to drink? Or Salem? She didn't know for sure.

What was in those drinks? What would it do to them?

And could she find them in time to warn them?

Suddenly everything clicked in Dru's mind with the quiet deadliness of a gun being cocked.

"This masquerade wasn't a volvajo at all. It was a trap." Rane was right, she realized. "You lured all of those sorcerers down here, but there was no contest. You just wanted them to wear themselves out up on those stages. Use up all their magical powers so they couldn't put up a fight. Right? And then you, what, drugged them? What's next, webbing them up, like me? Keeping them freshly wrapped for doomsday?"

He crossed the room and looked down at her. "I know you're angry at me, and for that I offer my most profound apologies. Obviously you don't approve of my methods. But you can't argue with my results." He adjusted the orange cushion behind her back and laid the fingers of his gloved hand briefly against her cheek. "Let's toast the success of the evening. I'll be right back with our drinks. Is a straw acceptable?"

Before she could think of a comeback, he left, closing the door behind him. She strained her ears for the sound of his footsteps receding, and waited a few more moments to be sure he was gone.

How long did she have before he came back and forced her to drink his concoction?

A minute?

She had to act. Now. There was only one thing she could do. She just hoped it would work.

29
NEXT TO YOU

Salem set down his empty glass and threaded his way across the dance floor, doing his best to keep Rane in sight without tipping her off that he was following her. The woman had zero sense of personal boundaries, and she couldn't detect sarcasm if it was dropped in her lap. But she was cunning. He had to give her that. Her razor-sharp hunting instincts made her impossible to sneak up on unnoticed.

Or nearly impossible, anyway. After so many years together, Salem knew her blind spots. And in times like this, that history of close familiarity made all the difference.

He avoided contact with the gyrating sorcerers around him, ducking beneath swinging arms and dodging sharp heels. The crowd was a seething ocean of black velvet, fishnets, hair, leather, feathers—and masks.

So many masks. With long, pointed noses. Or plumed with feathers. Or made of nothing but twisted metal wire. Everyone was trying so very, very hard to impress everyone else. It was difficult not to pity them.

Details leaped out at him with unusually sharp focus. A silver ankh. A gold tooth. A tattooed sigil at the base of a neck. Snatches of a vaguely familiar language. The sharp aroma of clove smoke. The brush of lace against the back of his hand.

The deeper he went into this crowd, the more it fragmented into discrete impressions that he couldn't seem to assimilate. It was as if his mind had cracked into pieces and started falling apart.

And what had happened to the music? All he could pick up now was a faint rhythmic buzz, like a speaker hooked up to badly grounded wire.

He blinked, fighting the creeping numbness at the edges of his mind. Something was wrong, something he couldn't put his finger on. It made it hard to think.

That concerned him deeply.

For a moment, he lost his concentration and stumbled. He bumped into a rotund clown in a black leather vest with spiked shoulder pads, making him spill his drink. Rotating in place like a tank turret, the big clown glared down at Salem from beneath white-painted eyebrows and a three-tasseled hat.

Apologizing would be a waste of time, Salem decided. He ducked around the clown, but with more difficulty than he expected. After just one drink, his movements were surprisingly sluggish and imprecise. Those drinks were stronger than he had anticipated.

Too strong. Salem drew up short. There had to be more than just alcohol lurking beneath those ridiculous flower petals and miniature umbrellas.

He turned back to the clown, who had already seemingly forgotten about him, and grabbed the massively overdecorated glass goblet out of his hand. Over his squalling protests, Salem spirited the drink away until he reached the edge of the dance floor.

Along the way, he reached deep inside his black silk shirt and pulled out his protective gold amulet by its woven leather thong. With his back to the crowd, he dropped the amulet into the glass.

The protective charm flared with magical light the moment it touched the liquid. As it sank down toward the bottom of the glass, it illuminated minuscule black streaks wriggling through the liquid, like living things. Worms, perhaps.

He lifted the glass and stared at them, trying to discern what they were. There was no way to know, without a lab and a series of tests. In different circumstances, he would have taken the drink home to study, using crystals and magical inscriptions to neutralize whatever was inside. But there was no time for that now. For the moment, there was nothing he could do.

Whatever these things were, they were certainly foul. Most likely, they were put in there on purpose. And now they were inside everyone who had had a drink.

Including him. The thought nauseated him.

Were these things magical? Toxic? Fatal?

Had Rane had any?

That thought pierced through him like a sword of ice. He hurled the drink against the rocky wall, hearing it smash in the darkness as he spun on his heel and marched out onto the dance floor.

Now he didn't give a damn about stealth. As if sensing the intensity of his fury, the crowd parted around him. Here and there, a few eyes flashed with recognition. Luckily for them, they stayed out of his way.

Rane was more or less where he had left her, still dancing in a way that would have mesmerized him, if his mind wasn't awash with the need to make sure she was safe. And if she wasn't dancing with some cretin in a wolf mask who apparently had an inordinate obsession with pumping iron at the gym.

As Rane danced, she scanned the crowd, her brass visor flashing beneath the lights. Alert. On guard. She saw him coming and deliberately turned her back on him.

Salem came up behind her and grabbed her elbow. "Have you had anything to drink?"

She jerked her arm away. "None of your business, dude. Don't be a creep."

"Hey. Is this guy bothering you?" the wolf said through his mask. His testosterone-fueled aggression might have been much more impressive if it hadn't sounded as if he were talking through a paper bag.

Salem looked him up and down, unable to hide his disdain. Clearly, the man was underestimating both of them. Salem didn't bother to reply. Instead, he said to Rane, "Are we going to do this the easy way, or do you get some kind of perverse pleasure out of making me repeat myself?" He waited expectantly. "Have you had even one sip?"

Her gaze traveled down his chest. He had forgotten to tuck the protective amulet back inside his shirt. As he hid it away, her eyes flashed with understanding. She folded her arms, biceps flexing, her mouth set in a thin line. "Why, what's up with the drinks? Start talking."

With her, everything was unnecessarily difficult. "It's a simple question. Did you or didn't you?"

"Hey," the wolf said to him. "You notice we're trying to dance here?"

Salem kept his gaze locked on Rane.

She blew a breath out of the corner of her mouth, having some kind of lengthy internal debate. "Are you sleeping with Ember?"

His patience evaporated. Anger and frustration rose up inside him until his pulse thudded in his ears. "I swear, woman, if you don't . . ."

She smiled tightly, waiting.

Despite the fuzziness in his brain, he got his temper back under control. "No," he said through his gritted teeth.

"Huh. Cool. Well, my body is a temple, so you can relax. No drinking tonight. Not that it's any of your business."

Relief flooded through Salem. So she was safe, at least. One box checked off of tonight's list.

But for him, and everyone else in here, the clock was ticking. Toward what, he didn't know. He needed to find out.

"Hey," the wolf said, edging past Rane to loom over him. "Something you want to say to me?"

Salem finally spared him a look. "The drinks are spiked. There are no judges for the contest. This masquerade is an elaborate trap. You're probably going to die."

The wolf pulled back. "What?"

Salem turned to Rane. "Where are your friends?"

Through the visor, she squinted at him a little, the way she always did when she was trying to figure him out. As if it were merely a matter of proper eye focus.

Meanwhile, the wolf apparently decided to ignore his warning and instead waved him along with a thumb, like a hitchhiker. "Time to go, man. Just move along."

Of all the sorcerers in this vast chamber, why had Rane chosen this one to dance with? He didn't seem like her type, except for the obvious obsession with athletic equipment, as evidenced by the size of his muscles.

Then the answer hit him, and Salem mentally cursed himself.

Of course, Rane wasn't really interested in dancing with this buffoon. It was merely a distraction. To draw him away from the sliding door, so Dru could get inside. Where she clearly didn't belong.

Why hadn't he seen that before? Such a transparent ploy. The spiked drink was clearly affecting his judgment.

As painful as it was to contemplate, he needed to go retrieve Dru before she could find Greyson. He turned on his heel and headed for the secret door.

If that shopkeeper found him before Salem did, she would foul everything up. Greyson was the key to doomsday, and that made him the world's biggest threat.

But Dru didn't seem to care about that. If she had her way, everybody would be sitting in a circle playing bongos and trading friendship bracelets. That was the difference between him and Dru, he decided. While she was trying to make peace, he was committed to doing whatever it took to save the world.

Too many times, he had watched her tie herself in knots trying to save people from their own stupidity, or prevent any collateral damage. But that was the nature of magic. It hurt you. It used you up and discarded you, until it left you as nothing but a burned-out shell that could only crave more.

Sometimes, magic could change the world. Or, in this case, destroy it. The Harbingers had unleashed the power of the apocalypse scroll decades ago, and it was too bad for Greyson that he'd ended up caught in the cross fire.

But now, as one of the Four Horsemen of the Apocalypse, the man was full to the brim with doomsday power. As long as he was roaming around free in his speed demon-powered car, then the apocalypse was still in play. The clock was ticking down to doomsday.

Salem couldn't allow that.

That was why he had broken into Greyson's house originally, looking for him, but all he had found was an undead creature lurking in the darkness. That had started all of this. Now, Salem still hadn't found Greyson. But he was getting closer.

He didn't absolutely have to kill Greyson, he supposed, if there was some other way to neutralize the threat. But so far, none of his research had turned up any alternatives. When the time came, Salem would do whatever was necessary, no matter how distasteful. Greyson had to be taken out.

That was why Dru couldn't be allowed to call the shots. She would try to stop him, if she knew his plan. But with the fate of the world hanging in the balance, there was no room to indulge her hand-holding, feel-good ways.

He had to stop this. Now. The door was just ahead now.

Just before he got there, Rane passed him with long, purposeful strides, her clingy gold lamé dress shimmering in the dance lights. The wolf was nowhere to be seen.

Salem squelched his surprise. Joining forces with him was the smartest thing Rane could do right now, obviously. There was no one else here tonight whom he could trust to cover his back. He was just secretly pleased that Rane had reached the same conclusion.

He wondered, fleetingly, if that was the sort of thinking that always prompted Dru to call him arrogant. What did it really matter, as long as he was proven right in the end?

Rane ducked her head inside the doorway, scanned the darkness, and then turned to survey the crowded chamber behind them. "We need to warn Opal. She's been drinking. So has Ruiz. What's going to happen to them?"

"No way to know yet," Salem said. "There's nothing we can do now except act quickly. Find Dru, find Greyson, put a stop to all this."

Rane nodded. "Okay. First, let's get Opal."

Salem tried not to roll his eyes. That woman lacked any magical powers at all. What could she possibly do, aside from wandering in and making everything needlessly complicated?

Apparently, that little item wasn't glaringly obvious to Rane, so he deflected it. "Don't worry about her," he said calmly. "Opal is busy enjoying the party. Such as it is. Meanwhile, you and I can track down your BFF before she makes things worse."

Rane pushed the visor up to reveal her fierce eyes. "She's not making things *worse*. She's on an important mission. Which is more than I can say about you. You want to accomplish something tonight? Stop sneaking around being all jealous-y."

"Please." He stripped off his mask and tossed it over his shoulder, glad to be done with the party. "Jealous? Hardly."

"Yeah, right. You were pretty freaking jealous out there. Admit it."

"Admitting anything is not my style." Staring up into her beautiful blue eyes, so fiery with energy, he suddenly didn't care what words came out of her lips. As long as they were spoken to him. Now that he had her all alone, had her full attention, he remembered how intoxicating it was to be the focus of all that raw, physical power. He'd missed it so deeply it left an ache inside him.

Rane waved a hand in front of his face. "*Hello?* Earth to you. Ready? Let's go."

He snapped his gaze away from her and peered into the dark metal stairwell, trying to ignore the distracting fact that she was standing so close to him. "Any idea what's down there?"

"Thought that was your job," she said. "I'm just here to get my freak on."

"Some things never change." Salem dug in the pocket of his long coat until his fingers closed on the bumpy shape of his skull-encrusted Zippo. He flipped the lid open and struck the wheel, chasing away the nearest shadows with the light of the flame.

Inside the stifling webbing, Dru shifted her grip on the dagger-shaped shard of spectrolite. Taking a deep breath, she focused all of her remaining magical power on the crystal, willing it to flare to life and cut her loose.

Nothing happened.

Confused, she tried again. She steadied her breathing, focused her thoughts, and willed energy to flow into the crystal.

Still nothing.

The sour taste of panic rose in the back of Dru's throat. She really was trapped after all.

She tried once again to charge the spectrolite, but it was no use. The webs had some sort of narcotic effect, sucking the magical energy out of her like a sponge. She had nothing left, except fear.

Any moment, Titus would return and drug her. She had no way to escape.

Violently, she fought against the cocoon, twisting one way and then the other, straining her muscles harder than she ever had in yoga class. Fat lot of good those classes were doing now, she thought.

All of her thrashing did nothing but roll her off the bench like a dropped burrito. She landed hard on the stone floor.

"Ow." Shaking her head, she peered around as best she could, looking for anything to help her escape. Then she noticed the vein of raw white quartz running up the side of the granite wall over the bench.

Quartz. The most common purifying crystal in the world.

In the shop, Dru used clear quartz crystals to purify just about anything. The clearer the crystal, generally the more powerful its effect. Milky quartz—clouded up by impurities when it formed millions of years ago—was considered junk for magical purposes.

But a sizable raw vein of quartz, undisturbed within the mountain, might be enough to help her cleanse away the narcotic effects of the cocoon. Which could give her a chance to charge up the spectrolite blade and cut herself loose.

But only if she could reach the quartz in the first place.

Breathing hard, Dru inch-wormed her way across the floor. She grunted with the effort of every undignified heave, until at last she reached the wall.

She stared up at the jagged vein of quartz. How could she touch it? Her arms were wrapped up.

No amount of wriggling got her any closer. Frustrated, she wedged the toes of her wrapped-up boots under the end of the heavy bench and tried to slide her back up the wall.

The exposed quartz was only a couple of feet over her head, but it might as well have been a mile away.

She stiffened her spine, straining to reach her cheek or forehead up to the quartz. Her entire body trembled with the effort, stretching every inch she could.

It still wasn't enough to make contact.

Tears of frustration burned in her eyes. This was all her fault. Everyone had warned her not to come here—Opal, Rane, even Salem—and still she had pushed blindly forward. Once again, she was in too deep. And all of her friends were in danger. Because of her.

Right now they could already be captured, or injured, or worse. And it was all her fault.

There was no one left to help her.

Not even Greyson.

She desperately missed his presence. The way he made her question everything she knew about magic, and about herself, and come up with better answers. The way he made her think not just about *what* she was doing, but *why*. He made her a better version of herself.

He had to be trapped somewhere under this mountain, and he needed her now more than ever. She couldn't give up. She had to find a way to get to him.

She wasn't going to die here. And she wasn't going to let Titus carry out his plans.

Not today. Not now.

Gathering her last bit of strength, she bunched her toes inside her boots and pressed hard, gaining a fraction of an inch with each push. She could feel the cool air coming off the wall, tickling the hairs of the top of her head.

Her shimmering go-go boots, anchored by the webs and the weight of the bench, started to give up their grip on her feet. Inside the leather, she pushed with her tiptoes.

One final effort and she covered the last inch. The skin of her temple brushed up against the rough surface of the quartz.

The moment she made contact, she focused all of her thoughts on connecting to it. Eyes squeezed shut, she reached out for its ancient energy. When she finally made contact, she discovered it was much more powerful than she expected.

The magical energy flowed through her head and down into her body like a stream of ice-cold meltwater pounding down a mountainside. She gasped at its sudden intensity. Her eyes flew open, and everything in the room looked brighter.

The vein of quartz, hidden within the depths of the living rock, had to be immense. Bigger than any crystal she had ever touched before. Her mouth filled with a gritty tingle. A metallic whine stung her ears. Her scalp prickled as her hair lifted up.

Inside the cocoon, a flickering rainbow glow began to shine through the webs. The spectrolite came to life in her palms, lit up from within by a primal energy that she couldn't contain.

She pushed, and the glowing tip of the crystal pierced through the cocoon of webs. Arms tingling, she sliced her way out. Frantically, she tore off the webs, leaving sparkling sequins behind in the sticky hollow of the cocoon. Finally free, she stamped her go-go boots to get the blood flowing into her feet again.

She looked around for some kind of tool to break loose a chunk of quartz from the wall. But there was nothing handy, and she didn't have time to dig through the plastic-wrapped furniture to find something she could use.

With the gritty remains of the mountain's energy trembling through her, she ducked out the orange door and checked to make sure that the tunnel was empty. Then she ran for all she was worth, clutching the still-glowing spectrolite blade.

She was going to find Greyson, she swore to herself, and save the world.

Or die trying.

30

LONG, COOL WOMAN

Beyond the sliding door, nothing moved but the flickering glow from Salem's lighter. It fell on bare metal stairs with circle-punched treads that led down into the darkness. Above, a few caged bulbs shone a feeble glow.

Salem peered down the shadowy metal staircase. Rust stains and decades of accumulated dust greeted him. "Lovely. Your friend Dru gets lost in the most glamorous places." He looked over his shoulder at Rane, intending to say more. But being this close to her, her familiar face softened by the light of the flame, made him forget what he was going to say.

Rane scowled back at him. "What now?"

Realizing she had caught him staring, he shrugged to cover it. "Since we're in a danger zone, I thought you would have transformed by now. But maybe it's casual day at the office?"

"You do your job. Don't tell me how to do mine." Rane laid one large hand on the worn handrail. With an echoing metallic ringing sound, her arm and then her entire body transformed into dark, cloudy steel.

With clanging footsteps, she marched past him down the stairs. "Let's go, Zippo boy."

He watched her go, endlessly fascinating by her long, lean body, even in metal. As she clanged across the landing and down the next flight of metal steps, he sighed. So much for the stealthy approach.

By the time they had descended several flights, his ears were ringing. He was about to suggest that she turn human again when they reached a rusty steel door stenciled with a yellow alphanumeric code.

Rane stopped marching and grunted in a way that Salem knew meant she'd found something. In the blissful silence that followed, he knelt at her feet, where a single silver sequin winked up at them from the textured metal floor. Carefully, he picked it up and held it near the light of the flame.

"Dru came this way," Rane said, her flat voice echoing. "That's from her dress."

"Or an equally stylish undead creature."

"Oh, was that a joke?" Rane asked in mock disbelief as he stood up. "Or did you just call Dru stylish? I don't know which is weirder."

"It must be the drink talking." Salem pushed the rusted metal door open. Chilly darkness waited beyond. It smelled of rust and fungus.

"Hey." Rane clamped a metal hand on his shoulder, stopping him. "Did you have one of those drinks? What's in it? Is it poisonous?"

"No way to know just yet," he said. "Looked like traces of scourge. But if it was deadly, this gothic tiki party would be long over. No, those drinks were spiked for another reason. The question is, what?"

They stepped out of the stairwell into a musty, mold-splotched cavern that stretched away into the darkness. Holding the hot lighter by the base, Salem played the flickering light around his feet, looking for any more signs of Dru's gradually atomizing disco dress.

Rane stooped to pick up a small sparkling object from the ground. Dru's masquerade mask. She held it close to her face and sniffed, then set it back on the ground. "Disco girl went this way." She marched away into the darkness, between rows of chiseled stone columns.

The flickering light from the Zippo fell on heaps of cobwebbed junk. Stacks of railroad ties. Unused ventilation ducts. Steel oil drums. Above the mess, someone had used red spray paint to write out a message on the stone columns.

"What's it say?" Rane pointed at the sorcio signs. "I didn't bring my secret decoder ring."

Salem studied the signs one by one, reading them twice to make sure he got the message right. "It's a warning. From a sorcerer who called himself Nomad. He says the lakes are poison."

Rane's face screwed up in confusion. "What lakes?"

Salem had no idea, but he didn't enlighten her to that fact. He was more concerned with finding Greyson and putting a stop to the apocalypse. He walked along the columns, reading the spray-painted symbols. "Apparently, Nomad's group tried to make camp here, thinking no one would find them. But they weren't alone." He directed her attention to the main part of the message. "Motorcycle gang. Undead. No survivors."

Rane crossed her arms. "Poor Nomad. I wonder if he made it out."

"Possible. The question is, when? This spray paint could have been here for years." He pointed at the last symbol, and then dropped his arm. "It says, 'Get out fast.'"

Salem considered that. Poison lakes. Undead creatures. It was entirely possible that Greyson was already dead, and the doomsday problem was solved. If that was the case, all they had to do was poke around until they found his body.

Rane turned to look at Salem, her steel eyes wide and shimmering in the light of the flame. "You hear that?"

He did, once she mentioned it. Scraping footsteps, dozens of them. But by the time he became aware of them, it was too late.

Staggering figures emerged from the darkness in all directions, clambering over the junk, snagging their webs on dusty corners. So many undead, all around them, that Salem couldn't see a way out.

It didn't matter. These creatures had caught him off guard once, and only once. This time, it would be vastly different. He would destroy them all.

Rane kicked over a metal drum with a resounding clang. As it toppled over and rolled, she drew back one well-defined arm and drove a steel fist into it. It dented and split, gushing a spreading pool across the stone floor. "Lighter!"

"Oh, the subtle approach," Salem said, tossing her the Zippo. "My favorite."

It never took Rane long to cause mass destruction. In a way, he'd been missing that. An oily orange-yellow flame sprang up at Rane's feet, illuminating the horde of undead closing in around them.

Salem was long past capturing these things to study them. This time, he was looking forward to destroying them outright.

He raised both hands, fingers spread wide, preparing to unleash his bottled-up fury.

He focused on the nearest creature, a staggering web-wrapped wretch in biker boots and the tatters of a leather vest. Its brown-stained jaws stretched open wide and let out a watery hiss.

Salem allowed himself a small measure of satisfaction. In an underground chamber this big, with no innocent civilians wandering around and no possibility of collateral damage, it was almost too easy. He could see why Rane relished the freedom of destruction.

He flexed his fingers and willed a blast of invisible force to erupt from his fingertips and shatter the thing before him.

But to his astonishment, nothing happened. Nothing but a throbbing headache that raced up the back of his skull and pounded through the fuzziness that surrounded his brain. His magic simply didn't materialize.

Salem stood frozen in disbelief as the corrupt thing staggered closer, untouched.

He tried again, digging down deep into his reserves of energy. The air wavered between his fingers, but it wasn't enough to even push the creature back.

He dug deeper. His head pounded. Black streaks clouded his vision. And yet he couldn't summon up his magic.

The spiked drink wasn't meant to kill sorcerers, he realized. It was meant to neutralize them. Rob them of their magic, leaving them defenseless. Making them easy to capture. Or kill.

The creature lunged at him, black dripping claws outstretched. Salem backed up and tripped, falling just as the thing swiped its claws through the air where he'd stood.

Salem's mind went blank with fear. His magic was gone. That had never happened before. The magic had always been there, volumes of it, just waiting to be tapped. And now, it was somehow all gone.

There was nothing he could do except stare up into the thing's empty-eyed grin as it loomed over him.

No, Salem thought, the sorcerer who called himself Nomad— whoever he was—hadn't made it out alive.

"Stay down!" Rane yelled. With a heavy rush of displaced air, a four-foot length of iron rail swung through the air, passing over his head like a low-flying jet.

It struck the undead creature square in the rib cage and obliterated it. Wet-looking bones and scraps of web exploded in all directions, clattering across the ground like hail.

Rane stepped into the swing, annihilating two more undead. Their dismembered legs tumbled across the stony floor. Their skulls bounced and rolled.

The rest of the undead horde wasn't yet near enough to strike, though it was steadily closing in around them. Rane hefted the iron rail in both hands, shifting her grip.

Her weapon looked as if it had been lifted directly from a railroad bed. In cross section, it was shaped like a heavyset uppercase letter T. Rane held it as if it were no heavier than a garden rake.

She stepped back over to Salem, her muscular legs standing wide, and surveyed the rest of the creatures circling around them.

"You just gonna lay there all day, sweetie?" She glanced down at him with a wild glint in her eye. The corner of her lips perked up in a feral smile, revealing shining teeth. "Or are you going to get up here and help me kick some freaky zombie ass?"

Dru crossed the underground railroad tracks, trying to retrace her steps back to the metal staircase, but she quickly figured out she was lost. The ride in Titus's Jeep had disoriented her more than she thought.

The next tunnel she found was much like the one she had just left, with orange doors and half-finished apartments. The tunnel after that was the same, but even rougher and not yet painted.

Sprinting down a long, curved tunnel, she spied a wide doorway that led into some kind of machine shop lined with workbenches. The nearest bench was stacked with cardboard trays full of rocks and crystals.

Dru skidded to a halt, silently thankful that her shimmering platform boots helped keep her from falling over.

She peeked around the edge of the huge, arched doorway. A line of fluorescent light fixtures hung down from the arched ceiling, but only the ones nearest the door were lit. Beyond the buzzing lights, the rest of the long chamber was cloaked in darkness.

She waited, eyeing the darkness within as she stole glances at the cardboard trays of crystals. From here, it was impossible to see exactly what was in those trays. There could be something she could use to defend herself.

Nothing moved. Finally, Dru decided she couldn't afford to wait any longer. She tiptoed into the room and rifled through the heavy trays of rocks.

The vast majority of them were actually brown barite roses, of greater or lesser quality. Judging by the shipping labels, most of them had come from Oklahoma, although a few had traveled from as far away as Tunisia. Apparently, Titus had brought in hundreds of the rocks and searched through them all in order to find one perfect specimen to give to Dru.

In a way, Dru was touched, even if everything else he'd done was misguided and freakishly creepy.

Buried under the cardboard trays of barite roses, she found a newspaper-lined tray of irregular citrine chunks, ranging in color from saffron yellow to mahogany brown. Beneath that, a tray of brain-shaped calcite clusters that had obviously been chipped off a cave wall somewhere.

She groaned in frustration. Citrine might help her save money, and calcite might help ease a hangover, but neither of them were good in a fight. She needed something she could use as a weapon.

At the bottom of the stack, she found a wooden tray filled with a jumble of crystals. Fossilized wood, purple amethyst, black tourmaline, and something wrapped in bright red plastic and packing tape.

Curious, she picked off the tape and unwrapped the plastic, revealing a gorgeous, transparent green crystal shaped like a miniature city skyline. Vivianite.

Her heart skipped a beat. Using vivianite, she could potentially open up a portal to the netherworld, if she could find one. She also grabbed the amethyst for protection. And the tourmaline, just in case she needed to ground any energy back to the earth.

She ignored the citrine, but there was a chance the hangover-curing properties of the calcite could have a healing effect on anyone who had drunk the potion.

A thought suddenly struck Dru. What if these crystals were actually here for her? What if Titus had collected this much calcite specifically because he intended to have Dru cure the sorcerers he had drugged with his spiked drinks?

She looked down at her armload of crystals. If that was the case, then what was the vivianite for? Could there actually be a portal to the netherworld somewhere in this vast underground fortress? Anything was possible, she decided.

Right now, she had more practical worries. She couldn't very well run around with her arms full of rocks. She needed something to carry them. Atop a workbench at the edge of the light was an old leather tool bag. It would have to do.

She upended the bag onto the workbench, dumping out crusty, old pliers, rusted screwdrivers, and about a hundred miscellaneous screws and bits of hardware. After shaking out the last of the dust, she loaded up her new crystals and hefted the bag. Heavy, but doable.

A massive cork board dominated the wall over the workbench, covered with paper schematics of the bunker in all of its various levels. Dru studied the map, trying to figure out where she was now and how she'd gotten there.

The tunnels of the underground complex formed an impenetrable maze. But much to her surprise, the schematics showed three lakes deep inside the mountain. Each one was crosshatched and labeled, POTABLE WATER, GRAY WATER, and DIESEL.

She read that last one twice, puzzled. A lake full of diesel fuel? But then she noticed the long, rectangular blocks on the schematic labeled GENERATORS. Apparently, they needed a giant fuel reservoir.

Someone, presumably Titus, had scratched out the name of each lake with a black magic marker. He had also drawn a sorcio symbol, a sideways figure eight with opposing swirls inside each half.

It was the symbol for scourge. Seeing it made her blood run cold.

There was more than just a river of scourge beneath this facility, she realized with growing horror. It was a vast series of reservoirs, each one connected by underground rivers and filled with millions of gallons of scourge.

A teaspoonful was enough to kill a sorcerer as powerful as Salem. What could Titus do with an entire sea of it?

There were more maps pinned up nearby. First, a topological map of the nearby Rocky Mountains, finely grained black lines showing elevation and squiggly blue lines showing rivers. Below that hung a map of the world's ocean currents. Both maps were covered with hand-drawn arrows and scribbled calculations.

Her throat tight with fear, Dru went back to the schematics of the mountain complex. With a pen, Titus had drawn arrows leading out of the reservoirs into tiny passageways, which she assumed were pipes or air vents. Eventually, the lines all converged on the curved central tunnel, which led out to the entrance. From there, he had simply drawn a thick black arrow that pointed off the edge of the map. Toward a river.

Dru kept looking from the underground map to the river map, and then to the ocean currents. A growing fear gnawed at her.

Could Titus truly carry out a plan this mad?

There was no time to lose. Dru ripped the tunnel map off the wall, folded it into a wad, and stuffed it into the leather tool bag, on top of the crystals. She turned to go. Across the room, a glimmer of light reflected off dozens of dead TV monitors.

She realized she was looking at some kind of control console, like the one in the party room. A line of gauges softly glowed yellow. Did any of the stuff still work?

She set down the leather bag and studied the rows of buttons and metal toggle switches. She didn't know anything about security systems, but she did find a chunky microphone on a black stand that looked promising. Could she warn the others while there was still time?

She hesitated a moment, worried that Titus would hear her. But it didn't matter anymore. It was too late to try to sneak around now.

She pressed a thick square button labeled TUNNEL 13. It let out a heavy, mechanical click. Then she picked up the microphone and pushed down its round red button. "Opal? Anyone? Can you hear me?"

31
THE WILD SIDE

Opal couldn't remember exactly how many of these deliciously fruity drinks she'd had, but it didn't matter. As far as she was concerned, this was the best party in the history of the universe.

She danced alone with Ruiz in the cozy control-booth nook, without a care in the world. For once, she was having such a great time that it practically seemed illegal. And on top of that, the drinks were free.

In between songs, they chatted about everything and nothing. The way Ruiz talked to her, the way he looked at her, made her feel amazing. Fantastic. She hadn't felt that way in more years than she could count. And she needed so badly to keep that feeling going. She never wanted it to end.

There was just one problem. Dru had some silly rule about not getting involved with customers. It really wasn't all that bad of an idea, in theory at least. But right there in the moment, the ordinary rules didn't seem to apply anymore.

Not when she was dancing to the beat, lights spinning around her, feeling warm and relaxed and sexy. She was miles away from her troubles, flying as high as the moon. Feeling young, feeling alive, feeling absolutely fabulous.

And right now, she thought about nothing else.

Everything around her faded away. The cavernous chamber of the nuclear bunker. The crowd of angst-ridden sorcerers dressed all in black. The grainy black-and-white film clips playing on the rough stone wall, showing explosions and blasted forests. None of that mattered anymore.

This, right here, right now, was the best night of her life. And if any of her troubles nagged at her, Ruiz was there to take her away from it all.

That easygoing, shoulder-shrugging way of his made her feel as if she could say anything. Do anything.

He made a joke about pulling off his *luchador* mask and ruining the whole masquerade party, telling everybody the cops were here and making them run for the door. She threw back her head and laughed.

When she looked at him again, his gaze sparkled.

Without even meaning to, Opal found herself drifting closer to him. Her whole body tingled, knowing what was coming next. Suddenly, she needed to wrap her arms around him and kiss him.

But she just couldn't shake Dru's warning voice in the back of her head.

Opal! Opal! Can you hear me?

Ruiz's lips were inches from hers. He paused, uncertain. "Um, did you hear that?"

Opal ran her fingers up his arm. "I didn't hear a thing, baby." She slid up next to him.

Opal!

"No, there it is again," Ruiz said. Head cocked to the side, he leaned closer to the control panel. "Is that Dru?"

"What?" Opal took a step and stumbled. How many of those drinks had she had, exactly? She couldn't remember. She planted both hands on the grimy steel edge of the control panel, wishing the room would stop spinning around her.

"Opal!" Dru's tinny voice crackled from a speaker between two dead TV monitors, their rounded glass screens grayish green and dusty. Her voice faded in and out, broken by static. "Opal, can . . . read me? Can you hear . . . are you?"

"Dru?" Opal brought her face closer to the speaker. "Where are you? How did you get in there?"

". . . emergency . . . could kill . . ."

Ruiz picked up a microphone on a chunky black stand and fiddled with its switches. "She can't hear you. The controls are dead. Hang on." He shoved the microphone into her hands.

"What am I supposed to do with this?" Opal asked. The microphone was surprisingly heavy, and solid enough to use as a hand weight.

"Just keep hitting that red button and trying it. I'm going to get you hooked up." Ruiz dug through the pockets of his coveralls and pulled out a couple of small tools. Grunting, he got down on the floor and yanked out a metal panel, revealing a nest of multicolored wires and green circuit boards.

Opal jiggled the microphone's red button. "Dru! Where are you?"

"Opal, if you . . . get everyone . . . trap . . ." Dru's voice shattered into a blast of static.

Ruiz muttered in Spanish and yanked something loose beneath the console.

"Dru?" Opal kept jiggling the button. "Dru!"

Nothing came back but static. The silence was ominous.

"Hurry up!" Opal said to Ruiz. "What are you doing down there?"

"Hey, this is a government setup, you know? So it was built by the lowest bidder. And it's like really old. All these plastic connections, all *basura*." Ruiz clamped his screwdriver between his teeth and dug deep in the console with both hands. "Hold on. Jus' a sec."

Opal tried the microphone again and again, calling Dru's name. As the seconds ticked by without a response, a wave of panic rose up inside her. Something was obviously horribly wrong. She wished she hadn't had so much to drink. But they were so *good*.

Without knowing where Dru was, or what had happened, there was nothing Opal could do. She could only stand there, helpless, trying to raise Dru with the clacking button on the old government microphone.

She stared at the dead screens of the control console, wishing they could show her what was going on. The dead gray ovals looked like a graveyard full of tombstones.

Yellow lights flickered on across the console. A row of needles jumped, and an electric hum reverberated from the speaker.

"Titus is coming back," Dru said clearly, her voice loud and strong. Then it broke up again, alternating bits of dead silence with chopped-up syllables that made no sense.

Opal keyed the microphone again. "Dru! We can hear you. Where are you?"

"Opal? Oh, thank—" The speaker crackled and went dead again as the light winked out.

Opal slammed the microphone down. "Ruiz!"

"Hang on," Ruiz said. "Almost got this. There!"

The lights came back up again, and with them Dru's voice. "—as far as I can tell. Millions of gallons of scourge. And I see generators, pumps, everything. The underground lakes are full of scourge, and Titus is planning to release it on the world. To raise the dead. All the dead in the world. I'm going to try to stop him, but you have to get everyone out of there!"

"Titus? For real?" Opal's mind whirled. "Scourge in a lake? What are you talking about?"

"A series of huge underground reservoirs of scourge. Imagine the biggest toxic waste spill in the world."

Opal tried to picture that, but she couldn't. She clicked the button. "A toxic waste spill? Here in the mountains?"

"This is the continental divide," Dru said matter-of-factly. "That scourge won't stay here in Colorado. It's going to flow both east and west from the Rocky Mountains. All the way to the Atlantic and Pacific. And from there to the entire world."

Ruiz crawled out from beneath the console. Even through his silver mask, she could see the fear on his face.

Opal clicked the microphone on again. "So it's just all going to get washed away, right?"

"No," Dru said tightly. "Titus's necromantic powers have been magnified by the coming apocalypse. This scourge will keep growing. Every time it reaches a dead body or even a bone, it will multiply. Until all the dead in the entire world have become undead creatures. Imagine the carnage. Millions would die. Maybe billions."

Opal and Ruiz traded long glances.

"Is she serious?" Ruiz said. "Because, man, that doesn't sound good."

"Can you warn Rane and Salem?" Dru asked.

Opal clicked the button. "I don't know where they got to. Last I saw, they went sneaking off together."

Dru went silent so long that Opal was afraid they had lost her again. "I need to find them," Dru said finally, sounding frightened. "Meanwhile, you need to get everyone out of there. This place is a trap. And don't let anyone drink any more. That stuff will mess them up."

Opal's gaze slid to the half-empty glasses perched on the edge of the metal control console, and she fought down a wave of nausea. "Dru, where are you?"

"I don't know, exactly. But I found a map. I've got to find Greyson. And Rane and Salem. We'll meet you outside. I hope."

"Greyson? What? Dru, get out of there, right now!" Opal waited. "Dru!"

But Dru didn't answer.

Opal looked out across the dancing crowd, all of the sorcerers oblivious to the looming danger. If they all took off their masks, she wondered how many she would recognize. Probably most of them had set foot in the Crystal Connection at some point or another. They would recognize her.

"Party's over." She pulled off her mask. "Ruiz, can you get the PA system working? Turn on all the lights in here?"

"The lights? Sure. No problem." He pulled off his silver mask, leaving his black hair sticking out in all directions, and studied the console. "Oh. Here we go." He spread out his fingers across a line of wide plastic switches and threw them all at once with a loud click.

Something thumped in the distance, and the cavern faded to pitch black. A murmur of worried voices broke out in the darkness.

"That's not it," Opal said.

"Yeah. Sorry." After a few more clicks, the lights all came back on, brighter than ever. Grinning, Ruiz pointed at the microphone in Opal's hands. "You're on."

Opal clicked the button. "Hey! Listen up, people!" Her voice reverberated off the rock walls, startling her.

The crowd milled about, looking up into the bright lights.

"Over here!" Opal waved her arms. "Hey! Party's over. Time to go home. Out the door, turn that way, head down the main tunnel to the entrance." No one moved. She lifted the microphone again. "Listen. You know who I am. You've been in my shop before. Right? All of you. Have I ever lied to you?"

No one answered, but now at least everyone was looking at her. She could see recognition in their eyes.

"There's a wave of undead about to flood this place. Anybody who stays here is probably gonna end up dead. Everybody's got to go. Now!"

A wailing alarm Klaxon drowned her out. Across the cavern, old yellow strobe lights began to spin on either side of the blast door. Voices in the crowd shouted, and they quickly turned into screams of fear.

Opal pointed toward the only exit. *"Everybody! Run!"*

Greyson snapped awake in the darkness of his cell. Something had changed in the cold, stale air surrounding him, but he wasn't sure what. His glowing red eyes scanned the tiny stone chamber, allowing him to see its dim outlines, if just barely.

Everything looked the same as it had when he'd been dragged in here. The floor was littered with dirty debris. Rock dust, gravel, scraps of wiring with brittle insulation, unidentifiable bits of plastic.

The creatures had left him in here for hours, possibly days, without food or water. It had taken enormous effort to struggle free of the webs that bound him, breaking the strands one by one against the rough metal edge of the vault-like steel door.

Now, those webs lay in a shapeless pile in the corner. Greyson was free, but there was no way out of this small room. On hands and knees, he had dug through the useless junk scattered across the floor, finding only a rusty braided steel cable. What he could do with that exactly, he wasn't sure yet. It certainly wouldn't get him through the thick metal door.

He had spent hours running his fingers across every gritty square inch of the stone ceiling that arched overhead and then abruptly ended in a wall of rock, like the termination of an unfinished tunnel. The only way out was through that door. And it was bolted from the outside.

Left alone in the dark, all he could think of was Dru. Where was she now? Was she safe?

Every so often, he swore he could sense her presence, as if she was somewhere just outside the door, looking for him. He couldn't shake the feeling that she was calling his name, over and over. But no matter how he strained his ears, all he could hear was the echoing silence of his own steady breathing.

It was just wishful thinking, he told himself. There was no way she could know where he was. No way to find him.

As time dragged by, his fate became more and more clear. There was no way out. Sooner or later, he would die here.

He'd always thought of himself as someone who lived a life without regrets. But he realized now, shivering against the cold steel door, that it wasn't true. There were so many things that he wished he could go back and change.

He wished he could have fixed things with his family. He wished he'd known the truth about his father, that he was much more than just a crazy old man who always dragged Greyson into his troubles. He wished he'd listened when his father and his sister talked about the magic that ran in their family. Instead, he had shut them out with accusations and ultimatums. Though they had tried to tell him the truth, he had ignored them and instead let his own bullheadedness drive them apart forever.

He wished he hadn't walled off the world after that, throwing himself into his work until there was nothing else left in his life. He could have spent less time fixing cars and more time fixing the things that mattered.

But most of all, he wished he hadn't walked away from Dru. He should have trusted her. Trusted in her knowledge, her compassion, and her inner strength. She would have figured out a way to break this demonic curse, if he'd given her a chance. He'd been afraid of hurting her, ruining her life, but now he knew he was just being selfish. It was his own fear that had driven him away.

She wouldn't have rejected him. Even if he was still some kind of monster. He only saw that now.

But it was too late.

Thirsty and exhausted, Greyson realized he must have fallen asleep with his ear to the steel door, listening to the impenetrable silence until his eyelids finally drooped closed. Now, as he breathed in a slow lungful of the cold, stale air, he figured out what had woken him.

It was the sharp sound of leather-heeled boots on stone. A single pair of footsteps echoed down the tunnel toward him. It sounded nothing like those skeletal creatures, who tended to shuffle and scrape.

These were booted feet, striding closer with what sounded like determination or barely restrained fury. Someone big, he figured. Someone on a mission. The same footsteps he'd heard walking on the road where he'd been captured.

Instantly, Greyson was on his feet, his whole body tense. This time, he would be ready. Quickly, he picked up the braided steel cable he'd found among the debris and wrapped it tightly around his fingers. The cold, rusty metal formed a crude set of brass knuckles. Not much of a weapon, but it was all he had, and he was going to make it count.

The footsteps strode closer, and a faint yellow stripe of light crept beneath the door, picking up the bottom edges of the junk that covered the floor.

For a brief moment, Greyson entertained the possibility that somebody might be coming to rescue him. But who would even know he was down here? And where was here, exactly? He had no idea.

The footsteps marched so quickly that Greyson was worried they would walk right on past. But they stopped, and the massive lock on the steel door screeched. An icy spike of adrenaline shot down Greyson's spine and across his shoulders. He was only going to get one shot at this.

The steel door groaned. With a shudder, the heavy hatch swung outward, until the yellow glow of a foot-long metal flashlight spilled in. Behind it loomed a man in a long red double-breasted jacket with shining gold buttons.

Lips drawn back in fury, the man pointed the flashlight at Greyson's eyes, nearly blinding him. "*Where* is she?" the man roared.

He stood a couple inches taller than Greyson, and didn't look like a pushover by any means, despite the George Washington outfit. Squinting painfully into the light, Greyson took in all the details he could: the man's distracted stance, the shrinking distance between them, the growing gap between the doorframe and the door as it swung open.

Everything after that happened on instinct.

As the man drew in a breath to shout something else, he lifted the flashlight, and Grayson snatched it with his left hand. Gripping the rounded end with the hot lens, he twisted and pulled. The man hung on for a split second, losing his balance as Greyson yanked him closer.

At the same time, Greyson drove his right fist—the one wrapped in steel cable—hard into the man's gut, doubling him over. His breath exploded out of him.

Greyson pulled the flashlight free, holding onto the bell-shaped lit end. In one motion, he swung it up overhead in a fast arc, driving it down hard on the back of the man's head like a club. His slicked-back hair flew with the impact.

With a meaty thump, the man dropped in the doorway.

Spots pulsed in Greyson's eyes from the flashlight beam, and the edges of his vision pounded with adrenaline. Breathing hard, he had to rein in the animal instinct that made him want to press the attack. Pay the man back for trapping him here. Finish him off.

Greyson shook his head to clear it. That wasn't who he was. That was the remnant of his curse, the part of him that made his eyes glow red. He couldn't give in to it, not ever again.

The man was down, and the door was open. That was all that mattered. Greyson stepped over him into the wide tunnel beyond, ready to run. He shone the flashlight around, looking for a way out, and came face-to-face with the undead.

They had him surrounded. Dozens of silent undead creatures stood there filling the tunnel, staring at him with hollow eye sockets.

He hadn't heard them approach, even though he'd been listening at the door for endless hours. Had they been stationed outside his cell all along? Why? Were they just waiting for him to wither away and die?

He didn't have time to process that unsettling thought. As one, the creatures raised their bony hands. Webbing swirled into existence around their fingers.

Greyson ducked and twisted, dodging streams of webs as they hissed toward him. Swinging the metal flashlight like a club, he bashed his way past two creatures, and then a third, before a web caught the flashlight and yanked it from his fist.

He let go, knowing it was no use trying to hold onto it. The flashlight tumbled, sending a jerky beam of light across the mob of shuffling undead creatures and their outstretched arms. Streamers of web shot through the light toward him, throwing spidery shadows.

Greyson held onto one end of the coiled steel cable and swung the length of it like a lasso. It sizzled through the air, knocking off the nearest creature's skull with a hollow crunch. He sprang through the gap and charged into the darkness of the tunnel, leaving the horde of creatures behind.

He only got a few steps before more webs tangled his legs, sending him crashing to the hard floor. He struggled to keep moving, but the creatures were on him too fast, tangling up his arms and chest in a tight cocoon, until he couldn't move.

As he struggled onto his knees, the man in red slowly got to his feet.

Breathing hard, the man slowly stripped off his torn red jacket and tossed it aside. With one gloved hand, he swept his dark hair out of his eyes and then picked up the flashlight. Its yellow beam, now pointed at the floor, made the space seem to shrink between them.

He regarded Greyson with untempered malice. "She's looking for you, Horseman. You're all she seems to care about."

Greyson glared back at him. "Who?"

But as soon as he asked, he knew. *Dru.*

If she was here looking for him, that meant she wasn't a prisoner like he was. His surge of hope quickly turned to fear as he realized just what she was up against. There was no way she could fight these things and win. There were just too many of them.

"She doesn't understand," the man said, slowly shaking his head as he stalked toward Greyson. "We all have our destiny laid out before us. You're here for a purpose, just as I am."

"I don't know why I'm here," Greyson ground out. His mouth tasted like rock dust from his fall. He spat it out. "Who the hell are you?"

"I'm the one who's going to create the new world. And you're the one who's going to destroy the old."

Greyson had no idea what that meant, but he didn't like the sound of it. There had to be a way for him to get out of this. Inside the cocoon, he tried to shrug his arms loose, but they were bound too tightly.

The man stepped closer, looming over him. When Greyson refused to tilt his head back to look up at him, the man gracefully knelt down on one knee, just out of reach.

His eyes lit with a fiendish hunger. "She thinks she can stop doomsday. She's wrong. If I can't convince her of that, I'll just have to show her. Tonight is the night." He tightened his gloved fist until Greyson could hear the leather creak. "That is why you're here. It's your destiny. The power inside you is the perfect catalyst. The final trigger for doomsday. She'll see for herself."

"Don't bet on it. If Dru's here, she'll find a way," Greyson said firmly. He held the man's dark gaze until the unspoken message passed between them. Greyson knew just what Dru could really do. He knew how strong she was, deep down, and he knew she'd never give up. "If anyone can stop doomsday, it's her."

The man's nostrils flared, and he rose to his feet. Breathing hard, he frowned at Greyson.

"You aren't worthy of her," he finally said through clenched teeth. Then he pointed down the tunnel, throwing his entire body into the gesture, like a commander leading his troops to war. As one, the undead creatures turned and marched, dragging Greyson behind them. Teeth gritted, he fought against them, trying to hold his ground or at least slow them down.

It was no use. Seemingly without effort, the undead hauled him away.

He just hoped that whatever happened to him, Dru wouldn't be forced to watch.

Deeper inside the machine shop, beyond the edge of the light, Dru saw a silhouette that made her breath catch in her throat. Not a human being. Something much bigger.

A car, swaddled in webs.

Long and sinister, pointed at the front with a piercing nose cone.

Black-speckled webs wrapped every inch of it, starting at the sharp nose and continuing up over the windshield, all the way back to the angled spoiler wing that rose up from the tail.

Dru stood stunned, staring at the unmistakable shape of Hellbringer glistening in the darkness, cocooned by the undead webs.

Hot tears filled her eyes and spilled down her cheeks. She covered her face in her hands, as all of the emotions that she had kept bottled up inside came spilling out. If Hellbringer was here, then Greyson was too. The two of them were inseparable.

She wasn't deluding herself. She hadn't been miscasting the spell. Greyson really was alive. And he was here somewhere.

Sniffing, she pulled out her wedge of spectrolite and charged it up, making it glow with a sparkling rainbow of hues. Starting at Hellbringer's nose, she slit the webbing all the way down the length of its long body, finishing at the tail wing.

As the webbing crumpled and fluttered away, she grasped the chrome handle on the driver's door and pulled. With a faint squeak, the heavy door swung open. The interior of the car was clean and empty. Not a trace of webbing inside, and no clue as to Greyson's whereabouts.

She slammed the door and sagged against the car's cold black paint, suddenly overcome with exhaustion. Even with a map, this place was a maze. She could spend weeks searching this labyrinthine underground complex without finding him. And it would only be a matter of time before Titus or his undead creatures caught up to her.

She pounded one fist uselessly on the roof of the car. Which way should she go? Where could Greyson be? There was no way she could track him down before Titus pumped his sea of scourge out into the world, raising all of the dead, everywhere.

They were all doomed.

Under Hellbringer's hood, something whined, as if stirring from a deep sleep. Despite the fact that part of her was indescribably happy to see the speed demon again, Dru couldn't contain her frustration. She slapped one hand on the hood. "Shush," she said.

Then she walked away and paced the shadowy floor. "Where is he?"

she wondered out loud. "I don't have my copper circle or my candle. I can't cast the spell again. The clock is ticking. There's like a hundred miles of tunnels in this place. It's impossible. Do you know where Greyson is?" She directed this last question at Hellbringer's black angular snout.

The speed demon, of course, said nothing.

Dru squeezed her eyes shut and pinched the skin between her eyebrows, fighting off the feeling of soul-crushing defeat. "Even if I walk out the door right now, I don't even know whether to go left or right."

A yellow light bathed her for a moment, then winked out and came on again.

She opened her eyes, confused. The light clicked on and off, surrounding her in a pulsing amber glow.

Hellbringer's left turn signal blinked steadily on and off. As she stared, Hellbringer's engine coughed and rumbled to life. The hot blast of its exhaust blew off the last tatters of webbing, sending them twirling away into the darkness.

She remembered when Hellbringer had come on its own to find them in the depths of the mountains. It knew, instinctively, where Greyson was. Hellbringer could take her to him.

"Do you know where Greyson is?" Dru shouted over the pounding roar of the engine. "Where is he?"

The driver's door swung open.

Heart thudding, Dru stepped around the door and sank into the cool depths of the driver's seat. She barely had time to place her hands on the steering wheel before the door slammed shut with a thunk as solid as a bank vault.

With a squeal of tires, Hellbringer lurched forward. Far too fast, they blasted down the length of the machine shop, shoving workbenches aside, until they made it out through the wide doorway. The tires howled like tortured banshees as Hellbringer turned and lunged down the left-hand tunnel.

32

BACK IN BLACK

As Hellbringer hurtled down the deserted tunnels, headlights burning through the darkness, Dru kept a wide-eyed lookout for Rane or Salem. But she saw no one, not even a single undead creature. Somehow, that made her even more nervous.

She couldn't tell how deep they were underground, but as the rough rock walls flew by, she could practically feel the weight of the mountain bearing down on her. It made it hard to breathe. Hard to think. Or maybe it was just the fear of what she might find.

The tunnel widened and tilted steeply down. They passed a gauntlet of walled-off machinery, then rumbled over a series of steel strips that turned out to be the tracks for massive sliding doors. A moment later, they emerged into a low-ceilinged chamber that extended out beyond the range of the headlights.

Hellbringer's tires crunched on gravel as they approached what at first resembled the edge of a cliff drop-off. But when the headlights caught the crests of distant waves and the light reflected back at them, Dru realized what she was really looking at: a vast underground lake.

But it wasn't water that sloshed and rolled as far as the eye could see. It was scourge. Black, oily, foul. So much scourge that the very air was thick with the stench of death and decay.

Ahead of them, a cluster of perhaps two dozen undead creatures marched steadily down the gravel beach and waded into the toxic scourge, disappearing one by one as the blackness swallowed them up.

Each creature towed a thick line of webbing behind it, and each line was firmly attached to a man wrapped in webs.

Dru blinked in shock, hardly able to believe it.

It was Greyson.

His arms and chest were wrapped up like a straitjacket. He fought against the tangle of webbing that dragged him inexorably toward the lake. Kicking, twisting, digging his bootheels into the gravel, he succeeded only in slowing down the undead. But he couldn't stop them.

Hellbringer's engine roared as the speed demon raced to attack the undead creatures. The car charged straight toward the lake.

"No!" Dru leaned forward and placed her hand on the textured black dashboard. "Forget them. Run over the webs instead. Can you do that?"

Hellbringer ignored her and charged resolutely toward the undead, the obvious enemy.

"The webs!" Dru ordered, trying in vain to turn the wheel. It wouldn't budge. "I can cut him loose! Stop right on the webs, pin them down, or he'll die!"

At the last second, Hellbringer relented and turned, kicking up sprays of gravel as it skidded across the beach and stopped. Its front tires flattened the ropy strands of webbing to the ground.

As one, the undead creatures lurched, their forward momentum instantly halted. Before they had a chance to turn and slog back out of the black scourge, Dru slid out of the car onto the gravel. Spectrolite flaring to life in her hand, she slashed at the dozen or so ropes of shimmering webbing.

As Dru hacked away, the thick silver strands snapped and whispered away into the lake. The undead, all knee-deep or farther in, foundered in the oily scourge. One by one, they slipped beneath the gurgling surface.

Dru scrambled around the front of the car. From beneath the other tire, taut yards of webbing led to where Greyson lay on the ground, his entire torso wrapped up in black-speckled webs.

"Dru!" He sounded just as shocked as she felt.

She knelt at his side, momentarily stunned that she had actually found him. That he really was alive and intact. Looking down at him, she couldn't truly believe he was real until she reached out and touched the scratchy stubble on his cheek.

She didn't realize she was sobbing until she saw her tears raining down onto his web cocoon. She was so choked up that she couldn't speak.

"Shh, it's okay," he said, over and over. "Can you cut me loose?"

"Yes, yes, sorry." She sniffed and wiped at her eyes before easing the glowing spectrolite blade through the webbing, carefully cutting it away. When his arms were free, he wrapped them around her and held her tight.

"I thought I'd never see you again," she blubbered into his shoulder. Then she straightened up, trying to get ahold of herself. "Why did you leave?" she demanded, still sniffling. "Why did you drive off like that?"

His glowing red eyes stared up at her sadly. "Look at me. I'm still cursed. I couldn't drag you back into all that. I couldn't ruin your chance to have a normal life."

She blinked away tears. "I don't care about any of that. I don't. Cursed or not, you're still you. And I could never push you away, no matter what." She ran her fingers through his hair. "I need you with me."

He cracked a smile, his stubbled cheeks dimpling. "That's the best thing I've heard in a long time." Then he squinted one glowing red eye at her. "What happened to your glasses?"

"Oh." She touched her face. "I got contacts. What do you think?"

Still smiling, he said, "Get the rest of these webs off me and I'll show you what I think."

"Oh. Right." She cut away more webs. They left behind a sticky residue, like an old price sticker. "How did you end up down here?"

"Some guy in red," Greyson said as she worked to free him. "He kept going on about his destiny. Said I wasn't worthy of you." He studied her face, as if searching for the answer to an unasked question.

She nodded, unable to stop the tears. "You are so worthy," she whispered, her voice rough.

When she finally freed him from the last of the web, he sat up and wrapped her in his arms again. His strength pushed away all the fear, all the danger, making her feel safe and secure. For the briefest moment, there was only the two of them, and she could have stayed that way forever.

She had never wanted to kiss him so badly as she did now. She turned her face to his.

In the distance, a deep voice bellowed, *"Drusy!"*

Her head snapped around to look.

Titus stomped along the beach toward them. His slicked-back hair had come undone, hanging around his head in disarray. His red double-breasted jacket was gone, leaving him in a torn white shirt smudged with dirt. He marched toward them with crazed fury in his eyes, his gloved fists bunched at his sides.

Greyson stood up and pulled her to her feet, standing protectively in front of her. "Stay back. This guy's bad news."

"Let me talk to him." She put a reassuring hand on Greyson's arm, then slipped her spectrolite into the open zippered pocket of his leather jacket. Carefully, she stepped around him and held out her open hands to show Titus that she was unarmed.

"*Drusy!*" he shouted, closing fast. "Why did you betray me? *Why?*"

Behind her, Greyson murmured, "Drusy?"

"He's a friend," Dru said, realizing that that explanation only made things sound worse. "An *old* friend." That was even worse. She cringed. "I'll tell you later."

Still marching toward them, Titus pointed one gloved finger at her. "This is not the way it's supposed to be. You were brought to me for a reason. You have a responsibility. To the world."

Dru held up her empty hands. "Yes. I do have a responsibility. To *save* the world. Not destroy it."

"You're under the misapprehension that those are two separate concepts. Your thinking is too literal." Titus shook his fist. "The world is going to end—"

"No!" Dru shouted. "It's not too late. You think the solution is to go with the flow and help make doomsday happen? It's not. You've dreamed up this convoluted prophecy to explain why you have these powers that you yourself admitted to me that you *hate*. You remember that? You got stuck with a bad power, Titus, and I'm sorry about that. But there is no cryptic master plan forcing you to kill people."

"There *is* a master plan." Titus stopped near the shore, planting his booted feet. He spread his arms wide, to encompass the vast lake before them. "And *I* am the master."

Dru held her thumb and forefinger an inch apart. "You want to take it down just a notch? Please? Let's step into the way-back machine and go way back to those days at my old apartment, when I was trying to help you get rid of your powers. Do you remember that? You remember how you trusted me back then? Because I was trying to help you then. And I haven't changed. I can still help you get rid of this power."

"Get *rid* of it?" He sounded as if she had slapped him.

"Yes. You got the short end of the sorcery stick, okay? And I feel bad for you. Anyone would. But sometimes bad things just happen."

Titus shook his head. "That's only your perception. In the grander scheme of things, all of this is happening for a reason. All of this was meant to be."

"Listen, you have a choice about what you do with your power. We all do," Dru said. "That's what's called free will. None of us are locked into one unchanging destiny. Life isn't a railroad, Titus. It's an open road. And ultimately, where we go is up to us."

"Bravo." He clapped slowly, looking unimpressed. "A clever bit of philosophy."

"Well, the railroad thing is from a box of herbal tea, actually. But that's not the point."

"I was given this power for a reason," Titus said emphatically. "I met you for a reason. Our existence, meeting here, at this moment before doomsday, that can't be a coincidence."

"Sure it can. Weird stuff happens all the time. I mean, look at me, I thought I was going to marry a dentist and settle down in Highlands Ranch and drive a minivan to soccer practice." She glanced over her shoulder at Greyson, who lifted an eyebrow in response. She patted his hand, and then turned back to Titus. "But instead, I'm a mile underground in a nuclear bunker arguing with you about the end of the world. I mean, come on, that's just a teensy bit weird, right? That's what happens."

"You can't avoid your destiny." Titus took a step closer. "It all adds up, Drusy, everything. My power. The Harbingers. The speed demon. The apocalypse scroll."

"Where is the apocalypse scroll?" Greyson called out, startling her.

Titus ignored him. "And now you're down here with me, Drusy. A crystal sorceress who can open up the gate to the netherworld. You have to know why the bunker is located here. You felt it when you stepped into the entrance, didn't you?"

Immediately, Dru knew what he was talking about. That subtle shift in the air she'd felt when she first stepped into the mountain tunnel. The sudden, sticky clamminess against her skin, as if she stood on the brink of another world. At the thought of it, goose bumps raised on her arms.

"These mountains are riddled with potential gateways," Titus said. "That's the reason for the crystals. The vivianite and all the rest. Everything I've done, it's all for you. So you can help me bring doomsday to the world, the way it's supposed to be." He held out his gloved hands, as if expecting she would run down the beach and leap into his arms. "That's why you're here. To help me."

"No," Dru said flatly. She could hear the coldness in her own voice, but she couldn't disguise it. The way he turned this all around and laid it at her feet filled her with revulsion. "I'll never help you."

"Of course you will. It's our destiny. Why else would you be here?"

She hesitated before she answered, but it was the only answer she could give. "I'm here to stop you."

Slowly, the manic confidence faded from Titus's eyes, replaced by a growing fury. As the cold rage spread across his features, Dru had the horrible sinking realization that she had gone too far. There was no talking Titus down from the ledge now.

He turned and raised his arms out over the scourge lake. The oily surface splashed and slopped, as if stirred from deep below. A foul wind sprang up, rippling across the shimmering black waves, tugging at Dru's hair and sequined dress.

Over the cold buffeting wind, Dru shouted, "I don't want to fight you, Titus!"

If he heard her, he gave no sign. He just stepped closer to the edge of the lake, raising his arms higher. The oily black scourge surged up like a rising tidal wave, a wall of filthy, toxic darkness that made her knees go weak with fear. Five feet high, then ten, and it kept growing.

"*No!*" Dru shouted, unable to keep the panic out of her voice. "Titus, *stop!*"

Behind her, Hellbringer's engine roared. Without warning, the demon car leaped past her, its back wheels spitting gravel as it charged directly at Titus. She didn't know what had spurred the speed demon into action. Maybe it was her fearful shout that triggered some kind of protective instinct in Hellbringer. Or perhaps the demon car simply took advantage of Titus's distraction to get revenge for its imprisonment.

In the end, it didn't matter why Hellbringer attacked. There was nowhere for Titus to run. Too late, Dru realized what was about to happen.

"Hellbringer, no!" She watched, horrified, as the car rammed into Titus, flipping him up over the windshield as it drove past. The impact sent him flying, howling in pain, toward the scourge. Titus's angry shout cut off abruptly as he plunged headfirst into the black lake and disappeared.

Hellbringer spun around, its tires carving long, curved gouges in the beach. It slowly crept back along the shoreline, like a hunting animal stalking its prey. But Titus was nowhere to be seen. Waves roiled unabated across the black surface of the lake.

The buffeting wind continued, and over it Dru could just make out a chorus of squeals from the scourge, sounding satisfied as it presumably devoured Titus.

With an effort, Dru pulled her hands away from her face, where they had flown the moment Hellbringer started moving. She couldn't believe what had just happened. A terrible trembling began somewhere deep inside her, propelled by emotions too violent to rein in. Disgust. Anger. Regret. All of them mixed with a rush of relief that Titus was gone, and she felt deeply ashamed for that. The man had to be dead.

"Oh, my God," she whispered. "What did we just do?"

Greyson put his arms around her and pulled her close. But even his presence couldn't reassure her. She couldn't be a part of killing someone. Not even Titus. As horrible as he had been, part of her still believed he could've been saved. She stared with horror out at the swirling black lake.

"Just to set the record straight," Greyson said, his voice rumbling through his chest, "Titus had that coming."

Dru shook her head. "No. Nobody deserves that."

"Should've told him that before his skeletons tried to take me water-skiing." Greyson released her. "Come on. Let's get out of here."

Together, they walked down the beach toward the demon-possessed car. Seeing it waiting for them, sinister and black, reminded Dru why she had initially feared Hellbringer. And why she could never forget that. It was, after all, a demon.

Seeing her apprehension, Greyson paused before opening the door for her. "Look, I'm sorry about Titus. But you tried your best. What really matters now is that we're safe."

Despite her misgivings, she had to nod. "You're right. We are safe."

As Dru started to get in the car, a deep gurgling sound from the lake made the hairs on the back of her neck stand up. She turned to see the scourge rise up like a black wall, towering over them. At the crest of it, she could clearly see a human form suspended in the oil, arms out-stretched, head tilted down to glare at her.

Titus.

"Get in!" Greyson got behind the wheel and revved the engine.

As they raced up the beach, Dru turned to watch the vast wave of scourge crash behind them, painting the gravel pitch black. The massive wave rose up again, chasing them like a vast, hungry creature about to devour them.

33

NEVER LET GO

Engine revving, Hellbringer charged headlong through the tunnels. Close behind them, the earth shook as the flood of black scourge crashed through the underground complex.

"Titus isn't dead," Dru realized out loud. "He's alive inside the scourge. And now he's even more powerful than before."

Greyson glanced over at her before returning his attention to the tunnel. Evenly spaced lights in the ceiling streaked past the windshield. "That black stuff looked pretty deadly to me."

"Deadly for people like you and me, yes. But Titus is different. He's a necromancer. He has absolute control over the scourge. And now he's become, I don't know, *one* with it. I saw his face." She turned around in the seat to see through the back window. Behind them, the rising flood snuffed out the tunnel lights behind them, one after another.

The sight terrified her.

"He's in there. He's part of it now," she said. "We have to find a way to stop him before he escapes this place and triggers doomsday."

They rapidly approached a T-intersection, and Greyson spun the wheel, sending them squealing down the left tunnel. The rock walls flashed by in the headlight beams.

"Do you know where we're going?" Dru asked.

Greyson's glowing red gaze cut up to the rearview mirror. "Away from that. Fast as possible. But if we hit a dead end, we're in trouble. Any ideas?"

"Hang on. I can find a way out of here." Dru pulled the wadded-up blueprint out of the grimy leather tool bag and unfolded it in her lap. Between the intermittent darkness and the lurching motion of the car, it was impossible to read.

Then a map light clicked on, and suddenly Dru could see. She patted the dashboard. "Thanks, Hellbringer."

"That was me," Greyson said, pulling his hand back from the light switch. "Another tunnel coming up. Which way?"

She ran her fingers frantically over the map, smoothing out the creases, trying to figure out exactly where they were. They had just come from one of the three lakes, so that narrowed it down. She remembered the walled-off machinery they had passed. Generators, maybe? She looked for the rectangles on the map.

"Two options," Greyson said, his voice tight. "Slow down and get caught, or take the wrong tunnel and get trapped. I don't like either one."

"Don't slow down, whatever you do! If that scourge catches us—"

"*Which way?* Left or right?"

Dru looked up from the map. Ahead, the tunnel split. Yellow numbers were stenciled on the walls of each tunnel, but she couldn't read them at the speed they were going. She had only seconds to decide.

"Dru?"

She found the intersection on the map. "Right, right! Go right!"

Greyson nudged the wheel, and they shot into the right-hand tunnel. As the yellow stenciled numbers flashed past Dru's window, she saw her error. "Shoot. I meant left."

Greyson smacked the steering wheel. "No time to turn around. It's right behind us."

As he spoke, the flood of scourge slammed into the intersection behind them, spraying off the corner and filling the tunnel. Hellbringer's engine picked up speed, and they powered uphill through the curving tunnel.

"Okay, okay," Dru said, running her fingers across the map, tracing various branches through the miles-long tunnels, trying to find a way back to the entrance. The complex wasn't designed to be easy to navigate. Most of the tunnels led to isolated branches and ended abruptly. If she accidentally steered them down one of those, they were done for. "At the next branch, go left, and then take another left."

He did, and a few seconds later, he took the next left.

"We keep passing these closed hatches," Greyson said as they streaked past a pair of closed blast doors, their striped edges sealed tight. "Looks like steel. Too tough to break through."

"He must have sealed the doors to channel the scourge out the front door." Dru followed the arrows Titus had drawn on the schematic in black pen. They all converged on the main entrance, where a single arrow in heavy black marker pointed off the edge of the paper. "If we can't contain the scourge, it will flow out into the rivers and lakes. Eventually it will hit the oceans, poisoning the water around the world, raising the dead from their graves. Everyone will die."

"Everyone who drinks the water?"

"Everyone. Everywhere." She met his gaze. "If the scourge doesn't get them, a worldwide plague of undead will."

His jaw flexed, and he nodded once. "So you're saying our survival is secondary. We have to stop the flood, dead or alive."

A cold wave of fear washed over her. He was right.

Just ahead of them, the right side of the tunnel wall fractured and burst apart. Black scourge gushed through, blasting boulder-sized chunks of stone into the tunnel. Trapping them.

Instantly, Greyson yanked the gearshift and swung the wheel.

Hellbringer's engine howled in protest, and the left wheels lurched up onto the wall.

Dru's stomach dropped as they tilted nearly sideways. With a crunch of steel and a spray of sparks, they scraped past the rocks.

She had an up close view of the tunnel floor as the scourge flooded over it. The black wave slammed against the broken rocks inches from her window.

They hit the floor on the far side, skidding at a nauseating angle into the wall. Hellbringer's nose clipped the rough stone, jolting Dru and sending her rock-filled tool bag careening against her ankles. She bounced off Greyson's outstretched arm as he held her against the seat.

He released her and straightened Hellbringer out. They shot away down the tunnel. He nailed the gas, and the gauges on the dashboard swung into the red.

Greyson said, "We've got to get—" But the rest of his words were drowned out by a chest-thudding rumble as the tunnel started to collapse behind them.

Rattled, Dru fought the urge to look back. Her fingers shook on the map. Swallowing down her fear, she forced herself to focus. "It's a straight shot from here until we pass through a bunch of stone columns."

Dru paused as her finger traced past Titus's library. Unless he had sealed that door too, all of those artifacts would be destroyed by the scourge. All of the Harbingers' research. All of the magical books, including the Wicked Scriptures. All of it, lost in the thundering flood of black oil that filled the tunnel behind them.

And where was the apocalypse scroll? Was it in his library? Could they risk turning around to look for it?

No, she decided. They had to keep going. All the way to the main entrance. Looking at it now on the map, she spotted a pair of penciled-in symbols she had missed before. The first resembled football uprights turned upside down. The second was a circle with a diagonal line drawn through it.

She recognized the sorcio signs from the Harbingers' mansion in the desert.

"*Sekura koridoro*," she translated out loud. "Secure passageway. Holy Shatner. It's a portal to the netherworld." She stabbed her finger down on the map. "No matter what, we have to get to the main entrance before the scourge does."

"Can do." Greyson's red eyes ticked up to the rearview mirror. "For now, we're gaining on it."

She looked back. At this speed, Hellbringer was outracing the flood. "We're going to need at least a minute head start for me to open the portal."

Gripping the wheel, he glanced over at her, a wordless question on his face.

She pulled the chunky green vivianite crystal out of the tool bag. "The moment we get out of the main entrance, stop the car. I'm going to open the portal and suck that bad mojo behind us right into the nether-world. All of it."

"Will that work?"

She nodded. "Scourge comes from the netherworld, originally. We can send it back there. The netherworld is a wasteland that devours everything. Sorcerers have used it as their dumping ground for millennia. If we're going to get rid of this scourge, that's where it needs to go." She didn't add that this was also the only plan she had. "Just get us to the entrance. No matter what happens. I mean it."

Greyson nodded grimly.

Hellbringer's roaring engine dropped a notch as the tunnel curved tightly uphill. Ahead, the way was strangely lit by the hot golden glow of firelight.

The tunnel opened into a vast chamber supported by chiseled stone columns. Dru recognized it as the place where she'd found the spray-painted symbols.

But instead of a dark and moldy maze, the chamber was now filled with a horde of undead creatures. And they were on fire.

Greyson slowed the car as they approached the flaming mob. Dozens of burning creatures, like skeletal bonfires, staggered blindly into each other or collided with the stone columns and collapsed into piles of smoking bones.

As Dru watched, oddly fascinated, a large metal drum tumbled end over end through the air. The drum sailed in a long arc overhead until it smashed against a stone column at the edge of the firelight. Bending in half on impact, it rained a spray of liquid down on the stumbling horde below.

In a blinding rush, greedy flames leaped from one creature to the next, setting them ablaze. They raised skeletal arms in confusion. Oily yellow flames raced up their web wrapping, reducing them to glowing cinders.

"No way around the fire," Greyson muttered. "We'll have to go straight through, fast as we can."

Dru spotted movement in the middle of the burning horde. "Hold on." To get a better view, she quickly cranked down her window, undid her seat belt, and pulled herself halfway out of the car. She squinted through the smoke.

Something moved quickly among the undead. A person. Made out of metal.

Rane.

Surrounded by the burning mob of undead, Rane swung some kind of huge club, smashing creatures left and right. But for each one she struck down, more crowded to take its place. No matter how many creatures she destroyed, she couldn't fight them all. There were too many.

Dru ducked back into the car. "It's Rane! We have to get her! Go!"

Hellbringer leaped forward. "Brace yourself," Greyson said.

As they raced toward the burning crowd, Dru started to put on her seat belt, but stopped. Maybe she shouldn't buckle into the seat if they were going to pick up Rane at high speed. Hellbringer only had two doors. And her window was still open. Before she could decide what to do, they hit the flames.

Hellbringer's long nose plowed through the blazing crowd, scattering flaming bones in all directions. The tires thudded and bumped as they drove over creatures and bashed the rest aside. In moments, they passed through the flames and reached the hollow center of the horde.

"Rane!" Coughing on the smoke-filled air, Dru got out before the car had completely shrieked to a halt. "Come on!"

Struck speechless, Rane stood openmouthed, still as a statue, shimmering like steel in the firelight. The tip of her long club drooped until it hit the floor at her feet with an iron clang.

Salem appeared from behind her, his face smudged with soot, cradling one arm as if wounded. For the first time ever, he actually looked relieved to see Dru. "Our ride is here," he said to Rane, as if he had somehow planned this all along.

Rane's disbelieving stare roamed the length of Hellbringer until it came to rest on Greyson sitting in the driver's seat. "No . . . *way*."

"Way," Dru said. She grabbed Salem by his good arm. "Into the back seat, big shot."

The hissing horde pressed closer around them. Streamers of web flashed past them, then sizzled as they caught fire. Rane shook herself and swung the club left and right, bashing creatures to pieces.

Dru wedged herself into the back seat beside Salem.

Rane climbed into the front, making Hellbringer's springs groan in protest. She slammed the door just as the burning creatures reached the car. The engine roared, and the sudden acceleration shoved them back into their seats.

Tires howling, Hellbringer plowed through the other side of the burning crowd and broke through into the dark tunnel beyond. One creature, missing everything below its rib cage, clambered up the length of the hood to press its flaming skull against the windshield.

One swipe of the chrome windshield wipers knocked it off. It bounced off the side mirror before spinning away behind them, leaving burning streaks in Dru's vision.

"Hurry. The flood of scourge can't be far behind us." Dru turned to look Salem over. "Are you okay? Are you bleeding?"

"He lost his powers," Rane said in a pouty stage whisper, reaching back to pat Salem's knee with one metal hand. "Poor little guy. Had too much to drink."

"So lovely we can all share this moment." Salem scowled. "But don't worry about me. Worry about them." He nodded his chin toward the windshield.

"Hang on!" Greyson said. Hellbringer's engine raced.

34

HOW THE GODS KILL

A pack of round yellow headlights stared back at Dru from the tunnel ahead. Motorcycles, at least twenty of them, each one ridden by a web-shrouded creature. They filled the width of the tunnel, cutting off all escape as they hurtled straight toward Hellbringer.

For some reason, Dru expected Hellbringer to stop. But either Greyson or the car itself hit the gas, charging forward.

"Brace yourself!" Greyson gripped the steering wheel hard enough to turn his knuckles white.

Dru planted her hands against the back of Rane's passenger seat, hoping her metal body would protect her. "Roll up the window!" Dru said. But Rane's four-foot length of iron rail jutted out through the open window, and she didn't let go of it.

At the last second, the motorcycle gang split and swerved around them, but not all of the riders were quick enough. One fell beneath the car's pointed nose, and Hellbringer bumped over it as if it were nothing more than a railroad crossing. The last bike rode up the long nose and hit the windshield. White spiderweb cracks fractured the glass.

A crash resounded through the car's roof as the motorcycle tumbled overhead and flew off the back of the car, scattering across the tunnel floor behind them in pieces.

The rest of the undead gang quickly regrouped and turned around to chase after them. In seconds, the motorcycles would catch up to Hellbringer.

Dru leaned up between the seats. "Can you outrun them?"

"Don't be ridiculous," Salem muttered. "They're too fast."

"We need to hit a straightaway," Greyson said as the cracks popped and vanished from the windshield. "In the curves, I can try and mash them against the wall. Hellbringer will heal. But if we crash, that's bad news for the rest of us. There's no way to fight them off."

As he steered them around the next curve, Rane gave him a look as if he'd made the dumbest statement in the world. "Dude, why do you think I brought this little flyswatter along?" She hefted the iron rail.

Greyson's red eyes looked up in the rearview mirror. "I can try to hug my wall. Give you some room to fight." He glanced at Rane. "Think you can hold them off until we get out of this tunnel?"

"That's a joke, right?"

"Then you're on." Greyson steered Hellbringer inches from the left wall, preventing the undead from coming up on the driver's side.

Rane pulled herself up to sit on the edge of the passenger door, facing backward, hanging onto the roof with one hand.

"Careful!" Dru yelled as the first motorcycle charged up beside them.

The rider raised one black-clawed hand. Webbing swirled into existence in its palm.

Rane swung the iron club like a tennis racket, knocking the skeletal rider cleanly off the back of the seat.

For a moment, the empty motorcycle popped a wheelie, tatters of webs flapping in the wind as its front wheel lifted up and over. Then it toppled, crumpling into twisted wreckage as it shed speed and fell behind them.

The other riders swerved around the wreck, pale headlights burning in the darkness of the tunnel. Then they surged forward to fill the gap.

Salem leaned across Dru to yell at Rane. "Get back inside! It's too dangerous!"

Rane ignored him.

The lead undead creature passed Hellbringer's tail wing and raised one clawed hand. It shot out a stream of webbing that smacked into the iron club and nearly wrenched it from Rane's hand. She held on tighter.

"Let it go!" Salem called.

"Screw that!" Rane yelled back. Hooking her metal feet inside the edge of the window, she whipped the iron club around in a circle. The motorcycle, pulled taut by the web, veered and swung into the wall like a tetherball on a string. It disintegrated into pieces, sending web-wrapped chunks of flaming wreckage flying in all directions. The explosion thinned the pack by two more motorcycles.

Grinning furiously, Rane let out a primal yell. "*Yeah!*"

The rest of the motorcycles squeezed close together, firing a volley of shimmering webs that smacked into Rane's arm, shoulder, and chest. They started to pull her out of the car.

"Look out!" Dru grabbed one of Rane's legs, and Salem grabbed the other, desperately trying to hold her in place. But since the woman was made of solid iron, there wasn't much they could do.

"Damn boneheads," Rane swore under her breath. She tried to twist loose from the webs, but more snagged her as the undead creatures kept firing. She lost her grip on the iron club, and it went clanging away down the tunnel.

Rane clung to the edge of the window frame with both hands. "D! Little help, here!"

"Just hang on!" Dru let go of Rane's leg and reached into Greyson's jacket pocket for her spectrolite blade. At first, she was too panicked to focus her magical energy into the crystal. But she forced herself to blot out the chaos around her and think only about energizing the blade. After a moment, she was rewarded with a glimmer of rainbow-colored light.

Even that small delay was too much. Rane momentarily lost her grip and went flying out the window.

"*No!*" Salem yelled. Dru screamed in fear.

Legs kicking in the air, Rane caught the trailing edge of the open window. Her heels bounced off the tunnel floor, sending up twin bursts of fiery sparks. Then the undead webs snagged her legs, too, stretching her out to her full length along the outside of the car.

Dru clambered into the front seat and leaned out into the buffeting wind. She slashed at the webs. The glowing spectrolite cast rippling streaks of rainbow light across Rane's metal face and arms.

But she could only reach as far as Rane's shoulders and back. Dru couldn't get to her legs. Frustrated, she tried to figure out how she could climb up onto the roof to cut the rest of the webs.

Rane hung onto the rear edge of the window frame by her fingertips. Her biceps bulged. Her lips drew back from her teeth as she grimaced, fighting to hold onto the side of the car.

More webs shot out from the tight pack of motorcycles, snagging Rane's feet.

The sheet metal surrounding the window started to bend, dimpling beneath Rane's metal fingertips. Black paint flaked and flew off, sucked away by the high-speed wind.

"I can't reach!" Dru fought down her rising panic. "I can't reach the webs! You have to—"

"D." Rane's breathy voice was oddly quiet and urgent. Its intensity cut through the howling wind. "D. Look at me."

Dru paused just long enough to meet her ferocious gaze.

Hellbringer's sheet metal squealed as it bent. "Save the world. Okay?"

As Dru opened her mouth to reply, the sheet metal gave away, ripping loose.

And Rane was gone.

Dru caught only a shocked glimpse of her tumbling iron body ricocheting through the tunnel in the red glow of the taillights, smashing the gang of motorcycles apart like a human cannonball.

Dru had known Rane long enough to know how much punishment her metal body could absorb. But this was far beyond anything she'd seen Rane take. Too much for anyone to survive.

Horrified, Dru stared into the empty darkness where Rane had vanished. Unwilling to comprehend what she had just seen.

Now free of the webs, Hellbringer charged ahead, engine howling, leaving the undead far behind them.

For Dru, the world went silent.

Hair flying, Dru hung out the window, shouting into the cold blackness behind them. "*Rane!*" She reached into the empty air, grasping at the wind as the tunnel swallowed her friend's broken body.

She was only dimly aware of a strong hand gripping the back of her dress, trying to keep her from falling out of the car.

Greyson pulled her, sobbing, back inside Hellbringer. In from the wind. Into the momentary reprieve that Rane had bought them with her life.

Dru pounded her fists against Greyson's shoulder. "Stop the car!" she yelled. *"Stop the car!"*

Greyson and Salem were saying words to her, urgent words that she couldn't understand. Nothing made any sense to her anymore. Her ears felt as if they were filled with a ringing pressure that would split her apart. It raged inside her, uncontrollable, inexpressible. Making it impossible to think, to comprehend anything.

Rane was *gone*. It was as if part of her had been ripped away, and the traumatized pieces that remained were left shattered and senseless, too wounded to survive.

Silvery moonlight bathed her as Hellbringer flew out the tunnel entrance. Greyson yanked the emergency brake and spun the wheel. The rear end of the car whipped around tightly, tires warbling across the gravel, until they faced back the way they had come. The sudden silence when they stopped only amplified the roaring in her ears.

Through pouring tears, Dru stared out the windshield, where the headlight beams cut through the cloud of dust raised by their passage. The open mouth of the tunnel entrance gaped at them in a wordless scream, the two radiation signs above it glaring down like Titus's crazed eyes.

Any moment, the black scourge would fill up the rest of the tunnel and come shooting out at them, disgorging certain death and destruction to millions of innocent lives.

Part of Dru wanted it to happen. As long as it swept her away in the flood, too, ending this unbearable pain. Because she knew she would spend the rest of her life seeing the final look in Rane's eyes.

Was it fear? Bravery? Both?

She would never know for sure. Because Rane was gone.

"D. Look at me."

She was lying somewhere in that tunnel, among the shattered undead. As the tidal wave of scourge filled up the bunker. And here, outside, Dru didn't feel she deserved to survive.

"Save the world. Okay?"

Dru stared into the darkness, trying in vain to blink away the stream of burning tears. The crushing pressure in her chest made it feel impossible to breathe. She couldn't inhale. She felt as if she would pass out.

Greyson pressed the green vivianite crystal into her cold hands, and she realized he was saying her name. Saying something about the portal. The netherworld. The scourge.

She stared down at the blocky green crystal in her hands. The seconds were ticking away. She had to act. She had to do this.

Right now.

With leaden arms, she opened the door and climbed out. Her chunky boot kicked the tool bag and spilled out the lump of brain-shaped calcite she had found earlier. With a thump, it landed on the dirty gravel and lay there gleaming in the moonlight like a misshapen skull.

She bent and picked it up as Greyson and Salem got out of the car. Calcite, raw from the cave wall like this, helped cure a hangover. She remembered her plan to cure the sorcerers drugged with Titus's spiked drink.

Sorcerers like Salem.

He sagged against the car, ashen-faced and stunned, eyes bloodshot and brimming with grief.

A glint of gold shone in the moonlight through the gaps in his slashed shirt. His protective amulet. She couldn't afford to let its shielding powers interfere with what she was about to do to him.

"Take off the amulet." Her voice cracked. "This is going to hurt." Then she shoved the green vivianite crystal back into Greyson's hands, as she held on tight to the white calcite.

Salem stared at her in shocked silence, uncomprehending.

Dru reached around the back of his neck and ripped the amulet off by its leather cord, then tossed it aside. In her other hand, she charged up the calcite until it glowed like a light bulb.

Then she thrust it against the center of Salem's chest.

He gasped and staggered back against the car, writhing in pain, but she kept the crystal planted against his sternum. Faint pin-scratching sounds filled the air as wormlike threads of darkness left Salem's body, drawn into the glowing calcite. They swirled and dispersed, turning the crystal dingy and speckled.

In moments, the glow faded from the calcite and it began to smoke like a snuffed candle. Dru cast it away into the darkness. "You're cured." She pointed at the tunnel entrance. Unable to keep the pleading tone out of her voice, she said, "Get her out of there."

Salem slowly raised his hands in front of his face. Magical sparks crackled between his long fingers, throwing his sharp features into relief. His eyes lit with a mad fury, and he charged toward the tunnel entrance, bellowing Rane's name at the top of his lungs.

35

EVERYTHING ENDS

Dru chased after Salem as he bolted toward the tunnel entrance, the tails of his black trench coat flapping behind him like the wings of some vast primordial creature.

He skidded to a stop outside the thick, saw-toothed edges of the open blast doors. Throwing his arms open wide, he raised his hands, long fingers outstretched. The air rippled around his fingertips.

Dru stopped short, breathing hard, as the cold air around them quickly warmed from the intensity of the spell. An unsettling pressure squeezed against her eardrums.

Debris flew out of the tunnel, pulled by Salem's magic. Broken bones from the undead, chunks of rock from the walls, twisted motorcycle parts. They all came hurtling out of the darkness into the moonlight, tumbling end over end until they sailed off into the dry grass.

An arcane glow surrounded Salem. The air itself began to shimmer with unseen energy so that every mote of dust lit from within, like starlight.

Dru backed away from the unearthly glow. Unidentifiable chunks of wreckage shot out of the tunnel, streaking by too fast to see. They blew rapid-fire holes in the gravel road around her feet, kicking up sprays of dirt like stray bullets. The noise was deafening.

Greyson stepped in front of Dru and pulled her to him, sheltering her with his broad back. Over the noise of the impacts, he yelled, "Get back in the car!"

"No!" Dru shook her head, not sure whether he could hear her. "I have to open the portal!"

He pushed the blocky green vivianite crystal into her hands. "Then do it. Right now. Before the flood catches up to us."

"No!" Her insides tightened with fear. "Not as long as there's any chance of getting Rane back!"

He stared down at her with his glowing red eyes, looking deep into her as if trying to determine whether she knew how much she was risking with every moment of delay.

She knew. She was risking everything. Risking everyone.

A voice inside her insisted that the fate of the world was far more important than any one of them. In fact, she was pretty sure that Salem had said that to her once. But even he wasn't going to give up on Rane.

It tortured Dru, knowing that opening the portal right now was supposed to be the right answer. But if she did, and there was any chance Rane was still alive, then she would guarantee that Rane was lost forever. And Dru couldn't doom her friend. It wasn't who she was.

Not if there was the slimmest chance of saving her.

After a moment, the look in Greyson's eyes changed from warning to admiration. He nodded slightly and pulled her close again. "I've got you," he shouted. Something bounced off his back, and he grunted. But he didn't budge.

Despite the danger, Dru couldn't resist peeking past his shoulder into the depths of the tunnel, straining for a glimpse of Rane in the darkness.

Or the scourge. It was in there, somewhere, flooding through the underground complex. Rushing up at them. How much time did they have?

Minutes? Seconds?

All of the wreckage that littered the final miles of the tunnel came flying out at them. Salem's magic pulled out countless bones flapping with webs, spinning motorcycle tires, twisted lengths of metal, jagged chunks of rock. They all catapulted out, streaking past them to clatter across the mountainside like an avalanche.

Staggering under the strain of his spell, Salem dropped to one knee. His arms shook, but they didn't lower. His long fingers spread even wider, and brilliant sparks danced around them, leaving jagged afterimages in Dru's vision. The motes of dust streaking past Salem burst into flame and burned out like scattered cinders. The air itself smelled charred by magic.

High-speed debris struck Greyson's back and bounced off his leather jacket, shoving him. But it didn't knock him off his feet. He held Dru tighter, protecting her.

Dru knew that Salem needed help, needed to increase his power even further. But there was nothing she could do. Even if she had some sort of crystal she could use to boost his spell, the added impact would probably kill him. Maybe all of them.

His arms trembled with the effort. He was on the edge of collapse.

Just as Dru feared the worst, a human figure came hurtling out of the tunnel into the moonlight. A spray of blonde hair, a shimmering gold minidress wrapped in dirty webs. Rane flew out headfirst, on her back, her arms dangling at her sides like a magician's levitating assistant.

A magician's assistant who weighed as much as a professional body-builder. Who was traveling at perhaps a hundred miles an hour. Straight at them.

Salem's eyes opened wide a split second before Rane collided with him with a resounding *whump*, slamming him to the ground like a sacked quarterback. Together, they slid a half-dozen car lengths down the gravel road before grinding to a halt.

Dru's heart leaped with hope. She prayed that Rane was still alive.

The ground shook with the wet rumbling of the sea of scourge. It pounded up the tunnel toward them, sloshing off tunnel walls and cracking through fissures in the mountain rock.

Putrid air blasted out of the tunnel, kicking up curls of dust from the ground. The air was tainted with the stink of death and mold. Underground decay. Primordial filth.

Whether Rane was alive or dead—or dying in Salem's arms at this moment—Dru couldn't be there with her. She had to stop the scourge. And she had to do it now.

Hot tears welling in her eyes, Dru stepped around Greyson and faced the roaring wind. She squinted into the darkness, trying to spot the oncoming scourge as it hurtled up from the depths of the earth. The tunnel was an endless pit of shadow.

Though she couldn't see the scourge, she could sense its foul presence in the goose bumps that crawled up from the base of her spine. She felt like a caged animal sensing an oncoming earthquake, unable to escape.

Every instinct inside her screamed at her to run. To gather up Greyson and Salem and Rane's body and just flee. But if she gave in to that instinct, they were all doomed. The entire world would suffer and die.

Unless she stopped it.

She gripped the heavy green vivianite in one hand, willing her magical energy to flow into its crystalline structure, down into the very molecules that had formed it eons ago.

She pushed aside the fear, worry, the grief, and thought only of the crystal. Making it burn bright enough to rip a hole in the universe.

Part of her was sure she would fail. As much as she tried to ignore it, she knew that it was right. This was so much bigger than the portal in the desert. So much more intense than anything she'd done before. It could so quickly go wrong.

But she couldn't give in to those thoughts. She blotted out the rest of the world. The tunnel, the wind, the onrushing wave of scourge. She breathed out and focused only on merging her energy with the green crystal in her hand.

A pale green spark lit within it.

She nurtured that spark with her own energy, growing it until it burned fierce and bright. Until it burned hot in her hand.

She held out her other hand, and Greyson's fingers folded around hers. His grip was warm and strong. At his touch, a bolt of magical energy shot through his arm and flowed into her.

As she merged her energy with his, she realized how much more powerful she had become on her own—and how his touch elevated her magic far beyond anything she had known.

Although they stood stock-still, she felt as if she were running full tilt downhill, off-balance, trying to keep from falling headlong into the darkness.

Eerie light glowed around the perimeter of the tunnel as the nether-world portal wavered into existence. From somewhere beyond Dru's range of hearing, a terrifying, hellish howl came screeching through her bones.

The air in front of her rippled. Hot energy crackled across her skin, clinging to the sparkling sequins in her dress until they prickled her like scorching hot pinpoints. Unearthly light surrounded her.

In the brilliant glow, she could see the oncoming wall of black scourge filling the tunnel, rushing at her like a runaway train.

A hundred yards away. Sixty yards. Forty.

Its oily mass reflected the light of Dru's magic. She could just make out a human figure within the roiling wave, arms reaching for her, mouth open wide in a wordless shout of rage.

Titus. Or more precisely, the inhuman creature he had become.

She remembered the haunted look he had given her all those years ago, shyly peeking out from under his dark hood. The longing in his eyes when he walked into her shop and gave her the crystalline rose. The cold look of inhuman fury that twisted his features on the shore of the underground lake.

She finally understood that no matter how much she had wanted to save him, she never had a chance. Because deep down, he had never wanted to be saved. Despite his insistence that he had never lied to her, he had still hidden the truth from her until it was too late.

Whoever Titus had once been, whatever potential he once had to do good, was all gone now. Everything inside him had long ago been consumed by his madness and his thirst for power. The Titus she thought she knew was dead long before she set foot inside this mountain.

Titus came hurtling toward her, a shadowy figure riding a wave of black oil. His fingers clawed at her.

He had taken Rane from her. Tried to take away Greyson. And now he was trying to bring about the end of the world.

She wouldn't let that happen.

She channeled her despair and fury into the vivianite until it burned so brightly green that all sense of color lost meaning. It became a supernova in her hand.

A strong arm wrapped across her back, bracing her. Greyson. His strength was a primal force that filled her with a resolve that couldn't be broken. Not by Titus, not by the scourge, not by anything. Together, they stood their ground.

Tears streaming down her face, Dru charged up the portal until there was nothing but naked white light piercing through her. She fought through the roaring wind and scorching pain until she emptied every last bit of energy into the abyss.

The white heat of the portal shuddered as the vile flood slammed into it. The air itself trembled under the impact of millions of gallons of scourge.

With a deafening screech, the vortex of magical energy warped, pushing her back as it bulged outward. Dru dug the thick heels of her boots into the gravel, fearing she would be crushed by the pressure. Waves of energy pummeled through her body, bruising her, shaking her. The punishment felt as if it would never end.

Just when she had nothing left to give, the rumbling ceased. In a silence as eerie as it had been loud, the white glow of the portal faded away.

Dru's ears filled with a fine, thin ringing sound. She felt like a vessel that had poured everything out and now lay empty and discarded. Her energy ebbed away, leaving nothing behind.

Her bones felt like jelly. Her muscles shook. The burning hot vivianite in her hand sparkled and flared, as if miniature thunderstorms raged in its sapphire-green depths.

She dropped it, crackling, onto the gravel. With a gasp, she sank to her knees.

Above her, the towering archway of the tunnel entrance was as black as charcoal, and completely empty. Not a drop of scourge remained. Thick curls of gray smoke streamed up from around the edge of the entrance, trailing away into a clear night sky magnificent with blazing stars.

Gently, Greyson pulled her to her feet. "You did it," he said softly.

She could only nod weakly. Sagging against him for support, she turned and hobbled toward the others. She was about to call out to Salem, but when she saw Rane, a hard lump formed in her throat, making it impossible to speak.

36

KISS THEM FOR ME

Salem bent over Rane, his spidery fingers dancing through the air over her body. One by one, the dirty webs rippled and flew off, as if blown away by an invisible gust of wind.

Beneath, her gold dress was scuffed and ripped. Her body was covered in vicious scrapes and ugly bruises. Her bottom lip had split and spilled blood down her neck. One eye was swollen shut. But the other eye slowly opened, clear and blue and very much alive.

"Rane!" Despite her exhaustion, Dru left Greyson's side and ran the last few steps. She dropped to her knees and wrapped Rane in a crushing hug.

"Huh," Rane wheezed. "Ow."

"Sorry. Sorry." Dru sat up and wiped away tears. A dozen overwhelming feelings flooded through her at once. "You made it, you made it. Oh, my God. You're all beat up. Anything broken? Are you okay?"

A toothy grin slowly spread across Rane's face. She raised one scraped-up arm and gave Dru an enthusiastic thumbs-up. "Rock 'n' roll," she croaked.

Tears welled up in Dru's eyes and overflowed. She sat back as Salem gently tended to Rane, checking her for injuries, helping her slowly sit up.

"Ugh." Rane shook her head, visibly dazed. "Where's Todd?"

Salem sat back and gave her a sharp look. "Who the hell is Todd?"

"Freckles," Rane said weakly, then held her head in her hands, muffling her voice. "He's got my number. No, wait. Dru's number."

Salem's eyebrows furrowed dangerously, wrinkling his entire forehead. His bloodshot eyes glared at Dru.

Caught off guard, Dru scrambled to remember who Rane was talking about. "Oh! *Todd*. From the emergency room?"

Rane, still holding her head in her hands, nodded. "I need a beer. And a steak. I'm so *hungry*," she whined. "And I need Todd."

At Salem's withering stare, Dru shrugged. "That's just her doctor. Not like another boyfriend or something." She winced, deciding maybe it would be better to stay quiet.

"Hey. Hey, you." Rane brushed dirt and debris off Salem's black silk collar and raised her hand to his cheek. "You *are* a big deal."

"I know," he said, gently holding her, but still scowling. "Of course. I know."

"Got anything to eat?" Rane whispered.

Looking serious, Salem started to answer, until Rane pulled him down and kissed him.

Dru blinked. After all this time, she hadn't expected that.

"Dru!" Opal's voice echoed from down the road. She emerged from the darkness, hobbling on her sassy honeybee platform sandals. Ruiz followed along beside her, laughing and clapping.

Greyson bent down and pulled Dru to her feet. Every muscle in her body ached in protest.

Opal's smile was huge as she swept Dru into a vaguely boozy-smelling hug. "You okay, honey? You all right?" Opal took a step back and planted one hand on her hip. As she looked Greyson up and down, her jaw dropped open in shock. "Greyson! I can't believe it. You're alive!"

He nodded curtly. "I get that a lot."

Ruiz crowded closer. "It was so cool. You should've seen it. Opal was like all yelling at all the sorcerers. Made 'em run for the door like little chickens. It was crazy, man, never seen anything like it. They all took off. That's gratitude for you, right?"

Opal, obviously still tipsy, leaned heavily on Ruiz. "This man here? He got the alarm wailing to make everybody run. Gotta love a man who's good with his hands."

Dru tilted her head back and explained to Greyson, "There were a bunch of sorcerers here earlier. Kind of a party. A really lame party."

Greyson nodded. His glowing red eyes scanned the darkness. "Where did they all go?"

"They all parked over there." Ruiz pointed into the darkness. "Pretty smart of you guys, coming in the back way. Less traffic that way. But look, you know, everybody took off, but I think maybe the shop is going to get a lot more customers coming up. Just my thinking." His eyebrows suddenly wrinkled with worry. "Hey, what about those drinks? What are they gonna do to us? We need to get to a hospital or something?"

"No, no." Dru shook her head. "You'll be fine. The drinks just temporarily neutralized everyone's magic powers. You and Opal shouldn't have anything to worry about. Just, you know, stay hydrated, get some electrolytes. That's what's really important. But maybe we should get Rane to a doctor. Or an all-night buffet."

"The hell did you do to my dress?" Opal shrieked. She waved her hands frantically at the dirty, torn, web-sticky remnants of the sequined disco dress. "Oh, I can't believe it. I knew this would happen. This is what happens *every* time I loan you clothes."

Dru cleared her throat, feeling more than slightly embarrassed. "Maybe if I take it to the cleaners . . . ?" At Opal's sour look, she put on her cutest smile. "You know, they've got more sequins at the fabric store. A couple of stitches, a little bit of craft glue, nobody will know the difference. I'm sure."

Opal slowly shook her head. "And there's no coming back for those boots, either. Nobody makes rainbow-colored shoe polish."

Dru cleared her throat again. "Let's focus on people. What should we do about Rane?"

"Oh, she'll be fine," Opal said. "That girl is a Neanderthal. She'll heal up overnight. Right, honey?"

She directed the question at Rane, who didn't respond because she was still busy kissing Salem.

"See? She's gonna be fine, trust me," Opal said. Then she let out a whoop as Ruiz pulled her aside and drew her into his arms for a kiss.

Blinking in surprise, Dru watched them embrace, wondering when and how exactly the Opal-Ruiz thing had happened. She shook her head.

"I'm just glad you found me," Greyson said. When she turned to face him, his gaze softened. "Things were getting a little rough down there. Then you showed up."

"I'd like to take all the credit, but . . ." Dru looked past him at Hellbringer parked in the darkness. "That speed demon is yours forever, it looks like. It knew where to find you."

He followed her gaze. "Guess I'll never have to worry about forgetting where I parked."

"That's not funny." She took his hand in both of hers and squeezed. "I thought I'd lost you forever. If it hadn't been for that car, you'd still be down there. I never would've found you."

"You would have. And you did." His belief in her seemed to be unshakable. "You don't give yourself enough credit."

She dropped her gaze. "For what?"

"Saving the world is a good start."

She placed a hand on his broad chest. A flood of emotions rose up in her. It had all been too much. They had all come so close to the edge. Inside, she felt shaken to the core.

"Don't cry," he said softly. "Everything is okay."

"No, it's not." Eyes moist, she shook her head. "You're still cursed. You're still a Horseman." She tried to calm down her whirling emotions, but she couldn't. "There's so much I don't understand about you. And me. And Hellbringer. And the apocalypse scroll." A jolt of realization shot through her. "We never found the scroll. I don't know if Titus had it or not. The dead rising from the grave, that was the fifth seal of the apocalypse. But the scroll has seven seals. That means two more seals, and—"

"Shh." He pulled her into his arms. "I know you. You'll figure it all out, I promise. But not tonight."

His presence calmed her. She nodded, already making mental notes about the research she had to do and the catalog of books she should study. Was there any chance Titus's library had survived the destruction? From here, it didn't look like it. Such a terrible loss. "I wonder if Salem would let me flip through some of his books. He's got so much stuff, it's crazy. Maybe Rane can make it work with him again?"

Greyson gazed down at her intently and just smiled.

"And Opal made a new friend," Dru added. "Everyone's getting a kiss tonight. Except for Hellbringer, naturally."

"Naturally." The corner of Greyson's mouth perked up in a smile. "No, go ahead. I'll try not to get jealous."

"I do like your car, it's true. But . . ." She held her finger and thumb an inch apart. "Only so much."

"Good," he said, drawing closer. "The question is, do you like me?"

Dru meant to answer that out loud. But instead, she wrapped her arms around Greyson and kissed him.

ACKNOWLEDGMENTS

First, a special acknowledgment to all of the fine readers who have joined me on this wild adventure with Dru and her friends.

My deepest thanks to my literary agent, the unstoppable Kristin Nelson, for her tireless vision and guidance.

Many thanks also to the brilliant crew of Nelson Literary Agency, including Brian Nelson, Angie Hodapp, Lori Bennett, James Persichetti, Sam Cronin, Tallahj Curry, and (of course) Chutney the Wonder Dog.

As always, a big thanks to everyone at Pyr for making this book a reality.

Extra-special thanks to my editor, Rene Sears, for her unflagging patience, encouragement, and ideas.

Thanks to my publicist, Lisa Michalski, for always finding a way to put my books in the spotlight.

Thanks to copyeditor Jeffrey Curry for finding all the stuff I missed.

Thanks to artist Nicole Sommer-Lecht for once again creating an enchanting cover.

Many thanks go out to all of my fellow writers and critique group members for their terrific insights and advice over the years, especially Nikki Baird, Z. J. Czupor, Mindy McIntyre, Joy Meredith, Val Moses, Michele Winkler, Kevin Wolf, and too many other writers to mention.

Above all, my heartfelt gratitude goes to my lovely wife, Cyndi, for endless inspiration, invaluable wisdom, and unshakable faith. I couldn't do it without you.

ABOUT THE AUTHOR

Laurence MacNaughton grew up in a creaky old colonial house in Connecticut that he's pretty sure was haunted. He's been a bookseller, printer, copywriter, and (somewhat randomly) a prototype vehicle test driver. When he's not writing, he bikes and hikes the Rocky Mountains, explores ghost towns, and wrenches on old cars. His books include *It Happened One Doomsday*, *The Spider Thief*, and *Conspiracy of Angels*. Visit him online at www.Laurence MacNaughton.com.

Author photo © Kelly Weaver Photography